Tiffany Reisz lives in Lexington, Kentucky. She graduated with a BA in English from Centre College and is making her parents and her professors proud by writing erotica under her real name. She has five piercings, one tattoo and has been arrested twice. When not under arrest, Tiffany enjoys Latin dance, Latin men, and Latin verbs. She dropped out of a conservative seminary in order to pursue her dream of becoming a smut peddler. If she couldn't write, she would die.

Praise for *The Siren*

'A beautiful, lyrical story... *The Siren* is about love lost and found, the choices that make us who we are... I can only hope Ms Reisz pens a sequel!'
—Bestselling author Jo Davis

'THE ORIGINAL SINNERS series certainly lives up to its name: it's mind-bendingly original and crammed with more sin than you can shake a hot poker at. I haven't read a book this dangerous and subversive since Chuck Palahniuk's *Fight Club*.'
—Andrew Shaffer, author of
Great Philosophers Who Failed at Love

'Tiffany Reisz is a smart, artful and masterful new voice in erotic fiction. An erotica star on the rise!'
—Award-winning author Lacey Alexander

'Daring, sophisticated and literary...exactly what good erotica should be.'
—Kitty Thomas, author of *Tender Mercies*

'Dazzling, devastating and sinfully erotic, Reisz writes unforgettable characters you'll either want to know or want to be. *The Siren* is an alluring book-within-a-book, a story that will leave you breathless and bruised, aching for another chapter with Nora Sutherlin and her men.'
—Miranda Baker, author of *Bottoms Up* and *Soloplay*

THE
SIREN

TIFFANY REISZ

First published in Great Britain 2012
Mills & Boon Spice, an imprint of Harlequin (UK) Limited,
Eton House, 18-24 Paradise Road, Richmond, Surrey TW9 1SR

© Tiffany Reisz 2012

ISBN: 9780263904529

Harlequin (UK) policy is to use papers that are natural, renewable and recyclable products and made from wood grown in sustainable forests. The logging and manufacturing processes conform to the legal environmental regulations of the country of origin.

Printed and bound by CPI Group (UK) Ltd, Croydon, CR0 4&YY

MIX
Paper from
responsible sources
FSC
www.fsc.org   FSC C007454

To Jason Isaacs—
otherwise known as The Most Beautiful Man Alive.

Thank you for being my Zachary and my Muse.

To Alyssa Palmer—*mon Canard*—if yours were the only eyes
that read my books, I would still write for you alone.

And to B.

1

There was no such thing as London fog—never had been. The London Fog of legend was only that. In reality London fog was London smog, and at the height of the Industrial Revolution it had killed thousands, choking the city with its poisonous hands. Zach Easton knew that in the offices of Royal House Publishing, he was known as the London Fog, the disparaging nickname coined by a fellow editor who disapproved of Zach's dour demeanor. Zach had no love of his nickname or the editor who'd coined it. But today he was eager to earn his epithet.

As he knew he would, Zach found John-Paul Bonner, the chief managing editor of Royal House Publishing, still hard at work even after hours. J.P. sat on the floor of his office, piles of manuscripts stacked about him like a paper Stonehenge in miniature.

Zach stopped in J.P.'s doorway and leaned against the frame. He stared his chief editor down and did not speak. He didn't have to tell J.P. why he was here. They both knew.

"Death—she comes to me on an Easton fog," J.P. said from the floor as he sorted through another stack of books. "A poetic enough way to die. You are here to kill me, I presume."

At sixty-four and with his gray beard and spectacles, J.P. was literature personified. Usually Zach enjoyed playing word games with him, but he was in no mood for repartee today.

"Yes."

"'Yes'?" J.P. repeated. "Just 'yes'? Well, brevity is the soul of wit after all. Help an old man off the floor, will you, Easton? If I'm going to die, might as well die on my feet."

Sighing, Zach stepped into the office, reached down and helped J.P. stand. J.P. patted Zach gratefully on the shoulder and collapsed into his chair behind his desk.

"I'm a dead man anyway. Can't find that damn *Hamlet* galley for John Warren. Should have had it in the mail yesterday. But happiness is good health and a bad memory they say, and I am a happy, happy man."

Zach studied J.P. for a moment and silently cursed him for being so endearing. His affection for his boss made this conversation far less pleasant. Zach walked over to J.P.'s bookshelves and ran his hand along the top of the case. He knew J.P.'s habit of stashing important papers where even he couldn't reach them. Zach found a manuscript and pulled it down. He threw it on J.P.'s desk and watched it kick up a small cloud of dust.

"Bless you," J.P. said, coughing as he put his hand over his heart. "You have saved my life."

"Now I get to be the one who kills you."

J.P. eyed Zach and pointed at the chair across from the desk. Zach reluctantly sat down, pulling his gray coat around him like a suit of armor.

"Easton, look," J.P. began but it was as far as Zach let him get.

"Nora Sutherlin?" Zach infused the name with as much disgust as he could muster, a considerable amount at the moment. "You must be joking."

"Yes, Nora *Sutherlin*. I've thought about it, looked at the sales projections. I think we should acquire her. I want you to work with her."

"I will do no such thing. It's pornography."

"It's not pornography." J.P. peered at Zach over the top of his glasses. "It's erotica. Very good erotica."

"I had no idea there was such a thing."

"Two words—Anaïs Nin," J.P. retorted.

"Two more words—Booker Prize."

J.P. exhaled noisily and leaned back in his chair.

"Easton, I know your track record. You're one of the top talents in the industry by far. I wouldn't have paid to import you here to New York if you weren't. Yes, your writers have won Booker Prizes."

"And Whitbreads, Silver Daggers—"

"And Sutherlin's last book outsold your Whitbread and Silver Dagger combined. We're in a recession, if you hadn't noticed. Books are a luxury. If it can't be eaten, no one is buying it right now."

"So Nora Sutherlin's the answer?" Zach challenged.

J.P. grinned. "Janie Burke at the *Times* called her last book 'highly edible.'"

Zach shook his head and looked up at the ceiling in disgust.

"She's a guttersnipe writer at best," Zach said. "Her mind's in the gutter, her books are in the gutter. I wouldn't be surprised if her last publishing house kept its offices in the gutter."

"She might be a guttersnipe, but she's our guttersnipe. Well, your guttersnipe now."

"This isn't *My Fair Lady*. I'm not Professor Henry Higgins, and she is no Eliza bloody Doolittle."

"Whoever she is she's a damn fine writer. You would know this if you'd bothered to read one of her books."

"I left England for this job," Zach reminded him. "I left one of the most respected publishers in Europe because I wanted to work with the best young American writers."

"She's young. She's American."

"I did not leave England, my life…" Zach stopped himself before he said, *"and my wife."* After all, it was his wife who'd left him first.

"This book has real potential. She brought it to us because she's ready to make a change."

"Give her twenty shillings for a pound if she wants change. I leave for L.A. in six weeks. I can't believe you want me to set everything aside and give my last six weeks to Nora Sutherlin. Not a chance."

"I've seen your in-box, Easton. It's not so full you can't work with Sutherlin while you tie up loose ends around here. Don't tell me you don't have the time when we both know you just don't have the inclination."

"Fine. I don't have the time or the inclination to edit erotica, even good erotica, if there is such an animal. I'm not the only editor here. Give it to Thomas Finley." Zach named his least favorite coworker, the one who'd given him his nickname. "Or Angie Clark even."

"Finley? That pansy? He'd make a pass at Sutherlin, and she'd eat him alive. If you punched him in the face, he wouldn't even know how to bleed right."

Zach nearly laughed in agreement before remembering he was fighting with J.P.

"Then what about Angie Clark?"

"She's too busy right now. Besides…"

"Besides what?" Zach demanded.

"Clark's afraid of her."

"Can't say I blame her," Zach said. "I've heard grown men practically whisper her name at parties. The rumor is she slept her way to her first book deal."

"I've heard that rumor, too. But she hasn't slept her way to this one. Unfortunately," J.P. said with a playful grin.

"I read on Rachel Bell's blog that she never leaves the house in any other color than red. She said Sutherlin's got a sixteen-year-old boy working as her personal assistant."

J.P. smiled at him. "I believe she prefers 'intern' to 'personal assistant.'"

Zach nearly choked on his own frustration. He'd been ready to leave for the evening, even had his coat on, when some demon voice in his head told him to check his work email one more time. He had a note from J.P. telling him that he was considering acquiring erotica writer Nora Sutherlin and her latest book for their big fall/winter release. And since Zach didn't have much to occupy him until he left for L.A. in a few weeks...

"I need you to do this for me. You and no one else," J.P. said.

"Why am I the only one who can handle her?"

"Handle her?" J.P. practically chortled the words before turning serious. "Listen to me—no one handles Nora Sutherlin. No, you're just the only one I've got who can keep up with her. Easton...Zach. Hear me out, please."

Zach swallowed and resigned himself to a moment's détente. It was a rare thing indeed when John-Paul Bonner called anyone by his first name.

"She writes romances, J.P.," Zach said quietly. "I hate romances."

J.P. met his eyes with sympathy.

"I know you've been through hell this past year. I've met

your Grace, remember? I know what you've lost. But Sutherlin…she's good. We need her."

Zach took a slow, deep breath.

"Has she signed the contract yet?" Zach asked.

"No. We're still ironing out the terms."

"Is there a verbal agreement in place?"

J.P. eyed him warily. "Not yet. I told her we'd have to look at the figures and get back to her, but we were leaning toward yes. Why?"

"I'll talk to her."

"A good start."

"And I'll read the manuscript. If I think there's any chance she—we—can make something decent out of her book, I'll give her my last six weeks. But the book doesn't go to press until I sign off on it."

J.P.'s eyes bored into Zach. Zach refused to blink or look away. He was used to having final say on all his books. He wasn't about to relinquish that power, not for J.P., not for Nora Sutherlin, not for anyone.

"Easton, one Dan Brown title will outsell in a month what the entire poetry section of a bookstore will sell in five years. Sutherlin's 'pornography,' as you call it, could pay for a lot of poetry around here."

"I want the contract in my hands, J.P., or I won't even meet her."

J.P. sat back in his chair and exhaled loudly through his nose.

"Fine. She's all yours. She's got a nice little place in Connecticut. Take the train. Take my car. I don't care. She'll be home on Monday, she said."

"Very well then." Zach knew he was likely safe. When the mood struck him, Zach could be merciless to an author about his or her book's shortcomings. The great writers took the criticism. The hacks couldn't handle it. If he was hard enough on her, she'd beg for another editor.

The argument now at a stalemate, Zach rose tiredly from the chair and with hunched and aching shoulders headed toward the door.

A small cough stopped Zach before he could leave the office. J.P. didn't meet his eyes, only ran his hand over the first page of the *Hamlet* reader's copy in front of him.

"You should read this book when it comes out," J.P. said, tapping the page. "Fascinating exploration of the feigned madness of Hamlet—'I am but mad north north-west...'"

"'But when the wind is southerly, I can tell a hawk from a handsaw,'" Zach finished the famous quotation.

"Sutherlin's only as mad as Hamlet was. Don't believe everything you've heard about her. The lady knows her hawks from her handsaws."

"Lady?"

J.P. closed the book and didn't answer the insult. Zach turned to leave again.

"You know, you're still young, Easton, and too handsome for your own good. You should try it sometime."

"What? Madness?" Zach asked, nodding toward the book.

"No. Happiness."

"Happiness?" Zach allowed himself a bitter grin. "I'm afraid my memory's too good for that."

Zach returned to his office. His assistant, Mary, had left Nora Sutherlin's manuscript on his desk along with a file folder.

Zach flipped the file open and barely glanced at Sutherlin's bio. She was thirty-three, about a decade younger than him. Her first book had come out when she was twenty-nine. She'd released five titles since then; her second book, entitled *Red,* had created a minor sensation—great sales, lots of buzz.

Zach studied the numbers in the file and saw why J.P. was so eager to acquire her. With each subsequent release, her sales had nearly doubled. Zach ran through the little he knew of erotica writers in his mind. These days erotica was about the only growth market in publishing. But it shouldn't be about the money. Just the art.

Zach threw Sutherlin's bio and sales projections in the trash. He'd stolen his philosophy of editing from the old New Critics—it's just about the book. Not the author, not the market, not the reader...one judged a book only by the book. He shouldn't care that Nora Sutherlin's personal life was rumored to be as torrid as her prose. Only her book mattered. And his hopes for the book were not high.

Zach examined the manuscript with suspicion. Mary knew he preferred to read his books in hard copy versions. But she'd obviously had a little too much fun printing out this one for him. Across the scarlet-red cover blazed the title in a lurid Gothic font—*The Consolation Prize*. Editors almost invariably changed a book's title, but he had to concede it was an interesting choice for a work of erotica. He opened the manuscript and read the first sentence: "I don't want to write this story any more than you want to read it."

Zach paused in his reading as he felt the shadow of something old and familiar whisper across his shoulder. He brushed the sensation off and read the line again. Then the next one and the next one...

2

Some days Zach hated his job. The actual editing he loved, taking a novel with pretensions of greatness and actually making it great. But the politics he hated, the budget crises, having to let a brilliant midlister go to make room for a better-selling hack… And now here he was, hauling his arse into Connecticut to meet some loony smut writer who'd somehow convinced one of the most respected lions in publishing that she deserved one of the best editors in literary fiction. Yes, some days he hated his job. Today he felt quite certain it hated him back.

Zach parked J.P.'s car in front of a rather quaint two-story Tudor cottage in the tame and pedestrian suburb. He checked the address, his directions and stared at the house. Nora Sutherlin—the notorious erotica writer whose books were banned as often as they were translated lived here? Zach could imagine his own grandmother in this house forcing tea and biscuits on small children.

With a heavy sigh, he strode to the front door and rang the

bell. Shortly after, he heard footsteps approaching—sturdy, masculine footsteps. Zach allowed himself the pleasure of imagining that *Nora Sutherlin* might simply be the pen name for some overweight bloke in his mid-fifties.

A man did open the door. No, not a man—a boy. A boy wearing nothing but plaid pajama pants and a cluster of hemp necklaces, one dangling a small silver cross, stood across the threshold from Zach and regarded him with a sleepy smile.

"Nineteen," he said in an accent Zach immediately recognized as American South. "Not sixteen. She just tells everybody I'm sixteen for the street cred."

"Street cred?" Zach asked, stunned that the rumor of the teenage intern had proved true.

The boy shrugged his sun-freckled shoulders. "Her words. Wesley Railey. Just Wes."

"Zachary Easton. I'm here to meet with your…employer?"

The boy, Wesley, laughed and brushed a swath of dark blond hair out of his brown eyes with the graceful languor of youth.

"My *employer* is right this way," he said, exaggerating the Southern accent for comic effect. Zach entered the house and found it cozy and homey, replete with overstuffed furniture and bursting bookcases. "I like your accent. You're British?"

"Lived in London the past ten years. You don't sound like a native, either."

"Kentucky. But Mom's a Georgia peach so that's where I get this mess from. I keep trying to lose it, but Nora won't let me. Has a thing for accents."

"That does not bode well," Zach said as Wesley grabbed a V-neck white T-shirt off a pile of folded laundry and pulled it on. Zach noted the boy's slim but muscular frame and wondered why Nora Sutherlin bothered with the intern pretense.

A nineteen-year-old lover might be rather disgraceful for a woman of thirty-three but certainly legal.

Wesley led him down an abbreviated hallway. Without knocking he pushed open a door.

"Nor, Mr. Easton's here."

He stepped to the side and Zach blinked in surprise at his first glimpse of the infamous Nora Sutherlin.

From all the rumors he'd heard, he'd expected some sort of Amazonian in red leather wielding a riding crop. Instead, he found a pale, petite beauty with wavy black hair barely contained in a loose knot at her nape. And no red leather in sight at all. She wore men's style pajamas, blue ones covered in what appeared to be little yellow ducks.

Her legs rested on top of her desk and she had her keyboard balanced across her lap. With quick nimble fingers she typed away, saying nothing and giving them only her beguiling profile.

"Nora?" Wesley prompted.

"I've got a crisp new Benjamin for the first person who can give me a good synonym for *thrust,* noun form. Go," she said, her voice both honeyed and sardonic.

Although irritated by her cavalier attitude and her unfortunate attractiveness, Zach couldn't help but scroll through his substantial mental thesaurus.

"Push, lunge, shove, attack, force, jab," he rattled off the words.

"His slow, relentless jabs sent her reeling…" she said. "Sounds like commentary on a boxing match. Goddammit, why are there no good synonyms for *thrust?* Bane of my existence. Although…" She set her keyboard aside and turned to face him for the first time. "I do love a man with a big vocabulary."

Zach's spine stiffened as the most unusually beautiful

woman he'd seen in years smiled at him. She stood up and walked on bare feet to him.

"Ms. Sutherlin." Zach took her proffered hand. "How do you do?"

From her small stature he expected a dainty grip. But she grasped his hand with surprisingly strong fingers.

"Gorgeous accent," she said. "Not a bit of the old Scouser left, is there?"

"You've done your homework, I see," Zach replied, troubled that she seemed to know more about him than he knew about her. He now regretted tossing her bio into the bin. "But not everyone born in Liverpool speaks like a young Paul McCartney."

"Shame." Her voice dropped to a whisper as she continued to gaze at him. "What a shame."

Zach forced himself to really meet her eyes and then wished he hadn't. At first glance her eyes appeared a deep green, but she blinked and they seemed to change to a black so dark they likely could not remember the green they had just been. He knew that she looked only at his face, but still he felt stripped bare by her penetrating gaze, torn open. She knew him. He knew it, and he sensed she knew it, too.

Determined to regain control of the situation, Zach pulled his hand back.

"Ms. Sutherlin—"

"Right. Work." She returned to her desk. Zach glanced around her office and saw even more books than were in the living room: books and notebooks, stacks of paper and dark wooden filing cabinets.

"One quick question, Mr. Easton," she said, dropping into her desk chair. "Are you, by any chance, ashamed of being Jewish?"

"Excuse me?" Zach said, not quite certain he'd heard her correctly.

"Nora, stop it," Wesley scolded.

"Just curious," she said with an indifferent wave of her hand. "You go by Zachary but your name is actually Zechariah like the Hebrew prophet. Why did you change it?"

The question was so personal, so entirely none of her concern that Zach couldn't believe he deigned to answer it.

"I've been called Zach or Zachary since the day I was born. Only when filling out formal documents do I even remember Zechariah is actually my name." Zach kept his tone cool and even. He knew that he could only win here if he stayed calm and didn't allow her to get the rise out of him she so clearly desired. "And the only thing I am ashamed of currently is this sudden downturn in my career."

He expected her to flinch or fight. Instead, she just laughed.

"I really can't blame you. Have a seat and tell me all about it."

Warily, Zach sat down in the battered paisley armchair across from her desk. He started to cross his ankle over his knee but froze in midmovement as his foot tapped an unusually long black duffel bag that sat on the floor. He heard the distinct, unnerving sound of metal clinking against metal.

"I've got to get to class," Wesley said, sounding desperate to leave. "That okay?"

"Oh, I doubt Mr. Easton will bend me over my desk and ravish me the second you leave," she said, winking at Zach. "Unfortunately."

The words and the wink forced an image into Zach's mind of doing that very act. He forced the thought out just as quickly as she put it in.

Wesley shook his head in amused disgust.

"Mr. Easton, good luck," Wesley said, turning to him. "Just don't act impressed, and she'll eventually settle down."

"Impressed?" Zach repeated. "I doubt that will be a problem."

Zach waited for his words to register. He saw Wesley's eyes narrow, but she only looked at him from under her veil of black eyelashes.

"Oh…" She nearly purred the word. "I like him already."

"God help us all." Wesley left on the heels of his prayer. Zach glanced back at Wesley's retreating form. He wasn't quite sure he wanted to be left alone with this woman.

"Your son, I presume?" Zach asked after Wesley departed.

"My intern. Sort of. He cooks so I guess that makes him more of a factotum. Intern? Factotum?"

"Houseboy," Zach supplied, putting his large vocabulary to use again. "And a rather well-trained one, I see."

"Well-trained? Wesley? He's horribly trained. I can't even train him to fuck me. But I don't think you drove all the way from the city just to talk about my intern with me, adorable as he is."

"No, I did not." Zach fell silent. He waited and watched as Nora Sutherlin sat back in her chair and studied him with her unnerving eyes.

"So…" she began. "I can tell you don't like me. Shows you've got good taste in women at least. Also shows you've heard of me. Am I what you expected?"

Zach stared at her a moment. The last three writers he'd worked with had been men in their late fifties and early sixties. Never once had he seen any of them in their pajamas. And never had he met a writer as uncomfortably alluring as Nora Sutherlin.

"You're shorter."

"Thank God for stilettos, right? So what's the verdict? J.P.

said he's giving you total control over the book and me. It's been a long time since I've let a man boss me around. I kind of miss it."

"The verdict is undecided."

"A well-hung jury then. Better give me a retrial."

"You're very clever."

"You're very handsome."

Zach shifted in his seat. He wasn't used to flirtation from his writers, either. Then again, she wasn't one of his writers.

"That wasn't a compliment. Cleverness is the last recourse of an amateur. I look for depth in my books, passion, substance."

"Passion I have."

"Passion is not synonymous with sex. I'll admit your book was interesting and not entirely without merit. At one point I even detected a heart inside all that flesh."

"I hear a 'but' in there."

"But the heartbeat was very faint. The patient might be terminal."

She looked at him and glanced away. Zach had seen that look before—it was defeat. He'd scared her away as he'd planned. He wondered why he wasn't happier about it.

"Terminal…" She turned her face back to him. A new look was shining in her eyes. "It's almost Easter—the season of Resurrection."

"Resurrection? Really?" Zach said, astonished by her tenacity. "I leave for Royal's L.A. offices in six weeks. Six weeks is not nearly enough time to involve myself with any project of worth or magnitude. But six weeks is all we have."

"You just said six weeks isn't long enough—"

"But it's all I have to give. Fix it in six and it's off to press. If not—"

"If not, it's back to the gutter for the guttersnipe writer, right?"

Zach stared at her in stunned silence.

"John-Paul Bonner's the biggest gossip in the publishing industry, Mr. Easton. He told me what you think of me. He told me you think I'll fail."

"I'm quite certain of it."

"If you're my editor, my failure will take you down, too."

"I'm not your editor yet. I haven't agreed to anything."

"You will. So why did you quit teaching?"

"Quit teaching?"

"You were a professor at Cambridge, right? Pretty good gig especially for someone so young. But you quit."

"Ten years ago," Zach said, shocked by how much she seemed to know about him. How on earth had she learned about Cambridge?

"So why—"

"Why my personal life is of such fascination to you, I cannot fathom."

"I'm a cat. You're a shiny object."

"You're insufferable."

"I am, aren't I? Somebody should spank me." She sighed. "So you're kind of an asshole. No offense."

"And you appear to be two or three words I don't feel quite comfortable saying aloud."

"I'd tell you to say them anyway, but I promised Wesley I wouldn't let you flirt with me. But I digress. Tell me what's wrong with my book. Say it slowly," she said, grinning.

"You have a very sanguine attitude toward the editing process. What will you say when I tell you that you must cut out the ten to twenty pages you're certain constitute the living, beating heart of your book?"

She said nothing for a long minute. Her eyes glanced away

from him and she seemed to lose herself in a dark place. He watched as she breathed in slowly through her nose, held the breath then exhaled out her mouth. She turned her uncanny green eyes to him.

"Then I'll say that I once cut the living, beating heart out of my own chest," she said, her voice devoid of its usual flippancy. "I survived that amputation. I'll survive this one."

"May I ask why you're so determined to work with me? I've done my research, Ms. Sutherlin. You have a rabid fan following that would buy your phone bill in hardcover and still manage to wank off to it."

"I'm also very big in France."

Zach gritted his teeth and felt the first stirrings of an impending headache. "Didn't your 'intern' say you would settle down at some point?"

"Mr. Easton," she said, rolling back in her swivel chair and throwing her legs back on her desk. "This is me settled down."

"I was afraid of that." Zach stood, prepared to leave.

"This book," she began and stopped. She moved her legs off the desk and sat cross-legged in her chair. For a moment she looked both very earnest and terribly young.

"What about it?"

She looked away and seemed to search for words. "It… means something to me. It's not another one of my dirty little stories. I came to Royal because I need to do right by this book." She met his eyes again and without a trace of levity or mirth said, "Please. I need your help."

"I only work with serious writers."

"I'm not a serious person. I know that. But I am a serious writer. Writing is one of the only two things in this world I do take seriously."

"And the other?"

"The Roman Catholic Church."

"I think we're done here."

"You're not much of an editor then," she taunted as he headed to the door. "It's much too early for an ending. I'm no editor and even I know that."

"Ms. Sutherlin, you're obviously emotionally involved in your book. That's fine for writing, but editing a book you love hurts."

"I like doing things that hurt." She gave him a Cheshire cat grin. "J.P. said you were the best. I think he's right. I'll do whatever it takes, whatever you say. I'll beg if it will help my case. I'll get down on my knees and beg if it'll help yours."

"I'm going now."

"J.P. also said they call you the London Fog around the office," she said as he turned his back to her. "Is that because of the long coat, the accent or your gift for putting a cold, wet damper on everyone's good time?"

"I'll leave you to decide that."

"Tell me what to do and I'll do it," she called out, and Zach was forced to admire her stubbornness. He couldn't believe he was tempted to consider rewarding it.

"A writer writes," he said, facing her again. "Write something for me, something good. I don't care how long it is, and I don't care what it's about. Just impress me. You've got twenty-four hours. Show me you can create under pressure, and I'll consider it."

"You'll be surprised what I can do under pressure," she said, but Zach had his doubts. The houseboy, the jokes, the flirting—she was no serious writer. "Any suggestions?" she asked, slightly more sincere this time.

"Stop writing what you know and start writing what you want to know. And," he said, pointing a finger at her, "none of your cheap tricks."

Her spine straightened as if he'd finally found an insult that stuck. "I assure you, Mr. Easton," she said in a tone both stern and reproving, "my tricks are anything but cheap."

"Prove it then. You've got twenty-four hours."

She leaned back in her chair and smiled.

"Fuck your twenty-four hours. You'll have it tonight."

3

Numbing.

As an editor Zach often forced his writers to dig deep, cast aside the obvious and find the perfect word for every sentence. And the perfect word to describe this book release party he'd been forced to attend? *Numbing.*

Zach stalked through the party saying little more than the occasional hello to various colleagues. He'd only come because once again J.P. had twisted his arm, and Rose Evely—the guest of honor—had been a Royal House writer for thirty years now. What a ludicrous party anyway—someone dimmed the lights to create a nightclub sort of atmosphere but no amount of ambience could turn the banal hotel banquet hall into anything other than a beige box. He wandered toward a spiral staircase in the corner of the room to surreptitiously check his watch. If he could survive two hours at this party, maybe it would be long enough to placate his social butterfly of a boss.

Scanning the crowd, he saw his twenty-eight-year-old assistant, Mary, trying to talk her new husband into dancing with her. His first week at Royal, he'd been pleasantly surprised to find out his spitfire of an assistant was, like him, Jewish. He'd teased her he'd never known a Jew named Mary before and started calling her his pseudoshiksa. Mary, for all her endearing brusqueness, only ever called him "Boss." J.P. stood with Rose Evely. Both J.P. and Evely had been happily married to their respective spouses for decades but nothing stopped J.P. from chivalrously flirting with any woman who had the patience to listen to his literary rambles. Everyone seemed to be enjoying themselves at this miserable party. Why wasn't he?

Once more he glanced down at his watch.

"I can save you, if you want," came a voice from above him.

Zach spun around and looked up. Smiling down at him from over the top of the staircase was Nora Sutherlin.

"Save me?" He narrowed his eyes at her.

"From this party." She crooked her index finger at him.

Zach's better judgment warned him that climbing that staircase could be a very bad idea indeed. Yet his feet overruled his reason, and he mounted the steps and joined her on the platform at the top. He raised his eyebrow as he cast a disapproving gaze over her clothes. That morning at her house, she'd worn shapeless pajamas that concealed every part of her but her abundant personality. Now he saw on full display what his mind had before only imagined.

She wore red, of course. Scarlet red and not much of it. The dress stopped at the top of her thighs and started at the edge of her breasts. She had miraculous curves that the dramatic floor-length red jacket she wore over her dress did nothing to hide. Even worse, she wore black leather boots that laced all the way above her knees. Pirate boots and a roguish grin on a beautiful black-haired woman…for the first time in a long time Zach felt something other than numb.

"How do you know I want to be saved from this party, Miss Sutherlin?" Zach leaned back against the railing and crossed his arms.

"I've been watching you from my little crow's nest here since the second you walked in. You've said maybe five words to four people, you've checked your watch three times in as many minutes, and you whispered something to J.P., which, guessing from the look on his face, was a death threat. You're here against your will. I can get you out."

Zach cocked a self-deprecating smile at her.

"Unfortunately, you're right. I am here against my will. I have to wonder, however, why you're here at all. Didn't I give you homework?" he asked, remembering his rash decision this morning to give her one chance to impress him.

"You did. And I was a good girl and finished it. See?"

He tried and failed to look away as she reached into the bodice of her dress and pulled out a folded piece of paper and handed it to him. The paper was still warm from her skin.

"This is it?" he asked, seeing only three paragraphs on the page.

"Don't judge a book by its mother. Just read."

Zach glanced at her once more and wished he hadn't. Every time he looked at her, he found something else to attract him. Her jacket had slipped down her arm and her pale sculpted shoulder peeked out. Sculpted? His petite little writer had some muscle to go along with her impressive curves. Tougher than she looked.

Remembering himself, Zach turned from her, tilted the page into a patch of light and read.

First she noticed his hips. The eyes might be the windows to the soul, but a man's hips were his seat of power. She doubted he'd cho-

*sen those perfectly fitted jeans and that black T-shirt that belied the
tautness of his stomach for the purpose of flattering his lower body,
but he had and now she lost herself in the thought of caressing with
her lips that exquisite hollow that lay between smooth skin and el-
egantly jutting hip bone.*

*She had to meet his eyes eventually. With reluctance she dragged
her gaze to his face, as dignified and angular as the rest of him. Pale
skin and dark Brutus-cut hair contrasted with eyes the color of ice.
Glacial, she decided his eyes were—they spoke of hidden depths. A
stark beauty, he was a man made to be admired by intelligent women.*

*Lean and tall but with the substantial mass of an athlete, he was
utterly masculine. The world had fallen away in his presence and
now that he was gone, she was left in the equally potent presence of
his absence.*

Zach read the words one more time trying all the while
to ignore the annoyingly pleasant image of Nora Sutherlin
caressing his naked hips with her mouth.

"I've noticed you usually shy away from long descriptive
passages in your book," he said.

"I know people think erotica is just a romance novel with
rougher sex. It's not. If it's a subgenre of anything, it's horror."

"Horror? Really?"

"Romance is sex plus love. Erotica is sex plus fear. You're
terrified of me, aren't you?"

"Slightly," he admitted, rubbing the back of his neck.

"A smart horror writer will never put too much detail in
about the monster. The readers' imaginations can conjure their
own demons. In erotica you never want your main characters to be too physically specific. That way your readers can
insert their own fantasies, their own fears. Erotica is a joint
effort between writer and reader."

"How so?" Zach asked, intrigued that Nora Sutherlin
would have her own literary theories.

"Writing erotica is like fucking someone for the first time. You aren't sure exactly what he wants yet so you try to give him everything he could possibly want. Everything and anything…" She enunciated the words like a cat stretching in sunlight. "You hit every nerve and eventually you'll hit the nerve. Have I hit any nerves yet?"

Zach clenched his jaw. "Not any of them you were aiming for."

"You don't know what I was aiming for. So what do you think of the writing?"

"Could be better." He refolded the page. "You use 'was' too much."

"Rough draft," she said unapologetically. She stared at him with dark, waiting eyes.

"The last line's the strongest—'*the equally potent presence of his absence*.'" Zach knew he should give the page back to her but for some reason he stuck it in his pocket. "It's good."

She gave him a slow, dangerous smile.

"It's you."

Zach only stared at her a moment before pulling the folded page back out.

"This is me?" he asked, his skin flushing.

"It is. Every last long, lean inch of you. I wrote it right after you left this morning. I was, needless to say, inspired by your visit."

Swallowing hard, Zach unfolded the sheet again. *Brutus-cut black hair…ice-colored eyes…jeans, black shirt…* It *was* him.

"Excuse me," Zach began, trying to regain control of this conversation, "but didn't I repeatedly insult you this morning?"

"Your kvetching was very fetching. I like men who are mean to me. I trust them more."

She tilted her head to the side and her unruly black hair fell over her forehead, veiling her green-black eyes.

"Forgive me. I might be speechless right now."

"Your orders," she said. "You told me to stop writing what I knew and start writing what I wanted to know. I want to know...you."

She took a step closer and Zach's heart dropped a few feet and landed somewhere in the vicinity of his groin.

"Who are you, Ms. Sutherlin?" he asked, not quite knowing what he meant by that question.

"I'm just a writer. A writer named Nora. And you can call me that, Zach."

"Nora then. I'm sorry. I'm not used to being hit on by my writers. Especially after verbally abusing them."

Nora's eyes flashed with amusement.

"Verbal abuse? Zach, where I come from 'slut' is a term of endearment. Want to see where I come from?"

"No."

"Pity," she said, sounding not at all surprised or disappointed. "Where should we go then? I promised to save you from this party, didn't I?"

"I really shouldn't leave," Zach said, terrified what would happen the second he found himself alone with Nora.

"Come on, Zach. This party sucks and not in the good way. I've had pap smears more fun than this."

Zach covered a laugh with a cough.

"I must admit you do have a way with words."

"So you'll edit me then? Please?" She batted her eyelashes at him in mock innocence. "You won't regret it."

Zach glanced up at the ceiling as if it could give him some hint of what the hell he was getting himself into. Nora Sutherlin...he had only six weeks left in New York until he left for L.A. Why was he even considering getting involved with

Nora Sutherlin and her book? He knew why. He had nothing else in his life right now. He liked Mary and enjoyed working for J.P. But he'd made no friends in New York, no connections of any kind. He hadn't allowed himself to even consider dating. One day he'd taken off his wedding ring in a fit of anger and couldn't find a reason to put it back on. He wouldn't consider inflicting himself on any woman right now. At least working with Nora Sutherlin might give him a much-needed distraction from his misery. She seemed like the type of woman who'd help you forget about your headache by setting your bed on fire.

Won't regret it? He already did.

"You do realize that working with you could be bad for my career," Zach said. "I do literary fiction, not—"

"Literary friction?"

"I can't believe I'm doing this." Zach shook his head.

Nora leaned in close to him. He was suddenly and uncomfortably aware of the long, bare curve of her neck. She smelled of hothouse flowers in bloom.

"I can." She breathed the words into his ear.

Zach exhaled slowly and pulled, reluctantly, away from her.

"I'm a brutal editor."

"I like brutal."

"I'll make you rewrite the whole book."

"Now you're trying to turn me on, aren't you? Shall we?"

"Fine," he finally said. "Save me then."

"Let's do it," she said. "If J.P. gives you shit about leaving the party with me, tell him it was my idea for us to go work on my book. J.P. won't spank me."

"I'm not certain of that," Zach said.

"I knew I liked that man for a reason."

"I need to say a few goodbyes if we're leaving." J.P. for

one. Then Mary. And he hadn't met her husband yet. And Rose Evely, too.

"Nope. Can't do that," Nora said. "Never say goodbye when you leave a party. That way you leave a mystery in your place. They'll have so much more fun talking about us than they ever would talking to us. Can't you already hear them? *Zach Easton just left with Nora Sutherlin. Are they…surely not… of course they are—*"

"We aren't," Zach said with finality.

"I know that. You know that. They don't know that."

Zach looked around the room. Everywhere he looked he saw eyes glancing furtively in their direction. The most intense gazing came from Thomas Finley, his least favorite coworker. Zach noted that Finley didn't so much stare at him as he did at Nora. And the look in his eyes wasn't particularly friendly.

"I prefer not being a topic of gossip," Zach said.

"Too late. At least with me, it'll be really good gossip." She strode down the staircase with an audacious kick of her heels on each step.

Zach followed in her wake. The crowd parted for her as she cut a bloodred swath through the center of the room.

Finally free of the suffocating party, Zach threw on his coat and breathed in the bracing winter evening air.

A cab stopped within seconds for Nora and she slipped gracefully inside. He took a sharp breath as her black-booted legs disappeared into the cab. One more time he asked himself what the hell he was doing before sliding in next to her.

Nora said nothing as he joined her, only turned her head and gazed out at the night. She seemed to be trying to stare down the city. He had a feeling the city would blink first.

Nervously, he rubbed the empty spot where he'd once worn his wedding band. Nora reached out and wrapped her hand around his ring finger. Facing him now, she raised her eyebrow in a question.

"Grace," he answered.

Nora nodded. "You married a princess."

Princess Grace—her mother called her that.

"She hates being called 'Princess.'" Zach heard the anguish in his voice.

Nora lifted his hand and brought it to her neck. She pressed his fingers into her throat. Her pulse throbbed through her warm, soft skin.

"Søren," she said and met his eyes. In those dark, dangerous depths he saw a glimmer of something human—not merely sympathy but empathy. And he felt something inhuman in response—not passion but pure animal need. For a brief moment he imagined his hands digging into her thighs and the bite of her leather boots on his back. He tore his gaze away before her uncanny ability to read him saw that image in his hungry gaze.

She released his hand just as the cab pulled up in front of Zach's apartment building. He opened the door and got out. He wanted to ask her up, wanted to spend a few hours forgetting his pain and all the reasons for it. But he couldn't, could he? Because of Grace, not that she would care anymore. Zach opened his mouth but before he could ask Nora up, she reached out to shut the door.

"See, Zach? I told you I'd save you."

Nora watched Zach stare after the cab before turning and walking into his building. What a beautiful wreck of a man. Kingsley always said beautiful wrecks were a specialty of hers. He should know. He certainly qualified as one himself.

"Where to, lady?"

Nora thought about it for a moment. For the next six weeks

she and Zach would rewrite her book. If he started kicking her ass tomorrow, might be cathartic to kick a little ass of her own tonight.

"Lady?" her driver prompted.

Nora rattled off an address for a Manhattan town house and nearly laughed as she saw her driver's eyes widen in the rearview mirror.

"You sure about that? That's no place for a nice girl to go after dark. Or ever."

This time Nora did laugh out loud. Every cabdriver in town knew Kingsley's address. No one with anything to lose would ever turn up there in his or her own car. Good thing she had nothing to lose. Not anymore anyway.

Nora looked back out onto the city night. Søren might kill her for getting involved with a guy like Zach, a guy still technically married. Pissing off Søren—yet another reason to go for it.

"Don't worry." She crossed her legs and leaned back in the seat. She'd tip the driver a Benjamin just for giving her a giggle. "I'm not a nice girl."

4

Everything hurt—back, arms, wrists, fingers, neck—
everything. Nora hadn't been this sore in years. Not
since the old days anyway. Zach hadn't been kidding—
he was a brutal editor. And she'd been right—he was kicking
her ass. Nora allowed herself a smile. She'd forgotten how
much she liked having her ass kicked.

She read through Zach's notes again on her first chapters.
Nice to see he had quite the sadistic streak in him. Of course
she couldn't imagine him taking a real whip to her—more's
the pity. But he had a gift for tongue-lashings. He'd been her
editor for all of three days and so far he'd already called her
a "guttersnipe writer" whose books were "melodramatic,"
"maniacal" and "unhygienic." *Unhygienic* had been her personal favorite.

Nora stretched her aching back as Wesley entered her office and collapsed into the armchair across from her desk.

"How's the rewrite going?" he asked.

"Horrible. It's day three and I've rewritten…nothing."

"Nothing?"

"Zach shredded the book." Nora held up a sheaf of paper. The morning after the release party Zach sent her a dozen pages of notes on the first three chapters alone. "You sure this guy's the right editor for you? Can't you work with somebody else?"

Nora picked up her tea and sipped at it. She'd rather not talk about the contract situation with Wesley. J.P. had told her Zach got final say on whether her book got published, but she hadn't passed that information on to Wesley. Poor kid worried about her enough as it was.

"Apparently not. John-Paul Bonner had to practically beg to even get Zach to meet me."

Wesley shrugged and crossed his arms.

"Not sure I like him. He was kind of, I don't know—"

"An ass? You can say 'ass' around me. It's in the Bible," she reminded him with a wink.

"He was a jerk to you. How's that?"

"Zach's a slave-driver. But I like that about him. Brings back memories." She sat back in her chair and smiled into her tea.

Wesley groaned. "Do you really have to bring up Søren?"

Nora grimaced. Wesley hated it when she brought up her ex.

"Sorry, kiddo. But even if Zach's an ass, he's still amazing at his job. I feel like I'm finally learning how to write a book. Books at Libretto were commodities. Royal treats writers like artists. I think this book deserves more than Libretto could give it."

Nora didn't mention that Libretto wouldn't publish it even if she wanted them to. Once Mark Klein found out she'd been shopping around for a new publisher, he cut off everything but contractually obligated contact with her. Wesley didn't need to know that Royal House was the only reputable publisher who'd given her the time of day. Despite their rocky start, she looked forward to working with Zach. He had a sterling reputation in the publishing industry, not to mention being stunning and fun to flirt with. Especially since he pretended he hated it when she did.

"What's this book about anyway?" Wesley asked.

"It's kind of a love story. Not my usual boy-meets-girl, boy-beats-girl story. My two characters love each other but they don't belong together. The whole book is them—against their will—breaking up."

Wesley plucked at a loose thread in the battered armchair.

"But they love each other? Why wouldn't they belong to-gether?"

Nora released a wistful sigh. "Spoken like a nineteen-year-old."

"I like happy endings. Is that a crime?"

"It's just unrealistic. You don't think two people can break up and still be happy eventually?"

Wesley paused. He tended to act before thinking, but he al-ways thought before he spoke. She studied him while he pon-dered her question. Gorgeous kid. He drove her up the wall with those big brown eyes of his and sweetly handsome face. For the millionth time since asking him to move in with her she wondered what the hell she'd been thinking by dragging this innocent into her world.

"You left him," Wesley finally said. Him…Søren.

"Yeah," she said, biting her bottom lip, a habit Søren had been trying to break her of for eighteen years. "I did."

"Are you happy without him?" Wesley turned his eyes back to her.

"Some days, yes. Then some days it's like I just got my arm blown off. But this book isn't about Søren."

"Can I read it?"

"Not a chance. Maybe when it's rewritten. Or maybe…"

Nora grinned at him, and Wesley suddenly looked nervous.

She got out of her chair and sat on the edge of her desk and put a foot on each arm of his chair.

"Let's play a game," she said leaning in close. Wesley sat up straight and pressed back into the chair. "I'll trade you my book for your body."

"I'm your intern. This counts as sexual harassment."

"Being sexually harassed is in your job description, re-member?"

Wesley shifted in the chair. She loved how jumpy she still made him even after over a year in the same house. A sandy-blond lock of hair fell over his forehead. She reached out to brush it back.

Wesley ducked under her leg before she could touch him and stood just out of reach.

"Coward," she teased.

Wesley started to say something but they both froze at the blaring ring that echoed from the vicinity of her desk.

The smile that had been in Wesley's eyes vanished as Nora dug out a sleek red cell phone from under a pile of papers.

"*La Maîtresse* speaking," she answered.

"The book," Wesley mouthed. His eyes pleaded with her.

With the phone still at her ear Nora walked up to Wesley. She moved so close he started stepping back. She took another step toward him, and he took another step back.

"Go do your homework, junior," she said, and Wesley gave her the closest thing to a mean look he had.

"You have homework, too," he reminded her.

"I'm not a biochemistry major at a fucking brutal liberal arts college. Scoot. The grown-ups are talking now."

She shut the door in his face.

"Talk, Kingsley," she said into the phone. "This better be good."

★ ★ ★

"Working late as usual, I see."

Zach glanced up from his notes on Nora's book and found J.P. standing outside his office with a newspaper under his arm. He checked his watch.

"After eight already?" Zach asked, shocked by his sudden immunity to the passage of time. "Good Lord."

"Must be reading something good." J.P. entered Zach's office and sat down.

"Possibly. Here—listen to this." Zach opened her manuscript to a marked page and read aloud.

"It is a pleasure to watch her work. From my desk in the office I need only to move my chair six inches to the right and I can see the kitchen's reflection in the hall mirror with such clarity that I feel like a ghost in the room.

"This is what I see—Caroline, who at twenty still retains the coltish legs of a much younger girl, pushes a stool to the counter. It wobbles nervously under her knees as she kneels on it with a steadying breath. She opens the cabinet that houses my wineglasses, my deliberately mismatched collection, all of which are older than her and one or two which are older than this adolescent country. She takes them one by one from the rack; their fragile stems shiver in her delicate fingers.

"I brought her to this moment by design. I could have tortured her with tasks, with arduous acts of service. Instead, I chose to torture her with boredom, curious to see what the devil would do with her idle hands. Interesting that in my home it is the objects most easily broken that draw her attention first. With a soft, clean cloth she polishes every glass. She holds the bowl like a bird, strokes the stem like the back of a cat, wipes every old whisper off the lip. I see her eyes count the glasses. I count them with her. Thirteen. Last night

I showed her the lash but did not use it on her. Thirteen…
one lash for every glass she touched without my permission.

"Thirteen…tonight I think I'll whip her first and tell her
why after."

Zach closed the manuscript and waited for J.P.'s reaction.
J.P. whistled, and Zach raised his eyebrow at him.

"I think that rather turned me on. Should that worry me?"
J.P. asked with a rakish grin.

"Since I'm the only other person in the room, I think it
should probably worry me a great deal more," Zach said. "It's
rather good, isn't it? The content is slightly unsettling but the
writing…"

"She's got talent. I told you. I hope this means you are no
longer planning on killing me."

"Killing you?"

J.P. grinned. "Yes, for twisting your arm over Sutherlin."

Zach laughed a little. "No, I'm not going to kill you anymore. But tell me—was I really the only editor who could
or would work with her?"

"I suppose I could have dug up someone else. No one near
as good as you, though. Anyway, Sutherlin requested you."

Zach looked up in surprise.

"She did?"

"Well, not by name." J.P. looked slightly sheepish. "She
told me to give her to whichever editor would flog her the
hardest. Yours was the first and quite honestly the only name
that came to mind."

"I'm hardly flogging her."

"What would you call it?" J.P. had a dark twinkle in
his eyes.

"I don't believe I will justify that insinuating tone in your
voice with a response. We were discussing the book after all."

"Yes, quite a stunning little book you waltzed out of Rose's party with Monday night."

"I'm a professional," Zach said calmly. "I don't shag my writers."

He omitted mentioning how shamefully close he'd come to asking Nora up after the cab ride to his building. He still couldn't believe she'd gotten to him that fast. In ten years of marriage he'd never once been unfaithful to Grace, never even wanted to be. And then in one day Nora Sutherlin was putting thoughts in his head he hadn't let himself have in years.

"I've seen her. I wouldn't blame you if you did. But it's just a shock. I'm surrounded by postfeminists and neo-Freudians. Whatever happened to that 'forgot the author, only the book matters' philosophy?"

"One cab ride and one good conversation hardly makes me a Freudian. I'll admit I was a bit of a prig about her. She is a good writer and the book has potential. If I'm warming up to her it's only because I'm warming up to the book. But she is starkers. That I was right about."

"She's a writer. She's supposed to be mad."

"At least she's also a mad worker. She's already sent me a full synopsis of every chapter and the new outline I ordered."

"How's the new outline?"

"Better," Zach said and glanced at his notes. "But still, more sex than substance. I think she's capable of substance. Just afraid of it."

"She does seem fairly married to her bad-girl writer persona," J.P. said, and Zach nodded his agreement. "It lends her credibility if she makes people think that she practices what she preaches. Getting her to retire her proverbial whip and take up the pen full-time won't be easy."

"But if she did…" Zach glanced down at the manuscript and remembered his reaction Tuesday morning when he'd forced himself to read it again, this time with an open mind. The words had simmered on the page, flared into life and burned. He'd gotten so engrossed in the story he'd forgotten that he was supposed to be editing it. "If she did, she could set the world on fire, and she wouldn't even need a candle. And don't you dare tell her anything I just said. I've got to keep her afraid of me if I'm going to keep her writing."

J.P. laughed to himself, and Zach stared at him.

"What?" Zach demanded.

J.P. took the newspaper out from under his arm and unfolded it. It was a copy of the *New Amsterdam Noteworthy,* a biweekly New York trade publication that carried the most recent news in publishing. J.P. threw the paper on Zach's desk. On the bottom front page was a small photo of him and Nora on the staircase at Rose Evely's party. Zach hadn't remembered a camera flash. Apparently the photographer had been far enough away he'd missed it. In the photo Nora leaned toward Zach with her mouth near his ear. It looked as if she was about to kiss him on the neck. Zach knew exactly what moment that was. It was when he'd said he couldn't believe he was doing this and she'd responded with a seductive "I can." The caption under the photograph read, "Nora Sutherlin— the only writer who could make Anaïs Nin blush."

"She doesn't look scared to me," J.P. said. "You look a little petrified, however."

"J.P., I—"

"I don't want to have to find another editor for Sutherlin. But I will if I must. I don't mind if the book sells because of the sex in it. But I don't want anyone thinking that writers have to do more than write when they come to Royal."

Zach rubbed his forehead.

"I swear it's just about the book. And no, you don't have

to find another editor for her. I know we can make something good together."

"I think you can, too. If you stay focused." J.P. sounded
skeptical.

"I am focused."

"Easton, I'm an old man. My hearing's going and I've got
two knees on the way out. But my eyes can still see. Since
the day you arrived here, you haven't once smiled like you
meant it. And when I walked into this office and caught you
reading her book, you were smiling like a lad who just found
his father's Playboy stash. I've tried writing in bed before. I
never seem to get much done."

Zach opened his mouth again, but J.P. raised his hand to
cut him off.

"You can keep working with Sutherlin. For now. Just take
a little advice—"

"I'd rather not."

J.P. reached across Zach's desk and grabbed the manuscript.
He flipped it open and whistled. No doubt his eyes had landed
on one of the myriad erotic encounters in the book.

"In the words of Charlotte Brontë," J.P. began, "'Life is so
constructed, that the event does not, cannot, will not, match
the expectation.' Or in the words of me… Keep it on paper,
Easton."

Zach clenched his jaw and did not reply. J.P. grabbed the
newspaper with Zach and Nora's picture and left him alone
once again with her book.

Closing his eyes, Zach conjured an image of Grace. God,
he was glad she was in England where she wouldn't see that
photo. But why worry? Even if she saw it, saw him with another woman, would she care? Of course not. If she did, she'd
be with him in New York right now.

With a tired sigh he turned to a page in Nora's book he'd

marked with a paperclip. Caroline is sleeping in a separate room from her lover after an argument. William wakes and walks on silent feet to her door. Cracking it just slightly, he pauses and listens until he hears her breathe. The image haunted Zach. The last year with Grace had become a nightmare of shutting doors and separate rooms. Still he could never let the night pass without at least looking in on his sleeping wife until that one terrible night when he found the door locked. The next day J.P. called and invited him to New York and to Royal House with the promise of the chief managing editor position at the L.A. offices when the current chief retired. Zach didn't even bother to ask what he would be paid before saying yes.

Why was he letting himself think about this? He had to stay objective about the book and its enigmatic author with her dark hair and red dress and her words that burned.

Keep it on paper, Easton…

Easier said than done.

5

*T*he phone rang at seven and the call itself consisted of only seven words—her hello followed by his "The club at nine. Wait blindfolded."

With shaking hands she hung up the phone and went to shower.

She arrived at 8:46. In most areas of her life she ran habitually five minutes late. But she'd learned the hard way never to keep him waiting.

He had his own room at the club, only one of seven people who did. And she had a key to his room, only one of two people who did.

His room was spare and strangely elegant considering its only purpose. Apart from three floor-standing candlesticks, his room was simply adorned. Rich white and black linens covered the bed. White sheets waiting to be stained.

She undressed completely and found the black silk scarf. Kneeling on the bed with her back to the door, she closed her eyes and wrapped the sash around her head. She hated this part, hated sacrificing her sight to him. It wasn't fear so much as greed. She wanted to see him, *wanted to see him hurt her, wanted to see him in her. He knew that's what she wanted. That's why he ordered the blindfold so often.*

She waited.

While she waited for him to arrive, she began the deep, slow breathing he had taught her long ago. She took the air in through her nose and pulled it into her stomach before exhaling out through her mouth. The breaths weren't simply to relax her although they did take the edge off her nervousness. The hypnotic breathing lulled her and helped her slip closer into subspace, that safe place where the mind went while the body was elsewhere being tortured. There was a third reason for the breathing he had never told her, but she knew was true—he'd ordered her to do it. Even the very air that went into her lungs did so at his command.

She exhaled when she heard the door quietly open. Straining her ears, she tried to hear everything he did. He didn't speak. He rarely spoke at these moments. She listened and heard with some relief the sound of only one set of feet. Sometimes he didn't come alone. She heard him strike a match and light the candles; she sensed the room brighten.

Five minutes or more passed in silence before he came to the bed. A shiver ran through her body as he placed his fingertips on the small of her back. The pleasure of the shockingly gentle touch was so intense it felt like something had pierced her back all the way through to her stomach. She sighed as he kissed her naked shoulder. She stiffened when he locked her collar around her neck.

He rarely used the leash in their private interludes. He reserved the leash to humiliate her when he paraded her through the club. When alone he simply slipped two fingers under her collar and dragged her like a dog to where he wanted her. The collar tightened when his fingers gripped the leather band. He pulled and she came with him as he brought her carefully off the bed. He was always so cautious with her when she was blindfolded, careful to never let her trip or hurt herself in any way. Hurting her was his privilege alone.

He pushed her forward and she felt the bedpost against her shoulder. Taking her arms one by one, he pulled them behind her back. She leaned her weight into the wood as he buckled the leather bondage cuffs on each wrist. He raised her arms over her head and secured them high to the top of the bedpost.

She stiffened as she felt his hands cover her face. They did nothing but rest there a moment before they moved over her head. Slowly, they ran over her neck and across her shoulders, up her arms and down them again. His arms encircled her and slid over her chest, breasts, and stomach and up her sides before gliding up and down the expanse of her back. One hand slipped between her legs as the other passed over hips and buttocks, down one leg and up again, then down the other. Finally, he ran his hands over the tops of her feet and then lightly passed them over the sensitive soles. She tried not to smile at the exquisitely gentle sensation of his hands touching every part of her body. She knew what he was doing. If more than three days passed without him taking her, he would perform this ritual of re-marking his territory. Her body was his territory, his hands were saying. Every inch of it.

She sensed him step away from her. She began her slow deep breathing again. When the first blow landed between her shoulders, she flinched but did not cry out. The second one came harder and this time she did flinch. By the tenth her back was on fire. After twenty she lost count.

Behind her blindfold, time ceased to pass in its customary manner. Five minutes of flogging lasted an hour. One night in his arms passed in minutes. An hour-long beating was something to be grateful for. The beating would seem to last forever. Even eternity in Hell was no Hell if he was there.

The flogging finally ceased. He pressed in close to her. She felt his strong, bare chest against her burning back. She breathed in and inhaled his scent. Even warm from exertion and arousal he still smelled like a deep winter night.

He placed his hands on her fluttering stomach and brought them slowly up to her breasts. A night with him always meant waning pleasure and waxing pain, waxing pleasure and waning pain. He brought her through the cycle over and over again. The pain brought her body to life. The pleasure was always most acute when it followed the pain.

Now it was pleasure alone she felt as he caressed her breasts and teased her nipples. His mouth found the spot between her shoulder blades that when touched sent a thrill straight into her stomach. One hand slid between her legs and touched her clitoris. With his finger and thumb he massaged it until she was so close to coming she felt the first muscle contraction.

He pulled away from her, leaving her panting and desperate for him. She prayed he'd let her down now, let her down and finally take her.

When she heard the whistling sound of something slicing through the air, she knew he wasn't done hurting her yet.

After so many years together she'd learned how to prepare herself for a flogging, for the whip and the strap. She knew tricks, ways to breathe, ways to hold herself, to alleviate the pain even as she received it. But when it came to the cane, nothing helped. And when the first strike landed on her lower thighs, she could do nothing but cry out. The second came on the heels of the first, a little harder and one inch higher. On the fourth strike she screamed and felt the blindfold turn wet with tears. The fifth was lighter only because the sixth and final strike was always the worst. The sixth landed in a diagonal across all five previous welts. She sagged in her bonds and cried. He didn't always beat her until she cried. She learned to love and fear those nights he did. He saved up her pain, counted it like currency and the more pain she endured, the more pleasure she could buy with it.

When he untied her from the bedpost, her arms fell like dead weight to her sides and her knees buckled. He caught her before she collapsed and laid her tenderly on the center of the bed.

His mouth was at her ear now. With words intimate and secret he whispered his love for her, his pride that she was his property, his possession, his heart. She was always his, would forever be his. New tears flowed now but they were ones wrenched from her by love and not torture. This was her favorite pain.

He kissed her now on the mouth for the first time. He kissed her like he owned her, as he owned her. He kissed her like her mouth was his mouth, her lips were his lips, her tongue was his tongue. They were one flesh. They needed no wedding ring, no ceremony to know that was true. She had the collar around her neck. She did not envy married women what they had. She would take his collar over a blood diamond and a cheap gold band any day and for all time.

He moved away from her again. She waited on her aching back and relished the absence of pain. When he returned to her he pulled the coverlet down underneath her so she lay on the sheets. He took her by the knees and wrapped a soft cotton rope around them. She relaxed and let him tie her to the bed. Her knees were up and pulled wide. She lay completely open now. No matter how hard she could try to close her legs, she couldn't. She never tried.

The bed shifted. She knew he knelt between her wide-open thighs. She inhaled sharply when she felt his fingers slowly enter her. He opened his fingers to widen her, to prepare her for his penetration. He pushed into the back wall of her vagina and pressed down until she flinched hard around his hand. Her passage was slick and wet for him. But he was large enough that he could tear her or bruise her if he didn't ready her for him first. There were times he took her so roughly she bled. Those were the nights he was lost to himself, lost in the darkness that hid beneath the shadow of his heart. But tonight he wasn't lost. He was with her.

She felt the wet tip of him poised at the entrance to her body. He pushed in slowly. She whimpered as she stretched and opened to take all of him. If she could have taken his whole being inside her she would. If she could disappear inside him and live in his skin she would.

He moved in her with long meticulous thrusts that filled and emptied her. His pace did not quicken. He gripped her wrists and pressed them into the bed. Many nights he would secure her wrists with rope, as well. But some nights he needed to hold her down with his own hands.

She lay beneath him and panted. Tied as she was she could do little more than take him. She wanted to beg but he hadn't given her permission to speak. She tilted her hips up as much as she could to take even more of him in her. With one hand still on her wrists, his other hand reached between them and caressed her where their bodies joined. The pressure built in her hips. A knot tightened in her stomach and she felt an invisible rope pull her toward the ceiling. She came hard and spasmed around him. He didn't stop.

The second climax came not long after the first one. He could manipulate her body as if he knew it better than his own. It terrified her at times how in control of himself he was even when inside her.

He thrust harder. He pushed in deeper, moved faster. She gasped as his grip on her wrists tightened to the point of pain. With one final push he poured into her. When he came at last it was in complete silence.

Still inside her he reached behind her head and untied the blindfold. She looked to the side and didn't meet his eyes.

"Look at me," he ordered and she did so gratefully. His steel-gray eyes glowed with his love for her.

"I love you, sir," she whispered.

The slap came so sudden and fierce that her whole body shuddered in shock.

"Did I give you permission to speak?"

This time she didn't answer. She shook her head. The movement dislodged a tear that had been lurking at the corner of her eye.

He smiled at her and dipped his lips to hers. He kissed her again and she relaxed into his mouth. His lips moved to her neck and up to her ear.

"I love you, too."

Still buried deep inside her, he began to thrust into her once again. She closed her eyes and leaned her head back as he wrapped his hand around her neck. Her collar bit into her throat.

She swallowed hard against his hand and breathed and breathed.

He'd only just begun to hurt her tonight.

"Hey, Nor, I'm home. Want some dinner?"

Nora blinked and rubbed her eyes, which had gone dry from staring at her computer screen for so long.

Wesley stood just inside her office and at first she could barely focus on him. She saw him but saw through him and past him at the same time.

"Sounds good." She glanced at the words on her screen. "I'm starving."

"Pasta?"

"Too many carbs."

Wesley rolled his eyes. "Fine. Salad and fish?"

"Fish? But it's not Friday."

"You're the Catholic. I'm Methodist. We eat fish whenever we want. Give me twenty minutes."

Wesley left her alone again. She printed out the pages she'd been typing and read through them.

The phone rang at seven and the call itself consisted of only seven words...

She read to the end and pressed the pages, still warm from the printer, briefly to her chest. Reluctantly, she slid the pages under her desk and fed them one by one through the shredder. She highlighted the text on her computer screen and hit Delete, flinching as the text disappeared. She closed the document and let the words disappear into the ether. She hated to do it. But she knew The Rule. She obeyed the Ruler.

Nora stood up for the first time in an hour and left her office. When she saw Wesley standing at the kitchen counter she actually could see him now. He smiled at her. She smiled back.

"So what did you write today?" he asked as he expertly sliced through the skin of a ripe red tomato.

"A really hot sex scene with a lot of S&M between a girl and her true love," she said and Wesley rolled his eyes at her, his usual response to her wickeder scenes. "But don't worry, I deleted it."

"How come?" he asked, popping a chunk of tomato into his mouth.

Nora leaned against Wesley, taking temporary comfort in his warm, strong chest. He wrapped his arm around her and rested his chin on top of her head.

"It wasn't fiction."

6

*M*y Caroline,
  I didn't want to write this story any more than you want to read it. It's us. Of course it's us. A name changed here, a date changed there…but still us. You have always been my only muse. I cannot paint or sculpt. I have only my words to render your likeness. Sometimes I wish I were both God and Adam so I could tear out my rib and create you from my own flesh. I would say I'd create you from my heart, but I gave that to you when you left me. But that's a cliché, isn't it? Sadly, that's all I have these days. The whole story is a cliché. I desired you. I ate of you. I lost you. That ancient story—older than the Garden, old as the Snake. I would have liked to call this story of ours The Temptation *but the word* temptation, *once the province of pious theologians, has now been co-opted by every third second-rate romance novelist. And although I loved you, my beautiful girl, this is not a romance novel.*

"Like it, Zach?"

Zach blinked at the interruption, lost as he was in Nora's new words.

"It's quite an improvement."

"An improvement? Oh, I meant the cocoa."

Zach sat in Nora's bright kitchen, the winter sun turning everything white. Nora's new draft of the first chapter sat in front of him and a cup of hot chocolate steamed at his elbow. He sipped the cocoa and felt like a lad again in his grandmother's kitchen.

"Very good," he said, inhaling the warm steam. "So is this."

He tapped the pages in front of him. Nora had taken his advice and created a frame story for her book. It would be a letter her narrator, William, was writing to Caroline, the woman he loved and lost. It was working beautifully already— the book and the partnership with Nora. He'd rarely gone to his writers' homes and certainly never sat with them at their kitchen table and drank cocoa. Nora was proving to be a different breed from any writer he'd ever before known. *"'This is not a romance novel…'"* Zach read from her new first chapter. "Excellent line. Evocative and provocative. Ironic, as well."

"Ironic?" Nora sipped at her own mug of hot cocoa. She sat across from him at the table and pulled one leg up to her chest. "It's true. It isn't a romance novel."

"Not a traditional one, of course. Your protagonists don't end up together, but it is a love story."

"A love story is not the same as a romance novel. A romance novel is the story of two people falling in love against their will. This is a story of two people who leave each other against their will. It starts to end the minute they meet."

"Why does it end? You seem like an optimist to me, but

the end is heartrending. The last thing she wants to do is leave him, and yet in the end she goes."

Nora left her chair and went to the kitchen cabinet by the refrigerator.

"I'm no optimist," she said as she opened the cabinet door. "I'm just a realist who smiles too much. And the reason William and Caroline don't stay together is that while he really is in the lifestyle, she's not. She's only in the relationship for him. It's their sexuality that's the problem, not the love. It's like a gay man being married to a straight woman. No matter how much he loves her, it's a sacrifice every moment they're together. The sex is secondary to the sacrifice."

"A very close second, I notice."

Nora laughed. She closed the cabinet door and knelt on the floor. She opened the bottom door and gave a victorious laugh.

"Found them." She pulled out a bag of marshmallows. "I have to hide the sugar from Wes."

"Has a sweet tooth, does he?"

"He has type 1 diabetes. And a sweet tooth. Bad combination. He's usually really good about what he eats, but I catch him staring pretty longingly when I have cocoa and marshmallows."

Zach wondered if it was actually the sugar Wesley had been staring at and not Nora. He couldn't take his own eyes off this woman. She'd been captivating in her signature red Monday night. And now in casual clothes she looked casually stunning. He watched her as she rolled back onto her toes and rose straight up off the floor with the well-trained grace of a geisha. He marveled at her offhand display of almost balletic agility while she leaned over the table and dropped a handful of marshmallows into his cocoa and hers.

"Zach, don't take this the wrong way, but you're even more

ridiculously handsome when you look happy," she said, dropping back into her chair and popping a marshmallow into her mouth. "You aren't, by any chance, enjoying working with me? The London Fog isn't lifting, is it?"

Zach took a sip of his cocoa to cover his embarrassment. He was used to women hitting on him but never before had any woman been so shamelessly forward with him.

"As this is the first time we've actually sat down and worked on your book together," Zach said and coughed uncomfortably, "I think a verdict on my meteorological conditions would be premature."

"What's the verdict on the book then?"

"The verdict is…you might actually pull this off. But not without some major revisions. Keep the letters at the beginning and end. But I want the body of the book in third, not first, person."

Nora looked down at her notes. She picked up her pen and wrote something on a sheet of paper. She looked at it a moment before sliding it across the table.

The first time William saw Caroline was on Ash Wednesday. She still had the ashes on her forehead.

"Like that, Zach?"

Zach read and nodded his approval. "Perfect. That's exactly what I want. Now rewrite the entire book like that."

"Yes, sir," she said and saluted. "What else? Since you're being nice to me, I have the feeling you're about to hit me with some more changes, yes?"

Zach grimaced, unnerved by how well this near stranger could read him.

"Just some minor ones—have you considered going a more mainstream route with your characters?"

"I like virgins, perverts and whores," Nora said without

apology. "I couldn't care less about the people who just fuck for fun on weekends."

"The sex shouldn't be the story, Nora."

"The sex isn't the story, Zachary. The sacrifice is. Caroline is actually vanilla, not kink. So she sacrifices who she really is to be with the man she loves—she sacrifices the good for the better."

"But they end it, yes?"

"That's the point of the book—sacrifice can only get you so far. William and Caroline are just too different to make it work. And although two people can love each other deeply, sometimes love alone doesn't cut it. We can only sacrifice so much of ourselves in a relationship before there's nothing left to love or be loved."

Zach's stomach clenched. Even now he ached for Grace with an impotent fury. Zach could only raise his cup of cocoa.

"I'll drink to that."

He and Nora *clinked* their tea mugs together in a mock toast. Across the table their eyes met, and Zach could see the ghost of his pain reflected in hers.

Zach's next question was cut off by Wesley's sudden entrance in the kitchen.

"Hey, you," Nora said to Wesley. "What's up?"

"I'm not here," Wesley said. "Keep working. I just need my coffee mug." Wesley threw open the cabinets and took an aluminum travel mug from a shelf.

"Where are you going?" Nora asked.

"Study group at Josh's. I'm helping him with calculus, and he's giving me his history notes."

"What are you majoring in, Wesley?" Zach asked politely, trying not to show how unnerving he found Nora's relationship with her young intern—unnerving and familiar.

"Biochem. I'm premed."

"That's wonderful. Your parents must be very pleased." Zach winced internally at how old he sounded.

"Not really." Wesley shrugged. "My whole family has worked with horses for generations. They want me to come home and stay in the business. If I have to do medicine, at least it could be equine medicine." He poured a mugful of coffee and screwed the lid on tightly. "I have this conversation with them every week."

"I think he should just let me talk to them." Nora batted her eyelashes at Wesley.

"You," Wesley said, pointing his finger at her, "don't exist. So don't even think about it."

Nora responded by wrinkling her nose at him in mock disgust.

"What?" Zach said. "Your parents don't know you and Nora are living together?"

A faint blush suffused Wesley's face. "There's a lot they don't know. They were going to pull me out of school and send me to the state school down there. It was money reasons, the usual, and Nora offered to let me live with her and work for my room and board. They just know I got a job to cover it and a place off-campus. They don't know what I'm doing."

"How did you two meet?"

"School," Nora answered for Wesley. "His school was obviously a little desperate—they asked me to be their writer-in-residence that semester. Wes was in my class."

"You were her student?" Zach asked, his hands going cold even as he said the words.

"The class met at one." Wesley smiled at Nora. "I needed to meet my Humanities requirement, and I would have taken anything that let me sleep late on Tuesdays and Thursdays."

"I'm very flattered." Nora stuck her tongue out at him.

"I'm very leaving. Later," Wesley said. He reached for Nora's mug and she slapped his hand.

"What are your numbers?" she demanded.

"One-seventeen. I can have a sip," Wesley protested.

"Not on my watch. Drink your coffee black, and keep your hands off my cocoa."

Wesley feinted to the left and stuck his finger in her cocoa and licked it off as he disappeared through the kitchen door. Zach felt a pang at the easy intimacy between Nora and Wesley. He missed his play-fights with Grace in the kitchen and the bargains they struck to make up. He would cook dinner if she would wear the lingerie he'd gotten her for her birthday. She'd do the dishes if she could be on top tonight…amazing how they both came out victors in those battles.

"So he's…nineteen?"

"You have a dirty mind, Zachary Easton. Wesley's as pure as, well, I'm not."

"You're telling me that Wesley's a virgin? The young attractive houseboy of an infamous erotica writer is a virgin?"

"Believe it or not, I do have some self-control. And even if I didn't, Wes certainly does—apart from sticking his damn hand into my cocoa every now and then. He's a good Christian kid and I respect him more than I can say for his decision to wait. Mark my words, Zach, I will put the first randy bitch who lays a hand on him in the hospital."

"And he doesn't mind what you write? What you do?"

Nora leaned back in her chair. "We made a deal. I can top, but not bottom."

"Are you secretly a gay man?" Zach eyed her curiously.

"I'm not so secretly kinky. Top and bottom are S&M terms, too. Wes leaves me alone about my sex life as long as I'm not the one coming home with the bruises."

Zach swallowed. "Did you ever come home with bruises?"

Nora bit her bottom lip.

"I won't bore you with the whole story of me and Søren," she said, glancing away. "Let's just say we've got history and leave it at that. Last year, I went to see Søren on the day we consider our anniversary. I do it every year. Can't stop myself for some reason. Anyway, I had a weak moment. I came home the next morning covered in welts and bruises and with a nice fat lip. Wes was horrified. He started packing."

Zach winced. The thought of welts and bruises on Nora horrified him, too.

"So you made your deal?"

"Right. If I go back to Søren one more time, Wes is gone."

"Moving out seems a rather extreme threat. Of course, moving in with you seems a rather odd decision."

"He's Methodist. I think he's trying to save me. Methodists are always trying to save people."

"Are you sure he doesn't have feelings for you?"

"He does have feelings for me. Namely irritation, frustration and disgust mingled with amusement. But that's not surprising since he's not in the game."

Zach sympathized with the boy. He had the same feeling for Nora, too. As well as intoxicated, amazed and aroused mingled with petrified.

"You said he was a virgin. How do you know he isn't like you?"

"K-dar," Nora said and tapped the side of her nose. "Kinksters can smell it on each other. And my Wesley smells like warm vanilla."

"Wonder what I smell like." Zach cursed himself for accidentally speaking the words aloud.

Nora cocked her head at him; Zach's heart started to race. She rose up out of her chair and slid onto the top of the kitchen table. She stretched across it and put her nose at his neck. Slowly, she inhaled. A slight rush of air whispered over Zach's skin and he immediately knew what every muscle in his body was doing.

"Not kink. But not vanilla, either. Smells like...curiosity. It killed the cat, you know."

"Nora," Zach said in a warning tone. J.P. would yank him off Nora's book in a heartbeat if he saw them right now.

"S&M is as psychological as it is physical and sexual, Zach. Imagine being as deep inside a woman's mind as you are inside her body."

Zach's hands gripped his mug, still warm from the steaming liquid inside.

"We're working," he reminded her, reminded himself. He remembered their photograph in the newspaper; her mouth had been at his ear just the way it was now. If he turned his head only a few inches their lips would meet.

"I write erotica. I am working. Want to earn some overtime?"

"Nora, we've got less than six weeks and more than four hundred pages to write. Now get off the table and stop wasting my time."

"Oh, fine," she said, sounding playfully disappointed. Zach exhaled with relief when she slid back and sat in her chair again. She reached under her notes and pulled out a copy of the trade newspaper that had their picture in it. She leaned back in her chair and threw her legs up on the table as she flipped through the paper. Zach stared at their picture again prominently displayed right in front of his face. The byline read Erotica Writer Nora Sutherlin Gets the Royal Treatment.

Nora turned another page and sighed. "And to think I thought the fog was finally lifting."

Zach stared at his computer screen for the seventeenth straight minute in a row. The words of the book review he'd sworn he would start writing for the *Times* tonight simply would not come. He had words, the wrong words, Nora's words, but not the words he needed.

Not kink, she'd purred into his ear, sending every nerve in his long neglected body firing. *But not vanilla, either...* Nora... Zach understood now why some people were afraid of her. He was afraid of her, of her power to take captive his every thought. He felt unmoored around her, unsafe, and yet of everyone he had met since coming to New York, he sensed only she could be trusted.

As deep inside a woman's mind... Zach tried and failed to stem the tide of images that her words conjured. Grace's soft skin, moon-white against midnight sheets, her back against his chest, his hands over hers, his mouth to her neck as he drove into her, knowing her flesh and yet still knowing so little of her soul. Her body had been so open to him once. But her mind? Her heart?

Zach shook his head, trying to pull himself out of his dangerous reverie. Grace, who he had made love to countless times, told him nothing. And Nora, on whom he had never laid a hand, said everything.

On a whim, Zach minimized his document and opened Google. Nora threw out S&M terminology like a doctor tossed around the names of exotic diseases. He wasn't entirely clueless when it came to matters of kink. An old lover of his had even accused him of being kinky because he preferred positions other than missionary. He certainly knew what S&M meant—sadomasochism, knew the French called it "the English vice" because his countrymen had an amusing obsession with corporeal punishment. Not him—he tried to avoid giving or receiving pain whenever possible. He'd been known to bite a little during lovemaking, something Grace was inordinately fond of, but actual hitting or whipping was something entirely out of his purview.

After they were done working on her book today, Zach had worked up the courage to ask Nora about Søren, her former lover who she spoke about with the reverent sadness of a knight speaking of a fallen king. She said they were a D/S couple like William and Caroline in her book. She'd been collared to him for years, and that leaving him had been akin to dying.

Zach typed in *D-S couple* and quickly discovered he'd mentally spelled it incorrectly. Spelled D/s it stood for Dominant and submissive. Interesting that while the *D* was capitalized the *s* was always lowercase to illustrate the lower status held by the submissive. The whole thing seemed rather strange and sexist to him, but he couldn't deny that there seemed to be quite a few male submissives and some rather impressive-looking female Dominants out there. He couldn't imagine a woman as vivacious as Nora being content to sit at a man's feet. His only guess was that this man, this Søren person, was a rather impressive specimen. He wondered what Søren did for a living—probably something innately alpha male like a pilot or a military officer. Or perhaps he was independently wealthy like Nora seemed to be. Something certainly afforded her an impressive quality of life. She drove a late-model black Lexus with a cheeky license plate that read "Say Ouch" and she lived in an elegant, historic home. He knew award-winning writers in England with a dozen or more books under their belts who still couldn't afford the house or the neighborhood she lived in.

Curiosity got the better of him, and Zach typed in *Nora Sutherlin* and hit Enter. She found several fan pages, some links to fan fiction and Nora's official website. Zach kept scrolling through all the mentions of Nora on the web. He clicked the link to someone's blog that carried an entry entitled "Last Night with THE Nora Sutherlin." But as soon as Zach clicked the link the page disappeared. He hit Back and tried to find it again, but the page had vanished. Maybe the blog server was down.

Zach gave up nosing on Nora and looked up more S&M terminology. As uncomfortable as the idea of coupling pain with sex, he did appreciate that people in the community seemed fairly responsible in their play. Every webpage he landed on carried the mantra "safe, sane and consensual." He stared for a long time at an image of a young woman wearing a brown leather collar that buckled and locked at the base of her neck. Zach remembered Nora had said she'd been "collared" to Søren. Collars were apparently quite an important part of the S&M scene. Nora had touched his naked wedding ring finger that night in the cab and then brought his hand to her bare neck. She'd equated being collared with marriage. Maybe that's why he and Nora had found common ground so quickly despite being such wildly different people—they were both going through a divorce of sorts.

But was he going through a divorce? Every day when he checked his mail, he expected papers from Grace's attorney. Every time his home phone rang, he expected it to be Grace telling him they needed to stop putting it off. But so far he'd received no calls or legal papers. Was she waiting on him to start the process? If so, she might have to wait a long time. He couldn't deny their marriage had fallen apart in the past year and a half, but he was in no hurry to put the final nail in the coffin. He'd hoped if he came to New York, she'd miss him enough to want to make it work again. But every day the phone stayed mute.

Zach closed the internet and exited from his empty document without writing a single sentence. He'd left Nora in her kitchen hours ago. Surely she'd sent him another email by now—she emailed him constantly. But his in-box sat empty but for a reminder from J.P. about the next staff meeting and a question from his assistant, Mary. Both could wait.

He clicked on New and typed in Nora's email address. Of course she would have an address with "littleredridingcrop" in it. Ludicrous as it was, at least it made it easy to remember.

Nora, he wrote and stopped. Why was he writing her? They'd discussed her book for hours today. There was no more to talk about for now. And considering they already had a reputation for working too closely together, he knew he didn't need to be writing her about anything but the book. What would he say if he did write her? He had those words, those sentences. But they had tumbled about in his head so much since meeting her that they had crashed against each other, against him, and broken into fragments.

Nora, I don't want to I won't it's been so bloody long I can't I think of you of her too much I still love but I I hurt her Grace Now it's hell worse Limbo I hurt too young too much…

Zach deleted it all, even Nora's address. He knew better than this, knew better than to get involved. He would not make this mistake again. She would not pull him off course.

It didn't matter, he told himself. He was gone in five weeks. Off to L.A. where he could start over again and perhaps get it right this time. But did he want to start over? At forty-two a new life seemed a far more terrifying prospect than it had at thirty-two when he and Grace married and moved to London.

The blank email sat waiting before him. He looked down at his fingers poised above the keyboard. Was it the words that failed him or his hands? They felt too heavy now. It made no sense. Without the weight of his wedding ring they should have been lighter.

The screen still waited, the cursor winking at him like an eye.

Zach typed in another address.

Gracie, he wrote, using the nickname that never failed to make her smile. Please talk to me.

Nora stood at the kitchen window peering into the dark. Sunset came so early in the winter that whole days seemed to pass in darkness. Zach had left her several hours ago, left her with a thousand ideas and admonitions. But now she could only wait and think and gaze at the light falling in from the lamppost outside the kitchen window. It illuminated the tremulous flakes of snow and cast white shadows that gathered round but did not touch her.

She turned toward a sound and saw Wesley standing in the doorway watching her with the same intensity as she watched the snow-lit play between the light and the shadows.

"How long have you been hanging out here in the dark?" Wesley asked, stepping into the lone pool of light.

She sighed at a shadow. "For as long as it's been dark."

Wesley reached out to flip the light switch.

"Leave them off."

Wesley dropped his hand back to his side.

"I didn't know you could write in the dark."

Nora gave him only the barest hint of a smile.

"You'd be surprised what I can do in the dark, Wes."

Wesley grimaced. "Zach know what you do in the dark?"

Nora shook her head.

"No. He thinks I'm just a writer. Let's keep it that way, shall we?"

"It's not anything I'll ever brag about."

"Wes, you knew what I was when you signed up for this job."

"And you knew how I felt about it when you asked me to move in."

Nora took a slow deep breath.

"And yet you moved in anyway. Why is that?" Wesley lifted his chin and only looked at her. "His silence says it all."

Nora stepped away from the window and took a wineglass from the cabinet.

"What are you doing?" he asked as he came deeper into the dark kitchen.

"If you're going to pout, I'm going to drink," she said, pouring herself a steep glass of red wine. "I read somewhere that red wine is good for diabetics. Want one?"

"I'm not pouting. And I don't drink."

"There's a lot you don't do."

Nora sat on top of the kitchen table across from him. She watched him, daring him with her eyes to either speak or leave.

"I've got homework," he said.

"Then go." Nora gestured to the door.

Wesley moved to walk past her. But Nora reached out and stopped him with a hand on his chest.

"Or stay," she said as she took a deliberate sip of her wine before setting the glass down on the table next to her. "Staying is better." She grabbed a fistful of his shirt and pulled Wesley to her, positioning him between her knees. His face was a blank mask and his eyes would not meet hers.

Nora laid her hand on his stomach, smiling as the taut muscle quivered through his T-shirt.

"Nora, don't—"

"Søren and I used to play a game on his kitchen table,"

Nora said, ignoring the plea in Wesley's voice. "Did I ever tell you about that?"

"No," Wesley said, visibly tensing as Nora raised his shirt and slid her hands underneath, pressing her palms into his warm skin. She saw his fingers curl into fists.

"Simple game—he'd fill a wineglass with one of his expensive reds and set it on the edge of the table. Then he would fuck me. Hard." Nora grinned as Wesley flinched. "If I thrashed too much, or fought him and knocked the glass off... then the wine wasn't the only red that we spilled that night."

Wesley closed his eyes as if trying to block out the image.

"The secret is," Nora said as she raked her fingernails up Wesley's chest and back down his stomach, "sometimes I'd knock it off on purpose."

"I won't play that game with you," he said as Nora continued relentlessly caressing the delicate skin of his chest and sides. "I won't play this game with you, either."

"But it doesn't have to be a game, Wesley." She narrowed her eyes like a cat's. "It can be very real."

"Don't do this." His voice was a plea. His breathing was getting harder, everything was getting harder now. "Not to me."

"Your heart is racing." She let her hand rest on the left side of his chest.

From his chest she traced a languid path down his stomach, his breath catching as she deftly unbuttoned the top button of his jeans.

"Nora..."

"I'm not holding you here. You can go if you want to. Do you?"

She grabbed his belt loops and pulled him even closer until his hips pressed against her inner thighs. She knew she shouldn't be doing this. But Wesley was a constant source of frustration. Sometimes she had to retaliate. And she knew that every now and then he forgot what she really was. It didn't hurt to remind him.

"I don't know," he finally answered.

"Now that is a refreshing bit of candor on your part. Since we're being so honest now, tell me, why are you being so pissy about Zach?"

Wesley's eyes widened. Nora bit her bottom lip as she waited for his answer.

"You like him."

"I do like him." She took another deep drink of the wine and set the glass down again. "But we've just met and we're not fucking. Not even I work that fast."

At that Wesley gave a grim chuckle and looked up at the ceiling.

"I couldn't care less if you were fucking him."

"My God, did you just say 'fuck'? You're a good, clean Methodist. You don't swear."

"You have no idea what I do."

"I do know what you do. I know you sleep with your bedroom door unlocked," Nora retorted. "Expecting company?"

"I know you stand in my door at night and watch me sleep. Expecting an invitation?"

Now it was Nora's eyes that widened. But she recovered herself quickly.

"You're pretty good at this game," she said, nodding her approval. "For a beginner."

"I told you. I'm not gonna play with you."

"Too bad. I think you'd like the prize." Nora went for the next button on his jeans, but Wesley grabbed her by the wrist to stop her.

"Harder," she instructed. Wesley let her go as if her skin had burned him.

"I thought so. Go," she said, dropping her hands to her sides. Wesley took a step back, his palm pressed into his stomach. "Go do your homework, kid."

She picked up her nearly forgotten wineglass and lifted it to her lips. But before she could drink, Wesley took the glass from her.

He held the glass in his subtly shaking hand before raising it and drinking. Finished, he lowered the glass and set it next to her on the table. He left the kitchen without another word.

Nora picked up the glass and stared inside.

He'd drained it to the dregs.

Nora set the glass back down and turned to follow Wesley. She hated when they fought even though it was almost always her fault.

Wesley would be fine, she told herself. He needed a little toughening up anyway. She'd never forget the first day she saw him. She walked into his classroom at Yorke, and the first thing she'd noticed was a pair of big brown eyes looking at her like he'd never seen anything like her before. And the minute he opened his mouth and those soft Southern syllables came out, she knew this kid was going to be no end of trouble. She'd made all her students talk about their favorite story. Wesley had said his favorite was O. Henry's *The Gift of the Magi*—the story of the wife who sold her hair to buy her husband a watch chain and the husband who sold his watch to buy his wife combs for her hair. Nora had called it a horror story. Wesley had objected and called it a love story. The debate had continued even after the class ended. Two people who give up their most precious possessions for love and end up with nothing—that's a love story? she'd demanded. Wesley had argued that they still had each other. She'd laughed and told him he might see things a little differently when he was her age.

She knew she'd been too rough with him tonight, but she

couldn't stop herself sometimes. After all, Søren had put her through ten kinds of hell when she was Wesley's age. And now she was grateful for the discipline he'd taught her, the fortitude he'd instilled in her. Now a guy like Zach could look her in the eyes and tell her she wasn't worth his time and energy, and she could look back and smile and ask him if that was the best he could do. Søren had made her strong and for that she'd be forever grateful. And Zach was making her a real writer, which was the one fantasy Søren could never make come true for her. And Wesley…she looked down at the empty wineglass and quickly refilled it in his honor—Wesley was just making her crazy.

Nora turned and saw her book and Zach's notes lying on top of the kitchen table.

"Goddammit, Zach," she said to herself and poured the wine down the drain. "Why did you have to tell me it was going to work?"

7

Five weeks left…

A tear formed in the corner of Nora's eye and fled down her cheek before she could stop it. She rubbed it off with her sleeve and made herself blink. She'd been staring at her computer screen for so long her eyes were watering. Stretching while she backed up her work, Nora decided to check her private email account before taking a bathroom break. She breezed through a note from her agent and deleted a few bits of spam. Just before logging out a new message popped into her in-box. From Zach, it bore the subject line "Regarding Sex."

"Why, Zachary," she said, chuckling to herself, "yes, I think I will regard sex."

The email dragged on for two pages and detailed every reason why she needed to cut out the majority of her sex scenes. She stopped reading after the fifth use of the word *gratuitous*.

You're no fun, she wrote Zach back. Can't I just keep three of my scenes?

Zach was obviously still at his computer. He quickly replied with one word.

No.

Two? she wrote back.

No.

Nora was about to fall out of her chair laughing. She could imagine his stern but strikingly handsome visage right now, his brow furrowing deeper with each annoying little email from her.

One? I promise I'll make it good. Please? I'll buy you a puppy.

I'm allergic to dogs, he replied.

Nora bit her lip as the wheels in her head turned.

Let's play a game, she wrote back. I'll give you fifty extra pages this week if you let me keep three of my scenes—heavily edited, of course.

She held her breath as she waited for his reply. An email finally popped up in her in-box.

Fine. But any sex on the page must serve both the plot and the character development. Now stop playing and start writing. You've got five weeks left and over four hundred pages to rewrite.

I'm keeping the puppy, she wrote back. She wasn't surprised when he didn't reply.

Nora was rereading Zach's most recent note on her new chapters when her hotline rang. She heard its Klaxon ringtone in her office all the way from the kitchen. Rolling her eyes, she stood up and headed in that direction in no particular hurry. When she got there, she found Wesley standing by the counter with the phone in his hand. He looked oddly tired and grim. He handed it to her without a word and walked past her. "King, I swear I'm going to beat the shit out of you if you don't stop calling me."

"Now you're flirting, *ma chérie*."

Nora ground her teeth together and took a deep breath. Was there any man in the world more infuriating than Kingsley Edge? Søren, she remembered. Only Søren.

"I am not flirting. I am working." She said the words slowly as if she were speaking to a child. "I have another job, recall?"

"I try everything I can to forget your other job, *maîtresse*. Your other job costs me money."

"Well, it makes me money."

"And that helps me how?"

"Kingsley, tell me what you want and then leave me alone. My editor is making me rewrite my entire book."

"*The* Nora Sutherlin taking orders from a man. I thought those days were long over."

Nora clenched her jaw. She would not let him goad her into a fight today.

"I'm *une petite peu* busy, *monsieur*."

"Never too busy for a client. For this client in particular."

Nora leaned her head against the cold metal of the refrigerator. Most of her clients were on her time; she saw them at her leisure. Just part of the mystique of being a Dominatrix. But there were a handful of clients not even she felt comfortable keeping waiting. She guessed it was Jake Sizemore, CEO of some company that made something that kept the world going. King never let her turn Sizemore down when he came to town.

"Fine. What do I need to know?"

"Just wear your finest and be there in an hour. *C'est ça*."

Nora scribbled the time and place down in her datebook. She'd been trying so hard not to take any jobs while working with Zach. Zach had all the signs of someone going through a fairly serious depression. She knew depression well, knew it was anger turned inward. That much depression signaled an impressive cache of anger lurking under that ridiculously handsome exterior. Her gorgeous blue-eyed editor already oozed disapproval of her at every turn. She could only imagine how bad his reaction would be if he found out that writing wasn't her only job. For over a year now she'd dreamed of quitting the game altogether, but without a signed contract from Royal, she was scared to give up her day job.

"I'm getting a little sick of this, you know, King?"

"You say that and yet I hear *la petite morte* under your breath. You know you love this job."

"I love the money. That's it."

"You love him, *chérie*."

Nora closed her eyes and swallowed the growl in the back of her throat.

"*He* has nothing to do with this." Nora refused to get into a discussion of Søren with Kingsley. Kingsley reported to Søren.

"*Ma petite,*" he chided. "You do this for his attention. *C'est vrai, oui?*"

"That's like saying criminals commit crimes to get the cops' attention."

She heard Kingsley's soft, heady laugh.

"*Exactement*. One hour, *maîtresse*."

Nora hung up and went to her bedroom. The house was too quiet. She couldn't hear Wesley anywhere. Usually at this time of day he was working on his homework and listening to music. Or if homework was light that night, he'd be playing his guitar and singing softly to himself. She remembered the first time she'd caught him playing and singing. She'd told him he sounded a little like the nineties band Nelson. He'd said, "Who's he?" and Nora had thrown a book at him.

She dressed in her black leather skirt with the back slit and her black-and-red brocade bustier. She found her black gauntlets and pulled them on. They laced up her arms and she had a horrible time tightening the laces and tying them off on her own. She went to find Wesley. He hated that she worked as a professional Dominatrix, but he tolerated it more or less. Before he'd moved in over a year ago she'd explained what she did, what she was. He'd been shocked. He didn't even know such things existed. He was relieved, however, when she explained she was in no way a prostitute and that she never had sex with clients—not the male clients anyway. They weren't even allowed to kiss her except on the toe of her boot. No, she was no prostitute, she explained. She was, if anything, a kind of massage therapist who simply inflicted pain instead of pleasure. Despite his shock, Wesley moved in anyway. She'd been so impressed by how well he took it, she'd even told him about Søren.

"Just don't ever let me in the same room with him," Wesley had said when Nora revealed the nature of their relationship.

"You think you can take Søren?"

"You said he was, what, forty-five? Eighteen versus forty-five? And any guy who beats up on women doesn't know what to do around a guy who'd only hit another man."

Nora had laughed then, so hard she'd almost fallen over. Could Wesley get any more precious? When she'd stopped laughing, she'd taken Wesley's chin in her hand and forced him to meet her eyes. Søren once told her she had the most dangerous eyes of any woman who'd ever lived. He told her when men looked in her eyes they saw their own darkest fears reflected back. Usually she tried to tamp down that particular trick of hers. This time she'd let Wesley see all her fears and all of his in one glance.

"Kid, Søren could eat you for breakfast and not even need to chew. Don't ever fuck with a sadist, Wesley. For Søren, torture's just foreplay."

"Why did you stay with him?" he'd whispered.

Nora had grinned at him, and she saw a new fear in Wesley's sweet brown eyes.

"I like foreplay."

Wesley…she couldn't find him anywhere. She stood in the living room and noticed a note taped to the door. It said he was at the library but he'd be home around six. And at the bottom of the note were the words he always said when she went out for a job—"You don't have to do this." No, she didn't have to. But she owed it to Kingsley. Nora grabbed her coat and toy bag and made a quick stop in the bathroom. She took a pill bottle from the medicine cabinet, swallowed one without bothering with water and left.

It took forty minutes to get to the hotel. Her clients were among the elite of the world—only the wealthiest and most powerful men and women could afford her. Quite a few were even household names. So it was rare she ever went in through the front doors of a home or hotel. But Kingsley hadn't mentioned the need for discretion so she didn't bother.

She strode through the front lobby of one of the grandest and oldest hotels in the city and worried for a second that someone from Royal might recognize her. She shook off the worry—no one who worked in publishing could afford this place. The lobby was littered with women dripping with Prada and men stuffed inside their Armani suits. Nora bit back a smile as she breezed past them in her leather and lace with her black toy bag slung across her back and her sunglasses on even though she was indoors and it was still winter. She wasn't ashamed of what she did. But it was fun to be around people who were nervous just being in the same room with her.

A couple standing near the elevator walked off when she joined them in their waiting. Vanilla people were so cute sometimes. She entered the elevator, hit the button for the nineteenth floor and headed up alone.

Nora stepped out, got her bearings and made her way to room 1909. A key card lay hidden under a newspaper in front of the door. She unlocked the door, stepped inside and saw a tall, blond man in black standing with his back to her.

"Hello, Eleanor," he said.

Nora gasped and her bag hit the floor with a nervous clatter of metal.

"Oh, my God…Søren."

Zach sat at his desk in his office at Royal. He checked his email one last time before shutting down the computer. He was surprised he hadn't gotten more of a fight from Nora about paring down her sex scenes. Perhaps she now understood the kind of book she was writing, was starting to understand she could write something erotic without being an erotica writer.

Straightening the papers on his desk, Zach found a copy of the contract that the legal department had worked up. It wasn't signed yet. And even if Nora signed it today, it wasn't valid until he signed it. He looked over the terms. J.P. had been very generous. Royal didn't dole out significant advances very often. Of course, Nora brought her own impressive fan base with her. Zach knew J.P. hoped she would bring a certain libidinous cachet to the rather staid old publishing house. It was a bold move that might actually pay off if Zach did his job right.

Zach smiled as he flipped through Nora's unsigned contract. When he and Grace had bought their first house, the paperwork hadn't been half this preposterous. Poor Grace. He remembered watching her at their tiny kitchen table in their first horrid little flat they'd rented sight unseen when they'd moved to London. They'd been married less than a year. She thought she was supposed to know what every word of the contract meant, what every clause referred to. She sat for hours poring over every page. He'd leave and come back and she would have another twelve questions to ask him. *What did first right of refusal mean? Did they know the assessed value? Did they need a variance if he worked from home?*

It was so damn endearing watching her spend an entire day trying to understand everything as if she thought she should that Zach finally had to come over, shove the papers away and make love to her right on top of their settlement statement. He remembered it so clearly, the shock on her face when the papers scattered to the four winds. She thought he was angry with her. But he remembered her smile when he kissed her so fiercely the table scooted a foot back. He remembered her red hair against the dark wood, how her legs had wrapped around him with almost childlike eagerness as he moved inside her.

He'd heard once there was nothing like buying a house together to make or break a relationship. That was the day he decided they were going to make it.

Zach put the contract down, leaned back in his chair and closed his eyes.

Maybe they should have bought more houses.

An hour later Nora left the hotel and strode to her car cursing Søren under her breath the whole way. She kept cursing, knowing if she let up on the fury for one second, she would collapse into tears. It had been months since they'd spoken. She did everything she could to avoid him. Sometimes she saw him at the club and they only looked at each other across the room while bystanders subtly moved a few steps back like unwitting townspeople caught between two gunslingers. Søren wasn't on the attack today, however. Worse—he'd wanted to talk.

Nora ran over their conversation again in her mind. The conversation, as all conversations with him were these days, was rather one-sided. She'd sat on the bed like a child in trouble for staying out too late and ground her foot into the plush carpeting as he stood in front of her and ticked off, one by one, all her multifarious sins. Nora had known him since she was fifteen years old. Shocking how much ammunition one could stockpile in eighteen years.

And then near the end he'd revealed why he'd gone to the trouble of setting up the meeting. Kingsley had told him she'd been acting different lately—quieter, angrier, desperate to work one day, reluctant the next. She'd explained she was heavy into revisions on her new book, that her new editor was a hard-ass who was giving her the chance and the challenge of a lifetime. Søren seemed skeptical, asking if there might be something she wasn't telling him. The hour he'd paid for finally up, Nora started to leave. On her way out the door Søren had stopped her with a word—"Wesley."

Nora had turned around slowly. Trying to keep her tone neutral she'd asked, "What about him?"

"Next time we meet, little one, we will have much more to discuss."

Her heart flinched when he'd used his old pet name for her. But she merely stared at his handsome face, hoisted her toy bag and left. After all these years, all the practice, she was getting good at that. Nora sat behind the wheel of her car and closed her eyes. She said a prayer of thanks Søren hadn't touched her. That's what had happened on their last anniversary. She'd gone to his home too late in the evening. She'd let him give her a glass of wine. They'd talked about mutual friends and even played a game of chess at the kitchen table he'd made brutal love to her on so many times. For a few minutes she'd let herself forget that she wasn't his property anymore. One curl had fallen forward across her face when she'd bent to move her bishop. Søren had reached out and brushed it behind her ear. He'd caressed her cheek with his thumb. Within minutes they were in his bedroom and she was strapped to the bedpost. He'd beaten her so hard that night she'd nearly gagged on her own tears. And when he finally gave up on the pain, he'd untied her and let her collapse into his arms. His darkness spent, he laid her in his bed and made love to her so tenderly she'd cried again. In the past when they were still together, he'd talk to her while inside her. Sometimes he would articulate in shocking detail the intensity of his desire for her. Sometimes he would simply claim her, calling her his property, his possession. That night as he moved in her he spoke in Danish, the language he fell into when his heart was its most open. He'd taught her some Danish when she was a restless teenager. It became one of their secret ways to communicate. She'd forgotten a lot of it in the four years they'd been apart, but she never forgot *Jeg elsker dig*. It was Danish for "I love you" and he whispered it again and again into her skin.

Afterward he'd stayed inside her and pulled them into a sitting position at the center of his bed. Her legs wrapped around his waist; her arms twined around his shoulders. He ran his hands up and down her beaten back as he kissed her bare neck. She rocked her hips slowly, relishing having him inside her again after so long.

"You miss your collar," he'd said—a statement, not a question. She'd taken it with her when she'd left him four years ago.

"I miss it." She tilted her head back to give him better access to her naked throat. She bent forward again and he kissed her bruised lips. If she pretended it was only today and that there was no yesterday and no tomorrow, she could stay with him forever.

"You can come back to me, Eleanor. Always."

"I can't." She shook her head. "They need you more than I do. I can't rip your life in half."

"It is my life," he'd reminded her. "You tore my life in half the day you ran from me."

"Don't," she said, and the tears burned bright in her eyes. Her chest heaved and she clung to him so hard her fingernails bit into his skin. "Don't say I ran. I didn't run. It wasn't running and you know it. You know I didn't want to leave you. I no more ran from you than I'd ever run into a burning building. I could never run from you."

He laughed at her vehemence.

"Then what would you call it if it wasn't running, little one?" He pressed his lips to her forehead.

"I crawled." She tried to smile for him. "It's what I'm good at after all."

He wrapped his arms even tighter around her. She prayed he'd chain her to his bed and make her stay there the rest of her life. But she knew he'd let her go at dawn. He wouldn't keep her against her will even if against her will was what she wanted.

"When you come back to me—" he began and she pulled back to meet his eyes.

"I won't."

"*If* you come back to me," he said, making a rare concession, "will you run or will you crawl?"

Nora had pressed her whole body into him at that moment. Resting her head on his strong shoulder, she watched as a tear forged a river down his long and muscled back.

"I'll fly."

To Søren she knew that night was proof that she still belonged to him. But to Wesley it was a waking nightmare when he'd seen the welts and bruises, her cracked lip, her purpling cheek. It took her a solid hour to convince him she didn't need to go to the hospital. For some reason telling him she'd had worse didn't seem to comfort him. For the second time in twenty-four hours, she'd had to beg.

"It's not violence," she'd tried to tell him. "It's love. Some loves only come out after dark, Wes."

"Not with me, Nora. Don't pull that writer romance crap on me. He beats you and you let him. And if this is love then he shouldn't love you anymore," Wesley had said on his way to the front door, his clothes in a duffel bag and his guitar case across his back.

"I wish he didn't. For his sake and mine. For yours, too."

Something in her voice changed his mind. He'd dropped his duffel by the floor and set his guitar down. He'd walked back to her and wrapped his arms gingerly around her. He'd been so careful not to hurt her. She'd cried then for the pain she'd caused him. Wesley had gone with her to her room and helped her take her shirt off. She lay on her stomach in her bed while he iced her bruises and put antibiotic ointment on her welts. They hadn't talked while he helped her. But when she was finally comfortable enough to sleep, Wesley had told her his decision. He couldn't stop her from working, but if she ever went back to Søren again, ever let him hurt her again,

Wesley was gone. It was like asking her to close her eyes and never open them again, but for Wesley, she'd agreed.

Nora drove home and put her regular clothes back on and decided that once and for all she was cutting off all contact with Søren. She knew it would be hard considering that they ran in the same circle but she would find a way. She would never talk to him again. Not after he'd tricked her into seeing him.

Nora paused in her bedroom and took slow, deep breaths. She checked the clock—6:36. Wesley should have been home from the library half an hour ago. She went to his bedroom—no backpack, no keys. She called his cell phone and no one picked up. She waited another half hour thinking he was just pissed at her for answering her hotline. But she knew Wesley—he wasn't the vindictive type. She called his cell phone again. No answer. By seven-thirty she was scared. By eight-thirty she was terrified. At nine she gave up and called the only person besides Wesley she trusted completely.

The phone rang only once.

"Søren, I need your help," she said as soon as he answered. The fear clutched at her throat like a claw. "I can't find my Wesley."

8

At nine-thirty Zach still remained in his office reading through Nora's rewritten chapters. Going with third person had opened the book up. The prose was more atmospheric in third person. He needed to talk to her about the end of chapter three, however. She was sliding into self-reflection when what she needed was a strong plot element.

He picked up his phone and dialed her number. She answered on the first ring.

"Nora, it's Zach."

"Dammit, Zach. I can't talk right now. I'm busy." She sounded angry for some reason. Angry and out of breath.

Busy and breathless…he knew immediately what she was busy doing.

"You're on my time now, Nora. I don't care what you're doing. The book is more important."

"Fuck the book."

"Nora, I went out on a limb to work with you. If you think—"

"You don't want to know what I'm thinking right now."

Zach sat back in his chair. What had happened to the Nora he'd shared cocoa with just a few days ago? She'd been so passionate about her book then, so interested in all of his ideas.

"I'm thinking you obviously don't have your priorities in order."

He heard Nora take a hard breath.

"Then fuck you, too, Zach." She hung up.

Zach set his phone down and stared at it. He expected to feel furious but instead his heart dropped. Apart from J.P. and Mary, Zach hadn't felt any connection with anyone since coming to New York. Then he'd met Nora and as exasperating as she was, she was also funny, beautiful and made him feel alive again. And she had been the first person who'd seemed to care about him. Now she'd yanked away from him, away from the book. He knew they wouldn't and couldn't ever be lovers. But he'd thought they might be able to forge something like a friendship while they worked together. What the hell had happened?

The phone rang again and Zach answered it immediately, hoping to hear Nora on the other end. Instead the chief managing editor of Royal West in L.A. started speaking. Zach had only spoken to her once or twice after he'd been offered her job once she retired. Now she was telling him he could come out sooner if he liked since she'd heard he didn't have much to hold him in New York. She wouldn't mind sharing her office for a couple of weeks while he got acclimated. Might ease the transition for the staff. Still reeling from his fight with Nora, Zach promised her he'd think about it.

After all, he agreed, there really wasn't anything keeping him in New York.

He hung up the phone again and pulled on his coat. Glancing down, he saw Nora's manuscript sitting on his desk. He picked it up and tossed it into the recycling bin.

"Fuck you, too, Nora."

Nora paced the hallways of her house with her private cell phone in her hand and her hotline phone in her pocket. Wesley didn't have her hotline number but she knew either Kingsley or Søren would call her back soon. Søren had connections at every hospital within eighty miles, and Kingsley had half the judges, attorneys and police chiefs in the tristate area in his back pocket. Between the two of them, one of them should be able to find Wesley.

She'd gone into his room and dug through his desk trying to find any of his friends' phone numbers. But they were all programmed into his cell phone and his cell phone was with him, wherever he was. She tore through his closet, his dirty clothes hamper, and found nothing to help her hunt him down.

Nora sat on the edge of his bed and opened his nightstand. She knew Wesley would be less than thrilled she was digging through his things. He'd probably get quite the shock if he saw what she kept in her nightstand. But she didn't find anything helpful or incriminating—ChapStick and a spare set of keys to his car. Under the file of his medical stuff she found a small photo album. Pulling it out she smiled through tears when she flipped it open and found it full of pictures from last summer.

Leafing through the pages of photos she remembered…

At first she'd been suspicious when Wesley had woken her up early on a Saturday morning in May and told her to get up and put on jeans and boots. He'd driven that day in his beat-up yellow VW bug, and they'd listened to weird music the whole way there. "Who is this?" she'd asked. "Wilco."

"Who's this?" "The Decembrists." Finally he'd demanded to know what the last album she bought was. She thought for a good five minutes before remembering—*Ill Communication,* the Beastie Boys, 1994. Wesley would have been a toddler and she'd been fifteen or sixteen years old.

After a long drive they'd arrived at a farm—a horse farm. Wesley had told her that he'd grown up around horses. From what he'd said it sounded as if his father worked as a horse trainer and his mother did the books at a horse farm in Central Kentucky. But that was the first day she'd actually seen Wesley around the big animals. For someone as blessed by Mother Nature as he was in the looks department, he often seemed nervous and unsure of himself. But the second they hit the stables he became a different person. Walking right up to them, he slapped their sides with sure hands. For a good forty-five minutes he took a turn on three or four different horses, saddling them, and riding them around the paddock.

"Being a little picky, aren't you, kid?" she'd asked him. "Just get a horse for yourself and let's go."

"I'm not picking one for me." He dismounted nimbly from a large Appaloosa. "I can ride anything. I'm trying to find one for you. You need something tame since you're a rookie."

"I'll take anything but a gelding," she'd told him.

"What's wrong with geldings?"

"We won't have anything to talk about."

Wesley had laughed then, open and easy, and for a moment she saw the man he would become in ten or twenty years—strong and kind, growing a little more handsome and a little less innocent with every year that passed. She envied the woman he'd end up with. Lucky lady indeed. Finally, after the fourth horse, he'd found her a young buckskin mare named Speakeasy.

"She's smart and submissive—perfect for a first-timer." Wesley handed her the reins.

"Smart *and* submissive—I should introduce you to Søren," she whispered in Speakeasy's twitching ear. "Do you like riding crops, too?"

Nora remembered following him back into the stables to watch him pick his horse. A teenage girl walked with Wesley giving him suggestions. Nora watched as the pretty girl cast adoring glances at Wesley while Wesley had eyes only for the horses.

"He'll do." Wesley picked out a large heavily muscled sorrel. "What's his name?"

"Bastinado," the stable-girl said. "The boss named him that. Don't know why."

"Is he bad about stepping on your feet?" Nora had asked.

"Very bad about it." The girl looked at Nora for the first time. "How did you know?"

"Bastinado—it's a fancy term for foot torture." Both Wesley and the stable-girl had stared at her with wide eyes. "What?"

Wesley saddled his horse with effortless proficiency. Nora watched his knowing fingers as they tightened the stirrups and adjusted the rigging. He swung up into the saddle, shoved his straw cowboy hat on his blond head, shifted his hips and took the leather reins as though he'd been born on a horse. Nora took a slow breath and silently repeated her Wesley mantra.

Look but don't touch…look but don't touch…

They'd gone easy that day since it was her first time on a horse. The sprawling farm had miles of trails connected to it. Wesley led them down paths that meandered all over the scenic hillside. They stopped every few minutes and took pictures. Nora flipped through the album and remembered when they'd passed over a small creek. Wesley must have sensed her apprehension because he took her reins and led both their horses easily through it.

Nora turned to another page and found her favorite photo. Wesley had bent over the saddle to pat Bastinado on the neck when Nora had snapped the picture. Wesley looked up just in time to flash her his million-watt smile. Nora closed the album and started to slide it in the drawer when she noticed another photo—this one in a frame and hidden all the way at the back. "Wes…" Nora breathed, looking at the picture of her and Speakeasy alone together. She remembered the moment the photo was captured. She had dismounted and was rubbing her horse down after they were done riding. She thought Wesley was taking a picture of the rolling pasture behind her. She'd pushed her sunglasses on top of her head and pressed her forehead to Speakeasy's. Tendrils of her hair had gone loose and wild around her face. Her eyes were closed in the picture and she wore a smile of pure happiness. She couldn't believe Wesley had framed the photo. She looked so silly in it.

Nora put everything back in his nightstand the way she found it and stretched out on Wesley's bed. She ran through every possible scenario in her mind—was he sick? Car accident? Lost his phone? Lost his mind? Did he have his insulin pen with him? Did he have his med-alert bracelet on? She knew Wesley. He'd call her if he was going to be five minutes late. Another college boy she wouldn't have worried about. Any other college sophomore was surely out at a party or a bar or back in some girl's dorm room. Not her Wesley—apart from occasionally sleeping in on Saturdays, he woke up at the same time every day, came home at the same time every day. He had to keep his meals regular because of his insulin injections. He had to get plenty of sleep. He worked out at the school gym every day. He didn't drink, didn't do drugs, didn't smoke, didn't have sex. He went to class, he went to church, he went home for Thanksgiving and Christmas…he was the most boring teenage boy alive. Alive…please let him be alive.

Nora closed her eyes and turned onto her side. She could smell Wesley's warm, clean scent on his pillows. For the first time in a long time she prayed with everything within her.

God, I know You're probably still pissed about Søren, and I really don't blame You. But please don't take Your wrath out on Wesley. Flog me all You want. He doesn't deserve it.

At 4:30 a.m. she was still wide-awake and staring at his ceiling when her red hotline phone rang. She sat straight up and found her hands were shaking so much she could barely hit the answer button.

"King, please tell me you know something."

"*Oui, chérie.* Your intern is a most interesting young man."

"Just tell me where he is. Is he okay?"

"He's in the hospital, but he is unharmed if rather the worse for wear."

"What happened?" Nora ran a hand through her hair. She leaned over and breathed through her fear and relief.

"A comely little nurse took a peek at his chart for me. Something called DKA? Is that familiar to you?"

Nora's hands went numb at the initials. "It's diabetic ketoacidosis. It can be fatal."

Kingsley rattled off the story sliding in and out of French as he did so. From what she gleaned from his hasty bilingual recitation, Wesley had gotten sick at the library and passed out after throwing up several times in the bathroom. He'd been admitted to the hospital in full-blown DKA.

"Which hospital?" she asked. "What room? Please tell me he's at General."

"*Oui.* I've already called Dr. Jonas."

"Tell him I'll give him the freebie of his dreams if he can get me in."

"No freebies, mistress. He's already promised to help any way he can. He would never cross *La Maîtresse*."

"Great. Wonderful. Where is he? ICU?"

"PICU," Kingsley said and laughed. Nora laughed a little, too. They'd put Wesley in the Pediatric Intensive Care Unit. "*Mais chérie*, you cannot go."

"Fuck you. Of course I can."

"His parents flew in. They're with him."

Nora swore. Wesley would kill her if she turned up at his bedside with his parents sitting right there. He did everything he could to keep her a secret from them. His parents would yank him back to Kentucky so fast his head would spin if they discovered he was living with an infamous erotica writer—especially one who worked as a Dominatrix. Jaded New York parents wouldn't let their kids near her much less these conservative Southerners.

"Forget it. Just tell me where he is."

Nora jotted down his hospital room number.

"Thanks, King. I owe you."

"*Pas moi*. Our mutual friend was the one who found where they'd taken your pet."

"Then tell him we're even now for him tricking me."

Nora hung up the phone and ran to her room. She threw water on her face and changed clothes again. At 6:00 a.m. she arrived at the hospital and found Dr. Jonas. He explained that Wesley ended up in the PICU because the ICU was full. Nora told him not to tell Wesley that.

He brought her down several hallways past dozens of hospital rooms. She glanced at the figure of a priest talking quietly to a family in tears in one room. Nora lowered her eyes respectfully and kept walking. Passing through a set of double doors, they entered the pediatric ICU. Teddy bears holding balloons were painted on the walls. Oh, yes, she'd never let Wes hear the end of this. Dr. Jonas put his finger over his lips and left her by room 518. She stood outside the open door and listened intently—a woman's voice with a heavy Southern accent, his mother's she guessed, loudly whispered to a man with a softer accent. In hushed tones they went back and forth about how they never should have let their son move so far from home for college. Fighting was a good sign. That meant Wesley was out of the woods. But her relief was short-lived. His mother sounded determined to have him back in Kentucky again while his father argued that he was old enough to be on his own, that they couldn't keep an eye on him forever. Nora found herself nodding her agreement with his father. But she could hear the distress in his mother's voice, the pain and the fear and the wrought-iron determination. Wesley's mom wanted him home with her to keep an eye on him. Nora felt the same way.

Nora didn't know what to do. She found Dr. Jonas again and made him call Wesley's attending physician. Wesley was in and out of consciousness after they'd brought him in, but he'd been awake and speaking a few hours ago. They'd stabilized his insulin levels and he'd be clear to go home in a day or two. Apparently Wesley wasn't absorbing his insulin as well as he needed to. He might need to start using a bigger needle. Nora ached with sympathy. Wesley loathed needles. He always injected himself in his upper left arm where he couldn't see the needle going in. Shoving needles into his own thighs or stomach would probably kill him before it cured him.

Dr. Jonas told her he'd call Kingsley if he heard anything else but there was nothing Nora could do for him now. She might as well go home.

Reluctantly, Nora left the hospital. She drove home and

decided she would let herself sleep. She checked the clock—almost 8:00 a.m. She'd been awake for over twenty-four hours.

Once in her driveway Nora turned off her car. But after that she lost the energy to do anything else. She leaned forward on the steering wheel and cried tears of relief, exhaustion and fear. Wesley's mother was the proverbial steel magnolia and she clearly wanted her son back home. Nora prayed Wesley had learned the fine art of telling someone off while living under her roof.

Telling someone off…

Nora leaned her head back against the headrest.

"Shit…Zach."

She turned the car back on and headed south toward Manhattan.

9

The next morning Zach headed straight to J.P.'s office without even bothering to stop in his own first.

J.P. looked up from his reading and blanched.

"I am reminded of the last words of Emily Dickinson at this moment," J.P. said. *"The fog is rising."*

"I'm done with her."

J.P. stared at him over the top of his glasses. "Easton, she could make Royal a great deal of money."

"Find another editor then. I don't care if we publish her or not. But I'm finished. Patricia Grier called me last night. She said I'm welcome to come out to L.A. a few weeks early and work with her. It's not a bad idea."

"It's a terrible idea. The staff won't know who's in charge. You won't know who's in charge. She'll undermine you. You'll undermine her. Regime change has to be quick and dramatic for it to be effective."

"It's Royal's West Coast office, not France in 1799."

J.P. took off his glasses and rubbed his forehead.

"Bring me her contract. I'll keep it."

Zach turned on his heel without another word and walked to his office. He paused at the door when he noticed it was cracked open. He remembered very clearly locking it last night since he'd left his laptop on his desk. Warily, he opened the door and entered.

"Hey, Zach," Nora said. She sat in his chair behind his desk with her eyes closed.

"What are you doing here?" he demanded. "How did you get into my office? It was locked."

"Magic." She opened her eyes and smiled.

"You look like hell," Zach said. Nora had dark circles under her eyes and her face appeared gaunt from lack of sleep.

Zach came around his desk and she stood up to give him his chair back. She sat on top of his desk and rolled back on it like a bed.

"I've spent the last twelve hours in hell. Sorry, I forgot to bring you a souvenir."

"I have all the souvenirs I need from my own trips there. What are you doing here, Nora?"

"Apologizing for going off on you last night."

"Apology accepted. Now you can go. J.P. is going to find another editor for you to work with. Probably Thomas Finley. He's an asshole. You'll like him."

"There are good assholes and bad assholes. You're the good kind. I only want to work with you."

"Well, perhaps you shouldn't have told me to first, fuck the book and second, to fuck myself."

Nora rolled up off his desk and turned to face him. She crossed her arms over her chest. She exhaled slowly.

"Wesley didn't come home last night."

"He's old enough he can go anywhere he pleases, Nora."

"But you don't know Wes. He calls. He calls all the time. If he's going to be five minutes late he calls me. I was in Miami a while ago and he called me to tell me he was going to the movies so if I tried to call him and didn't get him, I wouldn't worry. That's Wes. He didn't come home and he didn't call. I freaked out."

"I assume you found him?"

Nora laughed coldly. "Sort of. He's in the hospital."

Zach sat up in his chair.

"Good Lord. Is he all right?"

"He went into diabetic ketoacidosis at the library. No one called me because no one knows I exist. I'm not next of kin. I'm not any kin."

"Have you seen him?"

"I just came from the hospital where I spent half an hour eavesdropping on his parents while lurking out in the hallway. I can't go in since they're there. Zach, I feel…impotent. Bad feeling."

Zach looked away from her and stared out his window. His view was to the east, and if the world was flat and his vision was telescopic he could see all the way to England. He knew how Nora felt. Grace…her parents had come as soon as he called and told them she was in the hospital. As soon as they arrived he knew he'd made a mistake by calling them. The doctors immediately stopped talking to him and starting talking to them instead. He remembered his fury then, how he'd stepped between Grace's parents and the doctor and told the doctor in no uncertain terms that when a married woman was in the emergency ward, you spoke to her husband first and her parents second. He hadn't told the doctor to go fuck himself. He'd been far less polite than that.

"I'm sorry you had to go through that."

"When you called last night I was waiting for news. If God Himself had called me and started telling me the secrets of the universe, I would have told Him to go fuck Himself, too. You can't take me personally, Zach. Can I make it up to you? Coffee? Tea? Me?"

Zach laughed. Even exhausted she was still shameless.

"You need sleep, not caffeine or any other stimulant," he said, narrowing his eyes at her. She smiled and nodded in agreement.

"Okay, I'll leave you alone. Soon as Wes is home again, I promise I'll get back to the book. Can you email me whatever it was you were going to tell me last night? I'll read it and do whatever it is you want me to do."

Zach promised to do so and Nora started to leave.

"When's the last time you slept, Nora?" he asked before she walked out of his office.

"Twenty-six hours ago."

Zach winced. "You shouldn't be driving. Dead writers revise no tales."

"We'll put that on my tombstone," Nora said. Zach stared her down. "Fine. I've got a friend with a town house a few blocks from here. I'll go crash at his place."

"No stimulants, remember?" he reminded her. "Actors playing Hamlet are told to stay celibate lest they ruin their performance."

Nora threw a smile over her shoulder. Suddenly, she didn't look tired or worried anymore. She looked wild and beautiful and so alive.

"Celibate, Zach? Have you met me?"

Zach was still laughing after she'd left him. He looked up and saw J.P. standing in the door to his office.

"So the contract?" J.P. asked.

Zach looked at his boss.

"I think I might keep it a little while longer," Zach said a little sheepishly.

"And her?"

Zach reached under his desk and pulled Nora's manuscript out of the paper-recycling bin.

"I think I might keep her, too."

Nora pulled in at Kingsley's town house and walked inside without knocking. Nora announced herself to Juliette, Kingsley's beautiful Haitian secretary and the only other woman in the world besides her he was afraid of. Juliette gave her breakfast and took her up to Kingsley's opulent bedroom. She could sleep there since Kingsley was gone until tomorrow. Nora stripped out of her clothes and crawled between the sheets—sheets she'd spent more than a few nights on before. She took both of her cell phones out and laid them on the pillow next to hers in case Wesley, Zach, King or Søren called.

As she faded into sleep, Nora's mind went to Wesley's side—she hoped he was feeling better and would be home with her soon. As she pressed deeper into the luxurious sheets, a little part of her sort of wished Søren was there.

When Nora finally woke up it was almost nine at night. She'd slept for almost twelve straight hours. She showered in Kingsley's decadent bathroom and dressed in the clothes Juliette had brought for her and left on the chair next to the bed. When she got out of the shower, her hotline rang. She grabbed it and answered it with still wet hands.

"King—what's the news?"

"The good doctor says you are clear for a rendezvous with *ton petit garçon malade*. His parents succumbed to the doctor's insistence they let your pet sleep tonight. They are at a hotel."

"Tell Dr. Jonas next time I'll do that thing he likes with the peanut butter and the cock ring."

"It is without a doubt the sole reason he went to medical school."

Nora left Kingsley's town house and made her way back to the hospital feeling like a new person. Nearly shivering from the excitement at getting to see Wesley, she parked her car and headed straight to his room. Tiptoeing in, she saw Wesley lying in his hospital bed sound asleep.

She came up to the bed and looked down at him. His eyelashes fluttered against his tan cheeks and his chest rose and fell slowly. She bent forward and kissed him on the forehead. His eyes flew open and he looked at her as if she was something out of a dream.

"Nora, thank God." He tried to throw his arms around her. But he winced when he realized his arms were taped up with tubes.

"Don't move, kid. You're going to rip something out. I'm right here. How are you feeling?"

"Perfect now that you're here. I've been going nuts all day trying to figure out how to call you. But if Mom left the room Dad was here and vice versa. They finally left a few minutes ago. The doctor was really insistent they leave me alone tonight."

Nora grinned at him.

"Friend of yours?" he asked.

"Friend of a friend. It's good to have friends in strange places. I've got a cop who owes me a favor, too, if you ever get arrested."

"I'll keep that in mind." Wesley reached out and took her hand in his. "I'm so glad you're here."

"Me, too. I was here earlier creeping in the hallway. I heard your parents talking. Your mom wants you to move home."

"She does, but I'm not going to. I've got Dad on my side. We'll wear her down."

"You better. Good help is so hard to find. So what did the doctor say?"

Wesley groaned and Nora ran her hand through his hair. It felt so good just to touch him again, to be near him again. She couldn't believe it had been only one day they'd been apart.

"I've given myself so many shots in the arm that I've got scar tissue," Wesley said, rubbing his upper left biceps. "The insulin isn't getting through it well enough. I have to change my injection site."

"Thighs?" she asked. "Your cute little ass?"

"Worse. All my daytime shots in my stomach now and my thigh at night. You know, sticking a needle into your own stomach and leaving it there for five seconds is sort of over-rated."

"Tell me about it. Even the biggest kinksters don't play rough on the stomach. Very sensitive area. When can you come home?"

"They may let me out tomorrow or the day after. I feel a lot better. Just really tired."

"You look like you lost ten pounds and you didn't really have any extra to lose."

"You're the one who's too skinny, Nora."

"I have gained eight pounds since you moved in and started cooking every day."

"You needed those eight pounds. You were all gristle when I moved in."

"I have to be very tough to beat up on all my bad little boys and girls. I'm going to beat up on you, too, if you ever scare me like that again."

"I don't plan to. Promise."

Wesley smiled at her and she clutched his hand.

"Do you want me to run home and bring you anything? Clothes or anything?"

"Mom will use any excuse to go shopping. She was going to pick some stuff up for me tomorrow morning."

"Okay. I'll go and let you sleep then."

Wesley sat up and shook his head.

"Don't go. Please."

"I'll stay as long as you want me to, Wes," she said to the almost panic in his voice. "Scoot over and make room."

Wesley laughed but she wasn't joking. She carefully crawled into his hospital bed and slid under the wires and tubes. She stretched out next to him and Wesley wrapped an IVed arm around her back. She lay against his chest and closed her eyes.

"You know, I've fooled around in a hospital before but never in the pediatric ward."

"Nora, you're disgusting. Go to sleep."

"You sleep first."

"I don't want to sleep. I want to talk to you."

"Good. I don't want to sleep, either. What do you want to talk about? Horses?"

"You want to talk about horses?"

"Don't be mad but I was digging through your stuff trying to find your friends' phone numbers. I found the photo album from last summer. And the stupid picture of me with Speakeasy."

She looked up at him. Even in the dark she could see Wesley's blush.

"It's not a stupid picture. You look happy in it."

"Of course I do. I was with you."

Wesley smiled down at her. Nora kissed him on the cheek and rested her head once more against his chest. It was such a relief to hear his heart beating steadily against her ear.

"How did you find out where I was?" Wesley asked. He ran his hand up and down her arm. She knew the last thing he wanted to hear was that Søren had hunted him down for

her, and that Kingsley, her partner in crime, had used some
of his connections to get confidential information.

Nora shut her eyes and nestled in closer to Wesley.

"Magic."

10

Zach was relieved to find almost fifteen thousand new words from Nora in his email when he arrived at work two days after finding her half-unconscious in his office. Apparently she was working out her nervous energy from not having Wesley at home by writing five breathlessly intense chapters. He read through them and jotted down notes as he went. He was thrilled with what she was doing with the book. But he needed to steer her in a new direction before she wrote any more. The whole book couldn't be a sprint. She needed to stop and let the reader breathe for a chapter or two before kicking into high gear again.

Zach read through his notes again and dialed her office number.

"Sophocles's House of Patricide and Incest," Nora answered. "How may I blind you?"

Zach bit the inside of his cheek to keep her from hearing him laugh.

"Nora."

"Zachary," she said breathlessly.

"You're in a chipper mood, I see."

"You can see me? Where are you? Are you in my house?"

This time Zach let her hear him laugh.

"From this excessive display of mirth and jubilation, I assume your intern's come home."

"Yes, thank God. With a little subterfuge I managed to smuggle him back under my roof where he belongs. He is resting comfortably right now, and I am on cloud ten because cloud nine was full of pompous Englishmen. Wasn't my scene."

Zach cleared his throat. "Speaking of scenes—"

"Oh, God, the book. You know what, Zach, I am in a great mood. Nothing you can say or do will ruin it. Shred the chapters. Do your worst. Make it hurt. I'm ready."

Zach took a deep breath.

"They're fabulous."

He heard Nora snort a most unladylike laugh on the other end of the line.

"You're terrible at this game."

"I'm quite in earnest, Nora. They're excellent. Needs some minor cleaning up but spot-on all the way through. Now you just need to slow the pace down a little."

"Any suggestions?"

"Three words. Show—don't tell."

"How much are they paying you for this?"

Zach chuckled and gave Nora some concrete suggestions for where to take the next two or three chapters.

"And I want five more chapters by tomorrow morning," Zach said even though he knew that was an almost impossible challenge.

"Slave-driver," she said.

"Nora, we've lost a lot of time—"

"Zach," she said and he heard the smile in her voice. "Relax. It's me. *Slave-driver's* a compliment."

They said their goodbyes and Zach hung up the phone. He looked up and saw his assistant standing in the doorway of his office holding a box in her hands.

"Oh, God. Another one?" he asked.

"Afraid so, boss." Mary came inside his office. She put a book-size flat box on his desk.

"Have we figured out who is sending this nonsense yet?"

Zach picked up the box and warily tore off the plain brown paper wrapping.

"I think I know who it is," Mary said. "Wonder what it is this time."

"It was, what, anal beads two days ago. And a blindfold before that. And what was it last week?"

"Lube," Mary supplied. "K-Y Jelly specifically, I believe." Zach eyed Mary and suppressed a grin. Mary was his second favorite woman he'd met since coming to New York. "If you keep working with Nora Sutherlin, you'll be able to start your own sex shop."

"Anything would be preferable to this. I thought only adults were allowed to work in publishing," he said. Turning the box over in his hands, Zach considered just tossing it in the trash. Ever since he'd started working with Nora, a new "gift" would arrive in his office mailbox or on his desk every couple of days.

"Come on, you know better than that. I'll bet you anything it's Thomas Finley. He thought he'd get the job in L.A since he's been here the longest. He's been pretty pissed ever since J.P. promised it to you. But everyone knows he's still here only because he sucks up so much to the big bosses. He's doesn't edit books. He just spit-shines shit."

Zach laughed and decided Nora and Mary needed to meet if they hadn't already.

"I appreciate the loyalty as well as the imagery. But let's get this over with, shall we? Lovely," Zach said as he pulled out a pair of bright silver handcuffs with a set of tiny keys hanging off the middle link.

"Nice. Very shiny." Mary took them from him and examined them closely. "You have the right to remain silent," Mary began and slapped the cuffs on his left wrist. Zach gave her a dirty look. "Sorry. Too many *Law & Order* marathons, I think."

"Far too many."

Mary took the key and slipped it in the lock. She turned it but the cuffs didn't pop open.

"Shit," she breathed in shock. "The key doesn't work."

"Surely not." Zach took the key and tried it himself. Nothing happened. "Bloody hell."

"Boss, I'm so sorry," Mary said. "I'll call a locksmith right now."

"That bastard. If it's Finley, I'll kill him. Whoever it was wanted this to happen."

She raced from his office and headed to her own. He could only imagine how long it would take to get a locksmith here during the lunch rush hour.

He glanced down and saw Nora's manuscript in front of him. And then he looked at his door. He picked up his phone again.

"Ian McEwan's Cement and Incest Emporium—"

"Nora, really."

"I love caller ID. What can I do you for?"

"I have a small problem involving handcuffs," Zach said, glancing down at his wrist. "Do you know anything about locks?"

"If you knew how much of my life I've spent chained up, you wouldn't ask that question."

Zach paused a moment and said five words that were surprisingly difficult to get out.

"I need your help, Nora."

Zach waited for her to laugh or tease him. Instead, she gave him a small piece of advice that he decided to take and hung up the phone.

"I called the locksmith," Mary said, coming back into his office. "He said he'd be here in a couple of hours."

"Cancel him. I called Nora. She gave me a suggestion."

"What did she say?"

"She said, 'Three words—come to me.'"

Zach stood up and pulled on his long gray coat; he stuffed his hands into his pockets so no one could see the cuffs dangling off his left wrist.

"And I think I will."

Walking toward the elevator, Zach stiffened in fury as Thomas Finley strolled past him wearing an oily smirk on his face.

"Your jokes are not amusing, Finley," Zach said as he continued toward the elevators.

"That's because they're not jokes, Easton." Finley ducked into his office and Zach resisted the infantile urge to personally show Finley what was and was not amusing. Finley on the floor coughing up blood—that would be amusing.

Still fuming, Zach momentarily forgot about the handcuffs on his left hand when he stuck his hand out to hit the down button on the elevator. He heard a throat clearing and looked to the right.

J.P. stood at the receptionist's desk with his eyebrow arched in disapproval.

"Long story," Zach said. As much as he wanted to rant to

J.P. about Finley's torments, he was no schoolyard tattletale. He'd handle it himself when the time came.

"Might I ask where you are going thusly attired?" J.P. asked.

"Jail. Obviously." The elevator door opened and Zach stepped inside. He smiled at J.P. knowing full well that's exactly what Nora would have done. "It's just about the book."

If it was possible, J.P.'s eyebrow seemed to arch even higher.

"It's never just about the book, Easton."

When he put her in the handcuffs, she knew she was in trouble. The third time they ever saw each other she was wearing handcuffs. She wore them not for reasons of kink but of law enforcement. It was raining that night when she got caught for the first and last time. When she arrived at the police station and the cop pulled her out of the squad car, he was standing there just behind her mother. What was he doing here? she asked herself and then realized her mother must have called him out of fear and desperation. What a sight she was that night—soaked to the skin, bedraggled, wearing her school uniform with her hands cuffed behind her back. She'd glared at him from behind the veil of her wet hair, and he looked back at her with ironic amusement. But that wasn't the only look in his eyes. There was something else there, something it would take years before she fully understood.

She understood it now.

She sat on the floor gagged and handcuffed to the bedpost. In forced silence, she leaned back and watched him. A young woman with pink and blue hair was strapped spread-eagle to a St. Andrew's cross. With a cat-o'-nine-tails he tattooed the girl's back bright red with welts. The girl squirmed and cried out. She begged him to stop. He didn't stop.

After a few minutes the beating ceased. He laid the cat aside and strode over to where she sat on the floor. He knelt in front of her and ordered her to meet his eyes.

"Are you ready to apologize now?" he asked her. "Or shall I continue beating Simone?"

The only thing worse than one of his beatings was being forced to watch while someone else took the punishment that was rightfully hers. She slowly nodded her head.

"Good girl," he said. He stood up and walked over to the girl on the cross. He unbound her wrists and ankles. Simone stepped gingerly off the platform and knelt on the floor. She kissed the top of his bare feet and rose up again. He bent his head and in a voice too low to overhear, whispered something in her ear. The girl blushed and smiled. She asked for permission to kiss his hand. He granted it.

Simone kissed the center of his palm, gathered her clothes and left the room. They were alone again.

He walked back to her and squatted in front of her. He untied the gag and waited.

"You have something to say to me?" he asked.

"Yes, sir." She took a ragged breath. "I'm sorry I forgot to call, sir. I apologize for worrying you. I was so tired when I got home I went straight to bed."

"It takes mere seconds to call and let me know you arrived home. You are my most treasured possession. Your value to me is beyond what you can conceive. It is my duty to protect you. You know my rules. And you know better than to flout them."

She hated when she disappointed him. But it wasn't her fault she was so tired. He'd kept her up until 3:00 a.m. beating her and fucking her over and over again. It had taken everything she had to just make it to her bed that night. She knew she'd worried him when she hadn't called. But it was galling to be treated like a teenager with a curfew. She'd refused to apologize at first. She was twenty-six years old, for God's sake.

"Forgive me, please. I'll do anything."

He raised his eyebrow and she knew she'd made a mistake.

"Anything?"

Her stomach fell through the floor.

An antique black rotary phone sat on a table in his private quarters. He only ever used it for one purpose. He used it for that purpose now.

She didn't look up when the door opened. She knew from the shoes who it was who'd entered. Black riding boots. Men's riding boots.

She shouldn't have said "anything."

He returned to her and released her from the floor. He didn't remove the handcuffs, though. He kept her hands cuffed behind her back. He'd made her wear her old school uniform tonight in honor of the first time he'd seen her in handcuffs.

He unbuttoned her blouse and pushed it roughly off her shoulders. His mouth crashed onto hers and he kissed her until her lips were sore and swollen. He kissed his way down her neck and across her shoulders and breasts, leaving a trail of bite marks and bruises. He pushed her onto her back on the bed and wrenched her skirt up to her hips. He yanked her white cotton panties down her legs, over her white knee socks and saddle shoes. His fingers pushed inside her and spread her wide for him. He gripped her arm and shoved her onto her stomach. She felt his hands between her legs again separating her, prying her open. She braced herself and groaned as he pushed inside her. He rode her with fierce thrusts that left her gasping. She didn't want to moan or cry out. Not with an audience standing at the foot of the bed smiling and watching everything he did to her. But he wrenched the cries from her. She pressed her face into the bed and bit the coverlet trying to stifle the sound of her climax.

He kept thrusting and she was close to her second humiliating orgasm when he came inside her with a ferocious final thrust. She whimpered as he pulled out of her. She rolled onto her side and brought her legs up to her chest. Now they were both looking at her.

The man in the riding boots strolled toward her. He crawled onto the bed.

"Sir, please," she begged.

"You did say anything."

She swallowed and nodded.

"Yes, sir."

The man in the riding boots took her by the ankle and dragged her toward him.

"C'est à moi," the man said as he opened his pants. He pushed inside her and she raised her hips to take him deeper.

My turn.

Nora turned her head and checked the clock. Zach would probably be here soon. She laughed to herself at the thought of Zach getting stuck in handcuffs. How or why he'd been playing with handcuffs she could only begin to imagine. But knowing that sexy stuffed shirt of an Englishman there was no way he ended up in them for any of the reasons she ever had.

She stared at the words on her screen—*C'est à moi,* she read again and sighed. She exited from the document without saving it then stood up and headed to the living room.

Wesley lay stretched out on the couch with a chemistry textbook balanced on his chest and a highlighter between his teeth. He looked so warm and comfortable in his battered jeans and bleached-white socks and the double layer of T-shirts that she just wanted to stretch out on top of him and fall asleep on his chest. She was deliriously relieved he was home. But as happy as she was to have him back, she worried he was going to make himself sick again. He was supposed to start giving himself his insulin shots in his stomach, but he hadn't been able to make himself do it yet.

"You catching up on your homework?" she asked.

Wesley spit the highlighter out.

"Yeah. I've got three days of make-up work. I know what I'll be doing this weekend."

"Don't work too hard. I want to see nothing but decadent laziness on your part."

"I think I can handle that. Where are you going?" he asked as she pulled her coat on.

"Across the street. Zach's coming over. When you're done laughing at him, just send him over. Tell him to go in and look up."

Wesley eyed her suspiciously.

"Why would I laugh at Zach?"

She bent down and kissed him on the forehead.

"You'll see."

Zach hopped the train and headed north to Nora's. But when he knocked on the door it was Wesley who answered.

"Feeling better?" Zach asked.

"Much. Puking your guts out then fainting in a library bathroom is no way to spend a Monday night."

"Agreed. Nora seems quite pleased to have you back. You gave her quite the scare."

"It's only fair. She scares me half to death at least once a week." Zach laughed but Wesley's eyes showed no mirth.

"You're looking mostly restored." Zach envied the boy his youth. Three days in the hospital and Wesley still looked hearty and hale.

"Nora said I looked 'fit to be tied up.' I'm hoping she didn't mean it literally."

"Apparently someone meant it literally with me," Zach said, pulling his hand out of his pocket and showing Wesley the handcuffs dangling from his wrist.

Wesley laughed at him and Zach couldn't help but join in. It really was quite embarrassing and ridiculous.

"Don't feel bad, Zach," Wesley said when he was done laughing. "Nora made me help her with a scene once. I ended up hog-tied on the living-room floor for half an hour."

Now it was Zach's turn to laugh. Was there any woman in

the world quite like Nora? He was so glad she existed; even more glad there was only one of her.

"Where is Nora, by the way? She's going to try to help get these things off me."

"If anyone can, it's her. She wants you to meet her at church."

"Church?"

Wesley stood on the threshold of Nora's house with his arms crossed over his chest. He reached out and pointed to a building on the corner of the block.

"There. Go in. Look up. You'll find her."

Wesley shut the door and Zach crossed the street and reached the end of the block. Zach read the sign out in front of the church. St. Luke's Catholic Church, it said with the mass schedule underneath.

With trepidation, Zach slipped through the front doors of the small neo-Renaissance church. Apart from attending the weddings of a few friends he'd rarely stepped inside a church before. And he was certain this was his first time in a Catholic sanctuary. He glanced at the dripping candles and the stained-glass scenes of violence. In this setting the imagery in Nora's books made more sense.

Go in, look up, Wesley had instructed.

Zach strode to the center of the sanctuary and looked up.

"I'm up here, Zach."

Zach glanced up and found Nora at the back of the church leaning over the ledge of a small balcony section.

"What are you doing up there?" he asked, trying to keep his voice low. The acoustics were so good he felt as if he shouted every word.

"Choir practice. Show me the damage." Zach pulled his hand out of his pocket and held up his wrist to show her the dangling handcuffs.

"My, my, my…" She sighed, affecting a Southern drawl she no doubt stole from Wesley. "I see temptation has come a knockin' and you have answered the door…"

"Hardly, Blanche DuBois. I have a rather irksome prankster at my office. This was his pathetic attempt at a joke."

"Well, come on up. Let's see what we can do."

Zach found the tiny stairwell that led to the loft. In the loft he found smaller versions of the church's pews and an ancient-looking sound system. Nora sat on the balcony ledge and pointed to the pew in front of her.

"Come here, Kinky Easton." She beckoned. "Amateur. You know you should always do an equipment check before you play."

Today Nora wore jeans and a white blouse. With her hair down and loose about her shoulders, Zach was drawn to her despite himself. She reached for his hand and he felt a current go through him when her fingers touched his wrist.

"So what do you think?" he asked, trying to ignore the pleasant sensation of his hand in hers. "Some sort of wire cutters? Or can you pick the lock?"

"I can pick it. But I don't have to."

Nora reached into the pocket of her jeans and pulled out her keys. She flipped through a couple of them, stuck one in the lock and turned it. The cuffs popped open and fell off his wrist.

"Wonderful," he breathed. "Thank you."

"You're welcome." She stuffed the keys back in her pocket and picked up the cuffs. "These are police issue cuffs. The key on them should have worked."

"It didn't. Both Mary and I tried."

"Your prankster was really trying to cause trouble then. Handcuffs are mostly standardized in America and Canada. He wanted one or both of you to get stuck."

"You know your stuff, don't you?" he asked, impressed despite himself.

"I strive for authenticity in my work."

"So that's why you keep a handcuff key with you?"

She smiled slyly.

"Gotta be prepared. We guttersnipes are always ending up in trouble with the coppers."

"You know, I should apologize for being so rude about you. The work is going rather well."

The tiredness temporarily disappeared from her eyes.

"Thanks, Zach. I appreciate that."

"Don't thank me yet. We aren't even close to the finish line."

"I know. That's why I came here. This is a good place for praying and meditating."

"Praying? Really?"

"I grew up in the Catholic Church, believe it or not. Cradle Catholic, they call us. I was probably born in a pew. Knowing my father I was probably conceived in one, as well. I don't attend Mass much these days, but I do get homesick now and then."

"They must stand in line to hear your confessions."

Nora released a hollow, joyless laugh.

"No," she said, not quite meeting his eyes. "I don't go to confession anymore."

"So what brings you here then if you're no longer practicing? Faith or just nostalgia?"

"Maybe it's nostalgia for my faith." She shrugged and laughed again. "I still believe. I do. My life has been too blessed not to believe. Faith just isn't as easy as it used to be. Not since I left Søren anyway."

"Was it easier with him?"

Nora nodded. "It's easy to believe in God when you wake

up every morning knowing you are completely and unconditionally loved. Søren gave me that."

"But still you left him. Why?"

"There are only two reasons why you leave someone you're still in love with—either it's the right thing to do, or it's the only thing to do."

"Which was it?"

Nora exhaled slowly. "The right thing. I think. You?"

Zach turned his head and saw an icon of the Virgin Mary holding the infant Jesus in her arms.

"The only thing. I think. Suffice it to say Grace and I never should have been together to start with."

"Sounds like me and Søren. We definitely shouldn't have been together."

"Why?" Maybe if he could find out why Nora left the man she loved so deeply, he could begin to understand why Grace had pulled away from him.

"He had—" Nora paused and seemed to search for the right word "—other obligations."

"Is he married?"

She raised her hand and touched her neck. He followed her eyes. She gazed at a small iron Jesus impaled on his cross.

"Something like that." She shook herself from her reverie and met Zach's eyes again. "Come on. Let's get back to the house. You can look over my new chapters." Nora gave Zach her hand and he let her pull him up. But she didn't stop with up. She pulled him straight to her.

Face-to-face, their bodies were only separated by a hairbreadth. Nora looked down and back up again.

"Oh, dear. No room for the Holy Ghost."

"You are incorrigible, Ms. Sutherlin." Zach's smile died as he noticed the dark circles under Nora's eyes. "You look exhausted. Are you not sleeping?"

"I'm fine. But last night I kept waking up every hour and going in to check on Wes. You know, I got an IUD so I would never have to do the 'is junior still breathing?' thing. This is very unfair."

"IUD—you *are* a bad Catholic, aren't you?"

"The birth control is the least of my worries if I ever have to answer to the pope," she said, taking a step back. "I do as Martin Luther instructed—I sin boldly."

He followed her down the steps and along the rows of pews to a side entrance he hadn't seen when he came in. Inside the door was a foyer where Nora had left her coat.

"Do they make the sinners use the side door?" he asked.

"We'd all have to use the side door then. 'All have sinned and fallen short of the glory of God.' Romans 3:23."

"A Bible-quoting erotica writer—you are quite the oxymoron," Zach said.

"And a Moxie Whore-On sometimes." Nora winked at him. "If it helps, Søren used to say Catholicism was the perfect faith for someone into S&M."

"Why?"

Nora opened her mouth and closed it again as if she started to say something and then thought better of it.

"Show, don't tell," she said, taking his arm.

Together they walked back into the sanctuary taking another doorway on the opposite side that opened up to a long corridor. The walls of the corridor were adorned with framed prints of biblical scenes. Scenes from the Hebrew Bible were on his right—images that he remembered from his childhood in Hebrew school; he recognized Ruth and Naomi, Jacob's Ladder, the Crossing of the Red Sea, among others. On his left were scenes from the New Testament—images far less familiar to him. Nora brought him to the end of the hall and stopped in front of the third print from the end.

"This one's my favorite," she said, still holding his arm. "Antonio Ciseri's *Ecce Homo*. That's 'Behold the Man' if you aren't up on your Latin."

"A tad rusty. Is this from the Crucifixion?"

"From the Passion. This is when Christ is being presented to the angry mob."

"Ah, yes. When we bloodthirsty Jews killed Jesus, right?"

Nora smiled and shook her head. "You kidding? Jesus died for the sins of the world. Everyone who ever lived killed Jesus." She paused and smiled sadly. "I killed Him."

Zach said nothing as he studied the painting, struck by the artist's choice of bright colors to paint such a dark scene.

"Søren has this impressively twisted theology of the Trinity, you know. God the Father inflicted the suffering and humiliation, God the Son submitted to it willingly and God the Holy Spirit gave Christ the grace to endure it."

"Your Søren sounds…interesting," Zach said, attempting to be diplomatic.

"He was never *my Søren*. That's the one thing about being a collared submissive. I was his. He never was mine. But yes, he is interesting. The most caring sadist you could ever hope to meet."

"But you loved him?"

"And I loved him," she corrected. "Søren said Jesus was the only man who ever made him feel humble. He makes me feel humble, too."

"Søren or Jesus?"

But Nora didn't answer. Instead, she released Zach's arm and stepped toward the print.

"Just look at it. Look at Him. Isn't He the most beautiful thing you've ever seen, Zach?" She'd said his name but from the ethereal tone of her voice, it seemed as if she were talking to herself instead. "It's the Praetorium. Pilate was a kind of

Roman overseer of Jerusalem. He was trying to keep a very fragile peace so instead of immediately sentencing Christ to die, he orders Him to be scourged. Scourging meant a near fatal beating with a whip that had glass and bone and rocks embedded in the lashes. It was a serious punishment. He hoped that would satisfy the mob's bloodlust. But look at the painting—no wounds. The skin of his back looks perfect. But supposedly He's just been brutally, viciously whipped. Ciseri is emphasizing Christ's beauty, not His beating. He's showing Christ's feminine side. Admittedly it's very inaccurate, I know. Almost all depictions of the crucifixion are inaccurate. That little loincloth they always show Jesus wearing? Didn't exist. Victims of crucifixion were stripped completely naked to add to their shame and humiliation. Artists can't bring themselves to show just how fully human Jesus was."

Zach said nothing, strangely spellbound by Nora's words.

"Just imagine what this was like for Him, Zach." Nora shook her head as if she couldn't imagine it herself. "We talk about the Virgin Mary, but Jesus never married. He was a virgin, too. And there He was completely naked on display for the whole world to see, and right in front of Him is Mary Magdalene, who was his best friend, and His poor mother. His mother, Zach. He must have been so embarrassed, so humiliated. See these two women here. They get it."

Zach glanced at the painting and then at Nora.

"Look how Ciseri painted Jesus. See the curve of His back and shoulders. It is a classic feminine posture. His hands are tied behind His back and His robe is falling over His hips. And all the men are just pointing and staring and gawking. But the women—see them?—they can't bear it. One's looking down and she—" Nora pointed at a female figure who was turned completely away from the horrible scene unfolding behind her "—she can't even look. She has to hold on to the other woman just to keep from collapsing. And of all of them, she's the only one whose whole face we can see."

Nora fell into silent contemplation again and Zach watched her eyes. They were fixed on the two women in the foreground, huddled together in palpable distress. "They know what He's feeling. The women always know. They know it isn't just a beating or a murder they're being forced to witness. It wasn't even just a crucifixion. It was a sexual assault, Zach. It was a rape."

Nora took a deep breath and Zach felt his own breath catch in his chest. He wanted to say something but didn't trust himself to speak yet.

"That's why I believe, Zach," Nora continued. "Because of all gods, Jesus alone understands. He understands the purpose of pain and shame and humiliation."

"What is the purpose?" Zach asked, truly wanting to know.

Nora's eyes returned to the two women in the foreground clinging to each other in sympathy and horror.

"For salvation, of course. For love."

11

"You think I'm so damn obedient," Caroline said as she pulled away from William. She stood at the window looking out on their backyard where just yesterday they had sat and talked until dusk. If only there were more yesterdays instead of so many todays.

"You've never given me cause for complaint." She heard the confusion in his voice.

"It's always 'yes, sir' and 'no, sir' and 'as you wish, sir.' But it's not out of obedience."

"Then what is it, Caroline?"

She didn't want to answer. But she knew she couldn't keep lying to him with her every breath.

"Fear."

"Of what?"

"Of this...game you make us play. It isn't a game to you, though, is it?"

He came to stand behind her. She braced herself but he didn't touch her.

"No, it isn't. For me this is very real."

"I want it to be a game...so much," Caroline admitted. "Games can be won. You win the game and the game's over. And I want it to end."

"It can end," William said, his voice soft with sadness. "If you stop playing."

"But I can't. If I quit playing..." She didn't finish the sentence, couldn't bring herself to finish it.

"Then neither of us will ever win." William said what she'd been afraid to say.

"So what's the consolation prize?" she asked, trying and failing to find a smile for him.

William bent and rested his chin on the top of her head. He wrapped his arms around her and she sank into him and closed her eyes. This game had an hourglass for a timer and she saw the sand running out.

"I don't think there is one."

God, it was wrenching. Zach minimized the document and pushed back from his computer. He stood and walked around his office. Stopping at the window, he stared out at the city and the sky. Today was a gray day, cold and windy. It had been windy the day he'd left England: a sea wind, warm and fierce, and Zach recalled waiting at the airport almost hoping his flight would be canceled or even just delayed long enough for Grace to realize he really was going. But the wind had failed him that day. It had carried him aloft instead of forcing him aground. Sailors' wives once had little balconies on their roofs. What were they called? Widow's walks. That was it. Yes, the widow's walk, the place where they could go alone and stare out to sea and watch and wait. He envied them their macabre station. At least they could see the ship coming in. At least they had a place to hide their grief every day it didn't.

Zach stared at the sky and wished he could see all the way across the gray ocean. Gray was Grace's favorite color. She joked it was "like silver only sadder," and he'd tease her about all the gray sweaters in her closet, the dozens of gray woolen socks. Grace would have loved a morning like this. She would have opened the curtains, opened the blinds and dragged him back to bed with her to make hasty love before the sun intruded and changed the color of the day.

Tearing his eyes from the sky, he looked down at the gray streets below. Supposedly from this height everyone was supposed to look like ants. But they didn't look like ants to him at all. They still looked like people. He leaned his head against the glass and watched their progress. He was afraid for them and didn't know why.

Nora…was she why? When he'd made her cut the more graphic scenes of sexual violence from her book she'd replaced them with emotional violence. Now everywhere he looked he saw people as fragile as paper.

Nora's book had impressed him more than he wanted to admit. Most impressively she had turned the romance novel formula on its head. One of the cardinal rules of classic romance was that at no point, no matter how infuriating the heroine was and no matter how much the hero wanted to throttle her, he could never, would never raise his hand to her. But William was a sadist and used pain to prove his love. And where the romance novel began with the two characters trying to come together against forces both internal and external, Nora's novel began with them together and then let the forces slowly, torturously tear them apart. She was writing the antiromance novel.

Zach let his eyes focus on one of the small figures below him on the street. He couldn't tell if it was a man or a woman. He or she bustled across the street in a great hurry. He wondered if this was why Nora was drawn to religion despite herself. The Pagan gods sat on high and played with their subjects like pieces on a chessboard. Nora's god turned Himself into a pawn and let Himself be captured. He could see the attraction. Zach wanted to run down to the street below and follow whoever it was until he was certain he or she made it on time. He wanted to know everything turned out fine for at least one person in the gray city today.

Zach pulled away from the window and faced his desk again. As he returned to his computer he remembered Nora's original first line from the first draft of her novel—"I don't want to write this story any more than you want to read it." He realized it wasn't just William speaking to Caroline. It was Nora talking to him.

He sat down and opened Nora's revisions again. He made himself keep reading. As much as it hurt, he had to know what happened next.

Nora sat at her kitchen table writing furiously in her notebook. She'd given up on her computer a few hours ago. Her wrists were aching from typing, but she still had another chapter in her head she wanted to get on paper. After her long talk with Zach yesterday at church, she'd come home newly inspired. She had made a terrible mistake with her characters in her first draft. In the original ending of her book, Caroline was no longer able to bear William's darkness. In the original ending, Caroline left him. But Nora realized she'd done Caroline a great wrong. She was no sexual masochist; she was an emotional masochist and never would she leave the man she loved, the man she was certain needed her help. No, in the new ending William, out of love for her, would send her away. It was beautiful and brutal and how it had to end. William had told her that and she knew better than to cross him.

Wesley had spent the past two hours with her at the kitchen table catching up on more make-up work while she wrote. She wasn't worried about his homework. Wesley had a shockingly keen mind under that mess of blond hair and had made Dean's List all three semesters he'd been at Yorke. She'd made Dean's List once when she was in college. Søren had ordered her to just to annoy her. Just to annoy him, she'd done it. Wesley was a natural hard worker, however, and didn't need anyone telling him to do his homework or study. She told him once he could never be a writer like she was. He wasn't nearly lazy enough.

Wesley... Nora looked up and around the kitchen. Wesley had left over twenty minutes ago to check his blood sugar and take his insulin—something that usually took less than a minute—before he started cooking dinner. Nora went looking for him and found him leaning over the downstairs' bathroom sink.

"You okay, Wes?" she asked, trying to keep the panic out of her voice.

Wesley laughed and shook his head.

"You know, I have ridden some of the biggest, meanest, scariest stallions on the planet. You wouldn't think a little needle in my stomach would bother me this much."

Relieved that he wasn't sick again, Nora exhaled and entered the bathroom. Wesley stood up straight and she hopped up on the counter next to the sink.

"Still can't do it?"

"Nope. I think I have a mental block."

"I can help with mental blocks."

Wesley shook his head. "I have to do it myself, or I'll never get over this."

"You will do it yourself. You handle the needle. I'll handle the mental block. What's our target?"

Wesley pointed to a spot on the center of his stomach a hand's span beneath the bottom of his rib cage.

"Dr. Singh said I'm supposed to think of my stomach like a clock face when I rotate my injections. I start at noon for the first one and then move an inch for the second one. That way I'm not going to hit the same spot over and over again."

Nora nodded. "Clock face, huh?" She reached out and lifted the bottom of Wesley's T-shirt. He'd lost weight in the hospital so now his four-pack abdomen was a stark six-pack. He had nothing left on his frame but muscle. She let loose a wolf-whistle. "Sexiest clock I've ever seen."

"Nora," Wesley said and pulled his shirt back down. He was blushing. "Stop it."

"Wesley, you walk around the house without a shirt on all the time. Proof that you're a secret sadist, I think."

Wesley grimaced and Nora laughed.

"I am not a sadist. I'm nothing like him."

"You are a lot like him." She thought it was cute how Wesley tried to never say Søren's name. "You both worry about me too much."

"Anyone who's ever met you worries about you," Wesley countered.

"And you're both blonds. Except you've got dark blond hair and his is light blond."

"Well, he's Swedish or whatever."

"Danish. His mother was Danish and his father was English. Between the two of them, he's the least American American I've ever met. Another thing you two have in common—you're both musicians."

Wesley eyed her suspiciously. "Does he play guitar, too?"

"Piano. He could have been a concert pianist, but now he just plays for fun."

"He's one of those perfect guys, right?" Wesley asked,

crossing his arms. "His hair's never messed up, he never spills anything, never trips."

Nora nodded. "If that's your definition of *perfect,* he does qualify. I've lost track of the number of languages he speaks. And he can be very witty and charming when he wants to be. And he's ludicrously handsome. He's also pretentious and conceited."

Wesley grinned at her. "Keep going."

"And he's never ridden a horse in his life much less some of the biggest, meanest, scariest stallions on the planet. And," she said, reaching out for Wesley's T-shirt again, "he doesn't make me laugh and smile every single day like a certain someone I know."

Wesley raised his arms and Nora pulled his T-shirt off. Just to make it fair she unbuttoned her blouse and let it join Wesley's shirt on the floor. Wesley seemed to be trying very hard not to stare at her wearing just her jeans and bra.

"So we're shooting for here?" she asked and touched a spot on his stomach a few inches above Wesley's belly button.

"Yeah. That's noon."

"Gotcha." She flicked noon with her fingers hard enough Wesley flinched.

"Ouch!" He laughed. Nora flicked again.

"What are you doing?"

"In S&M, if you're about to give someone a beating, you start off soft to desensitize the skin. A little pain at first can prevent a lot of pain later." She kept flicking until their target spot had turned bright red.

"This might be worse than the needle."

Nora looked at him and raised her eyebrows.

"Okay, I see what you did there," Wesley said and Nora finally stopped flicking him. "Now what?"

"Take this and turn around," she ordered, handing him his insulin pen. "Lean back against me."

Wesley turned his back to her and Nora wrapped her arms around him. His young skin was smooth and warm, and when the swell of her breasts made contact with his back, she sensed him shiver. She reminded herself she was trying to help him, not seduce him.

"Okay, look down at my hands." Her hands were on his rib cage. "Breathe in so deeply that you inflate your lungs like a balloon and my fingers spread apart."

Wesley took a deep breath as instructed and Nora felt her hands open up.

"Now exhale slowly for five seconds and then breathe in again."

Wesley obeyed, taking another breath in and then exhaling one more time.

"This time," she said, "breathe in just as deeply but when you exhale, pop the air out hard and stick the needle in. I'll count to five and then you pull it out."

One more time Wesley pulled in air. "Now blow it out hard," Nora said.

Wesley pushed the air from his lungs and from the tiny flinch she felt she knew he'd stuck himself.

She counted to five slowly and dropped a small kiss on his back between each number. At five he pulled the needle out.

He turned around and beamed at her.

"That's my boy," she said, and Wesley hugged her.

"That wasn't as horrible as I thought it would be."

"It's a good trick," Nora said as Wesley released her. "Works if you get a body piercing, too. I speak from experience." Wesley had never seen where she was pierced.

"No, thanks. The tattoo was enough for me."

Nora's eyes widened with shock.

"What? You have a tattoo?"

Wesley groaned.

"Yes, I have a tattoo. A little one."

"Wesley—you're telling me that you had a mental block over injecting insulin in your stomach but you got a tattoo?"

"I didn't have to give myself the tattoo. And believe me, I didn't watch."

Nora pursed her lips and looked him up and down.

"Well, I've seen you shirtless and I've seen you in boxers so it's got be somewhere in this area." She pointed at his pelvic region and Wesley blushed again. Caught. "I knew it. Show me, show me."

"I am not going to show you. It's stupid."

"I'll show you my piercing."

"How about I show you my tattoo and you don't show me your piercing. Deal?"

"My idea was better but whatever. Show me."

Wesley exhaled loudly through his nose and started unbuttoning his jeans. Nora applauded. Rolling his eyes at her, Wesley pulled down his jeans and boxers just enough to reveal a small tattoo on his right hip. Nora leaned over and looked at it.

"It's a trumpet," she said, surprised by the strange image.

"It's the bugle from the call to post at Churchill Downs for the Kentucky Derby. One of the horses Dad worked with did really well at the Derby a couple of years ago. He got the horse's name tattooed on his shoulder. When I turned eighteen, I got the bugle. I only got it on my hip so Mom wouldn't see it."

"It's very sexy." Nora reached out and traced the tattoo with the tip of her finger. Wesley inhaled as her finger touched the sensitive skin. He was so responsive to everything she did that she couldn't help but wonder what he'd be like in bed. But she didn't kid herself. She knew his responsiveness had very little to do with her and a lot to do with his being nineteen and still a virgin.

"It's not supposed to be sexy. It's a tribute to the most important horse race in the world."

Wesley pulled his boxers back up and buttoned his jeans.

"So the Kentucky Derby's a big deal?" Nora asked. "Must be if I've heard of it."

"It's the most exciting two minutes in sports."

"Two minutes?" she scoffed. "I better get a dozen roses and a big apology if all I get is two minutes."

"It's a very long two minutes if you have a horse in the race. It's not just that race, though. The whole thing lasts all day. There are races before and then all the people watching and the women in their crazy hats and everybody's drunk on mint juleps, which are disgusting if you ask me, but don't tell anyone I said that." Wesley looked at her and took a quick little breath. "You should come with me this year."

Nora raised her chin and studied Wesley. He didn't quite meet her gaze.

"Did you just ask me out on a date, Wes Railey?"

"Nora, we live together. Asking you on a date would kind of be a step backward."

"Yes, but we're roommates. We don't *live* together. And don't you think it'll be a little hard to keep the erotica-writer-roommate thing a secret if I show up with you wearing a sombrero at the Kentucky Derby?"

Wesley reached down and picked up their shirts off the floor. He pulled his T-shirt on, but Nora was in no hurry to get dressed. She enjoyed watching Wesley trying not to watch her too much.

"I sort of told Dad about you."

"You're kidding. Did he freak out?"

"I didn't go into detail. I just sort of let him think I had a girlfriend so he'd really back me up about not moving home. He was starting to get worried his son was, you know—"

"A stallion not interested in mares?"

Wesley laughed. "Right. He was thrilled."

"I never figured you for a liar. I'm impressed."

"I didn't lie. You're a girl who's a friend ergo—"

"Girlfriend. Well, if I'm going to be your girlfriend, this virginity thing has got to go. But after dinner," she said and finally pulled her blouse back on.

She started to leave the bathroom but Wesley grabbed her hand.

"You didn't say if you'd go with me or not."

Nora smiled up at him. She couldn't believe how serious Wesley was being.

"Yes, Wes. I will go with you to the most exciting two minutes in sports. When is it?"

"First Saturday in May."

"I'll book the flight. You get the tickets."

"I already have the tickets. I go every year. My family would cancel Christmas before they missed the Derby. I only missed last year because of finals. No school in Central Kentucky would ever hold a final on Derby Day."

"We're all damned Yankees up here, aren't we?"

"I like you Yankees. Y'all talk funny."

Nora twined her fingers in his and studied him. Since getting out of the hospital, he'd seemed older, calmer, more sure of himself. And he also seemed more intent on spending time with her. He read in her office while she wrote. When she moved from her office to the kitchen, he went with her. She liked having him as a shadow. Since getting him back home she'd wished more than a few times that they were lovers so they could sleep in the same bed. As much as he shadowed her by day, she shadowed him at night. Ever since he came home from the hospital, she found herself waking up several times a night to make sure he was okay. She'd half considered getting a baby monitor and hiding it under his bed.

Nora took a step toward him and heard the devil on her shoulder telling her to kiss him, really kiss him for the first time. She tried to hear the angel on her shoulder but she remembered her angel had long ago turned in his letter of resignation. She wrapped an arm around Wesley's neck and rose on tiptoes.

From the kitchen came the unmistakable sound of her hotline phone blaring its Klaxon ringtone at her. Wesley sighed and rested his chin on top of her head.

"It's okay," Nora said and kissed him quick on the cheek. She still had a lot of writing to do for Zach, and it would take a whole team of stallions to drag her away from Wesley tonight. She leaned into Wesley's chest, and he wrapped his arms around her. "Just let it ring."

12

Four weeks left…

What the hell was he doing?

Zach wondered how many times since meeting Nora he'd asked himself that question. He was getting into double digits at least. He paid his cabdriver and faced Wordsworth's Bookshelf, the venue for Nora's book-signing today. He shouldn't be here. *Saturnalia* wasn't even a Royal House title. The previous books didn't matter, but for some reason Nora was starting to.

Zach entered through the grand double doors and found the signing area at the back of the store. It was a small sort of stage with a table and a chair roped off on three sides. Wesley stood on the platform talking to a man in his fifties with a kind face and absolutely no hair on his head. Zach stepped inside the roped off area. A table sat in front of a wall and was stacked high with copies of Nora's most recent bestseller. The bald man excused himself to fetch a pitcher of water and a glass.

"Nice tie," Zach said to Wesley. "Quite natty."

"Natty—British compliment, right?"

"Right."

"Nora's orders. Not really a tie guy."

"Her orders? Where is our autocrat anyway?"

"Hiding somewhere. Her last book with Libretto came out two months ago. This is her last event for them. She loathes these things."

"As extroverted as she is, I would have thought signings would be her forte."

"She's all bark, Zach." Wesley's eyes scanned the crowd that was beginning to form behind the red ropes. "Being around a lot of people bothers her when she's not in total control of the situation."

"Control freak, is she?"

Wesley pointed to his chest.

"Note the tie."

Zach laughed at Wesley's disgusted, but amused face. It still seemed strange and uncomfortable that Wesley was so devoted to a woman so much older than he. He knew how dangerous romantic hero-worship could be.

"Looks like it's about to start," Zach said as the bald man put the pitcher and glass on the signing table. Zach counted about forty or fifty people already in the queue and more joining by the minute. "Should I go fetch our elusive author?"

"Would you mind? I want to stay here and keep an eye on things."

Zach noticed Wesley paying close attention to the people waiting for Nora. Wesley's eyes studied every man in line. There were more men than Zach would have expected. Erotica was usually marketed as a subgenre of romance and yet there were at least a half a dozen adult men and a few teenage boys in the line holding shiny new copies of Nora's latest release.

"Worried about the fans?" Zach asked.

"You would be, too, if you had to open the fan mail."

"Point taken. I'll go find Nora. Any suggestions?"

Wesley met the eyes of one young man in the crowd. Zach noted nothing particularly menacing about him although he did seem nervous and impatient and was casting envious glances at him and Wesley standing inside the ropes. He wore an army-green jacket and heavy combat boots. Not the typical romance fan. But then again, nothing about Nora or her books was particularly typical.

"Try upstairs," Wesley suggested. "The kids' section."

Zach had trouble accepting the idea that Nora would be hiding with Winnie the Pooh and Harry Potter. Of course, he would never have imagined her hiding in a church, either. He took the escalator to the second level and followed dinosaur footprints painted on the carpet that led him to a brightly colored alcove. He turned a corner at the picture books and heard a familiar raucous laugh.

On a tiny stage Nora sat with a book in her hand, her coat laid across her lap to cover her too short red leather skirt. Three small children—one boy about five or six years old and two tiny girls sat wide-eyed and spellbound listening to Nora.

"'Beware the Jub-Jub bird,'" Nora recited as she held the book open so the children could see the pictures, "'and shun the frumious Bandersnatch.'"

"What's a Bandersnatch?" the smallest girl asked, tripping over the awkward word.

"It's like a bird-dolphin-hippo-snake thing," Nora explained matter-of-factly. "But more frumious. Got it?"

The kids nodded and giggled as Nora turned the page. Zach coughed to get Nora's attention.

"Oh, what do you want?" Nora closed the book and glowered at him.

"Your presence, madam," Zach said, putting on his most posh Oxford accent, "is required on the main floor."

Nora groaned and stood up.

"Sorry, kiddles. I have to go."

The older girl tugged on Nora's sleeve.

"Miss Ellie," she said, "is that your boyfriend?" she asked in a whisper everyone could hear.

"No," Nora said in a stage whisper of her own. "He's my babysitter."

Nora left the children with obvious reluctance.

"I'm your editor. Not your babysitter. And who is Ellie?"

"The question is 'Who was Ellie?' And better question— what the hell are you doing here?"

"Wesley invited me. He said book-signings made you nervous."

"Book-signings make him more nervous than they make me. They just annoy me. You sit there like some queen on a dais with all of seven people out there and four of them are related to you."

"Well, there's eight people counting me," Zach said. "If you hate signings then why are you doing one at such a large bookshop?"

"Because Lex asked me and I couldn't say no." Nora sighed. "Saying no has never been my strongest suit."

"Lex?"

"Bald guy—Lex Luthor. Owns the place. I used to work here so we keep in touch."

They reached the down escalator and Zach noticed a man with shoulder-length dark hair pulled back in a ponytail standing at the railing and staring at Nora. He wore a Victorian-cut gray suit and riding boots and next to him stood the most exotically beautiful black woman he'd ever seen in his life. The man said something in French to the woman and the woman smiled. The man leaned against the railing and winked at Nora. Nora stepped onto the escalator, looked calmly up at the man, raised her hand and flipped him off. The man's stunning companion only laughed.

"Who is that?" Zach asked once they were out of earshot.

Nora shrugged as they reached the first floor. "No idea."

Zach heard her mumble something else but couldn't quite make it out over the applause. They parted ways and Zach rejoined Wesley.

Nora stood on the platform and waved at the assembled crowd of nearly a hundred. Lex stood next to her and opened the books to the title page for her while Nora chatted with her fans.

"No reading?" Zach asked Wesley.

"Nora doesn't do readings at 'straight bookstores' as she calls them. She doesn't want to get arrested for public indecency. And no Q&A session, either."

"For the same reason, I suppose," Zach said and smiled.

Nora sat a few yards away but Zach could hear her bantering with her devotees. One young woman asked Nora where she got her inspiration. Nora answered, "Catholic school."

Zach laughed to himself, enjoying the repartee, but Wesley paid no attention. He kept scanning the crowd and not once did he take his eyes off the men who waited in line. Zach let Wesley watch the crowd while Zach watched Nora. For all her protestations she seemed to be having a wonderful time. She looked radiant in her red suit even if her skirt was too short to be entirely appropriate. Another young woman brought out a riding crop and Nora attempted to sign its narrow length. An older man in a suit got Nora's permission to kiss the tip of her shoe while the man's wife took a picture.

"So how long have you lived with Nora?" Zach asked Wesley, hoping to distract him from his unnecessary vigilance.

"A little over a year."

"And how long have you been in love with her?"

Wesley looked sharply at Zach before laughing ruefully.

"A little over a year…and a few months."

"She doesn't know?"

"Nope. She only asked me to move in because I sort of hinted that I might have to move back to Kentucky. I thought if I told Nora I might be moving…"

"You wanted to see how she would react," Zach said with a sad half smile. "And she called your bluff." Zach couldn't stop himself from recalling the day he told Grace he was moving to the States. *If that's what you want, Zachary,* wasn't the answer he'd been hoping for.

"That she did." Wesley grinned at Nora who looked away from her fan long enough to return the smile.

"I see it worked for you. Didn't work quite so well for me. I think I underestimated you, Wesley."

"I hope I overestimated you," Wesley said, and Zach felt a quick pang of guilt.

"I'm not your competition, young man. I am still married after all."

"Doesn't matter," Wesley said with far too much bitterness for someone so young. "Holy vows have never stopped her before. Yours won't, either."

"Yours seem to have stopped her."

Wesley said nothing for a moment, and Zach knew he'd misspoken.

"She told you I was still a virgin?"

Zach heard Wesley's wounded pride.

"I'm sorry, Wesley. I accused her of taking advantage of you and she was simply defending herself."

"It's okay," Wesley said. "I'm not ashamed of it. I'm just… waiting."

"For her?"

"You think I'm an idiot, right?"

"Of course not. But whether you like to admit it or not, she is fourteen years older than you. These sorts of relationships rarely work out even under the best of circumstances. Not if experience is any indicator."

"Yeah, well, whose experience?"

Zach looked from Wesley and back at Nora. He stared at her but didn't see her. Instead, he saw a door and the door opened and standing in the doorway was Grace, and no woman in the history of the world had ever looked so brave or so scared or so beautiful standing in a doorway.

"Mine."

Wesley didn't answer. Zach didn't know what to say to comfort him. If he had any words of comfort, he would have told them to himself. But there was nothing but the cold, hard truth that loving someone and being loved back was only the beginning, not the end, of all the pain.

The young man in the green jacket came to Nora with his book to sign. Zach heard Nora asking for his name and if he wanted her to write anything in particular in his book.

"How about, 'To my number one fan, Fuck me,'" the young man said leaning over the table. "And then sign it in blood."

Zach's stomach dropped when the man pulled out a small thin, knife and started to climb onto the table. Wesley was already on his way to Nora. It was a good thing, too, because Nora had pushed back out of her chair and the man loomed only inches from her. He saw her back pressed to the wall.

It seemed to happen in slow motion. Wesley jumped up on

the signing platform and dragged the man back by his jacket and threw him down hard to the floor.

"Zach, get her out of here!" Wesley shouted at him.

The urgency in Wesley's voice jarred Zach from his state of shock. He ran to Nora and grabbed her by the arm.

"No, Zach," she said, trying to get to Wesley. For a second time since meeting her he was shocked by how much strength was hidden in her small frame.

"This way," Lex said and Zach finally steered Nora away from the crowd and toward the bookstore's stockroom. As he dragged her away he glanced up to the second floor. The man in the gray suit had pulled out a cell phone and was dialing a number. Zach hoped it was 911. They reached the stockroom and Lex locked the door.

Nora was already on her way to the door when Zach stopped her, blocking the door with his body.

"Get out of my way," she ordered with shocking ferocity. "Wes is out there with that lunatic."

"I'm sure he's fine," Zach said, not sure he believed his own words. But he knew if the man was dangerous then it was Nora who he was after, not Wesley. "Stay back here until it's safe."

"He's right. I'll go check on things," Lex said and hung up the phone. "I'm sure security's got him by now."

"Please," she begged, "make sure Wes is okay."

Lex left them in the stockroom and Zach locked the door again.

"Yet another reason why I avoid signings," Nora said, pacing the floor. Her high heels echoed ominously against the cold concrete floor.

"I see. This happens a lot at your appearances?"

Nora shook her head. "I've had my fair share of crazies. But this is the first one with a knife."

"Well, violent erotica will give the crazies ideas."

Nora looked up at him sharply.

"Are you blaming my books for this?"

"Of course not. It's only that stories with sexual violence in them will attract violent people. It appeals to the baser instincts."

"Baser instincts? Violent people? My readers are housewives and college girls and a few straight guys who are trying way too hard to find out what women want in the bedroom. I don't write for insane people. Is it Salinger's fault that Mark David Chapman misread *Catcher in the Rye*?"

"That is not what I'm implying. But when you market yourself as a sex object, it can't come as a shock when someone decides you can be bought."

"Bought?" she scoffed and met Zach's eyes. She looked at him so coldly he was almost afraid of her. "I can't be bought, Zach. And even if I could I'm out of your price range."

"Nora—" he said, trying to apologize.

Lex opened the door with Wesley right behind him. Nora raced across the room and ran straight into Wesley's arms.

"You okay, kid?" She ran her hand over him as if checking him for injuries.

"I'm fine. The cops have him. He's apparently a Bellevue resident off his meds."

"He didn't hurt you, did he?"

"Nah," Wesley said. "He went down hard, fast and easy."

"Sounds like one of my characters," she said, wrapping her arms around Wesley.

Zach met Wesley's eyes from across the room. His voice had been glib with Nora, but Zach could see the sheer panic written across the boy's face.

"Come on. We're going home," Wesley said, letting Nora go.

"Home? That's ridiculous. All those people are out there. We've got to finish the signing."

"No, Nora." Wesley's voice was stern and intractable. For a moment Wesley seemed older than Nora. "We've got to give the cops a statement and then we're going home. You can finish the signing when Lex gets some more security in here." Lex voiced his agreement with Wesley, and Nora promised she'd reschedule as soon as possible.

"That guy didn't hurt you, did he?" Wesley asked as he opened the door for Nora.

Nora stopped and looked back at Zach. Zach stomach's flinched from the look of pure pain in Nora's eyes.

"No worries, Wes. Just sticks and stones. It's the words that hurt."

13

Zach returned to his flat after the book-signing but found himself unable to concentrate on work. All he could do was replay Nora's words in his head. *"I can't be bought, Zach…"* It didn't take long to realize how unconscionably he'd acted. A fan had attacked Nora, and he had blamed the victim.

He checked the time—still only five o'clock. He couldn't spend the rest of the day agonizing over Nora. Racing from his building he made only one stop on the way to the train station. He stood on Nora's porch trying to collect his words. He wanted to have them just right so when he said he was sorry she would know he meant it. But he knew something would change between them if he crossed her threshold for any other reason but her book. Zach took a step toward the door but it opened before he could knock. Wesley was standing there with a sardonic half smile on his face.

"Nora told me to let you in. She said you were starting to look a little cold."

"May I see her please?"

Wesley took a step back and let Zach enter.

"In her office," Wesley said. "She's writing."

Zach followed Wesley to the office and remembered how very different things were just three weeks ago. He'd come here determined to be rid of Nora and her book. Now here he was ready to beg for another chance to make their partnership work.

Before they reached the door to Nora's office, Wesley stopped and turned to him.

"You know, your opinion means more to her than anything," Wesley said. "I came home today after the signing and came pretty close to throwing up. She just went into her office and got back to work."

Zach nodded, humbled by this nineteen-year-old child.

"I've come to apologize if she'll let me."

"She'll let you. Maybe she shouldn't, but she'll let you."

Wesley knocked on Nora's office door and entered without waiting for her response.

"Nor? Got a minute?" Wesley asked. Nora was at her desk in black silk men's style pajamas. Her hair was piled high on her head and held up with two ballpoint pens serving as chopsticks. She was typing away furiously, not even stopping to look at them.

"What are you still doing here, Wes? I thought you had something at church tonight."

"Yeah, I'm supposed to help chaperone the middle school retreat this weekend," Wesley said, walking around the desk to stand behind her chair. "But I'm not going to leave you alone after today—"

"Yes, you are. You just go and keep those kids from making out in the coat closet. Sexual repression must begin as early as possible. Go, Wes. You deserve a night off from my dramas."

"Are you sure?" Wesley put his hands on Nora's shoulders and tilted her chair back toward him. She leaned her head against his stomach and looked up at him.

"Yes. Go. Have fun. You've earned it."

"If you let me go, I'm going to eat pizza," he warned her and smiled down at her.

"One slice," she said, raising her arm and waving her index finger in his face. "One."

"What if it's thin crust? That's low carb."

"Hmm…" Nora held up a second finger. "Two. But no more than two."

"Yes, ma'am. I'll be home tomorrow morning. Zach?" Zach turned to face Wesley who was looking at him with determination. "You'll keep an eye on Nora tonight, right?"

"Wes, I'm fine," Nora said. "You were in the hospital last week. I have survived much scarier shit than what happened today."

"Yeah, well, I haven't," Wes said. He touched Nora's shoulder and she laid her head briefly against his hand. Wesley's touch and Nora's response was light and chaste, but Zach felt he'd witnessed something very private between them. "I'll see you later."

"Be safe," she said. "It may snow again tonight."

Wesley left them alone and Nora returned to her typing. Zach didn't wait for an invitation that was likely not forthcoming. He sat in the armchair across from her desk and watched her. He heard the house door open and close and Wesley's car start and back out of the driveway.

"Nora, will you please look at me?"

"I can't. I'm working. I've only got three weeks to get the last three hundred pages out of the gutter."

"The rewrite is in fantastic shape. I think you've earned a night off, too," Zach said.

Nora stopped typing. She swiveled in her chair to face him. She pulled her knees to her chest and wrapped her arms around her legs.

"Can I tell you something?" she asked.

"Anything, of course."

"My books," she began, and Zach saw the bright shadow of a tear forming in her eyes turning them from black to green, "are the only thing I do that isn't selling myself. No, it's not even something I do—it's what I am. And no one can buy that part of me. Not you, not Royal, not some psychotic asshole who thinks my books are letters written straight to him."

"I'm sorry, Nora. I didn't mean to blame you for that madman's behavior today. I haven't been scared like that in a long time. I just took my fear out on you since Wesley beat me to the person who actually deserved it."

Nora stared past him and seemed to watch something only she could see. Whatever it was, it brought a faint, sad smile to her face.

"You know I didn't start writing books until after I left Søren. I could barely get out of bed that first month. I thought I was losing my mind. Some days I thought I was dying. I started creating worlds in my head, other people, other lives. I slipped out of my skin and into theirs, and while I was there I wasn't grieving anymore. I was feeling what they were feeling. Writing resurrected me, Zach. Trust me, I know what it feels like to sell yourself. Writing my books is the opposite of selling myself. Do you believe that?"

Zach swallowed.

"Yes, I believe that." He met her eyes.

"Okay," she said. "We're okay. I could have told you all this over the phone, you know."

"I know. But you pegged me as a Scouser the day we met. So I thought I'd say 'I'm sorry' the way a Scouser does."

"And how is that?"

Zach reached inside his trench coat and brought out a brown paper bag. From it he pulled a bottle of Irish whiskey and set it in front of her on her desk.

"Interesting," she said eyeing the bottle.

"What is?"

Nora opened the bottom drawer of her desk and brought out two shot glasses and placed them next to the bottle.

"How much Catholics and Scousers have in common."

Zach stared at her across her desk and suddenly found himself doing something he hadn't done in a very long time—he laughed loudly and freely and it felt so foreign and wonderful that if he'd been braver, he might have kissed Nora right then and there.

Standing, Zach reached for the bottle. But Nora beat him to it. She held it in her hand and gave him the most dangerous smile he'd ever seen.

"Zach…let's play a game."

It took five minutes before Zach regretted coming to Nora's.

"Truth or drink?" Zach asked as he shed his coat. "You will recall I'm in my forties."

"There's no age limit on alcohol-induced stupidity," Nora countered. "And this is an easy game. I ask a question and either you answer it or you take a shot. Same rules for me. Whoever gets the drunkest loses, or wins, depending on your mood."

"This game is hardly fair. You are far more forthcoming than any other person I've ever met." Zach tossed his coat over the back of Nora's armchair.

Nora leaned forward across her desk.

"Trust me, Easton. You've got secrets you want to keep.

I've got secrets I have to keep. I think we're pretty evenly matched here."

"Is that so?" he asked, his curiosity piqued. "Let's find out then."

"Game on," Nora said. "You go first."

Zach knew his first question immediately. "I'll ask you the question you didn't answer today—who is, excuse me, was Ellie?"

"Ellie was me once upon a time. My mother and friends always called me Elle or Ellie. Søren, being rather formal, calls me Eleanor. I was born Eleanor Schreiber."

"A German Catholic then. This poor Jew is even more intimidated. So Nora Sutherlin is your pen name?"

"It's the name I work under, yes," she said, and Zach thought he saw a shadow of one of her secrets cross her face. "But that's two questions. My turn—why did your wife leave you? Or was it you who left her?"

Zach leaned forward, poured his whiskey and took a shot. He swallowed a cough as the liquor burned his throat and stomach all the way down. He hadn't done any hard drinking in a long time. He was afraid if he started he would never stop. Here with Nora he still felt as if he was at a funeral but now at least it was a jazz funeral.

"Fair enough," Nora said. "Your turn."

"On the subject of our respective exes, why did you leave your mysterious and formal Søren?"

Nora seemed to think about it. She reached forward, poured her shot and downed it.

"Søren's off-limits," she said. "More for his sake than mine. My turn to ask—are you going to sign my contract?"

"Honest answer, I don't know." Zach worried Nora would be hurt by his reticence. "It's going well, better than I'd hoped. But there's still a great deal of work to do on it. And

I never know if I like a book until I've read the last page. The ending makes or breaks every book. I hope that doesn't upset you."

"Water off a drunk's back." Nora raised her shot glass to him in a salute. "Your turn."

"Why is Søren such a secret?"

Nora smirked at him and downed her whiskey without the hint of a cough or discomfort.

"You're trying to get me drunk. I appreciate that. I will tell you this—I highly doubt Søren is a secret for the same reason your wife, ex-wife, whatever, is."

"Who is also off-limits."

"Let's forget wives then. How about lovers? Ever had a threesome?"

"There's no warm-up here, is it? It's just straight for the jugular."

"I'm known for my directness, gorgeous. Answer or drink."

"The answer," Zach said, "is that I'm going to drink."

Nora hooted with laughter.

"I'll take that as a yes then," she said as Zach swallowed hard and set his shot glass down with an emphatic clink.

"It is a yes, but I wanted the whiskey anyway."

"My kind of guy. Who, what, where, when, and can you draw me a picture?"

Zach leaned back in the armchair and felt the heat from the drink and the memory quickly rushing to his head.

"I will admit I barely remember the evening. It was when I was at university, as a student not a professor, and I was at a birthday party. I believe there was some Irish whiskey involved in that night, as well. I was seeing a young lady, and her rather liberated flatmate decided to join us in bed after the party. Lovely girls, both of them. One's married to an M.P. now."

"I'm jealous," she said. She left her chair and crawled up onto her desk and sat on top of it cross-legged. "I've never had a threesome with two other women. All of mine have been with one man and one woman. Or two men." She looked down at him and winked.

"Can't believe there's anything you haven't done. Is there anything else?"

"One or two things. Keep asking, you might find out what they are."

Zach knew she expected a question about her sex life. He decided to try a different approach.

"Apart from the occasional heroic rescue you don't really seem to need the services of a live-in personal assistant. Why did you ask Wesley to move in?"

Nora blinked and reached for her shot. Her hand pulled back and she met Zach's eyes.

"Wesley… That kid blew my mind from day one. He was so damn sweet. I'm not around sweet people very often. When I had him in class I found myself doing something I hadn't done in a long time."

"What was that?"

"Smiling. I'd been working so much, living a pretty hard life. Wes was the opposite of me in so many ways—soft where I was hard. Probably hard where I'm soft, too." She laughed again. "He made me feel human again…like the kind of person who could stay up too late watching stupid movies and talking. I'd forgotten how to be normal, or maybe I never knew how. My life got weird at a pretty young age and it's been weird ever since. But Wes came along and suddenly I had another reason to get out of bed in the morning besides money."

"Are you in love with him?" Zach asked.

"That's two questions," Nora said, wagging a finger at him.

She downed her shot. "That wasn't me admitting to being in love with the kid. That was me being driven to drink yet again by that twerp."

"Frustrating roommate, I imagine."

"Very. No one that sexy should be that off-limits. I could say the same about you."

"I'm your editor, Nora. I don't think we should be involved," Zach said, squirming a little in his seat. "J.P. would kill us both."

"You're not scared of J.P. and we both know it. It's me you're scared of—why?"

Zach gave the question some thought. The three shots had gone quickly to his head on his empty stomach. He felt light-headed and warm. He knew Nora deserved an answer no matter how badly he didn't want to tell her.

He picked up his shot glass.

"Again, I'll answer. But not without some liquid fortification," he said and took his drink. He bent over for a moment and breathed. He looked up and saw Nora looking down at him, waiting patiently. "You're beautiful enough and wild enough that you make me think things I never thought I would think again and feel things I didn't think I'd ever feel again. And you make me afraid I'll start forgetting things I don't ever want to forget. You're dangerous."

She nodded her head and didn't look flattered.

"You're not the first man who's called me that. When I was sixteen, Søren told me that there were suicide bombers on the Gaza Strip who were less dangerous than I was. At that age, I took it as a compliment."

"Were you engaged in domestic terrorism at the time?"

"No, I told him I knew he was in love with me. That was his response."

"You were sixteen. How old was he?"

"Thirty."

"I thought Søren was off-limits for discussion."

"He was. But I'm getting drunk fast and have very little self-control under the best of circumstances. You could get Søren ten times as shit-faced as we're getting and he'd still have the self-control of a desert father."

"He must not be that disciplined if he made love to you at such a young age."

"Young age? That bastard made me wait until I was twenty years old, Zach. You are sitting in the office of probably the most famous erotica writer since Anaïs Nin and she's telling you that she didn't lose her virginity until she was twenty," Nora said and shook her head.

"I'm aghast. Why so long?"

"If he just wanted sex he would have taken me on day one, I have no doubt. But with D/s couples, the sex is the least of it. He wanted obedience, total submission. Keeping me a virgin waiting for him for so long proved he owned me even more than fucking me would have. He was also preparing me for everything he had planned. S&M is not for children or the faint of heart. He had to wait to make sure I was neither. My question now—how old were you?"

Zach stared at her. She reached out and he handed her his shot glass. She refilled it and handed it back.

"Younger than twenty," he said and raised his glass to drink.

Nora cleared her throat and waved her hand in a "give it up" gesture. Zach put his glass down.

"Oh, very well, I was thirteen," Zach said and had a sudden memory of running off into the trees behind his school with his best mate's pretty older sister and coming out ten minutes later with a smile on his face.

"Holy shit," Nora said, laughing. "Good thing Wes is watching those middle school kids tonight."

"She was only fourteen and while it was a rather awkward and quick affair, it was hardly traumatizing or particularly scandalous."

"My first time was orchestrated and took all night, and I could barely move for a week after. I guess since I put Søren back up for discussion, we can talk about your wife."

"Not drunk enough for that."

"Well, keep drinking and at least tell me why it's so hard for you to talk about her."

While they'd been talking, the sun had set. Zach sipped at his whiskey while Nora flipped on her desk lamp. Warm light suffused the dark room and cast amber shadows everywhere he looked. Turning his head, Zach saw his reflection in the window. But he didn't see himself. He saw the door behind him and the door opened and in the doorway stood Grace who should have been anywhere in the world but standing in his doorway...

"Talking about how it ended, why it ended...it feels too much like it ended. And I don't know if I'm ready for that, Nora. I'm sorry."

"I understand not wanting something to be over. Can you at least tell me how it began?"

Zach tapped his knee with his half-empty shot glass.

"It began very badly. I would say we were doomed from the start."

Nora slid off her desk and sank to the floor in front of him. He thought it looked like an excellent idea. He joined her on the floor and leaned back against the chair.

He watched Nora take down the whiskey bottle and pour another shot.

"That year after I left Søren, I became obsessed with one

question—when was it, when were we, irrevocable? When did all the little tumblers fall into place and our fate was locked in and it became impossible for us to be anything other than what we became? When was the guilty moment?"

"Did you find your answer?"

Nora shook her head. "Never. I suppose doom and destiny are just two sides of the same coin."

"I don't have to ask or wonder. I know my guilty moment. But you left your lover and mine left me. You could go back to yours, couldn't you?"

"Zach, Søren isn't some boyfriend you have a fight with and then kiss and make up. He's the invading army you surrender to before it burns your village down."

"He sounds even more dangerous than you are."

"He is. By far. He's also the best man I've ever known. Tell me about Grace. What's she like?"

Zach paused before answering. How could he describe his wife to anyone? To him Grace was the open arms he fell into when he crawled into bed at 2:00 a.m. after staying up reading a new manuscript. She was the laughing water thief in the shower at least one morning a week. She was the quiet comfort and the hand he'd been unable to let go of at his mother's funeral three years ago. Unable to get the words past his throat, Grace had taken his notes from his hand and read his eulogy for him. She was every evening and every morning and every night, and during the day when they were apart he was always happy knowing evening and night and morning were coming again.

"Grace is…well-named. She's intelligent, far smarter than I. A poet and a schoolteacher," Zach said as the alcohol swirled around his head. "She has red hair and the most perfect freckles I've ever seen on a woman." Zach closed his eyes. The first time he'd seen her completely naked when they'd made

love in his bed the first time, he'd almost stopped breathing.
"Even on her back all the way to her hips…the most perfect
dusting of freckles."

"Freckles? That's just ruthless, isn't it?"

"Merciless. No woman that beautiful should also have freckles." Zach laughed mirthlessly. "She would lie across my lap in
the evenings and read her obscure Welsh poets while I worked
on a manuscript. Once she fell asleep on my lap. I used my red
pen to connect all the freckles on her lower back. She was livid.
We laughed for days about it."

"You had a good marriage. What happened?"

Zach stared at Nora. She sat two feet away from him but
it seemed an ocean of truth and lies and memories lay between them. He held out his shot glass. She refilled it with a
shaky hand. Zach drank the whiskey and enjoyed the burn
all the way down.

"This is a terrible game." He closed his eyes and leaned
back against the chair.

"I know a better one."

Something in Nora's voice sobered him up momentarily.
He opened his eyes and Nora now sat even closer to him. She
had something behind her back.

Zach reached out and brushed her cheek with the back of
his hand. He raised his hand to her hair, pulled the ink pens
out and watched the dark curls fall around her face.

"How long has it been?" Nora asked, her voice soft and
insinuating.

"Thirteen months." He didn't have to ask what Nora meant
by her question. He didn't have to think before he answered it.

"How long's it been for Grace?"

Zach took a hard breath.

"Less than thirteen months. Friday…she emailed me. Bill

questions, addresses, all sorts of marital flotsam. She casually mentioned some bloke named Ian."

Nora winced.

"How casually?"

"Not casually enough for me to not picture them in bed together. It's my own fault. When we decided there was a chance our marriage was going to work—we made each other promise no secrets and no lies. I told her I could get over anything, even straying, as long as she didn't lie to me about it. I hate lying more than anything." Zach shook his head. "Here we are eight months separated and she still can't lie to me about anything, damn that girl."

Zach looked at Nora and saw something flash across her eyes, some secret worry of her own.

"I'm sorry," Nora said and Zach could tell she meant it. Zach ran a single finger over Nora's forehead and down her face. With his thumb he caressed her full bottom lip.

"Thank you. So what's the new game? This one's about to drive me to quit drinking."

"Perish the thought. Ever played 'I've never'?"

"I've never played I've never." Zach knew he was as drunk now as he'd been in a long time.

"Fun game. Very easy. I say something I've never done, and if you've actually done it then you take a shot."

"What haven't you done?"

"A few things. For example, I've never…" She leaned in toward him. She moved close enough he could smell her perfume and even taste it on his burning tongue, close enough to feel the heat radiating from her body. "I've never let an erotica writer handcuff me to her desk and go down on me."

Something caught in Zach's throat. He looked into Nora's eyes and felt the foundations of his resolve shudder. He'd never

let a woman handcuff him and do anything to him. But tonight…he looked down at his shot glass.

"Never done that. Never will."

"You sure about that?" Nora stared him down. He reached
out to touch her knee, and she slapped the handcuffs on his
right wrist. "Look familiar? I thought we should put your
prankster's gift to good use at least once."

"You're out of your mind."

"And you're so turned on right now you can hardly breathe.
Your pupils are dilated, your skin is flushed, and it's not from
the whiskey and we both know it."

Zach met her eyes and said nothing.

"Thirteen months, Zach. You don't need to be afraid of
me anymore."

He had a vague memory of standing on Nora's porch thinking that if he crossed her threshold tonight for any reason other
than her book everything would change between them. Zach
took the shot glass in his hand. He looked down at the amber
liquid and then back into Nora's eyes. Raising the glass to his
lips, he downed his shot. He watched a grin spread ear to ear
across Nora's face. For a single moment she was all smiles.

"Good boy."

For someone he thought was as drunk as he, Nora moved
with a swiftness and precision that almost terrified him. She
pushed him on his back, yanked his arms over his head and
cuffed his wrists around the leg of her desk. Straddling him at
the stomach, Nora unbuttoned her black silk pajama top and
let it slide off her arms. He felt the wisp of silk brush his face
before she threw it aside and on top of his coat. Under her
shirt she wore a black bra that revealed far more than it concealed. He couldn't take his eyes off her curves, off her pale
skin and shoulders.

Nora slid her hands under his T-shirt. Her hands on his

bare skin sent every nerve firing. She bent over and kissed the center of his stomach. Unzipping his jeans, she worked them down low enough to expose the top of his hips. Zach inhaled sharply when she bit his hip bone.

"Nora—"

Nora rose up and covered his lips with one finger.

"Søren used to call me his Siren," she whispered, bending over him until she hovered an inch away from his face. "He said the things I did with my mouth could blow any man off course. Don't you want to know what he meant by that?"

Zach didn't answer but Nora didn't seem to care. She started at his neck and kissed her way down his body. A soft sigh escaped his lips as she took him in her mouth. Not even all that alcohol could blunt the pleasure of what her tongue, her lips did to him. Her hair covered her face like a veil. The tendrils of her curls tickled his stomach.

So long…it had been so long since he'd felt something so intense, so sharp that he could almost mistake the pleasure for pain. Zach ached to touch Nora but when he tried he remembered the handcuffs.

"Relax, Zach. Just enjoy." Nora paused to kiss his stomach again. "Your only job right now is to surrender."

Surrender? He'd forgotten how. He took a deep breath and laid his head back as she kept working on him. Pressure built deep in his hips.

"Nora," he gasped a warning that she didn't heed. He flinched hard and came with a ragged breath. Through the haze of alcohol and orgasm he saw Nora sit up on his thighs. She picked up the whiskey, poured it and downed him and the shot in one swallow.

She looked down at him.

"I love a whiskey chaser."

★ ★ ★

Zach opened his eyes and immediately regretted the decision. He closed them again when he realized he wasn't in his
flat. He was still at Nora's.

With grave reservations, Zach dragged himself to a sitting
position. The movement jarred his already ringing skull and
had the unfortunate side effect of jarring his memory into
recalling last night's events. Nora and he had… No, almost.
Zach leaned back and rested his aching eyes. Shame flooded
his system when he remembered how he'd succumbed to her
and let her… God, he let his writer go down on him.

Zach opened his eyes again and looked around. He sat fully
dressed and on Nora's living-room sofa, not in her bedroom.
Where she was he had no idea. He stood and wandered to
her office but she was nowhere to be seen. He picked up her
phone and called for a taxi to take him to the train station.
He hung up and found the downstairs bathroom. On the mirror Nora had taped a note—"Morning, Sunshine," it read.
"Catholics-1, Scousers-0." Zach ripped the note off the mirror and tossed it in the wastebasket. He noticed she'd left a
toothbrush out for him and a bottle of aspirin. He made quick
use of both. When he opened the medicine cabinet door to
return the aspirin to the shelf, his eyes caught Nora's name on
a pill bottle. He knew he was being shamefully nosy but he
couldn't stop himself from squinting his aching eyes to read
the label. Why on earth, Zach wondered, would Nora take
a beta-blocker, the same drug his father had to take for his
heart trouble? Zach couldn't believe someone who seemed
as alive and vibrant as Nora could have such a serious health
problem. With a shaking hand, Zach returned the bottle to
the cabinet and shut the door.

Stumbling from the bathroom, Zach heard a noise coming
from the direction of the kitchen. Every part of him wanted

to grab his coat and leave before anyone noticed he'd awoken. But he knew he'd have to face the morning-after awkwardness sooner or later. And after finding that terrifying pill bottle, he had to see Nora and make sure she was well.

He found Nora and Wesley bustling about the kitchen attempting to cook breakfast in a manner that appeared more combative than collaborative.

"Jesus H. Christ, Wesley," Nora said with feigned anger. "Cheese omelets have to have cheese or they're just flat scrambled eggs."

"Woman, Wisconsin is out of cheese now because of your omelet." Wesley smacked her hand as she tried to put more cheese on the eggs. "Set the table and stop being a backseat chef."

Nora took plates out of the cabinet and Zach winced at the clattering sound of the ceramic dishes knocking against each other.

"Could we possibly use paper plates?" he asked as he stepped into the kitchen. "They're quieter."

Nora turned and smiled at him. He saw nothing in the smile but friendliness and concern. Had he imagined what happened between them last night?

"Morning, Zach. How are you feeling?" she asked.

"Coffee," he said. "Please."

"Coffee. I know that feeling well." Nora poured him a cup of black coffee, which he took with gratitude. "We're having breakfast for lunch. You should join us."

"You okay, Zach?" Wesley asked. He stood with his back to the stove with a frying pan and a spatula in his hand. "You look like you've been rode hard and put up wet."

Nora snorted a laugh.

"What?" Wesley asked.

"It's a horse thing."

"Of course it is." She flashed a wicked grin at Zach as soon as Wesley turned his back. Dammit, he hadn't imagined last night at all.

"I'm fine," Zach said, answering Wesley's question. "Hungover and disgusted Nora isn't."

"She was puking her guts out when I got home at eight this morning," Wesley said, and Nora threw a napkin at him. Wesley batted it away with his spatula. "I think you both need a sermon on the wages of sin."

"No sermons, please. Just greasy food," Nora begged.

"Can you stomach an omelet, Zach?" Wesley asked.

Zach forced his eyes to focus on Wesley. He had a dish towel thrown over his shoulder as he stirred his eggs with expertise.

"I'm not sure I can eat anything…for the next week. The coffee is fine, thank you."

"What were you two doing last night? Trying to be Hemingway or Faulkner?" Wesley asked.

"I was going more for Oscar Wilde," Nora said. Zach looked up at her and she winked. "He was…Irish."

Wesley didn't seem to pick up her double meaning. He merely slid the omelet onto Nora's plate and sat down to his own.

"Whatever we were doing was clearly a bad idea and will not happen again," Zach said.

The smile fell out of Nora's eyes. She started toying with her omelet.

Wesley took a healthy bite of his breakfast.

"I can make toast or—"

A blaring ring that seemed to originate from the top of the refrigerator interrupted Wesley's question.

"Good God, what is that?" The sound bored a hole into Zach's head.

Nora and Wesley exchanged a look. Nora stood and grabbed a red cell phone off the top of her refrigerator and silenced the ringer. Before she answered she checked the number.

"Shit. It's not King." She looked at Wesley with something like fear in her face, more fear than she'd shown yesterday at the book-signing. Zach saw the same fear mirrored in Wesley's eyes.

"Is it—" Wesley asked, and Nora nodded.

She took a quick, deep breath.

"Yes, sir?" she said, finally answering the phone.

Wesley stood up slowly and started to walk to the door.

"Wes?" Nora said and Zach heard a quaver in her voice.

"What?" Wesley turned around to face her.

"It's Søren."

"Yeah, I know."

Nora looked ghost-pale.

"I mean, it's Søren for you. He wants to talk to you."

Wesley's eyes widened in shock. "Why?"

"I don't know. Just talk to him, please."

Wesley took the phone from her with obvious reluctance.

"Hello," Wesley said and Zach winced with sympathy at the pain in the boy's voice.

Nora stood with her arms crossed and leaned back against the counter. Wesley listened a moment and walked out of the kitchen, out of earshot.

"What on earth is that about?" Zach asked.

"I don't know." Nora seemed genuinely concerned.

"Søren and Wesley chat often?"

"No, they've never met, never spoken. Wes hates Søren." Nora sat down at the table again. After what seemed like an eternity but what was probably only a minute or two, Wesley returned to the kitchen. He handed the red phone back to Nora.

"What did he want, Wes?" Nora asked.

Zach studied Wesley's face. The boy looked flushed and fearful.

"He thanked me."

"Thanked you for what?" she asked.

"For pulling that guy off you yesterday. He said that as he was no longer in a position to protect you, he was grateful you had someone who was seeing to your safety."

Nora laughed a little.

"That sounds like him. What did you say?"

"I said 'you're welcome.' I didn't know what else to say. Nora, how did he even know about what happened?"

"If it involves me, he knows."

"Why did he call me?"

"Because he's Søren," she said. "And he was grateful to you. That simple."

"I didn't pull that guy away from you for him, Nora. I did it for you."

"I know you did. But Søren—"

"He still thinks he owns you, doesn't he?"

"He still loves me."

Wesley turned away from Nora. He picked up his plate and dumped his uneaten omelet in the trash bin. He looked back at Nora on his way out of the kitchen.

"I thought he was in your past," Wesley said, and Zach saw the twin demons of sorrow and jealously in Wesley's expression.

"I can't help it if he doesn't want to stay there," Nora said.

Wesley left, and Nora started playing with her food again. She didn't take a single bite.

"Nora, are you all right?"

Nora stood up and let her breakfast join Wesley's in the trash.

"Come on, Zach. I'll take you home." Nora held out her hand.

Zach looked at her hand but didn't take it.

"I've called a cab."

14

William pushed her onto her back and forced her arms over her head. He'd done this so many times he didn't even have to think about how much strength to exert to keep her down with one arm while his free hand bound her wrists to the bedpost. He pulled the knot taut but not tight enough that it would cut off the circulation to her hands. He would hurt her and hurt her but he would cut off his own arm before he harmed her. Looking down, he saw her face turn to the window. Sunlight poured in and turned her eyes and her pale hair white as the feathers of a dove. A soft gasp across her lips as he pushed slowly into her. Her head tilted back and a sob escaped her throat.

He pulled out of her and she dragged her knees to her chest and rolled onto her side, her arms still pinned over her head.

"I don't know," she answered the question he hadn't been able to ask. "I'm sorry, sir."

"Talk to me, Caroline. What is it?"

"I don't know," she said again. She took a deep breath and then *another. She slowly rolled onto her back again. "We don't have to stop."*

He leaned forward and untied her wrists and gathered her into his arms. The gesture seemed to release whatever was tied up inside her. Sobbing, she collapsed against his chest.

Pulling her as close to him as he could without crushing her, he said the three words that most terrified him.

"Maybe we do…"

Nora stopped typing and stretched her hands and wrists. She was tempted to delete everything she'd just written. It felt like melodrama to her. But then again most relationships falling apart often genuinely degenerated into melodrama. There was no dignity in grief, a truth she knew all too well. After leaving Søren she'd turned into a ghost for almost a year. It wasn't until she grew bored and disgusted with her own sorrow, the days spent half-sick on dirty sheets, that she picked up a pen and started jotting down sentences—sentences that turned into paragraphs that turned into pages and pages of demons she exorcised out of her own soul. Still she hadn't been able to get her life back together. It wasn't until her mother had laid down the final ultimatum—get up or get out. For once Nora listened to her mother. She'd done both. She'd humbled herself at the feet of Kingsley Edge, the King of the Underground and Søren's oldest friend. She'd do anything, she told him, just so she could afford her own place to write and grieve in peace.

"Anything, *chérie?*" he'd asked her. "Anything at all?"

"Just a job, King. I'll cocktail waitress at the club, I'll mop floors…I don't care."

He'd laughed and stared her down. Her years with Søren had taught her to never meet a Dominant's eyes unless ordered. But that day she had. She looked at him and knew that in her eyes shone all the hurt and desperation that a year of hell had hammered into her like armor.

"*Non,*" he'd said, taking her chin in his hands. He'd smiled then, and she knew she was in the biggest trouble of her life. "Not a waitress, not a maid. No more serving for you. I have a much better idea...."

"Nor?"

Nora turned her head and saw Wesley standing in the doorway to her office.

"Hey, kiddo. Sorry, I was in another world. What's up?"

"Nothing. How's the book coming?"

"Okay, I guess."

"Did Zach like the new chapters you sent him?"

"I don't know. I haven't talked to him in a couple of days."

Wesley came into her office and sat down in her armchair. He studied her, and she hated the intelligence behind those brown eyes. She should have hired a stupid intern.

"Saturday night...something happened between you two, didn't it?"

"We didn't fuck, if that's what you're worried about."

"I'm worried about you."

"You worry too much. I'm fine. The book's coming along fine."

He stood up and looked at her. She met his eyes and smiled. She never had to lie to him as long as she could still smile. Poor kid bought it every time.

"All right, I'm going to Josh's. I'll see you later."

"Study hard. Learn all those quadratics and isotopes and such."

"You really were an English major, weren't you?"

"And an English minor," she reminded him as she shooed him out of the office. Standing up, she paced the floor, grateful for her solitude. She looked at her office phone. It hadn't rung all day, or yesterday, or the day before. Zach hadn't spoken to her since Sunday when he'd given her an awkward goodbye and climbed into a cab. She kept emailing him her pages. He'd send them back with comments and suggestions but no personal notes, no encouragements, no insults, nothing. She handed fistfuls of her heart while he circled her comma splices.

Nora turned away from her black office phone and found her red cell phone. She hit the number eight, the only number she had programmed into her speed dial.

"*Oh là là,*" Kingsley said in his usual seductive drawl, "clearly reports of your demise have been greatly exaggerated. Or am I talking to a ghost?"

"You're talking to Mistress fucking Nora and I'm bored and pissed off."

"Your usual sunny self then. How can I assist you?"

"Who's on my waiting list?"

"*Tout le monde, maîtresse.* Absolutely everyone."

"Pick somebody and set it up."

"*Mais bien sûr, ma chérie.* I'll call you back in five."

In less than five minutes King called back with a name, a place and a time—one hour from now.

Nora ran to her bedroom and threw open her closet. She pulled out her client's favorite costume—her tailored white Marlene Dietrich suit. She adjusted the pale blue suspenders, threw on the jacket and stood in front of the mirror tying her tie.

"Nor?"

"Shit." Nora turned around to find Wesley in her bedroom looking pale and cold. "Thought you had study group."

"I ran off without my notes," he said with a tremor in his voice. "I came back for them. Nora—"

"Save it. I need a night off."

She grabbed her matching white fedora but didn't put it on. Finding her coat and her keys, she headed for the front door.

"Nora, you said everything was fine."

"It is fine," Nora said at the door.

"Please, please be safe." His voice caught in his throat.

"Don't worry, kid. She's five-two and a hundred pounds. I can take her. And I will." She rolled the hat up her arm and set it on her head. "Don't wait up."

Nora made good time to the club and parked in her usual spot. She checked her coat and took the secret entrance in the coat closet that led downstairs. At the last door on the left she paused and took a breath. She opened the door and couldn't suppress a smile at the sight that greeted her.

"Sheridan…" Nora nearly purred the girl's name as she entered her room at the club. Sheridan lay stretched out on Nora's bed wearing nothing but a white lacy garter and a smile. Nora snapped her fingers and Sheridan came up on her knees at the edge of the bed.

In the beginning Kingsley had taught Nora the rules of being a paid Dominant. He was no pimp and never allowed his employees to have sex with clients on his time clock.

Rule number one, he'd intoned in his erotic French accent. *Do not kiss your clients. They may kiss you…but only on the toe of your boot.*

"Hello, Mistress."

Nora cupped Sheridan's face in her hand and gave her a long, thorough kiss. Sheridan tasted of strawberries and Nora breathed into her lips. Kingsley and his rules were powerless against the petite blonde beauty of Sheridan Stratford, star of *Empire City,* the number one drama on television. Only twenty-three, Sheridan had been a client of Nora's for two years now. She'd come running to Kingsley after four years of being unable to have an orgasm during vanilla sex. In her first session with Nora, Sheridan had climaxed five times.

Sheridan held on to Nora's suspenders as Nora ran her hands from Sheridan's shoulders down to her hips. Right now Sheridan's skin was a pristine porcelain canvas waiting for Nora to mark it. But first…

Nora pushed Sheridan down and onto her back. With her knees Nora wrenched Sheridan's thighs apart. Out in the real world, Sheridan had earned the moniker "America's Sweetheart" because of her innocent blue-eyed beauty and sweet smile. In nearly every role she played a virgin. Virgin? Sheridan hadn't been a virgin since age fourteen when her father's best friend had turned her over his knee, spanked her and fucked her right on her councilman father's big oak desk. She'd developed an appetite for extreme sex, intense BDSM, and couldn't orgasm unless submitting to a Dominant. Her father's best friend had kept on his Armani business suit while deflowering Sheridan and now Sheridan had a delicious little fetish for men's clothing.

With one hand Nora held Sheridan down by her throat while her mouth tasted the tips of Sheridan's small but perfectly formed breasts. Nora's other hand slipped down Sheridan's flat stomach and teased her already swollen clitoris.

"You started without me." Nora met Sheridan's eyes as she pushed two fingers into Sheridan's wet body.

"Am I in trouble, mistress?"

Nora laughed, low and throaty.

"Do you want to be in trouble, little miss?"

Sheridan nodded humbly and smiled so sweetly it took everything Nora had in her not to kiss the smile right off her face.

"Yes, mistress," she whispered and the smile remained.

Nora raised her hand and slapped it off instead.

Sheridan gasped as Nora grabbed her by the back of the neck; her fingers tangled in the girl's blond hair, and she dragged her to the head of the bed. From under the bed, Nora pulled her famous red riding crop.

"Hands here," Nora ordered and Sheridan came up on her knees and gripped the black metal headboard as instructed.

Nora found Sheridan's clitoris again and kneaded it. In a few moments Sheridan started panting and pushing her hips into Nora's hand.

"Pick a number between one and five," Nora instructed, and Sheridan groaned. Poor little thing hated this game. Nora never revealed in advance what Sheridan was picking. One to five orgasms? One to five beatings?

Sheridan's small hands twisted nervously on the black metal of the headboard.

"Five, mistress?" her worried voice replied.

"Five then, little miss." Nora pulled her hand away from Sheridan. "Five welts."

Sheridan released a moan of fear. A well-justified moan as Nora brought her crop down hard and swift between Sheridan's shoulder blades. Another blow landed in the center of Sheridan's back. Another on her lower back. Nora hit even harder on her bottom and hardest still on her thighs. With each strike, Sheridan cried out. It hurt. Of course it hurt. Sheridan didn't love it until it hurt.

Nora dropped the crop and ran her hand down Sheridan's welted back. She, like Søren, knew how to beat someone brutally without leaving marks. But Sheridan cherished her welts and bruises just as Nora once did. The public believed Sheridan didn't do nude scenes because of modesty. Modesty? The girl once let four men fuck her in one night while Nora watched and directed the action. No, the only reason Sheridan kept her clothes on in public was because of what Nora did to her in private.

"I'll tell you a secret," Nora whispered as she traced a finger around a bright red slash on Sheridan's back. Nora slid between Sheridan and the headboard. Once more she lightly sucked on Sheridan's nipples. With both hands, Nora opened up Sheridan's wet folds and looked up at the gasping girl. "It wasn't just five welts you were choosing."

"No, mistress?"

"No...you also picked five fingers."

Sheridan shuddered as Nora pushed first two, then three fingers into her. Nora considered pausing for lube but Sheridan was so wet right now, lube would be a moot point. A fourth finger followed. Finally Nora turned her hand and pushed her thumb into Sheridan and Sheridan cried out in shocked pleasure.

"Don't you dare, little miss," Nora warned.

Sheridan's breaths came in short bursts as she forced herself not to orgasm. Nora never let her come on her own... only on command.

Spreading her fingers, Nora pushed in deeper.

"Now," Nora said as she lightly pinched Sheridan's clitoris. The girl released a desperate gasp as her inner muscles spasmed wildly around Nora's hand.

As Nora pulled out, Sheridan released a little whimper. It seemed such a crime to take Sheridan's money for these sessions. Nora would pay good money herself just to hear that sound.

"I'm going to tell you another secret, little miss." Nora gathered a fistful of Sheridan's hair again and pulled her off the bed. She shoved Sheridan forward so the girl stood with her legs a foot apart and her hands on the bed.

"Yes, mistress?"

Nora gathered supplies before coming to stand at the opposite side of the bed. She threw down a crop, a flogger, a cane, a paddle and a whip—five implements of torture. Then she lay down in a straight line five vibrators of increasingly larger sizes.

"It wasn't just five fingers, either," Nora said as Sheridan started panting again in anticipation at the sight of all the pain ahead of her, all the pleasure.

"Mistress…" Sheridan breathed. "I only paid for an hour."

Nora laughed.

Rule number two, maîtresse…*give them everything they paid for and not a minute more.*

Nora came back to Sheridan and caressed the girl's trembling back, kissed her shivering shoulder.

"Shh…" Nora instructed as she ran a single finger down the side of Sheridan's exquisite face. "What Kingsley doesn't know won't hurt him."

Nora took off her jacket and tossed it aside. She reached for the cane and Sheridan whimpered.

That sound…worth every minute, worth every penny.

Before this night ended, she'd break Sheridan open—body and soul.

Some days Nora loved her job.

Several hours later Nora pulled up her suspenders and stuffed her tie in her pocket.

Sheridan still lay in bed, the sheet twisted around her hips leaving her petite back, scored with welts and bruises, bare to the eye.

"You did very well tonight, little miss," Nora said. "A pleasure as always. Until next time."

"Nora?" she said and Nora turned around. Sheridan sat up

and pulled the covers primly up to her chest, an odd gesture considering the last three hours of sex and S&M they'd shared.

"What's up, Sher?" Nora sat on the bed next to the pale, small beauty.

"I don't know if there'll be a next time. I'm getting married."

"Married? People still do that?"

Sheridan laughed. "God knows why, but yes."

"You've told him—"

She nodded. "He says…he'll try. We're working on it. He won't be as good as you, but then again who is?"

Nora smiled in agreement.

"I'll miss you, beautiful." Nora leaned forward and kissed the girl with a passion she rarely allowed herself to share with her clients. She pulled back and looked into Sheridan's wide, tired eyes. "But you do what you have to do. Are you sure you have to do it?"

Sheridan shrugged and looked so small and sad that for a moment Nora hated the girl's fiancé with an anger she usually reserved only for her fights with Søren.

"Can't do this forever, can we?" she asked. "I mean, I have to have something in my life besides money and work and waiting for you to have a few hours for me. You've got your books, Nora. I want to have something like that, something that matters more than anything. Can you understand that?"

Nora nodded and didn't say anything. She just pressed her forehead to Sheridan's and rested it there. She kissed her quick on the forehead and stood up.

"Call me if he needs me to show him the ropes, little miss."

Nora headed to the door.

"I'll miss you, too, mistress."

Nora turned around and doffed her hat like a matinee idol.

"Be a good girl," Nora said and left before she changed her mind. "Or else."

Sheridan stayed on her mind all the way home. *Can't do this forever, can we?*

Nora went into her office and turned on the desk lamp. She threw her hat onto the armchair, turned on her computer and opened the working draft of her book.

She thought about Zach, how he'd told her in the beginning that he thought she'd fail. She wondered if a part of him still thought that. Part of her certainly still thought that. But she wouldn't fail. She'd show Zach who she really was. Nora Sutherlin was a writer, a good writer. And once he finished the book and signed the contract then she could finally tell him she was a Dominatrix—an ex-Dominatrix by then.

She leaned back into her chair and yawned. She reread the scene she'd been working on earlier. Deciding she didn't like it, she erased it and started over.

15

Zach pulled Nora's latest chapter off his office printer and picked up his red pen. Skimming the lines, he rubbed the bridge of his nose tiredly. He needed to talk to Nora about the last few chapters she'd sent. They were going well, but he was afraid she was starting to lose her way again. She was obviously in love with her characters and wanted to spend as much time with them as possible. But her musings slowed the story down. He had to give it up and face her again. It had been five days since that night. He still couldn't think of it without hating himself a little more each time he remembered how he'd been unable to stop himself from touching her face…her skin was so soft and warm…and how he wanted to see her hair down and loose…so he pulled out the pens and let it fall…and her voice seemed to get inside him and stoke a fire he thought he'd long ago extinguished.

He raised his head, picked up the phone and dialed. After two rings Wesley answered.

"She's not here, Zach. Want to leave a message?"

"Does she have her mobile on her? Do you know where she is?"

"She's in your office, Zach."

Zach looked up and found Nora standing in his office doorway. She knocked twice on the open door and waited.

"Never mind, Wesley. She's here." Zach hung up. "How are you, Nora?"

"We need to talk about the blow job."

Zach stood up and rushed around his desk. He pulled her inside the office and shut the door behind her.

"The blow job scene in my book." She raised her voice as Zach sat at his desk again.

"You will be the death of me. You realize that, don't you?"

"I have no idea what you're talking about. I'm here to discuss my book with my editor. I still have an editor, don't I?"

"Of course. I've been busy this week."

"Busy ignoring me."

"I have responded to everything you've sent me."

"Yes, with notes and polite suggestions. I don't need polite suggestions. Polite doesn't help me. How do I know what I'm doing right if you aren't telling me what I'm doing wrong? I need you to be angry again, not polite. I think I liked it better when you hated me."

"I never hated you." Zach forced himself to meet her eyes. He took a deep breath and sat up straighter in his chair. "I never hated you or the book. It's only…about Saturday night—"

Nora opened her mouth and he raised his hand.

"About Saturday night," he began again. "I need to apologize."

Nora looked at him in wide-eyed surprise. "Zach—"

"Please, let me finish. I'm terribly sorry about what happened. I had too much to drink, and I was still reeling from

Grace's last email. That's no excuse, I realize. I shouldn't have taken advantage of you in your condition. It was foolish and reckless and I—"

"Zach, seriously. You have to stop," Nora said and laughed.

Zach stared at her. She shook her head.

"You know why I'm here? I came to apologize to you," she said.

"Whatever for?"

"I thought I was here to apologize to you for taking advantage of you in your condition, but apparently I'm the victim here. Novel sensation for me, being the victim. Not sure I like it."

"Nora, I'm your editor."

"Yes, my gorgeous editor with his poshy British accent and his ice-colored eyes and tennis player arms with the veins running from the wrist to the elbow. Oh, no, please don't ever force me to go down on you again, Mr. Easton. It's a fate worse than death."

"This isn't a bloody joke."

"No, it's not a joke. It's a blow job."

"Will you please stop saying that?"

"Fine. I fellated you, sucked you off, gave you an Oscar Wilde. But call it what you will, Zach, I handcuffed you to my desk and blew you back to England. And for some reason you aren't thrilled that happened. It's a bit of a, forgive me, *blow* to the ego, but I'll survive. What I want to know is why you're taking it so personally."

Zach sat back in his chair and counted the days until he was on a plane to California. If he were on a plane to California right now, a plane to anywhere, he wouldn't be having the most humiliating conversation of his life.

"I take it personally because that night was the first night I'd been intimate with any woman other than my wife in over ten years. That may seem rather bourgeois to you, but I'm afraid I'm terribly bourgeois when it comes to matters of infidelity—"

"She's moved on."

Zach ignored the comment.

"Not to mention taking advantage of a woman I have some modicum of power over."

"Power? You think you have power over me? You wouldn't know what to do with yourself if you had power over me. You are helping me make my book publishable. You work for me as much as I work for you."

"I have the power to decide if your book gets published. I alone have the final say."

Nora stood up and walked around the desk. She sat on the top and crossed her legs. Her knees and thighs were at Zach's eye level. Zach refused to look at her legs, her sheer stockings and short red skirt and the boots that went up to her knees. He met her eyes and waited.

"If I gagged you right now and put you flat on your back and fucked you seven ways till Sunday right here on this fine mahogany desk…would you sign my contract?" she asked.

"Absolutely not. And that's not going to happen." Zach forced back the flood of images her words conjured in his mind.

Nora slid off the desk and onto her knees next to his chair.

"What if I just gave you my best Oscar Wilde again every day for the next three weeks? Would you sign my contract then?"

"Nora, you can't buy your contract with sexual favors." Zach reached down and pulled Nora up off the floor. "I told you I wouldn't sign it until I'd read the very last page and I meant it."

"I know you meant it. That's my point. I probably could

buy off a lesser man with sex, a lesser editor. But you and I both know that even if we'd had sex ten times Saturday night, you still wouldn't sign my contract until the book was perfect. You might think less of me, or yourself more likely, but you'd read the book with the same eyes that see every flaw and the same mind that knows how to fix it. You're just afraid to be mean to my face because you think I'll think it was about Saturday night. Be as mean to me as you want, Zach. Trust me." She leaned forward and met him eye to eye. "I like mean."

Zach looked into her eyes and saw they burned black as night. In them writhed the shades and shadows of the things she'd seen and done; things that he couldn't and didn't want to imagine.

Nodding, Zach glanced away.

"Very well. I'm sorry I've disappointed you this week." He stood up. "You'll have my snide, churlish, cantankerous and bitter best from now on," he pledged.

"God, I love a man with a big vocabulary." Nora wrapped her arms around his neck. Despite how much he wanted to leave them there, Zach took her arms and pulled them off him.

"But this can't happen," he said. "Saturday night can't happen again."

"It can, and will in a few days. Saturday night happens at least once a week."

"No more jokes. You know what I mean."

"And you know I'm right. We could fuck all we wanted—"

"Perhaps I don't want to."

Nora took a step back and Zach cursed himself for his inability to say what he meant without hurting her.

"Zach, you had how many shots Saturday night, and I was still able to get you off with, let's be honest, minimal effort on my part? Don't pretend you aren't attracted to me."

"Attracted or not, we can't sleep together. And not just because of the book."

Nora moved closer. She seemed to be studying him.

"You act like you're afraid of me, Zach. But you're not afraid of me at all, are you?"

"I'm terrified of you."

"No, you're not. I know guys like you. You worship women, put them on pedestals, think they're fragile and perfect. That's why even though it was you on your back in the handcuffs Saturday night, you're the one doing the apologizing. Zach...you're afraid of yourself."

"I'm not—"

"You are. I've never known a grown man to be so afraid of his own desires. What happened to you? What did you do that's made you so afraid to let go?"

"This meeting is over."

"Tell me. Whatever it is, I promise I've done worse."

"Believe me, Nora, you've never done this."

"It was Grace, wasn't it? What did you do to her?"

Nora's words pummeled into him but he couldn't tell her to stop. He knew whatever pain she inflicted he deserved.

"Please," he whispered.

"You know how to beg. That's a good start."

"No more games, either. I'm not like you."

"We're more alike than you want to admit."

"I'm not—" he paused and looked for the right word "—*free* like you."

"You could be." She took another step closer. "I can show you if you'll let me. The world I live in, you've never seen such freedom. Freedom like you can't even begin to imagine. Try, Zach."

"I can't." The sadness settled over him again.

"Come with me," Nora said. Zach felt himself falling under

the spell her words were weaving. "Let me show you what life is like lived in the moment. No past, no future, just the one perfect moment you're standing in and there's no guilt and there's no shame and there's absolutely nothing to be afraid of..."

Zach closed his eyes and tried to imagine her world. But once his eyes closed he could see only darkness and he could smell only the copper of fresh fallen blood.

"I'm sorry."

Nora was still looking at him when he opened his eyes.

"Fuck your sorry," she said with angry eyes and turned on her heel. "I've got a book to write."

16

Three weeks left…

"Why do you stay with me?" William asked. With his fingertip, he traced the outline of a welt that ran shoulder to shoulder across her back.

Caroline turned over in bed to face him. "Because of the Wives of Weinsburg," she said as if it were the most obvious answer in the world.

"I'm afraid I'm not familiar with the ladies of which you speak." William ran his hand over her hip and she shivered at the sensation. For all the pain he inflicted on her, he resolved every day to inflict equal pleasure.

"They may only be a legend. I like to think they were real. Once the city of Weinsburg in Germany was under siege. The enemy emperor was dangerous but not unmerciful. When it became inevitable that the city would fall, the men of Weinsberg pleaded for their women, that they be allowed to flee with their lives. The emperor relented and allowed the women to leave the city with only the valuables they *could carry on their backs. The day came and the gates of the city opened and the emperor watched in shock as the women stumbled through the gates nearly breaking under the weight of their husbands and fathers who they carried on their backs. Their love humbled the emperor and he declared all would be spared."*

"For these women who may or may not exist you stay with me?" he asked, laughing at her as usual.

Caroline reached out to touch his face but pulled her hand back. He'd taught her so well not to touch him without permission. There were moments he regretted how well he'd trained her.

"Every day you battle an enemy I cannot fight with you or for you. But if there is ever a chance for a reprieve, then I will bear you across the world on my back to see you finally at peace."

William smiled at the twenty-year-old child who loved him more than he could or would ever deserve.

"But what if the enemy you think I fight isn't the enemy at all?" he asked, reaching out to take her face in his hand. He forced her to meet his gaze and for a moment he let his eyes fill with all his darkest desires. "What if this enemy is only me?"

Caroline didn't flinch at what she saw. He had taught her that, as well.

"Then I will save you from yourself."

Poor Wesley, Zach thought. Did that poor smitten lad have any idea that he was the inspiration for Nora's latest hopeless, love-struck heroine? Did Nora even know it herself? *I will save you from yourself...*he could hear Wesley saying those very words to Nora. He hadn't learned yet you couldn't save someone who didn't want to be saved.

Zach wanted to be saved. He tried to conjure the image of Grace, six inches shorter than he and light as a sparrow, trying to lift and carry him on her back. She'd had the chance to save him once. That day he told her about the job at Royal House, that he would be moving to the States, she could have saved him with a sentence—"I'll go with you." She could have saved him with a word—"Don't."

Zach opened his email. Nora—you cut half this chapter or I'll cut half this chapter. Either way half of it is getting cut.

He hit Send without remorse. Nora truly worked better when he was at his most brutally honest with her. He didn't have to couch a criticism inside a compliment. She didn't want compliments. She wanted her book to be better.

Zach closed his laptop. Stretching out on his sofa he stared around his flat. Grace would be horrified by its austerity. If she ever saw it she would tease him that *minimalist* was not a synonym for *empty*. But when he'd come to New York he knew it was temporary. He'd have about eight months at the East Coast offices until the current chief editor in L.A. finished off the last of her projects and then he was off to yet another city. He saw no reason to have anything but the bare minimum—a sofa, a bed, a television that he only ever tuned to the occasional Everton football match, and a landline phone sitting on the floor. Why even bother with an end table for the living room? Just one more damn thing to pack.

He picked up his lager and took a drink. Only seven o'clock on a Monday evening and he already felt so exhausted he considered just calling it a night. Only his masculine pride kept him from going to bed at such a geriatric hour. Even his sixty-six-year-old widowed father never went to bed before eight.

Thoughts of his father stirred a fearful thought—Nora's pills in the medicine cabinet. He still couldn't believe that she was as ill as the bottle portended. Perhaps it was only a mild condition, an arrhythmia or something innocuous and treatable. He tried to talk himself out of his fear but couldn't quite rationalize it away.

Zach picked up a handful of Nora's pages and skimmed the lines. *Why do you stay with me?* He had never spoken those words to Grace, though they echoed in his head almost every day of their marriage. Their marriage had begun in terror and shame and then in time changed into something he didn't want to live without. Zach knew why he stayed. But why had she?

Standing, Zach rubbed his neck and tried to think of something or someone else for a few minutes. But his only other thoughts were of Nora and that was an even more dangerous rabbit hole. Nora... It had been over a week since their drunken night of idiocy. He remembered how her mouth felt on his skin, how foreign it felt to be touched by a woman's hands again, how strange it was to be awake and conscious and thinking of something other than losing Grace, not thinking about anything at all except that whatever Nora was doing he would be content to let her keep doing until the day he died. Only afterward did the guilt set in—the guilt that for a few minutes he let himself stop feeling guilty.

Zach performed a quick mental calculation. Seven o'clock in New York equaled midnight in London. He knew Grace would still be up. A night owl in the worst way, she took long naps after coming home from school and then stayed up far too late reading.

He picked up his phone and dialed. It rang once and no one answered. A second ring and still no answer. Zach's heart dropped with every unanswered ring. Between the seventh and the eighth ring Zach whispered, "I miss you, Gracie," and hung up the phone. On the floor next to the phone Zach sat with his head in his hands. Midnight and she wasn't home. A school night and she wasn't...

For a horrible second an image of her with another man tore through his mind. But he knew he couldn't be angry or jealous. After that night with Nora, he'd lost all right to be hurt.

Nora…he remembered what she'd offered him when she'd come to his office last Thursday…a chance to see the world she lived in, to see what it was like to live free of guilt or restraint. He envied Nora her freedom. He wondered if her mysterious former lover, Søren, was the source of her vivacity. Nora said the first day they worked on her book together that Søren had owned her. He couldn't even imagine what that meant, what such a relationship would be like. But perhaps only someone who had been a slave could truly appreciate the worth of freedom.

Let me show you what life is like lived in the moment. No past, no future…no guilt…no shame…nothing to be afraid of…

No guilt, no shame, no fear—he'd forgotten what it felt like to live without his three most constant and cruel companions. Could Nora really do that for him? Even just a few minutes of freedom seemed worth any price he had to pay.

Zach looked down at the useless phone and his empty flat and made a quick decision. He stood up and grabbed his coat. He fled his building in one minute and hopped on the train in ten more. He wouldn't turn into his father, he told himself. Not tonight.

On their third morning together, she woke up in his bed and found it empty. Slowly, she sat up, careful of her bruised and aching body. Last night had been the roughest yet, and she smiled at the memory of the sensual crimes he committed against her flesh. He'd spent two years mentally preparing her for what he would demand of her once they finally consummated their relationship. Although she'd known what was coming, had even watched him with others, she hadn't truly known how much it would hurt until the first blows landed on her virgin back their first night together as lovers. Waking up the next morning with welts on her body and blood on her thighs and his sheets, her first thought was not of regret or fear, but that it had all been worth it—the wait, the pain, the sacrifice that now felt like no sacrifice at all. She belonged to him and always would. He'd said those words to her but now she felt them singing in her skin. The collar he'd locked around her neck now encircled her heart. She raised a hand to her neck and found it bare. He'd taken off her collar in her sleep. Knowing he did not expect total submission from her right now, she rose from the bed and followed the sound of running water to the bathroom. She found him in the shower and without asking permission joined him under the steaming water. He was not angry. She knew he wouldn't be. Everyone she knew was intimidated by him—by his intelligence, by his imposing height and strength, by his ethereal beauty—but she knew him as a man of flesh and earthy desire who loved her beyond comprehension. She knew his kindness, his generosity, and although he could make the surface of her body ripple with fear when as he locked her in her bonds at night, underneath that fear moved deep ocean currents of trust. For five years he'd been teaching her how to trust him. And as he bent his head to kiss her, she laughed into his mouth, proud of how well she'd learned the lesson.

His hands, as gentle this morning as they'd been brutal last night, explored every corner of her body. She ran her fingers through his hair and slicked it back. When he moved his mouth to her neck and drank the water from the hollow of her throat, she taunted, "No toys, no chains—how are you going to dominate me now?"

It happened so fast that she didn't even have time to gasp. She was pinned with her stomach flat against the shower wall. At first she wasn't scared.

"Like this," he whispered in her ear. "This is how." And he pushed into the one part of her body he hadn't yet penetrated. The pain was beyond anything he'd ever inflicted on her. She screamed in the back of her throat, screamed broken formless words, words ripped in half as she was. She knew there was a way to stop it, but in her panic and her agony, the way was forgotten. On her lips she tasted blood and realized she'd bitten her own arm. He continued to thrust *as her tears mingled with the water and ran down her face. It was over then as quickly as it began. He pulled out of her and left her in the shower. Her legs gave out and she sank to the floor. The water continued to beat down on her. When he came back to her, he was dressed.*

Slowly, she forced herself to look up at him and in a hollow voice she whispered, "I forgot my safe word." Horror dawned in his eyes. Slowly, he knelt on the floor, knelt like he meant to pray. He reached for her and she shrank back instinctively in fear. He waited and did not move to touch her again. Finally, she pulled herself slowly up. He held open a towel and she stepped into it, leaning into his body as he wrapped it around her. Picking her up he carried her back to the bedroom. He sat in the armchair by the window and held her to him, rocking her in his strong arms while she cried.

He did not apologize and she did not expect him to.

She never forgot her safe word again.

Nora read the words with a slight smile on her lips before deleting the last hour of writing with a wistful sigh. She opened her email and found a new set of notes from Zach on the last chapters she'd sent him. Although he liked where she was taking it, Zach was back in attack mode and she couldn't stop grinning as she read some of his more sarcastic comments.

"Nora— Forgive me for copyediting, but it must be said— you have raped the semicolon yet again. Stop it. It wasn't asking for it no matter how it was dressed. If you don't know how to use punctuation then do away with it altogether, write like Faulkner and we'll pretend it's on purpose."

Bite me, Easton, Nora said to herself as she corrected her sexually compromised semicolon in chapter eighteen. *Seriously, bite me.*

"Nora— Aristotle said character is plot. Aristotle is dead and can't hurt you. I'm alive and I can. Plot is plot. Find one and keep it."

You want to try to hurt me, Zach? I'd love to see you try.

Nora looked up as Wesley entered her office. She smiled but he didn't smile back. He merely sat her red cell phone on her desk, turned around and walked out.

With relief Nora noted that her one missed call was from Kingsley and not Søren. She called back, but only out of courtesy.

"Bonjour, ma chérie, ma belle, mon canard," Kingsley started in on her as soon as he answered.

"King, calling me 'your duck' isn't going to change the fact that I'm still busy."

"Too busy for a 10K evening with a dear friend of yours?"

"Tell him it's 20K or the waiting list."

"The waiting list then."

"We are in a recession after all. Just tell him to tell his wife how much he's paid me in the last year. That should earn him enough of an ass-kicking to last him until I'm done with the book."

"I'll pass your well-wishes along to the happy couple."

Nora hung up on Kingsley and left her office. She followed the thrumming of a guitar to Wesley's room.

"That's pretty. What it is?" she asked.

"The Killers." Wesley stopped playing the song and adjusted his capo. "Ever heard of them?"

"If they came after Pearl Jam's Ten then probably not."

He looked at her and laughed a little.

"A little after. You going out tonight?"

"Nope. I hung up on King. And in three weeks if Zach signs my contract I will put on my best pair of stilettos and slam my heel through my hotline once and for all."

Wesley smiled and started picking out a melody. Nora started to leave.

"What if he doesn't sign it?" Wesley asked.

Nora considered the terrifying possibility that after read-

ing the finished novel, Zach would still think it wasn't Royal
House material.

"I guess the hotline will have to stay hot a little while longer."

Nora watched Wesley's face.

"I like Zach," he said. "I didn't at first, but I do now. He's
a really good guy."

She cocked her head and looked at him.

"I agree. Wholeheartedly."

"I think you should tell him, you know, about the other
job."

Nora's stomach tightened.

"I will. I promise I will. But not yet. I want him to read
the book with clear eyes. If I tell him what I do he'll think
I'm just writing a knock-off memoir with the names changed
instead of real fiction. If and when he signs the contract, then
I'll tell him," she promised.

Nora left Wesley in his room and headed to the kitchen. She
only made it as far as the living room when she heard a knock
on her door. She glanced at the clock. Who would be stopping
by her house at almost eight o'clock at night?

Nora went to the door and opened it. Zach stood on the
other side looking flushed and sheepish and so handsome she
had to force her heart to slow its frantic beating.

She said nothing, only raised an eyebrow and waited.

"I know why he calls you his Siren," Zach said without
preamble.

Nora grinned at him.

"You finally decide to let me blow you off course?"

"Yes. I think. I'm not sure, but I know I can't keep living
like this, Nora."

Nora reached out her hand and this time Zach took it in
his. His strong hand felt so good wrapped around hers she

was afraid that now she had it she wouldn't ever let it go. She yanked him into the house with her left hand while her right hand hit the eight on her phone.

"What now?" he asked as Nora lifted the phone to her ear.

"We're taking a little trip. King, don't talk," she said when Kingsley answered. "I'm hitting the club tonight. Call and have them hold my table. One guest." She glanced at Zach. "And Kingsley…mum's the word."

Nora hung up the phone and looked at Zach.

"Where are we going?" Zach asked.

Nora could hear the fear still hiding under the excitement in his voice.

She met his eyes and without smiling answered him.

"Hell."

17

Zach entered Nora's office and switched on her desk lamp. From what Wesley said just before he left, it sounded as if Nora would be a while getting ready. Might as well pass the time with a book. Considering Nora's tastes he had no doubt he could find something to distract him from the screaming voice in his head telling him he really didn't want to do this.

The lamplight spread its warm yellow glow over Nora's desk. Wesley must have tidied up. Her usual disarray had been transformed into well-ordered chaos, if there was such a thing. He picked up a small box she'd labeled Scribbles and Bits. He opened it and found dozens of quotations from various sources on multicolored note cards.

One card read in Nora's slanting script, "No pain, no palm; no thorns, no throne; no gall, no glory; no cross, no crown. —William Penn." That did sound like something Nora would commit to memory. Another quote came from the Roman playwright Platus: "I do believe it was Love which devised the torturer's profession here on earth." Appropriate. A pink card read, "The man who has never been flogged has never been taught.—Menander of Athens."

The last card simply said, "The Lady or the Tiger?" over and over and over again.

Zach put the cards away and closed the box. He saw her day planner tucked next to her keyboard. He knew he was being unconscionably nosy, but his curiosity got the better of him. Seemed to be today's theme.

He flipped the red leather-bound calendar open. She and Lex apparently had rescheduled her book-signing for a month from Saturday. She'd dragged Wesley to the opera a few weeks ago. She and G.F. had been in Miami in January. He flipped to the week before he and Nora had met. On that Monday she'd written, "T.R.—M.D. 8:00 p.m." Another notation later that week read, "S.S.—W.A., 9:00 p.m." But the next day had another M.D. appointment at 5:00 p.m. He glanced through all the previous pages. Anywhere from two to four times a week, Nora had some sort of M.D. appointment. But as soon as they'd started working on her book the M.D. appointments had dropped off almost completely. What sort of doctor saw a patient on evenings and weekends? Why had Nora stopped going to her appointments when they started working together?

With shaking hands, Zach closed the calendar and stepped to her bookshelves. Lovely, he thought, smirking at the books on the top shelf—sex manuals. He skimmed the titles: *The Joy of Sex, The Kama Sutra, The Guide to Anal Sex for Women*. The last title he read twice. The second shelf did hold some surprises, however—psychology and sociology texts, weighty cerebral tomes on the psychology of power and pain. On the third shelf down sat children's books, their covers worn from multiple readings—the *Harry Potter* books in British first editions, *Alice in Wonderland, Through the Looking Glass, The Wonderful Wizard of Oz, The Chronicles of Narnia*. But one book appeared more loved than the rest. Its thin red spine was worn and frayed. Zach slipped it off the shelf—*The Jabberwocky* by Lewis Carroll. Some clever illustrator had taken the text of Carroll's poem and reimagined it as a story all its own. Zach leafed through the lurid, lush illustrations, the pages grown soft and porous from so many readings. On a hunch he turned back to the front end-pages and found an inscription. In handwriting both masculine and elegant it read, "My Little One, Never forget the lesson of the Jabberwocky. And never forget that I love you." It was signed only "S" with a fierce diagonal slash through it; the mark of the mysterious Søren. He closed the book and slipped it back on the shelf.

Turning back to Nora's desk, he noticed again that long black duffel bag he'd accidentally kicked the first time he sat in this office. He stuck out his foot and toed the bag, hearing again the chiming sound of metal against metal.

"Open it, Zach."

Nora entered the office grinning at him, but Zach was too stunned to smile back. He only stared as she moved even closer, the heels of her boots clicked hollowly on the hardwood floor as her ankle-length leather skirt quietly creaked with each soft sway of her hips. The pale flesh of her thigh peeked out from the hip-high slit in her skirt over a black lace-trimmed stocking. She wore a black corset laced over a flesh-toned bustier. And with her neck bare, her hair artfully arranged over her shoulder, the effect was utterly obscene.

"Gotta love a woman in uniform," she said, and Zach caught a whiff of her perfume—subtle and seductive. It made the little hairs on the back of his neck stand on end.

"You will hear no complaints from me."

"Thank you, Zachary. Give me a hand, will you? I can't get them tight enough on my own."

Nora held out her arms, completely bare but for a pair of black fingerless leather gloves that covered her forearms. She turned her arms over, and Zach saw the gloves hooked over her thumbs and laced up her arms like a corset.

"What are these?" He took Nora's wrist in his hand and methodically pulled the laces tight.

"They're called gauntlets. Kind of a feminized medieval warrior look."

"Thought you only wore red when you went out." Zach laced her other gauntlet.

"Don't believe everything you hear about me—just the bad stuff. You're pretty good at this. You've laced a corset before. You like lingerie?"

"I've never been known to object to it. Must be frustrating to have clothing you need help putting on."

"This is usually Wes's job. He's the one who finds it frustrating."

"His job? And to think I tended bar for cash while I was at university. This is a far cry from punching out drunken football hooligans."

"A lover and a fighter? You need to give Wes some lessons on how to properly enjoy his college experience."

"Where is Wesley anyway? He seemed to leave in a hurry."

"Oh—" Nora waved her hand "—off pouting somewhere."

"Pouting? Might I ask why?"

"Wes doesn't want me, but he doesn't like it if I want someone else. Kid's gotta learn that he can't have his cake and not eat me, too."

Zach laughed.

"He's also pissed," Nora said, moving even closer to him, "because he knows what I'm doing tonight."

"And that is?"

"Seducing you."

Zach took a step back.

"Nora, I haven't changed my mind. We can't work together and be lovers, too. J.P. will kill me to start with. And if he doesn't I might kill myself."

Nora raised her eyebrow at him, crossed her arms and leaned against his side.

"So are you just window-shopping tonight?"

Zach crossed his arms to match her and gave her a smile.

"Perhaps I'm just hoping you'll be inspired to finish the book before I leave."

"Is that a challenge?"

"How about this…" Zach began and couldn't believe what he was proposing. "I'll give you your homework. You get it done in a timely manner by day and—"

"And by night we play?" Nora's eyes were shining. "This is a fun game, Zach. I could win this one."

"And…" Zach turned to face her. "If you do manage to complete the book a few days ahead of schedule then technically we'll no longer be working together. Perhaps then we can discuss bringing the handcuffs out of hiding."

"Handcuffs?" she scoffed. "Handcuffs are the least of your worries. Open it." She pointed her toe toward her long black duffel bag on the floor. "I dare you."

Zach let a few seconds pass before he bent over and grabbed the handles. He hefted it onto Nora's desk, stunned by its weight.

"What on earth is in here?"

"It's my toy bag."

"Toy bag?" He eyed her skeptically. "Store your Legos in here, do you?"

"Not quite."

He glanced at her once more before slowly unzipping the bag. Nora moved to stand next to him, her left hip pressing against his right leg. Nora reached past him and pulled from the bag a long chrome bar.

"Do you know what this is? It's called a spreader bar. Just a basic pipe with eyebolts on the end. You take a snap-hook and a pair of these——" she reached into the bag again and brought out a wide leather bracelet with a gold buckle sewn into it "——leather cuffs. Adjustable. They go around the wrists or the ankles. Both if you want to put someone in a spread-eagle position."

Nora arched an eyebrow at him and reached back into the bag.

"This is a flogger. Here. Give me your arm."

Zach held his arm out with extreme reluctance. Nora brushed his forearm lightly with the tips of the flogger's leather strips.

"It tickles." He rubbed his arm.

"Pain or pleasure, it's made for either. So am I."

"I'll stick with pleasure. I've always preferred the carrot to the stick."

"Where we're going, the stick *is* the carrot." She put the flogger away. She dug into her bag again. "This lovely device," she said as she held out what looked like two spreader bars joined in the middle, "is called an X-Bar. It cuffs the wrists and ankles behind the back. Perfect for immobilizing someone in a kneeling position. As a man, I'm certain you can imagine the benefit of immobilizing a woman on her knees."

Zach coughed and exhaled.

"Usually, I just prefer her to volunteer for that particular activity." His tongue felt heavy and dry in his mouth.

"In my world, if she shows up, she did volunteer. Or in your case, you showed up and I volunteered."

Zach could feel the cold metal of the handcuffs around his wrists again.

"I can't win with you, can I?"

Nora laughed.

"Of course not. The only way to win in this game is to surrender. Come on, Zach," she said, seeming to drop out of character for a moment. "You and I both know I could have had you weeks ago. In the cab, remember?"

Zach recalled the night of the release party. He'd convinced himself it was his own restraint that had prevented him from asking Nora up. But he knew it was only because Nora had closed the door before he could invite her inside.

"Why didn't you?"

"You weren't ready then."

"And I'm ready now?"

"Well… You did show up again, didn't you? You should know by now," Nora said, and Zach made himself look in her eyes, "I wouldn't chase you so hard if I didn't know you wanted to be caught."

"Just because you want something doesn't mean you should have it."

"Really?" Nora asked with a raised eyebrow. "And what did you want that you shouldn't have had?"

Zach looked away and pointed at something in her bag. "What's that?"

"Ah…" Nora sighed. "He's lost in the fog yet again." Still, she reached into the bag and pulled out a black silk scarf. She twined it through her fingers and over her wrists, letting it cascade into her palms like black water.

"Blindfold?" Zach made an educated guess.

"Or gag. Or wrist restraint. The blindfold seems tame, but I'm very fond of them. Do you have any idea how much trust it takes to let someone take you blind? Want to find out?"

"Nora…"

"Okay, Zach. I promise I'll keep my hands off…more or less. No sex until the book is done. Well, you won't have any sex. Knowing me, I will," she said over her shoulder.

Zach laughed until he saw she wasn't smiling.

"Come on." Nora threw on her coat and belted it. She strode toward the door. "Time to go."

"Need your bag?" he joked.

"Not where we're going."

18

Zach followed Nora outside. He started to walk toward her car parked in front of the house. But she beckoned him instead to her garage.

"This way, handsome. I've got a little surprise for you."

Nora pulled her key ring out of her coat pocket and hit a small black button. The garage door slowly yawned open. Zach never dreamed she kept an actual car in her garage. Her black Lexus and Wesley's beat-up VW always sat in the driveway or on the street. But inside the garage he saw some kind of vehicle covered in a suede car cover.

"You Yanks." Zach shook his head. "You think you need a whole army of cars."

"This isn't just a car, Zach." She grabbed the corner of the cover and pulled it off in one extravagant motion.

"My God…Nora," he breathed at the sight of the inferno-red machine. He'd never been much of a car enthusiast but something very male in him wanted to just run his hands across it from fender to fender.

"Once upon a time," Nora began, "I spent a week with a sheikh. This was his version of morning-after roses."

"You just keep this in your garage?"

"What? Just your everyday Aston Martin."

"This is James Bond's car."

"Yes, but he can't have it back. Don't tell, but I'm going to give it to Wes as a graduation present in a couple of years."

"If you ever fire him and start looking for a new intern…" Zach reached out and touched the hood.

"I'll keep your résumé on file," Nora said, looking at him as he stroked the top of the car. "You're hard right now, aren't you?"

"Fully erect." Zach didn't crack a smile.

"Typical male." Nora rolled her eyes. "Get in."

Zach slid onto the passenger seat and inhaled the heady scent of the most expensive leather interior in the world. He closed his eyes and leaned back in his seat. It held him like a hand. He could die here.

Nora slipped into the driver's seat. The car purred to life.

"Nora…who are you?"

"Just another guttersnipe. Ready to see my gutter?"

Zach leaned up and opened his eyes.

"Where exactly are we going?" he asked as she slinked through the streets and headed toward the city.

"It's a club," Nora simply said.

"What kind of club?"

"The only kind of club I would ever go to."

"What's this club called?"

"It doesn't really have an official name. It doesn't officially exist. Those of us in the know call it the 8th Circle."

Zach tried to remember his Italian literature class.

"It's been too long since I've read Dante. The eighth circle—was that where the sins of lust were punished?"

Nora's lips curled into an ironic grin.

"That was the second circle. The eighth circle was the destination for those who abused their power—panderers, seducers, simonists, false counselors."

"Simonists?"

Nora's smiled widened.

"Corrupt priests."

"Abused their power...very clever."

"The name is all too apt."

Zach turned to her and didn't ask what she meant by that. He'd already lost his train of thought as he watched Nora shift gears with the practiced ease of a race-car driver. Her touch was easy and smooth; the engine responded to her every whim. Zach couldn't stop watching, couldn't stop imagining her dexterous hands on him.

"How did you learn to drive like this?" Zach asked, trying to ignore his growing arousal.

"I can drive anything—any car, any kind. I've been driving a stick shift since I was thirteen."

Zach started to open his mouth to ask her another question. But Nora took a sharp turn to the left and pulled into what appeared to be an abandoned parking structure attached to a dingy squat concrete block of a building. Windowless, lifeless and covered in graffiti, the building seemed the last place in the city Nora would want to enter.

"Why did you stop?"

Nora pulled in and parked next to a sleek, silver Porsche.

"Because we're here."

"Here?" Zach looked around in disbelief as they both left the car. The place seemed dismal and far too quiet. Only the wind sliding around the concrete columns made any sound at all. He looked back at the Aston Martin.

"Are you sure it's safe to leave it here?" Zach asked even though it was just one of many luxury cars in the garage.

"This is the safest parking garage in New York. Trust me."

Nora brought them to a gunmetal-gray door and pulled out her keys again. She slid one into the lock and turned it. Zach expected the roar of a nightclub to greet them but he heard nothing but silence.

He found himself standing at the end of a long hallway. It seemed to be part of an old hotel. The walls and carpets were a deep red; small aging chandeliers hung from the ceiling and cast broken light over the paisley squares of threadbare carpeting. They came to the end of the hall where an old-fashioned coat check booth stood. Nora rang the silver desk bell and shed her coat.

A girl came out of the back and flashed them both a courteous smile.

"How may I serve you?" she asked. Her smile wavered and widened as the young woman seemed to suddenly register Nora's identity. "Mistress Nora," she said, bobbing a perfect curtsy. She looked positively starstruck. The girl wore a classic cigarette girl costume, blue and black striped, and her lush dark hair was coiffed Bettie-Page style.

"Hello, dear," Nora said with a magnanimous air as she gave the girl her coat. Zach surrendered his, as well, grateful to be rid of it. In the stifling hallway, he instantly felt more comfortable in his jeans and T-shirt. "Are you new? Did King bring you in?"

"Yes, mistress. Mr. K. brought me in a few weeks ago."

"King always did have good taste," Nora said, eliciting a blush from the beaming young woman. "Have you made it to the floor yet?"

"No, mistress," the girl said, her voice aflutter with nervousness. "I'm so sorry. It's just…I'm such a fan."

Zach smiled at the girl. "You should enjoy her next book, too. It's coming along very well."

The girl looked puzzled.

"You write books too, mistress?"

Nora laughed but didn't meet Zach's eyes.

"You're adorable," Nora said to the girl. "I'll talk to King about getting you on the floor."

"Thank you, mistress," the girl breathed. She seemed to re-member herself and said with a more professional tone, "Can I get anything for you, mistress? For your guest?"

"A white scarf, please. And my case. The black one."

With another curtsy the girl left and promptly returned with a plain white handkerchief and a small box that looked like a flute case only much longer.

Nora took the white scarf and wrapped it around his bicep.

"What on earth—"

"The Circle revived the flag and scarf signal system from the old guard leather scene," Nora explained. "We revised it quite a bit to suit the specific clientele that comes here. The scarves are signals or advertisements. Here white means you're an S&M virgin who only wants to observe. Should keep the wolves at bay."

"Should?" Zach asked skeptically. "I really need a stop sig-nal? A simple 'no, thanks' wouldn't do?"

"Trust me, as gorgeous as you are, Zach, you would be in big trouble down there without a little armor on."

"Wouldn't red make for a better stop signal?" Zach asked, not wanting to be labeled as a "virgin" anything.

"A red scarf would signal you were into blood-play."

"Ah, I see."

"Could be worse," Nora said as she finished knotting the scarf around his arm. "It could be a brown scarf."

"And brown means?"

The young woman and Nora gave each other conspiratorial glances.

"Keep the wolves at bay…should I be nervous, Nora?"

Nora didn't answer. She snapped open the black case and
took out a riding crop, black with white braiding and quite
professional-looking. She took a step back and twirled the
crop with stunning expertise. With a quick flick she struck
it against her own leather-clad calf. The sound echoed down
the hall like a gunshot.

"Kingsley Edge was the first person who put a riding crop
in my hand. It was like Arthur with Excalibur." She winked
at the girl and the girl could only smile in awe. Zach tried
not to roll his eyes. Disheartening to think Nora had better
luck with women than he did.

"Come, Zachary," Nora said, tapping her leather-clad calf
with the crop.

"Yes, mistress," he said, with minimal irony.

Nora started to turn but stopped in midstep.

"Tell me your name," she ordered the girl.

"Robin," she replied.

"Ah, a little bird," Nora purred. She reached out and caressed the girl's burning cheek with the back of her hand.
"I'll remember that."

Nora lowered her hand and stepped away. She pushed the
down button on the elevator and the door slid open. They
entered and Zach saw there was only a down button inside.

"This elevator only goes down?"

"Apparently so." Nora held the handle of her crop in her
right hand and the tip in her left. She held it, he discovered
with a jolt of recognition, like a scepter. Even her posture,
usually intimate and conspiratorial, had transformed. She held
herself like a queen, her chin high, her back straight. She wore
the hauteur well.

"Then how will we get out?"

Nora looked at him as if the thought had never occurred to her.

"I suppose we won't."

"That girl worships you but she doesn't know you're a writer. How did she know you, Nora?"

"Down here everyone knows me. Oh, and to answer your earlier question," she said as the elevator slowed. "Yes, you should be nervous."

He heard the muted grinding of the elevator coming to a shuddering stop. The doors opened. Nora turned her face to the dark outside the doors, and in a low voice said, "Let the wild rumpus begin."

Nora stepped forward and across the threshold. Zach called her name as she disappeared into the dark. Her hand reached back; Zach grasped it and let her pull him across blindly into the abyss. It took a few moments for his eyes to adjust. Zach stepped back when he realized he now stood teetering at the top of a steep staircase. But Nora stepped forward and went down, and he had no choice but to go down with her.

He felt the music before he even heard it. It beat into his chest, a pounding, visceral symphony of violence. Nora descended the staircase, and he had to trust her since he could barely make out his own feet below him. As they reached the middle of the staircase a deafening roar erupted as the throngs below recognized Nora. When they reached the bottom step a horde of near naked bodies congregated to throw themselves at Nora's feet. She brushed past them, kicked some away, and swatted a few dismissively like flies with her riding crop. The more viciously she dealt with them, the more they groveled.

Looking around, Zach saw sights his eyes could process but his mind could not. Above him hung bodies hoisted high on suspension harnesses. A woman in leather dragged a man to a cross and lashed him to it. A line of people queued up to take turns flogging him. A naked woman was tied spread-eagle to a large spinning wheel. A huge bear of a man whipped her as the wheel turned and turned. Another woman strapped to an X-Bar volunteered her services to a man covered in head-to-toe vinyl except for the part of him in her mouth.

Into all this wet, red hell Nora strode without blinking, without flinching, without missing a step. She floated light and buoyant across the black waters, her eyes burning like flags afire. Zach imagined they could be seen for miles.

She pulled him through the herd of admirers toward an open wrought-iron elevator shaft at the other side of the floor. Guarding the elevator was a man roughly the size of a house wearing chaps and a spiked dog collar. Nora transferred her riding crop from her right hand to her left, and with her free right hand delivered a slap so fierce to the man's face that Zach winced.

Zach moved forward ready to take the brunt of the man's retaliation, but he merely smiled, bowed to Nora and stepped aside.

Nora stepped into the elevator and Zach followed.

"What the hell was that?" Zach demanded, referring to the slap.

"The password," she called back.

No doors closed on the lift as it started to rise. Zach huddled near the back wall for safety, but Nora stood at the very edge and blew a kiss to the howling, cheering crowd below.

The elevator brought them three stories up to an old world bar. Tables of black lacquer sat everywhere and at the center of each pale yellow candles burned and dripped wax over the shiny surfaces. Behind the bar hung a huge mirror and every sort of alcohol one could conceive of. The din of the crowd was still audible but distinctly subdued. A portion of the bar opened like a balcony. Zach could see the chaos still raging below.

Nora brought him to a table near the center of the bar. She stood by her chair and waited. Seconds later a dark-eyed, well-muscled young man wearing low-slung leather pants came up behind Nora and pulled her chair out for her.

"Have a seat, mistress," he said. "If it pleases you."

Nora laughed and turned in her chair to face him. He knelt at her feet and waited with a smile.

"Griffin Randolfe Fiske," she said in delighted recognition. She put the tip of her riding crop under his chin and forced him to meet her eyes. "What the hell are you doing down there, you dirty Dom?"

"Just seeing how the other half grovels," Griffin said, running his hand through his near-black hair. Even on the floor on his knees, it was obvious to Zach Nora's friend was no submissive.

Zach guessed Nora's friend was in his mid-twenties. Handsome and tan with armband tattoos around both biceps, Griffin appeared to be a close friend of Nora's—very close.

"Who'd you piss off this time?" Nora flicked the little silver tag hanging off his collar.

"The usual."

Nora shook her head.

"You know Søren has the right to revoke your key, Griff," she warned, casually twirling the riding crop in her nimble fingers.

"Yes, but you like me so he won't."

Nora gave him a sidelong glare with a smile underneath.

"I don't like you. I tolerate you."

"Yeah, you tolerated my brains out in Miami two months ago."

Nora scoffed. "I was feeling unusually tolerant that day."

"Weekend," Griffin corrected. "Who's blue eyes over here?"

Zach started as he realized Nora's friend was now sizing him up.

"Master Griffin Fiske, meet my editor, Zachary Easton," she introduced them.

"A pleasure to meet you." Zach reached forward to shake Griffin's hand. But Griffin kissed the center of his palm instead. Zach yanked his hand back.

"He's gorgeous, Nora. Hot accent, too. Fucked him yet?"

Nora shrugged. "Just a blow job."

Zach had the sudden urge to throttle Nora.

"Blow job on a British guy?" Griffin asked with some concern. "You're a braver bitch than I. No offense," Griffin said, turning to Zach. "I have a foreskin phobia."

"Zach's Jewish."

Griffin nodded his approval. "Mazel tov."

"Griffin, are you going to get our drink order anytime soon or will I have to report you to a certain someone for dereliction of duty?"

"Drink order, mistress. Give it to me."

"Zach, do you want anything?"

Did he want anything? He wanted to get back in the Aston Martin right now and head straight for home. He'd thought he'd lived a wild life before he and Grace married—dozens of lovers, sex in cars, in parks, once with the maid of honor in the bathroom during a wedding reception, twice with the daughter of the dean of his college…loads of drinking, carousing, wild nights followed by tired but happy next mornings. But nothing he'd ever done compared to what was going on right in front of his eyes. A girl no more than twenty-five was being dragged by her hair past their table by a man about his age. He pushed her onto the elevator floor and put his foot on the back of her neck. Nora and Griffin barely even glanced in their direction.

"Anything that will put me into a coma," Zach decided.

"No comas tonight. The Circle's got a two-drink maximum," Nora said.

"Two-drink maximum?"

"Griffin, explain," Nora ordered.

"You see, blue eyes," Griffin said, still kneeling on the floor. "This place doesn't actually exist. No one knows it's here. Not the cops, not the IRS, nobody but members, and the guy who runs this joint has so much blackmail shit on every member that we don't breathe a word about this place to outsiders. So to avoid any unnecessary scrutiny, we play it very safe down here. No drugs, very little alcohol and safe words, safe words, safe words."

"So, two-drink maximum," Nora finished. "Better make it a good two."

"Gin and tonic," Zach said, picking the first hard drink that came to mind.

"Just mineral water," Nora said.

"Oh…" Griffin said, his dark brown eyes turning gold with mirth. "Sounds like somebody wants to play tonight."

"Up. Go," Nora ordered and Griffin jumped straight from the floor to his feet in kip-up—a move Zach had only seen in the occasional kung-fu movie.

"Such a punk," Nora said, watching him walk away. "Thinks he's a sex ninja."

"Friend of yours?" Zach asked.

"Kink buddy. But he talks too much so I have to gag him every time we fuck. Cute, isn't he?"

"Delightful. He's…" Zach didn't complete the question.

"Bisexual. Very."

"Was it absolutely necessary to tell him that we—"

"I blew you. You liked it. Get over it," she said as a naked woman wearing only a tail feather held in place in a way Zach didn't want to think about sashayed past their table. Nora didn't even bat an eyelash at her. "Ever heard of John Fiske?"

"Of course. Chairman of the stock exchange, isn't he? He's your friend's—"

"Yup, that's Junior," she said, inclining her head in Griffin's direction. "The Fiske family is new money, old money, money money. Griff is New York's biggest trust fund baby. He drives Søren up the wall. Søren's very dignified. Griffin...not so much."

"So who owns this club?"

"Kingsley Edge—he's Søren's best friend. Best friend when Søren isn't trying to kill him that is. King runs the place but Søren's top Dom here so he calls the shots when he's in attendance. He can order anyone to do anything and they have to do it. Here all the Dominants are ranked by experience and level of dominance. Griffin's lucky number seven."

"Who's number two?"

Nora leaned back in her chair, snapped her fingers and pointed at herself.

"I am."

Zach's eyes widened in shock.

"You are?"

"Zach, this isn't a game, you know. I don't just write it. I live it. I'm a Domme, a female Dominant. There aren't a lot of us around. Most Dominants are men. Technically I'm Switch since I can top and bottom, but if I show up on your doorstep, get ready to say ouch. I'm not good at it—I'm amazing at it. So good at it that I'm as famous down here for my skills with a whip as I am in the straight world for my skills with a pen."

"My God," Zach breathed.

"No need for that. You can just call me 'ma'am.'" Nora

winked at him. Zach looked at her and knew she spoke the truth. He knew she was kinky but he never dreamed before now she was some sort of legend. No wonder she'd scared him from the moment they met—she really was dangerous.

"Your G&T." Griffin returned to the table with their drinks. "And your mineral water, mistress. Anything else?"

"Yes," Nora said. "Kneel."

Griffin knelt again on the floor at Nora's feet.

"Zachary, Griffin is demonstrating for us the attendant slave posture. Kneeling, hands resting on knees, thighs—" she said and put a foot on Griffin's inner thigh and pushed "—wide-open. Very good, slave."

"Thank you, mistress."

"Slave, please recite for my guest the first rule of S&M here at the 8th Circle."

"Hurt, but do not harm, mistress."

"And the second rule."

"Respect the safe word always, mistress."

"And the third rule?"

Griffin looked at Zach before answering.

"No vanilla sex allowed…mistress."

Nora broke into a wide grin. "Good boy. You are dismissed for the moment. But stay close."

Griffin rose to his feet and leaned over.

"I'll stay so close you'll think I'm inside you," he said in a stage whisper meant for Zach to hear and nipped at Nora's neck. Zach tried to ignore it.

"Hurt but do not harm?" Zach asked. "What's the difference?"

"Hurt is a bruise on the outside." Nora sipped her mineral water delicately. "Harm is a bruise on the inside. If you're a masochist, pain feels like love to you. Not being hurt is what hurts."

"Are you a masochist?" Zach asked, fascinated despite himself.

"Not exactly." Nora smiled almost shyly. "Not everyone who practices S&M is an actual sadist or masochist, not in the pathological sense anyway. With Søren, I loved submitting to pain. I loved the submission, though, not the pain itself. There are a handful of actual masochists down here, though, if you want to meet one. Fair warning, they can be almost as dangerous to play with as the sadists."

"Warning taken. You don't seem like those people down there." Zach nodded toward the pit.

"Those people down there are doctors, lawyers, stockbrokers, politicians, you name it. If I'm not like them it's only because I don't have a real job. And I have played in the pit before, I'll have you know. It's like Sodom and Gomorrah down there sometimes. Tonight's Monday so the play's a little tame."

"You say 'play' like this is all a game. But people are actually getting hurt down there, Nora."

"I have one word for you, my uptight English editor—rugby."

Zach winced. Rugby—the sport as rough as American football but without all the padding.

"A lot of people think we're crazy, Zach. Some even think we're evil. But I'm a Switch so I've seen both sides of the whip. I know you can't imagine it, but this is love to a lot of us. When Søren hit me, it was because he loved me, because that's how we loved each other."

"Sounds horrifying."

"Horrifying is the last thing Søren is. Dangerous, yes. I'll give you that. But S&M's only dangerous if you play with someone you don't trust or if you forget your safe word." She stopped, looked up at the ceiling and smiled. He could see something like a memory flash across her eyes. "Trust me, whatever you do, Zach, don't forget your safe word."

"What's a safe word?"

"A safe word's your last out. That's the dark secret of S&M—the submissives actually have the final say. And your safe word can be anything—popcorn, barn owl—whatever as long as it's not a word you'd use in a scene. If you need to tell the person topping you that you have to stop completely, you end it by using that word."

"You can't just say 'stop'?"

"A lot of submissives enjoy feeling overpowered and truly dominated. God knows I did. 'Stop' doesn't mean 'stop' in S&M. It's just part of the scene. You should have a safe word down here. Everyone does. Except Søren, of course."

"Why is he exempt?"

Nora smirked and rolled her eyes.

"Because Søren doesn't get topped. Go ahead. You can pick anything—the street you grew up on, your favorite food, the middle name of the long-lost love of your life. Got one?"

"Sure, fine," Zach said, picking the first word that came to mind. "Calais."

"The city in France?"

"*Oui.*"

"*Bien.* I'll remember it. If I start to push you hard enough you need to really get out, just say that and everything will stop. Saying 'no, Nora, I don't think that's such a grand idea' doesn't always work on me."

"I've noticed." Zach took a sip of his drink. "So my writer is the most famous Domme in New York."

Nora grinned. "Zach, I'm the most famous Domme—" she began and then closed her mouth. Her ears seemed to perk up. She tilted her head sideways.

"Do you hear that?" she asked.

Zach listened.

"I don't hear anything."

Nora inhaled and exhaled slowly.

"Fuck."

Nora jumped to her feet and raced to the balcony area of the bar. Zach ran to join her.

"What is it?" Zach asked.

Griffin came to stand behind them. Zach heard him chuckling.

"Stop me if you've heard this one—a priest, a rabbi and a griffin walk into an S&M club…"

"This is why I gag you during sex, Griffin," Nora nearly growled.

"You brought a date to the Circle," Griffin chided. "What did you expect him to do?"

"I expected King to keep his mouth shut."

"You know King answers to a higher power."

"Nora," Zach said with exasperation, "please tell me what's going on."

Nora turned to face him. He saw real fear in her eyes.

"Søren."

"Søren?" Zach repeated and looked down. A man stood at the top of the staircase where he and Nora had entered. Zach couldn't make out any of his features at first. All he noticed was the man's commanding height, his incredible presence. All play below had ceased at his entrance. He strode down the staircase slowly, imperiously. The world stopped for him. The chaos on the floor fell silent. Everyone everywhere, Nora included, seemed to be holding their breath.

Zach narrowed his eyes at the sight of Nora's former lover. He noticed something strange about the man's clothes.

"Zach, I should have told you. There's a lot I should have told you."

"Søren..." Zach said in utter shock. "He's a priest?"

"My priest."

19

A hundred whispers and hints from conversations over the past few weeks came back to Zach in an instant. Nora Sutherlin's former lover who still haunted her like the shadow of a ghost was a Catholic priest. And if it weren't for the fear in her eyes and the dread in his stomach he might have laughed.

"Zach, look at me," Nora ordered, and Zach wrenched his eyes away from the scene below.

"It's all right," Zach said, trying to reassure her.

"No, it isn't," she said. "He's here for a reason and it's probably not a good one. If he wants me, I have to go with him. I won't have a choice."

"Of course you have a choice," Zach said.

Nora shook her head. "Not down here. House rules. Griffin?"

"Yes, my Mistress in Distress?" Griffin said, clearly taking great pleasure in Nora's extreme agitation.

"I'll need you to stay with Zach if you can. Just don't let him out of your sight. That's an order."

"I'm all over it. And him, too, if he'll let me."

"He won't let you," Zach said, and Griffin grinned at him.

"And Griffin." She reached out to take Griffin's face in her hands. "For God's sake and for the first time in your life, keep your mouth shut."

Zach expected one of Griffin's witty retorts but the young man merely nodded. Zach saw something pass between them, some sort of secret understanding that he was apparently not to be privy to. He'd already seen Nora's former lover was a priest. What else was left to shock him?

"He's coming," Griffin whispered and Zach's heart beat hard in his chest.

Zach sensed a presence behind him. He turned and found himself face-to-face with Nora's former lover. Almost face-to-face. Although Zach stood six feet tall in bare feet, Søren dwarfed him by at least two or three inches. It wasn't only his height that was so formidable. Strikingly handsome, he was in his mid-forties but while his lean and angular face looked younger than that, his eyes held aeons in their steely depths. On rare occasions Zach had encountered members of England's lingering aristocracy. But in his simple black clerics, this man appeared more aristocratic, more imperious and commanding than any baron, any duke, any prince he'd ever glimpsed. Now Zach understood the source of Nora's fear. If God himself was intimidated by this man, Zach wouldn't have been surprised.

"Eleanor," Søren spoke first. "Would you care to introduce me to your friend?"

Zach heard the remnant of an accent in his voice. With the name Søren, Zach might have expected a Scandinavian accent and with his impeccable blond hair and steel-gray eyes,

Søren certainly looked the part. But in the echo of his inflection Zach heard the slightest trace of something more familiar, the faintest English accent.

"Søren—" Nora's voice fluttered. "This is Zachary Easton, my editor. Zach, this is Søren, my…"

"*Priest* is the word Eleanor is looking for, I believe." Søren spoke with authoritarian hauteur. "You are her editor, Mr. Easton, so I believe helping her find her words is your job, yes? I don't believe I see a red pen on your person. Are you off duty tonight?"

"Nora just wanted me to help with her research for her book." Zach sensed Søren weighing him. Zach had an inkling that no matter what he did or said, he would be found wanting.

"Research?" The word seemed to amuse him. Nora stood silent next to Zach; her skin flushed and her hands gripped her riding crop handle with white-knuckled force. "Yes, Eleanor is quite thorough in her research. Eleanor, accompany me please. I need a moment with you."

"Actually, we were about to leave." Zach stepped between Nora and Søren.

Søren raised his chin and gazed down on Zach with an expression of ironic detachment. His eyes took in the white flag around Zach's arm and he raised an eyebrow in apparent amusement. Zach stared at the white collar around Søren's neck before meeting the priest's eyes again. But Søren seemed untouchable—no guilt, no embarrassment, not even the slightest hint of shame haunted his eyes. Søren slowly raised his hand right next to Nora's ear. He snapped his fingers, and Nora flinched at the echoing sound. Søren pointed to the floor at his side, and Nora stepped out and stood where Søren had indicated. Zach wanted to pull her back and run with her as far and fast away from this man as they could. But

Nora met his eyes for the briefest moment, and he saw someone he'd never seen before reflected back. *No one handles Nora
Sutherlin*, J.P. had said and Zach had begun to believe it. Now
he knew he'd met the one man who could.

"House rules," she explained with an apology in her wan
smile.

Søren inclined his head regally and took a step forward.

They walked away toward a black door next to the end of
the bar. Søren held the door open for Nora and as she stepped
past him to enter the room, he gripped her by the back of
the neck. Zach took a step forward, but Griffin put his hand
out to stop him.

"Don't even think about it, man," Griffin warned. "I'm
not his biggest fan, either, but you come down here, you obey
the rules and you respect the ruler."

"Is she all right?" Zach asked, scared for Nora but feeling
impotent to help her in this strange world.

"She'll be fine. He won't hurt her."

"Are you certain of that?"

Griffin looked at the door that had just closed behind Nora.
He looked back at Zach.

"No."

Nora tried to stay calm as Søren escorted her to the dimly
lit bar stockroom. She counted her breaths and tried to slow
her racing heart. It didn't work. Søren opened the door and
Nora risked one quick look back at Zach standing with Griffin. He watched her with a question in his eyes. She didn't
know how to answer it.

She wasn't surprised when Søren grabbed her by the neck
as she slipped through the door. The neck was the most vul-
nerable part of the human body—Søren always went for her

weak spots and having just humiliated her in front of Zach meant only one thing: he wanted her.

The door shut behind them. In an instant, Søren had turned her toward him. She was in his arms, his mouth on hers. He tasted like fire and wine. She pressed into him, the dawn of her body meeting the horizon of his. It had been so long since she'd given herself over to him. She didn't care that Zach was waiting right outside. For a moment she didn't even remember Zach or the promise she made Wesley. She stiffened as he grasped her by the wrist. With one adept movement he had her arm twisted behind her back, her stomach flat against the wall.

Panting with need, she closed her eyes as Søren lifted the back of her skirt. She knew what was coming and didn't try to fight it. She breathed him in, inhaling his perfect scent, the scent of winter that clung to him in every season. His mouth lingered at her neck; his warm breath on her bare skin sent a shiver through her whole body. She waited for him to penetrate her but he was too cruel for that. She heard Søren release the slightest throaty gasp, and he came instead on the back of her thighs.

Nora swallowed a groan of frustration. He loved punishing her by withholding himself. Instead of taking her, he'd merely marked his territory. Bastard. Søren pulled away as she yanked her skirt back down and turned to face him.

"Now that the pleasantries are out of the way, let's talk, shall we, little one?"

"What did I do now?" she demanded. "Obviously I'm in trouble…again."

A quiver of tension shot through her as Søren raised a single finger and ran it from under her ear, down her neck and across her naked shoulder. He leaned forward and whispered.

"Deep trouble."

★ ★ ★

Zach sat next to Griffin on one of the barstools. He tried not to appear too gauche next to this unabashedly half-naked young man.

"So what do you think of our little acre of Hell?" Griffin asked, reaching over the bar to grab a bottle of water.

Zach glanced around—he saw naked flesh and leather wherever he looked. A young woman wearing not much more than her pale pink collar and cuffs sat at the feet of a slightly older man. The man said something to the girl and she nodded obediently. She tucked her toes under and rose straight up off the floor just the way Nora had in the kitchen that day. Suddenly Zach didn't see the girl but a younger Nora. And in place of the older man was Søren smiling darkly down at her as she sat on the floor at his feet.

"Nora and Søren…how long were they together?" Zach asked, barely hearing Griffin's question.

"He owned her about ten years, I think." Griffin twisted the cap of his water and took a drink. "But she told me she's known him since she was fifteen. Love at first sight, apparently. For both of them."

"Ten years…" Zach couldn't wrap his mind around it. His own marriage had lasted ten years. "She said he's a sadist. I assume she means he's…"

"A sadist," Griffin said simply. "He's sexually aroused by inflicting pain and humiliation. And he's phenomenal at it. The Pope there is Machiavelli's wet dream."

"Phenomenal? It doesn't seem that difficult to hurt someone."

Griffin scoffed. "Look, any jackass with a baseball bat can beat up somebody in the street and in five seconds they're begging for it to stop. Søren can beat you up and in five minutes you're begging him to never stop. That's his gift."

"He's a priest. A Catholic priest. He has vows—"

"Which he doesn't break except with Nora, as far as I know. A Catholic priest who only has sex with one consenting adult woman? Jesus, they'll probably make him a bishop. Real sadists don't need to fuck. They need to fuck you up."

"I can't believe Nora could stay with someone who hurt her for so long. She's so…"

"Dominant? Yeah, she's one helluva Switch. She's as dominant now as she used to be submissive. You wouldn't recognize her if you saw her six years ago. Of course you wouldn't see her face anyway because it'd be buried in his lap."

Zach had started to take a drink of his gin and tonic but he set his glass down again.

"He forced her to do that in public?"

"Hell, yeah. Fucked her a few times in public, too. Well, not public—private parties. I got invited once. The only time I ever got to top that woman. One of the best nights of my life. He beat her, fucked her, passed her around. He and King would tag team her a lot. Most dominant thing you can do is give your submissive to someone else to play with."

"Nora allowed that?"

Griffin choked on a laugh and turned to meet Zach eye to eye. "Allowed it? Man, she fucking loved it."

Zach shook his head. "I don't believe it. Who would enjoy being treated like that?"

"Believe what you want. All the submissives down here would sell their souls to belong to him. That's why he's number one. He's the real thing. He doesn't play to get laid. And he doesn't do it for money like some people. He does it for pure sadistic pleasure."

"But Nora…why does she do it?"

"Lots of reasons. But for him mainly."

"Surely he doesn't approve of her being a Dominant."

Griffin gave him a sidelong smile. "What? You never pulled the ponytail of the little girl you liked on the playground? This is his playground," Griffin said, sweeping his arm out to indicate the bar and the writhing pit below. "He'd never allow anyone but him to own her. So if she wants to play on his playground, she does it as a Domme. He doesn't like it but he won't stop it. Still loves her too much."

Zach turned his head and saw the young woman in the pale pink collar return to her master. With her eyes and head lowered she presented him a glass of wine. The man set the glass of wine aside, took her by the hair and pulled her face between his legs. Zach tried to look away but found he couldn't. The man leaned his head back in arrogant bliss as the girl wrapped her lips and tongue around him.

"God, I love it here," Griffin said, and Zach could hear arousal in his voice. "I've gotta get a sub."

Zach tried to ignore how aroused he was becoming by watching the girl. The man dug his fingers into the back of the girl's neck as his hips twitched. Zach wrenched his gaze away as he finally let the girl go.

"Nora and Søren were just like that?" Zach asked, still in shock.

Griffin shrugged indifferently.

"Nora says he's a great priest."

"So what do you want to talk about? We've been having the same fight for five years. I guess we can have it again. Yes, I miss you. Yes, I miss it. No, I'm not coming back."

"You would assume this was all about you, wouldn't you?" Søren said.

"If it isn't, then what?" she demanded, angry at herself for still being so affected by him even after all this time.

"I told you when I saw you again we would discuss Wesley."

Nora took a step back.

"No, not him. He's not on the table. He's not up for negotiation."

Søren's eyes flashed at her. "Fitting as I do not negotiate."

"I'm not giving Wesley up."

"He's not one of us, Eleanor, and you know it. You never should have allowed him into your home. This is a dangerous game you are playing and one or both of you will be deeply hurt by it."

"Wes isn't a game. He's my best friend. Jesus, Søren, he's my only friend." Nora hated admitting it but she knew it was true. Everyone in her life—Zach included—she'd either slept with or planned to.

"Friend? He's your pet and you are using him. A game is only fair when both parties know they are playing it."

"You don't know anything about us. You haven't even met him."

Søren took her chin in his hand, gripping it to the edge of pain.

"Do you think," Søren asked slowly, "that there is any corner of your life you can keep from me?"

"Why do you care what happens to Wes?"

"One of us has to. Is he a virgin still?" Søren demanded and Nora turned away from him. "Answer me, young lady."

"Yes," she said, too well-trained to ignore a direct order. "We're just friends."

"Only for love would you ever sleep alone. I could have had you when you were fifteen years old, Eleanor. And although I burned for you, although my desire for you grew until the calendar of my life counted down only the days and months and years I had to wait until I could make you mine, I still kept you a virgin. Why?"

Nora rolled her eyes. "Because you're a sadist."

Søren reached for her and held her by the shoulders. His hands on her bare skin sent electricity running through her whole body.

"Because I loved you. I wouldn't take you until you were ready. You keep Wesley for yourself as I kept you for me. But you were born for this life and he was not. You will harm him if you keep him any longer."

"I would never hurt Wes." A knot tightened in her throat.

"It will end badly, Eleanor. As will that, if you aren't careful," Søren said, indicating Zach sitting at the bar with Griffin. Griffin glanced at the mirror and winked. Of course, Griffin knew it was a two-way mirror that hung behind the bar. She and he had snuck back here for some quick kinky sex more than once. "Your editor. He seemed surprised when we met. You haven't told him everything about us. What else haven't you told him?"

Nora twisted her riding crop in her hands.

"Eleanor…" Søren scolded in his most insufferable paternalistic voice. "How will he feel when he discovers that writing isn't your only source of income?"

"I was going to tell him. I will tell him. When the book's done."

"He cares for you, Eleanor. I can see it in his eyes. He's letting himself care for you and it terrifies him. He won't take betrayal lightly."

"Then I won't betray him. The book is more than halfway done. And Zach…he's amazing. He's smart and funny. He's—"

"Married. I thought I taught you better than that."

"They're separated. They even live on separate continents."

"Are you attempting to convince me or yourself?" Søren asked. Nora closed her eyes, exhaling as Søren slipped his hands down her arms. "If he hasn't taken you yet, and I'm sure you've offered, it is because he still loves his wife. Broken love is the most dangerous love. It will slice you open with every touch."

"Like your love?"

Søren dipped his head and kissed her from her neck to the tip of her shoulder. She exhaled with bliss as his lips met her skin. No other lover had ever made her feel what Søren could.

"You haven't broken me yet," he said into her ear. It took everything she had to keep from turning around and sinking into his arms. "Are you following my rule still, Eleanor?"

Nora bit her bottom lip. "Yes. Mostly. More or less."

"Eleanor…" he said in a warning tone.

"I do write about you," she admitted. "All the time. But I always delete or shred it."

"Then why do you write about me, about us, if you destroy your own words?"

"They aren't just words. They're memories. I like to read them, hold them in my hands. And then I can let them go. A little bit at least."

"You will never love anyone as you love me," Søren said and as much as she wanted to slap him for his arrogance, she couldn't disagree. "Not even Wesley. Not even him." Søren's eyes came to rest on Zach at the bar talking with Griffin. "But I think you care for him more than you realize. This must be terrifying for you."

"It is terrifying," she admitted. "Zach's my editor. He's the first person who ever treated me as a serious writer."

"I told you that you should be a writer when you were seventeen years old," he reminded her.

Nora smiled at the memory. She'd written a short story

for her English class that had gotten her into big trouble at her Catholic high school. Only the intervention of her priest had kept her from getting hauled in front of a whole team of doctors and psychiatric personnel.

"I assumed you were a little biased where I was concerned."

"Perhaps I was," he admitted with a smile. "But I knew talent when I saw it. So what will you do with him?" Søren nodded toward Zach.

Nora watched Zach through the two-way mirror. Griffin leaned in close and Zach managed to recoil without even moving—a very English feat.

"It's not just about sex this time. Not entirely. Zach's got secrets, bad ones. I want to help him but I don't even know where to start. What do you think?"

Søren looked at her and she had to fight her training to keep her eye contact with him. Once in a private moment like this she would never have met his eyes without his permission. But that was so long ago. Søren sighed and shook his head.

"My Eleanor…someday perhaps I'll learn to tell you 'no.'"

With that Søren stepped to her side. She watched his face as he studied Zach through the glass. In all her life Nora had never known anyone as perceptive as Søren. He could read a soul with the merest glance. He'd known what she would become from the moment he first saw her. He had told her so. It had always been her favorite bedtime story. *Tell me about that day,* she would beg. *Eleanor,* he'd begin, his stories always in third person, *had pulled her sleeves down over her hands. She was ashamed of the burn on her wrist. But as she reached for the cup, her sleeve slipped back and he saw what she was.* Nora always interrupted with an eager, *What was she?* And Søren would pull her into his arms and answer, *She was mine.*

"Guilt." Søren's pronouncement wrenched her from the past. "Old guilt. He wears it awkwardly as if he hasn't quite learned how to carry it yet. He committed no crime although he may believe he did."

"Old guilt—I have to get it out of him," she said, amused that she and Søren were at once adversaries and conspirators. "He's choking on his own secrets. I have to break him. But how? That insufferable British dignity is impenetrable. The last thing he needs is some time on the rack and a good whipping."

"I agree. It would merely insult him. I have seen that guilt before. He hurt someone once."

Nora heard a turn in his last statement, heard the teacher's hint.

"He hurt his wife."

"Then you know what you have to do." Søren smiled proudly at her. She was always his best pupil.

"Make him hurt me?"

"Yes, little one. Make him hurt you."

"So you're Nora's new Maxwell Perkins, right?" Griffin asked Zach.

"Well, I am her editor. But Perkins and I have quite disparate philosophies of editing."

"Good. I'd hate to see her books get all fucked up because her editor can't keep his hands off her prose."

"So," Zach said evenly, "you read?"

Griffin shot him a dirty look.

"I may be a slut, Max, but I'm not a dumb slut. I read Nora's books. They're amazing. Of course, my favorite book of hers is the one she hasn't written yet."

"And that is?"

"The Nora Sutherlin Story."

"It would be a page-turner," Zach agreed. "Is he actually going to keep her all night?"

Zach glanced at his watch. Nora had been gone only a short while but he was already impatient for her return.

"If he wants to. The minute he steps into this place, martial law is in effect."

"Does she come here often?"

"Used to come all the time. Had to. But she dropped off the face of the earth about a month ago."

"That was when we began work on her book," Zach explained.

"And when she began work on you, too, huh?" Griffin grinned at him. Zach tried not to let himself be embarrassed. After all, Nora and Griffin were clearly occasional lovers.

"What do you mean she had to come here?" Zach asked after a moment's silence.

But Griffin only laughed and slapped him on the shoulder.

"Come on. Let's check out the pit."

"I really should get back to my guest." Nora didn't want to leave Søren, but she knew she needed to. God only knew what Griffin was telling Zach right now.

"Not quite yet. We still need to plan how to celebrate our anniversary next week. Or have you forgotten what next Thursday is?"

"If I forgot every other day of the year, I would remember that one. But we aren't celebrating it. Not this year or ever again."

"I see." Søren gave her a cool, appraising stare. "Was last year not to your liking?"

Last year…what he did to her that night was beautiful and brutal and it hurt to even remember.

If you come back to me, will you run or will you crawl?
I'll fly.

Nora shook her head, tried to forget how much she still wanted him.

"Last year was a mistake. It shouldn't have happened. It went too far."

"You are never satisfied until it goes too far."

"I nearly lost Wes over that night."

"Yes. What was that promise you made? That if you ever gave yourself over to me again he would leave you? Was that it?"

"You can't blame him, can you? He doesn't understand us."

"I am certain he does not." Søren reached out and caressed her cheek. Those fingers, she thought. Those hands. Hands that knew every corner of her body as their owner knew every corner of her heart. "My Eleanor…such a creature of Divine Discontent."

"Divine Discontent?"

"God's dirty little secret. He will make you suffer, little one, until He makes you wise."

"No more sermons. Please," she pleaded.

Søren responded with only the merest suggestion of a smile on his lips. "If you won't come see me on our anniversary, I suppose I'll have to give you your gift early. Good thing I brought him with me."

He pulled something from his pocket and opened his hand for her. A key with a delicate white ribbon in place of a key chain lay across his palm.

"What is it?"

"The key to the White Room, of course. It's where your anniversary present is waiting for you."

His hand still open and waiting, Søren took a step toward her.

"He's a virgin, Eleanor," he whispered into her ear. "You can close your eyes and pretend he's Wesley."

Nora wanted to withdraw, wanted to push Søren away. Zach was out there waiting for her. And she knew better than this. Søren's gifts were always double-edged swords, and there was no way to take them except by the blade. She heard the voice of reason reminding her that she should find Zach and get him out of here. And then she remembered what she promised him—to show him a place of no regret, no shame and no fear.

She took the key from Søren's hand.

"I see He's not finished making you suffer," Søren said.

Nora didn't reply. Closing her fingers around the key so tightly the teeth bit fiercely into her hand, she slipped from the room and into a back hallway. Nora felt Søren's eyes on her. She didn't look back.

20

Zach followed Griffin to the balcony section of the bar. Leaning over the railing, they studied the show below.

A lovely dark-haired woman with sinister-looking chopsticks in her hair and wearing a kimono stood on a platform below them. She twined a black rope around a shapely red-haired girl who stood calm and naked next to her.

"That's Lady Noy. She's the queen of Asian Rope Bondage around here." Griffin pointed out two women down in the pit. "And that babe she's tying up is Alyssa Petrosky."

"Petrosky?" The name sounded vaguely familiar.

"Yeah, that Petrosky. She's the governor's stepdaughter. She's a pretty infamous submissive down here. Really into exhibitionism."

"I can see that." Zach marveled as Lady Noy finished her work and hoisted the girl into the air with a complicated rope and pulley system. The girl lay back in an elegant asymmetrical arch and seemed completely at peace with both her nudity and her bondage.

"And that's Agent Byers—he's high-level FBI," Griffin said, pointing out a man strapped to a cross and being flogged by a woman half his age. "And a sub, too."

"Are you allowed to tell me all this?"

"What? You're going to tell someone? No one would believe you if you did tell. And if you spill a word, Kingsley Edge will destroy you. He watches all our backs—it's part of the membership fee. I'd bet you my bank account that he's already got a file on you."

"On me? Are you serious?" Zach asked. He remembered how Nora seemed to know so much about him at their first meeting.

"You get within five feet of Nora and you get a file. And it sounds like you've been a helluva lot closer than five feet."

"I'm hardly blackmail material," Zach protested.

"Really? Anybody out there you'd prefer not know that Nora blew you?"

Zach flushed and said nothing. Yes, there certainly was.

"Point taken," Zach said.

"You gotta know, Zach—Nora's not just some smut writer with a wild sex life. She's the motherfucking queen of the Underground. And Kingsley Edge is, obviously, our king."

"And him? What is he?" Zach didn't even want to say Søren's name.

"He's whatever's higher than a king and queen."

"An emperor?" Zach guessed.

Griffin smirked. "A god."

"A god," Zach repeated and looked down at the worshippers beneath them. The FBI agent Griffin spoke about was now being dragged from his cross and the woman in leather wrapped a collar around his neck and attached a leash to it. She led him on his hands and knees across the floor.

"I can't believe you put collars on human beings," Zach said with renewed disgust.

"The collar is everything down here. Subs love their collars."

"Do all submissives wear collars?"

"Not all of them. House submissives, those are subs that work here at the Circle, wear house collars to show they're on the payroll. They look like this," Griffin said, pointing at the collar he wore as part of his punishment. Where a dog tag usually would be hung a small silver number eight inside a circle. "But in private a Dom will use a collar either for utility, for love or both. A collar can be as meaningful as a wedding ring to some couples." Griffin laughed. "Holy shit...you should have seen Nora and Søren back when they were still together. I'd only been coming here a year before she left him. But I got to see them in their glory days. Collars are leather usually, black or brown, right? Guess what color her collar was?"

"I don't know. Red?"

"White," came a voice from behind them. Zach and Griffin turned around and found Søren watching them in a white collar of his own. "What else would it have been?"

The halls and stairways of the 8th Circle were a labyrinth to most, but Nora knew them better than her own home. She could have found her way around blindfolded. A few times in the past she'd had to. She turned corner after corner and descended a small staircase to the lowest level of the building. At the end of the quiet hallway stood a door identical to all the others except this door and its knob were painted completely white.

Nora stood before the door and took slow, deep breaths. She couldn't even imagine who or what waited behind the door. The White Room was reserved only for the highest-level Dominants—not even Griffin had earned White Room privileges yet.

Slowly, she opened the door and hung her riding crop on the knob outside to show it was occupied. The White Room door had a lock, one of the few at the Circle that did, but Nora knew better than to lock herself in with a stranger. She'd learned that the hard way.

Nora took a cautious step inside. At the center of the room stood an iron four-poster bed heaped with luxurious white linens and pillows and surrounded by a semitranslucent white bed-curtain. For all its pretensions of purity and innocence, Nora knew for a fact that some of the most lurid sex acts in the history of the world had been performed in this room.

She crept to the bed and pushed the bed-curtain back. In the center of the bed lay a young man sleeping on his side. Nora studied him for a moment as her heart beat ferociously in her chest. He appeared to be about seventeen years old. He had straight black hair that fell past his shoulders and the longest, darkest eyelashes she'd even seen on a boy. They rested on his pale cheeks and fluttered in his sleep. Her eyes roamed down his body. He wore a frayed T-shirt, jeans with tears in the knees and white socks, one with a hole in the toe. He'd taken off his shoes but not his watch. It was leather and as wide as a bondage cuff. He'd covered his other wrist with a black wristband. He appeared tall but his hands and feet seemed disproportionately large. He hadn't finished growing yet. Nora sighed and cursed Søren with everything within her. The boy—her gift—was inexpressibly lovely.

Nora leaned forward and brushed an errant strand of hair off the boy's cheek and tucked it behind his ear.

"Oh, Søren," she said as she sighed to herself. "You shouldn't have."

★ ★ ★

Zach searched for a suitable reply. He found himself strangely speechless in Søren's presence. The priest seemed to find Zach's discomfort amusing.

"Where's Nora, sir?" Griffin asked for him.

"She will be occupied for some time with Circle business. While she's off, I thought I should entertain her guest for her," Søren said with a magnanimous air.

"But Nora told me I had to stay—"

Søren's hand snaked out with the subtle speed of a cobra and grabbed Griffin by the throat. Zach stepped forward but Griffin shot him a warning look. At least it appeared Griffin could still breathe.

"Mr. Easton, may I call you Zachary?"

Zach attempted to tamp down his nervousness before answering.

"Do I call you Father Søren? Or sir?"

"I understand you aren't Catholic. And you aren't part of this community. You may call me Søren, of course. Would you care for a tour?"

Zach sensed that Nora's priest desired his company for a reason or reasons he didn't care to find out. But he decided to use it as a bargaining chip.

"Will you let Griffin go?" Zach asked.

Søren seemed to find this amusing.

"I'd hardly be a sufficient tour guide with a corpse in my hand, would I?"

Zach glanced worriedly at Griffin who thankfully still seemed calm even as the priest continued to hold him in his vicious grip.

"I suppose not. A tour would be fine."

Søren let Griffin go. Zach noted that on Griffin's neck

right under his jawline were distinct red impressions of the priest's fingers. "Shall we then?"

Reluctantly, Zach left Griffin at the balcony. As flirtatious as the young man was, Zach far preferred his genial company to Nora's priest.

"What's Nora doing?" Zach asked as Søren guided him from the balcony to an unmarked exit at the opposite end of the bar.

"Eleanor is doing what she is always doing, Zachary— anything she wants to."

At Nora's touch the sleeping boy's eyelashes fluttered open. She bit her bottom lip to stifle a laugh as the boy scrambled into a sitting position.

"It's all right. Don't be scared," she said as if talking to a frightened animal. "It's only a dream."

He looked at her with silver eyes moon-wide. His face flushed and he pulled his knees tight to his chest.

"Do you talk?" she asked.

"Not usually." He raked his hands through his long hair and shoved it behind his ears.

"You can talk me to me. You can say anything you want to me. I want you to. Do you understand?"

The boy nodded and Nora nodded back. She was gratified to hear a small, nervous laugh.

"Okay, I understand."

"Good boy. Do you know who I am?"

He nodded again and Nora raised her eyebrow.

"Yes. Father S., he told me about you, that he knew you."

"What did he tell you?" Nora asked.

"He said you were an old friend of his. I mean, not old—"

"We've known each other a long time," she said, coming to his rescue.

"Right. And he said you were the most beautiful woman who ever lived."

Nora blushed slightly. "What else did he tell you?"

The boy inhaled sharply and met her eyes.

"He said you'd help me."

Nora cocked her head slightly. She reached out and touched the top of his foot.

"Do you need help?"

The young man didn't answer at first.

Slowly, the boy relaxed his arms from around his legs. He started to take off his watch but his fingers fumbled too much and he exhaled in exasperation.

"Sorry," he said.

"Here. Let me."

The boy tenuously stretched out his arm. Nora unbuckled his watch and nearly gasped when she discovered why he wore a watch with such a wide band.

Down the center of his wrist stretched a white scar and the crosshatch outline of stitches. He held out his other arm and slid off his wristband and showed her the matching scar and stitches. The wounds appeared fully healed. With her knowledge of scars she guessed his suicide attempt had been around a year ago.

"Why?" she asked.

"My dad, he caught me..." He took a hard breath. "I had stuff in my room he found. He saw the bruises and burns. He said he refused to have a sicko for a son. He left a couple of months later. Mom—she's not okay anymore."

"That isn't your fault," Nora said. "Your father's the sicko, not you. And he left for his own reasons. My family's fucked up, too."

"I know. Father S. told me that, too. He said we had a lot in common. I couldn't believe it when he told me he knew you."

"You knew who I was before he told you?"

"Yeah," he said, blushing. "I've read your books."

Nora ran her hands up and down the boy's forearms. She traced the scars with her fingertips.

"He said if I went a whole year without hurting myself, then he would let me meet you," the boy said in a whisper. "Sometimes it was the only thing that kept me from trying again."

Nora's heart dropped. She hated how much Søren's unusual mercies made her feel in one breath all eighteen years of her love for him. She looked up and met the boy's eyes. They shone like polished silver; his pupils dilated.

"What's your name?" she asked.

"Michael."

"Michael…Michael was God's chief archangel. Michael, has anyone ever told you that you're beautiful?"

He blushed and shook his head. "No."

"You are, angel." Nora reached out and ran her hand through his long black hair. Michael sighed with pleasure and closed his eyes. He opened them again when Nora pulled her hand away.

At the back of her mind Nora knew Zach was out there alone with Søren, but she wouldn't rush this moment or this scared boy, not for the world. She knew she shouldn't be here, knew she shouldn't have left Zach at Søren's mercy. But she remembered how Søren had saved her a lifetime of misery when he'd told her what she was, what she could be. She understood why Michael had tried to kill himself. She'd never been tempted to kill herself but she couldn't deny Søren had saved her life a time or two. As Nora studied Michael she told herself it was her duty to stay, to help him any way she could.

"Michael, I'm going to take your virginity tonight."

If she had any doubts that the boy was too young, too

fragile, they evaporated when he looked back at her and met her eyes without blinking and for the first time without fear.

"Father S. said that's what you would do."

Nora's priest proved to be a somewhat taciturn tour guide. Zach sensed Søren was waiting for him to speak, testing to see how long he'd remain silent. Nora must have learned that trick from him. Zach followed him through the bar exit and down several long hallways and corridors. Although Søren said little, Zach was not left in silence. Many of the doors hung open and Zach could see what was happening inside the rooms. They passed another door, this one closed, and Zach heard a woman scream. He stopped, unsure what to do, but Søren, who had surely heard the scream, as well, continued as if such a sound was commonplace and beneath his notice. Which it probably was.

They turned another corner.

"I know what you're trying to do," Zach finally said. "Trying to intimidate me with the personal tour of hell. Nora's already told me she's a Dominant. She's told me everything. I know you're just trying to scare me away from her. It won't work."

Søren smiled coldly and Zach realized that the man was untouchable.

"Eleanor does seem very forthcoming, doesn't she? She's always followed the philosophy that the best place to hide is in plain sight. But I take offense at your insinuation. I would never try to dissuade you from being with the woman you most desire. Eleanor is the woman you most desire, isn't she?"

Zach didn't answer. He tried to stare Søren down but the priest only smiled and kept walking.

"We have more to see. Come along."

Reluctantly Zach followed.

"You may ask any questions you like, Zachary."

"Your voice," Zach said, wondering if the priest would answer questions about himself. "You have an English accent. A very faint one, but it's there."

"Very good," Søren said with approval. "You would notice. Most Americans don't. They simply assume I'm over-educated. I was born in America, but I attended school as a child in England. My father was English. And he was evil. I pray daily that it is only the trace of his accent I've inherited."

"You seduced a young woman in your congregation. You don't think that's at all evil?"

"Since I became a priest, Eleanor is the only woman with whom I've been sexually intimate. No children, either, I assure you. But you are welcome to ask Eleanor if she ever once felt taken advantage of or abused. I believe you'll find her answer enlightening."

"Why do you keep calling her that?" Zach couldn't reconcile his Nora with the priest's Eleanor. "She changed her name to Nora years ago."

"She was born Eleanor and it was Eleanor with whom I fell in love. She has made decisions in her life that I do not approve of these past five years. I prefer to remember her for who she was, not for what she's become. She can forsake her name and her past. I never will."

Søren's words stirred another memory. "She hasn't forsaken it," Zach told him, wanting to prove he knew something about Nora the priest didn't. "Not entirely. I went to one of her book-signings not long ago. She was reading to some children. They called her Ellie." Zach glanced at Søren's face, but other than a glint of a smile, the revelation seemed to have no impact on him.

"Yes, well," Søren said as they passed under an archway into another hall, "Eleanor always did have a way with children."

★ ★ ★

Nora slipped off the bed and brought Michael with her. She bade him stand still while she knelt down and reached under the bed. She pulled out a metal briefcase, entered the numeric combination and snapped the locks open.

"Are you scared?" she asked.

"A little." Michael looked down at her.

"Here, I'll give you something to help with the fear. It's called a 'safe word.'"

"I've read about safe words…in your books."

"Good. Since you're an angel, yours will be 'wings.'"

"Wings," he repeated.

She dug through the briefcase for all the supplies she needed—rope, condoms, scissors. "If at any point you want to stop everything and just go home, you can say 'wings' and we're done. We've all safed out. It's completely okay."

Nora shut the suitcase and slid it back under the bed. She rose up and faced him. With him in his bare feet and her in her high heels, they were almost the same height.

"Let's practice," she said. "I'm going to ask you to do something and you're going to say your safe word to stop everything. Okay?"

"Okay."

Nora took a step back and looked him up and down.

"Take your clothes off," she ordered. Michael raised his arm and grasped the neck of his T-shirt.

"Wait," she said and he stopped. "You're supposed to say your safe word, angel."

He lowered his arm slowly.

"But what if I don't want to?"

Nora grinned at him and came so close to him she could almost hear his heart pounding in his chest.

"Then don't."

Michael raised his arm again and stripped out of his T-shirt. He bent over and pulled off his socks. When he got to the top button of his jeans, his courage seemed to fail him.

"Here. Let me help," she said. Nora reached out and laid her hands flat on his stomach. They traveled down to his waistband and to the buttons. She made quick work of them and slipped a hand into his pants.

"No underwear," she said, and Michael blushed again. "You really are one of us, aren't you?"

His mouth was near her ear. "I want to be." He shuddered as Nora took him in her hand. She stroked his hard length before releasing him to pull his jeans all the way down.

Michael stepped out of his jeans and stood naked in front of her.

"Do you know what these are?" she asked from the floor.

"Cuffs," he said.

"Very good. Bondage cuffs. Two sets. One set for your ankles." She clasped the first one around his left ankle and then his right before standing up again. "And one set for your wrists. You'll like these."

Michael held out his arms. Nora took his left arm in her hand. She raised it to her lips and slowly kissed the scar on his wrist. He breathed in as her mouth met his ravaged skin. She buckled the cuff around his wrist and kissed the scar on the other. She buckled his other wrist and took a step back.

He examined the cuffs on his wrists. He looked down at the cuffs on his ankles. Michael met her eyes. In his face she saw herself at age eighteen when Søren first began her training. That moment when he first revealed to her what she would become to him, how he would possess her completely when the time came...looking down at her bound wrists and ankles; it was the first time she knew what love looked like.

"Thank you," Michael breathed.

Nora coughed a hint.

"Thank you…mistress."

21

Søren brought Zach to another hallway—this one strangely silent and empty. Although quiet, it was far more colorful and elaborate than the other more non-descript hallways and rooms Søren had shown him. Here every door was decorated—some with extravagant S&M scenes, some with startling graffiti. One door had a faux coat of arms painted on it—a unicorn fellating a griffin. Zach had no doubt whose room that was. They stopped before a door painted only with words.

"'We're all mad here,'" Zach read the famous *Alice in Wonderland* quote aloud that was scrawled across the door in Gothic lettering. "I think she's right."

"There is a method to our madness. Sadomasochism was once considered a mental illness. Now for many psychologists it is an object of study rather than derision. One in ten people are said to have experimented with S&M...although I would be surprised if the number were not higher."

"I would be in that nine."

"I'm sure that will change. Eleanor is nothing if not persuasive." Søren smiled at him with a smile Zach knew women must find charming but he found alarming.

"She won't talk me into this." Zach waved his hand at the ominously closed doors.

"Everyone should try it at least once. S&M has a curious effect on those who practice it." Søren sounded professorial now. "The Dominant undergoes a surge of testosterone while the submissive experiences a euphoria that has been likened to the effects of opiates. But for most of us the physical sensations are the least of why we do this."

"Why do you do it?"

Søren paused and seemed to consider the question.

"To call what Eleanor and I had 'bliss' would insult it. Owning her, dominating her, training her to react to the slightest command, the merest crook of my finger, the barest change in my tone, and to love someone so much that anything less than complete and utter possession is unacceptable... that is the purest joy."

"But she left you," Zach reminded him.

"Disobedience is as much a proof of authority as obedience. You cannot be a rebel without acknowledging a government. You cannot be a heretic until you are first a believer. And I could leave the priesthood, but I would still be a priest. The church would endure with or without me. Some vows are merely promises. But some are sacraments. Like marriage," Søren added and met his eyes for a moment. "Yes, she did leave me, and I let her go. But she will return. Still, I imagine it isn't simply the mix of pleasure and pain that you find disturbing, is it?"

"The hierarchy is disturbing. Women being enslaved to men. Women have fought against such treatment for hundreds of years and yet here—"

"Yet here they willingly and bravely choose to explore those aspects of their sexuality that are less than socially acceptable. Another study revealed that a shockingly high percentage of women have rape fantasies. What is the likelihood that your wife is in that minority that has not?"

"I won't discuss my wife's fantasies with you."

"Did you ever discuss them with her? Forgive me. You don't have to answer that," Søren said in a way that was both offhanded and pointed. Zach knew Søren wasn't asking for forgiveness at all. "Yes, we have a power structure here. Some require a power structure as they are born submissives. Others require a power structure as they are born subversives."

"Which is Nora?"

"Which is she?" Søren smiled. "Shortly after Eleanor and I became lovers I introduced her to the blindfold. She loathed it at first."

"Why?" Zach asked.

"I'm sure it is nearly impossible for you to imagine a virginal Eleanor, but once she was actually both timid and shy. The loss of her sight during our interludes terrified her. So naturally I employed the blindfold often."

"Naturally."

"One evening I noticed something strange. Just before I blindfolded Eleanor she would close her eyes. It seemed counterintuitive. Surely someone so afraid of forced blindness would keep her eyes open to drink in every precious second of sight. Then I realized what she was doing. By closing her eyes first she was choosing the darkness, blindfolding herself in a way, and subverting me with her very surrender. Astonishing. I had never been so proud of her. That's what this place is. This is where we come to close our eyes."

Søren opened the door with the *Alice in Wonderland* quote. Zach let Søren enter the dark room first. When a light appeared Zach stepped inside. Søren stood by a massive bed piled high with red and gold linens. He had an oil lamp in his hand. The lamp sent lambent light into every corner of the room. It seemed to be only a bedroom, albeit one festooned like a French bordello.

"Decadent, isn't it? Eleanor has never learned the meaning of subtle. Perhaps you could help her with that."

"So Nora has her own room here?"

"Yes. The top seven Dominants are given their own quarters for personal use. As you can see," Søren said, bending down and picking up a white lace garter off the floor and laying it on the rumpled bed, "she has been making use of it."

Zach looked at the discarded lingerie and grinned.

"White…I wouldn't have expected it of Nora. She's always in red or black."

"I doubt it belongs to Eleanor," Søren said.

"Then why—" Zach began and stopped before he said something foolish. Of course, Nora had been with another woman. He tried to be bothered by the fact, but the images that tiny slip of lace brought to mind evoked feelings distinctly different from disgust.

"You appear troubled, Zachary. What is it?" Søren asked, and Zach did not trust the note of concern in the priest's voice.

"She joked about threesomes with other women. I suppose it wasn't a joke."

Søren gave him a dark look.

"Eleanor is always joking. Eleanor is never joking. Best to learn that as soon as possible. Care to see the rest of the suite?"

"Suite?"

"Eleanor's earned very posh accommodations here."

Søren raised the oil lamp to shine a light on a door to the left of the massive bed.

"How does one become a top Dominant here?" Zach asked

as he walked around the bed to the door. As soon as Søren's back was turned, Zach took the white garter off the bed and shoved it in his pocket.

"The same way anyone else would ascend to the heights of her chosen field." Søren opened the door. "Practice."

Zach inhaled sharply as he entered the second room of Nora's suite.

"Good God," he breathed. In the center of the room stood a massive wooden X. Leather thongs were attached to the tops and bottoms of the wood planks—a large-scale cross of her very own. Zach had no doubt what Nora used it for. He'd seen the pit, seen a man lashed to it and beaten until he came.

Eyes wide with shock, Zach turned his attention to the walls. On hooks and racks, in rows of military precision hung whips, floggers, bamboo canes, crops…a hundred various in-struments of torture. On a small table lay an assortment of spreader bars like the one Nora had in her toy bag at home. He opened a drawer and found cuffs and collars, leashes and leads. In addition to the cross was a large examining table, the kind found in a doctor's office. Except this one came equipped with four-point restraints.

Søren's voice came from over his shoulder.

"Impressive, isn't it?"

"No," Zach said. "It's appalling."

"Really? Such a strong word to describe sensual activities shared between consenting adults."

"Hurting people for pleasure? For sexual pleasure?"

"Holding Eleanor down while she struggled underneath me and begged me to stop…that was beauty."

"Rape isn't beautiful."

"But you see, it wasn't rape," Søren said, his tone light and conversational. "She enjoyed the struggle, enjoyed feeling overpowered and taken. I take rape very seriously, Zachary. My mother was a rape victim."

Zach turned and looked at Søren in shocked sympathy. His distrust of the man wavered.

"I'm sorry," he said with sincerity. "That must have been traumatic. For you and her."

"It was."

"May I ask how old you were when it happened?" Zach asked, trying to find the origin of Søren's violent sexual proclivities.

"It happened roughly nine months before I was born. But that is neither here nor there. You seem uncomfortable with women fully owning their sexuality."

"That isn't true. Women have as much right to their bodies and desires as men. Nora accuses me of being a stuffy Englishman and she isn't far off the mark. But I am no prude."

"You say that and yet the thought of a woman allowing herself to be violated appalls you."

"Of course it does. There are limits to what's healthy."

"Healthy...interesting word choice. Are you much familiar with the disease leprosy?"

Zach furrowed his brow at the odd question.

"No more so than the next man, I suppose."

"I mention it for a reason." Søren began to make a slow circuit of the room. "During my summers at seminary I worked in a leprosy camp in India. There is a disturbing amount of misinformation about the disease. The idea that it is the disease that infects the limbs and causes them to rot and fall off? Pure myth. Leprosy, Hansen's disease as it should be called, is a disease of the nerves. It destroys the nerves that experience pain. And once the ability to feel pain is gone, then it is a simple matter to burn the hand off while cooking dinner over an open fire, or to step on a small nail and not realize it until a doctor pulls it from a festering wound a week later. There were mornings," Søren said as he took a whip from its hook on the wall and examined it, "I awoke to the sound of screams. Without the capacity for pain it is all too easy to slumber in peace as a rat chews off your fingers in the night."

"Pain is a necessary evil," Zach said, fighting off the chills produced by Søren's hypnotic speech. "But still an evil."

"Pain is a gift from God. It imparts understanding, wisdom. Pain is life. And here we give pain as freely as we give pleasure."

Zach watched Søren's hand as he gripped the handle of the whip and coiled it neatly. Every movement the priest made was precise, his fingers as deft as an artist's, his muscles lean and taut as a dancer. And on his face he wore an expression of quiet peace, of intelligent disinterest. A true believer, Zach could tell. But a believer in what? Words from *Paradise Lost* came to Zach's mind—"Better to reign in hell than serve in Heaven." Somehow, Zach realized, Nora's priest had found a way to do both.

"If pain is a sign of love," Zach said as Søren hung the whip on the wall once more, "then I must love a great deal." He thought of Grace now, wondered what she would say if she knew where he was, what he was doing.

Søren's eyes found his and the look he gave Zach was one of the most profound compassion.

"I am certain that you do."

Zach held the priest's gaze as long as he could, but the moment grew too intimate and Zach turned away. A good priest, Griffin had called Søren. He was certainly adept at inspiring confessions.

A mural adorned the fourth wall of the room. Zach picked up the oil lamp and threw light against the familiar monster on the wall.

"The lesson of the Jabberwocky," Zach said, studying its line and angles. Søren came to stand at his side. "I saw a book at Nora's. The Jabberwocky. You, I presume it was you, wrote, 'Never forget the lesson of the Jabberwocky' inside it. But it's a nonsense poem. It has no lesson."

"But it does," Søren countered. "A handsome prince fights a terrible, beautiful dragon and slays him then carries the head home strapped to his saddle. The lesson is obvious. When one is a monster, one does well to beware knights in shining armor. A good lesson for Eleanor."

Zach heard the meaning behind Søren's words. "Nora is not a monster. She's not perfect obviously. But she's a good person, and to call her a monster is ridiculous."

"You know her that well, do you?" Søren asked, turning to face him full-on. "Before tonight she scared you, didn't she? Her fearlessness, her brazenness, I'm sure it's terrifying at first. Foreign to those who lead the proverbial life of quiet desperation as I imagine you do. She scared you with the sheer force of her life and being. But now you look around and think her courage is merely a byproduct of her damage. You imagine I abused her, changed her. And you would save her, as Wesley imagines he can? You would be her knight in shining armor? Yes, before you feared her and now you pity her. I assure you, Zachary, you were right the first time."

This was her favorite part.

Nora ordered Michael to lie on his back in the middle of the bed. She pulled out from under the bed a silver spreader bar. She laid the bar, a length of rope and a pair of scissors on the bed next to Michael's hip. She lit three candles and let them burn on the table next to the bed.

"Don't be scared, angel," she said. "You are completely safe here. You have your safe word. You can stop this at any time.

You don't have to do anything but lie there and take what I give you. Do you understand?"

Michael eyed the scissors warily. He took a deep breath.

"Yes, mistress. I understand."

Nora took two snap hooks and locked Michael's ankles to each end of the bar. She threaded rope through the buckle on his ankle cuffs, tied the cuff to the bedpost and neatly snipped off the excess rope. She came to the head of the bed and took each of Michael's wrists in her hands. She spread him out like an X and tied him down. He could move neither his hands nor his feet. She bent and bit the soft skin above his wrist—a shiver passed through his body. His eyes looked to the ceiling and stared placidly at nothing. Nora knew that look, had worn it herself a thousand nights in Søren's bed.

"Michael, stay with me."

"I'm here." His eyes focused again on her face. She knew how easy it was to disappear into the moment. But she wanted him to remember it, to be with her every step of the way.

"Good boy. How do you feel?"

Michael tugged on his bonds but not in a struggle. He seemed simply to take pleasure in their existence.

"Free," he said and she knew exactly what he meant.

Nora slipped off the bed and unzipped her skirt and let it fall to the floor. She crawled back onto the bed and sat next to Michael's hips. She ran her hands over his skin…smooth and cool to the touch. She caressed his face, stroked his arms and lingered along his inner thighs.

Finally, when it seemed he could wait no longer, she straddled his hips, took him in her hand and guided him inside her.

Michael arched underneath her as she wrapped herself around him. She watched as his eyes closed in shocked wonder and opened again darkened with knowledge. He gasped as she pushed and clenched her muscles tight around him. She bent over, dipping her mouth to his, his lips eager and art-less and tasting of snow. She remembered the last kiss Søren gave her before he penetrated her the first time. Such pleasure coupled with such pain…the pain, like the flash of a camera, rendering the moment forever fixed in her mind. Michael would remember this moment, too. She would make sure of it.

She pushed against him again and let herself enjoy his body inside hers. Closing her eyes for a moment, she imagined someone else under her, inside her, someone with blond hair instead of black, someone with brown eyes instead of silver… Nora felt her climax start to build and she pushed it back and opened her eyes.

Rising up, she reached for the candle burning beside the bed. She brought it to her carefully, not letting any of the wax drop. Michael's eyes followed the glowing wick as Nora held it over the center of his panting chest.

"And now how do you feel?" she asked, rocking her hips to evoke another gasp.

Michael turned his gaze from the candle to her face. He wore an expression of fearful trust, of trusting fear.

"Safe," he said.

Nora smiled down at him and let the scalding wax fall.

Søren doused Nora's oil lamp and shut the door behind them. Zach followed Nora's priest down another set of stairs and hallways. He stopped in front of one of the doors but did not move to open it. They faced each other across an invis-ible threshold.

"Why did you bring me down here?" Zach asked.

"I thought you needed to see what Eleanor is. You thought you knew her until tonight."

"I do know her."

"No, you merely think you know her. It's one of her best

tricks. She flirts, she teases, she confesses everything but reveals nothing. It's the oldest magician's trick—smoke and mirrors, misdirection. You are absolutely certain she's here—" Søren snapped his fingers at Zach's right ear "—when all the while she's right over here."

Zach looked at Søren's right hand and saw the priest holding up his wallet.

"Nice trick." Zach snatched his wallet and shoved it back into his pocket. "But I think I know Nora better than that."

"Do you really? Tell me, what do you think her darkest secret is?"

"You," Zach answered. "She was once lovers with a Catholic priest. I know that now and I couldn't care less."

"Me? Her darkest secret? Hardly. She keeps me a secret for my sake, not hers."

"We've all done things we're ashamed of. Everyone has a past."

"Eleanor has a past, yes. But she has a present, too."

Zach took a step forward and with more courage than he knew he had within him stared Nora's priest down.

"You're jealous," Zach said.

"Am I?" The idea seemed to amuse him.

"Yes, because she's found a life outside of you and away from here. She told me you want her back. But she won't come back. She loved you once. But now you're just a game she's tired of playing."

"I assure you the game has only begun."

Zach didn't back down.

"This game you're playing with me is over. Show me anything you want to show me. Tell me all the horror stories you've got. But I know what Nora Sutherlin is."

"Do you? What is she?"

"A writer."

"Yes, she certainly is. And a very talented one. But a writer is not all she is, Zachary."

"I don't care about her private life. Whatever you say, she's no monster."

Søren sighed and Zach saw something unexpected in the man's eyes, something like sympathy.

"No, you are right. She is no monster," Søren said, turning his attention to the door. Zach followed the priest's gaze. Unlike all the others the knob on this door was painted white and from it hung a familiar-looking riding crop—black with white braiding. And from within the room came a faint sound, a whimper of pain both poignant and plaintive like the cry of a child. Zach found Søren's eyes on him. "But she is no saint, either."

22

Zach heaved a sigh of relief when they returned to the bar at the end of his tour of the 8th Circle. Søren led him to a table elevated on a platform at the corner of the room farthest from the balcony. Clearly it was the best table in the house and reserved for Søren alone. When he and Zach took their seats, a small army of attendants, Griffin included, rushed the table to serve them.

"Care for a drink?" Søren asked as he reached out to casually stroke the hair and collared neck of the lovely young woman who waited at his feet.

"I'm afraid I've reached my two drink maximum."

Søren gave him a slight smile. "I do have some sway here."

"Another G&T."

"Of course." Søren leaned forward and the young woman rose up on her knees. He cupped his hand around her face and whispered something in her ear. She blushed, smiled and whispered something in reply. Søren paused and seemed to consider her words. He turned his head, whispered again and the girl rose and hurried to the bar.

"May I ask what that was about?"

"Simply giving her our drink order." Søren snapped his fingers at Griffin and pointed to the floor. Immediately Griffin went down on his hands and knees at Søren's feet displaying for them a perfectly flat back.

"Giving her our drink order required hushed whispering?" Zach asked.

"Not at all," Søren said with dark amusement glimmering in his steel-colored eyes. "But even a drink order can be an intimate act when done properly." He raised his legs, resting his feet on Griffin's back. The girl returned with Zach's gin and tonic and a glass of red wine for the priest. Søren took the glass from her hand and pressed a kiss inside her palm. After another brief exchange of whispers, the girl floated off. Zach raised an eyebrow at him.

"Just saying a simple thank-you," Søren explained.

Zach glanced down as Griffin looked up at him and winked. He started to argue with Søren—nothing about him seemed remotely simple—but at that moment Nora entered the bar through the side door and strode toward their table.

Rarely in his life had Zach been so glad to see someone. He ran his eyes up and down her—she seemed completely unharmed by whatever activity had distracted her for the past hour. She gave Søren the most perfunctory of curtsies and stepped onto the platform, ignoring Griffin's attempts to bite her ankles. She collapsed dramatically onto Zach's lap and Zach wrapped an arm around her waist. Such possessive alpha male maneuvers were never his style, but he couldn't resist showing Søren that he and Nora weren't completely in his thrall.

"Where have you been, my dear?" Zach wanted to see

how Søren would react to outright flirtation. He dropped a
kiss on her bare shoulder.

"Sorry that took so long." Nora took a quick drink of
Zach's gin and tonic. "Had to do a favor for a friend."

Zach breathed in and recognized a sweet and heady scent
on her skin—a familiar scent that Grace's skin had carried
after they'd made love. She hadn't been with Søren, he knew.
Or Griffin...Zach remembered the lingerie in his pocket and
wondered if she'd run off with another woman.

"Quite all right, Eleanor." Søren dipped his middle finger
into his wine and delicately ran the wet tip slowly around
the rim of the glass. "I kept your guest entertained in your
absence."

Nora shot Griffin a dirty look, but Griffin only shrugged
a helpless apology from the floor.

"Well, Zach and I both had a long night then," she said
to Søren. Leaning back against Zach's chest, she asked, "You
ready to go?"

"Absolutely," Zach said and stared at Søren. Zach saw no
jealousy in Søren's eyes, but no mercy, either. Zach realized
he could never win in a game with this man, especially not
on his territory.

"With your permission, sir," she said to Søren.

"Of course. I will show you out."

"That won't be necessary." Zach stood by Nora and took
her hand. She moved her fingers in his grip, wrapping them
tightly around his thumb.

"I insist," Søren said. Nora squeezed Zach's hand in a warning. Apparently Søren was not to be denied.

Søren stepped to the floor and set his glass of wine on Griffin's back, balancing it on the flat plane between his shoulder blades. "Stay," Søren ordered Griffin who stayed stiff and

motionless on the floor. Søren offered Nora his arm and Zach was pleased to feel her reluctance to let him go.

Søren and Nora led as Zach followed closely behind. They went back down the elevator and across the pit where the play had grown louder as more Circle denizens had joined in. Zach expected Søren to leave them at the elevator, but the priest entered it with them, taking a key and inserting it under the down button. The doors closed and the elevator ascended. The door opened onto the first entry hallway and Zach stepped out.

"Excuse us, Zachary," Søren said, still inside the elevator. "I need another word with Eleanor."

Søren flicked his wrist and the doors closed once more leaving Zach alone in the empty hall.

"Søren, let me out," Nora demanded. "Zach and I want to get home."

"He can wait. We have things to discuss."

"We have nothing to discuss."

"Not even Michael?"

Nora sighed. There was no point in fighting Søren.

"Yes, of course. Michael was lovely. Thank you very much."

"You are certainly welcome. I take it Michael is no longer a virgin?"

"No, of course not."

Søren nodded. "How funny."

"What is?" Nora said, exasperated.

"Tonight you took the virginity of a boy you've never met...and yet you still think you can keep Wesley safe from you."

"It's different. Michael's obviously one of us. Wes is vanilla. Michael's a sub. Michael was born—"

"Michael was born fifteen years ago."

Nora could only gape at him.

"You gave me an underage boy for our anniversary?" she breathed in shock.

Søren smiled and moved closer to her. She backed into the farthest corner of the elevator.

"Yes, I did." He stroked her face with the back of his hand. "Which you would have known had you asked. But I knew you wouldn't ask. And so tell me again how safe Wesley is with you."

"You bastard." She tried to turn her face away from his hand but she had nowhere to go. "God, you'll do anything to make a point, won't you?"

"Yes, but it wasn't for that reason alone. I had to give him some incentive to stay alive."

"And I was the incentive?"

Søren brushed her hair with the back of his hand. "You have kept me alive all these years."

Nora shook her head, moved away from his hand.

"I will do whatever I can to protect you even if I'm only protecting you from yourself. You are a creature of appetite. You take what you desire without thought or remorse. And that is how God created you and it is much of why I love you. But do not stand there and claim to be otherwise. Not with me. I know you. You must make a choice, little one—bring Wesley into this world with you or let him go."

"I won't do either. And he stays with me for as long as he wants to."

Søren stared her down with a look of pure skepticism.

"Fine," she said. "I admit it. I can't be trusted with him. But it doesn't matter because he can be trusted with me."

"Wesley...you don't even know him. The things he has kept from you—"

"Wes is perfect the way he is. I don't care if he has secrets. He'll tell me when he's ready. I won't ask him to change."

Søren turned away from her.

"Of course you won't. God forbid you allow anyone to make any kind of sacrifice for you. Because if Wesley changed for you, then you would be indebted to him. And you won't allow that. You are so in love with your own profligate freedom that you refuse to even be grateful to another person lest you be weighed down by the smallest shred of guilt or obligation." Søren faced her again. "Your obsession with your own liberty is why Wesley is still a virgin and I am still a priest."

Nora raised her hands to her face. "Don't bring that up. Please."

"I offered to leave the priesthood for you and instead you left me."

"You never wanted to leave," Nora said, facing him angrily. "You just wanted to keep me any way you could. I couldn't let you give up your life for me."

Nora tried to pull away as Søren reached out for her hands. But his grip proved too strong. He moved her hands away from her face and looked at her.

"You are now and always my life." His voice was so soft and true that she couldn't even look back at him.

"You love being a priest. The priesthood is a sacrament. You can't quit it. It's who you are."

"Yes, I love it. Yes, it's who I am. And yes, I was willing to give it up so we could be together. But you couldn't allow that."

"I still won't. And I won't turn Wes into something he doesn't want to be, either. You say it's because I refuse to be indebted to anyone. I say it's because I won't let you two fuck up your lives for me."

"And we have no say in this?"

Nora finally found the courage to meet his eyes. Even after five years, no, eighteen years, she still couldn't look at his face without falling in love with him even more. Time sharpened the edge of her love for him. It cut into her more and more with each passing year.

"No," she said. "You don't. And neither does Wes. Whatever he wants to do or be, that's his decision. I don't own him. And you don't own me."

Søren rose to his full height. What charity had been in his eyes was now gone. He put his hand on the elevator key but did not turn it.

"I have seen both hell and purgatory. I assure you, purgatory is the more fearsome punishment."

"I can be me and be with Wes, too. I don't have to choose."

"You will eventually. You will have to choose between this life or the one Wesley promises. You think because you're a Switch in the bedroom, you can be a Switch in all aspects of your life. You will have to decide one day if you're a professional writer, or just a professional who writes. And whatever you decide, you must tell Zachary who you really are. If you care about him at all, he must know."

Nora growled. Søren was merciless tonight.

"I'm surprised you didn't tell him. I know you were trying to scare him off."

"Only testing his courage to see if he was worthy of you. He impressed me, but still he's quite in love with his wife. I'll allow him to hurt you, Eleanor, but if he dares harm you, I will not be happy with him."

Nora repressed a shiver of fear. She'd seen Søren *not happy* with someone who'd hurt her before.

"I appreciate the chivalry. I think I can handle Zach on my own."

Søren cupped the side of her face and forced her to meet his eyes.

"Marriage is a sacrament, too, Eleanor. If Zachary offers to finally leave his wife for you, will you run from him as you ran from me?"

"I told you—I didn't run from you."

"You can't have him *and* Wesley. Neither of them will allow that."

"I don't *have* Wesley. The kid's been with me for over a year and he's still a virgin. Obviously I don't have him."

"You have him as much as I had you even when you were still a virgin. You believe he remains celibate because of his faith?"

"Of course he does."

"Wesley is celibate now for the same reason I was celibate eighteen years ago."

Nora scoffed. "What? Because he's a priest?"

"No," Søren said, leaning in to meet her eye to eye. "Because he's waiting for you to grow up."

Nora's spine stiffened in fury. She took a deep breath and met Søren's eyes. "You don't own me anymore, Søren." She said the words slowly, carefully, enunciating one syllable at a time. "Now," she said, shoving her anger down, "is there anything else, sir?"

"No. There is nothing else. You've made up your mind about him. You won't let him go. And you won't turn him into one of us. And so you will let him turn you into the one thing you most fear becoming."

"What? Happy?"

"Boring."

Nora gasped and raised her hand to slap Søren's perfect face. But she'd forgotten how fast he could strike. He grabbed her by the wrist before she could touch him. He pressed her flat back against the elevator. Pinning her right hand above her head while his free hand slipped through the slit in her skirt. Hard and fast he shoved two fingers deep inside her.

"Stop," she ordered but he only pushed deeper. She panted and cursed him, hating him for how well he knew her body. His probing fingers found her most secret places and dragged her to the edge.

"You were a child when I fell in love with you," Søren said into her ear. His warm breath on her neck sent shivers through her whole body. "You're still a child."

"I don't want this," she said, even as her body betrayed her. Her inner muscles clenched tight around his fingers, her body grew wetter and wetter with each deft movement of his hand.

"I have kept nothing from you. I gave you everything I am. I have risked my calling for you. I will not allow you to destroy yourself."

"How am I destroying myself?" She gasped the words. It was getting harder and harder to breathe. "By loving someone else?"

"By denying yourself. You don't love him. You only love that he loves you. This is what you love." Søren turned his hand and slipped a third finger inside her. His thumb found her clitoris and rubbed it. "Giving yourself to me completely. Tell me this isn't who you really are."

"It isn't," she said even as she spread her legs wider and pushed her hips into his hand again and again.

"Liar." Søren punctuated his word with a dexterous twist of his fingers, and Nora came hard on his hand, gasping with each sharp, spiking contraction. She leaned against him as the pleasure waned, and he stroked her hair. For a moment she let herself forget she didn't belong to him anymore.

Nora stood up straight as Søren pulled his hand out of her.

He took a black handkerchief out of his pocket and began casually wiping off his fingers.

"I hate you sometimes." Nora said the words without venom or remorse.

Søren reached out and caressed her burning face.

"You've been saying that since you were fifteen."

"You want me to pick you over Wes," she said, shaking her head. "I won't do it."

Søren leaned in again. His hand moved to her neck, his mouth brushing her shoulder.

"The choice was never Wesley or me," he said, cupping her breast. Nora felt a rising panic. If she didn't stop him he would take her here on the floor with Zach just outside. If she didn't stop herself, she would let him. "The choice is Wesley or you."

Søren gripped her by the neck. His fingers dug into her soft skin. It hurt and yet for all the world she didn't want it to stop. She wanted him to shove her onto the floor, wanted him to hurt her, bruise her, mark her and take everything from her...but she remembered her promise to Wesley, felt a new panic at the thought of losing him. The house would be so empty without him...

Nora pressed close to him. She would never want anyone as she wanted Søren.

"Jabberwocky," she whispered into Søren's ear.

Søren's hands were off her in an instant. Even she was shocked that she'd spoken the word. In all their years together, this was only the second time she'd safed out.

Søren looked at her. She expected to see fury but he seemed strangely pleased.

"Let me go, Søren," she said, too tired to fight him anymore. "I'm on my own now. I love who I love and I fuck who I fuck."

Søren reached for the key again but did not turn it.

"You love whom you love. You fuck whom you fuck. I see you do need your editor after all. Go." With an arrogant smirk he flipped the key and opened the door. Nora rushed out and into Zach's waiting arms.

"Aren't you forgetting something, Eleanor?" Søren called out after her. Nora grimaced and took a deep breath. She tried smiling at Zach before she turned back to Søren, now standing on the threshold between the hallway and the elevator.

Returning to him, she bobbed the necessary curtsy. But it was not enough for Søren. He took her face in his hands and kissed her forehead. His fingers were still damp from being inside her.

"My little one…" he breathed, turning his face so that his cheek pressed against her forehead. He had done that so many times to her. How many? A million? It never failed to make her forgive him. She met his eyes and smiled, her anger momentarily forgotten. He was still too powerful a force in her life to leave things unfinished between them. She pulled away reluctantly, wondering if she would have to spend the rest of her life leaving this man.

"Oh, *cloro al clero*." She sighed and Søren laughed. It was the real laugh she heard so rarely these days and missed so much. She smiled back and returned to Zach with only the hint of regret in her heart.

Zach still waited patiently for her. Something had indeed changed in him during his time with Søren. She reached out for her coat, but Zach gave her his hand instead and pulled her close to him. Just because she could, she unwrapped the white scarf from around Zach's bicep. Zach looked down at her and she winked. She tossed the white scarf at Søren's feet. Søren glanced down at the scarf and then up at her again.

"How easily you forgive, Eleanor." Søren stared at them

with his wise and all-knowing eyes. "How freely you absolve the sins of others. Tell me, little one, when the time comes, how will you absolve yours?"

Nora had no answer. Søren merely smiled again and took a step back into the elevator. The doors closed and Søren descended into the pit below.

Hell was due for another harrowing.

23

Zach greeted the cool March night air with gratitude as they exited the stifling atmosphere of the club and returned to the parking garage.

"I'm sorry, Zach," Nora said as they reached the car. "I should have warned you about Søren."

"I can understand now why you were reluctant to. It must have been very difficult to have a relationship with him... for so many reasons."

Nora threw her coat in the car. "Tell me about it. It was like being with a married guy, except this guy happens to be married to God and the entire Catholic Church. That's a lot of competition."

"I'm glad you left him. He's—" Zach searched for the right word "—terrifying."

"Thought I was terrifying."

"You were. Then I met him."

"You've never met a Jesuit before, have you?"

Zach gave her a blank look.

"Søren was trained as a Jesuit. They're an infamous militant religious order. Otherwise known as 'God's Marines.' They used to eat Protestant heretics," Nora said with a dark grin. "But these days they're known more for their rather liberal stance on abortion, homosexuality and…priestly celibacy."

"Very liberal stance, I see. Are you sure he's on God's side?" Zach asked.

Nora laughed. "Very sure. And believe me, God's relieved that he is. But don't overreact. Søren was just fucking with your head. It's his favorite part of the body to fuck with. Well, maybe second favorite."

"I can't believe you're defending him."

"Well, he *was* defending me."

Zach looked at her. "What do you mean?"

"Back there with you. He's worried you're going to hurt me if you and I get involved. I mean, technically you're still married. Søren's really protective of me still. He wasn't just trying to be a bitch to you, Zach. He was making sure you knew that if you hurt me, you'd have to answer to him."

Zach blanched a little. He remembered the day he'd had to answer to Grace's father about what had happened between them. That had possibly been the second worst day of his life. And Grace's father was a teddy bear compared to Nora's Father.

"Nora, I'll no more answer to him than you should have to. He dragged you away and ordered you around like you were his own personal property. You aren't even with him anymore. House rules or not, he has no right to treat you like that."

Nora took her keys out of her coat pocket and held one up.

"Here. Want to go back in and tell him that?"

Zach stared at the key and remembered the dread he felt around Nora's priest.

"Yeah," Nora said, spinning the key ring on her finger. "I thought so. How about this one?" she said, holding up another key.

"Is that the key to the Aston Martin?" Zach raised an eyebrow.

"It is. Forgive me for Søren?" she asked dangling the key.

Zach took the key ring from her hand. "I'll forgive you for anything."

"I'm going to hold you to that, Zach."

Zach slipped in the driver's seat while Nora entered on the passenger side.

"You can drive a stick shift, can't you?"

"Of course. Just haven't ever done it on the right side of the road," Zach said and grinned at her.

Zach started the car and felt the engine's gentle vibrations run through his body.

"Now behave yourself," Nora said. "I've got a friend on the force, but he says he's fixed all the speeding tickets he can for me."

"If I get a ticket in an Aston Martin, I plan to frame it and put it on my desk." And with that Zach gunned the engine and spun out of the parking garage.

"So what did Søren say to you tonight?" Nora asked. Zach looked at her. She sounded a little too casual.

"He did more showing than telling."

"I suppose you approved of that. What did you think of my room?"

"I think you should clean it a little more often," Zach said, pulling the white garter from his pocket and tossing it at Nora. "Yours?"

Nora laughed as she played with the delicate piece of lace.

"I see Sheridan left me a souvenir. Naughty little slut. Too bad she's engaged now or we could have a threesome with her."

Zach's groin tightened a little at the erotic tone in Nora's voice. He hated what a stereotypical male he was when it came to the thought of two beautiful women together.

Zach was silent for a few moments as he worked up his courage.

"Nora, talking with Griffin this evening—"

"Oh, God, Griffin. He's the reason gags were invented. What did he say?"

"He told me about what it was like when you and Søren were together. About what he did to you. Why did you stay with him so long?"

Nora only laughed.

"Zach, there's an alley up here on the left. Pull in and park. I want to show you something."

Nervously, Zach obeyed. He turned the car off and looked at Nora. She unbuckled her seat belt and before Zach could react, she had reached across him, reclined his seat and straddled his lap. She ran her hand down his chest and unzipped his pants. Zach inhaled sharply as she took him in her hand.

"I'm flattered." She grinned at him through the dark. "Is this for me or the car?"

"Nora, I told you—"

Nora ran her fingers up and down him so possessively he panted.

"Pay attention, Zach. I'm only going to say this once." Bending close, she bit him lightly on his neck. She kissed a path from his throat to his ear as she stroked him with knowing fingers. "I know you want to fuck me. And I know you wish you didn't. So how about we compromise and you can sit here and say, 'No, Nora,' 'Don't, Nora,' 'Stop, Nora,' and I'll ignore all those protests and slide right down on your cock anyway? And I'll do it because *no* and *don't* and *stop* aren't your safe word. So you can finally get fucked and still sleep like a baby in your big lonely bed tonight feeling all clean and shiny and virginal because, after all, you did say 'no' and that awful Nora Sutherlin just wouldn't listen."

Zach swallowed hard. He remembered his safe word, knew all he had to do was say it and Nora would stop touching him. He didn't say it. Nora let go of him and grabbed his wrist. She brought his hand between her legs and pushed his thumb and forefinger into her. She was so warm inside Zach groaned aloud.

"I'm wet," Nora said. "And you're hard. I've got an IUD, no STDs and nowhere I have to be for the rest of my life. I know exactly what Griffin told you Søren used to do to me. I was there, after all. So yeah, maybe I did beg Søren to stop beating me, maybe I did scream when he caned me, maybe I did cry out when he slapped me, and maybe I did beg him to not share me with King, maybe I did lie underneath him and cry while he fucked me in the middle of a room full of people, or yanked a fistful of my hair and forced me to go down on him at that very table we were sitting at half an hour ago. But I never said my safe word, the one thing I could have done to stop it. And I'll give you one guess why I didn't stop it."

Unable to stop himself, Zach pushed into her a little deeper, spread his fingers apart a little wider. Nora inhaled, her breath caught in the back of her throat. Zach's free hand held her thigh where her stocking met her bare flesh. He couldn't remember the last time he'd been this painfully aroused.

Zach met Nora's eyes.

"You didn't want to stop it," he said.

Nora nodded at him. "You can be taught. Zach, I was never Søren's victim. We were lovers, we were equals, and what we did together was a game we were both very good at playing.

Some nights he would make me orgasm so hard my lower back would hurt the next day. When's the last time you felt something that good?"

"On the floor of your office," Zach admitted.

Nora's eyes glowed bright black in the dark of the car. "You know, you're the second man tonight who's had his fingers inside me. Does that bother you?"

Zach recalled Nora's flushed face when she raced from the elevator once Søren finally let her go. She was so wet that he could hear it as he turned his hand.

"No."

"There's hope for you yet, Zachary Easton." Nora leaned in again and put her mouth at his ear. Her breasts pressed close to his face. "I still remember what you taste like."

Every nerve in his body fired at once.

Nora turned her head so her ear was now at his mouth.

"I'm still waiting to hear that safe word," she taunted. Zach didn't answer. A tendril of her hair brushed his cheek. He didn't speak; he wanted her to do exactly what she threatened. More than anything he wanted to have sex with the world's most erotic woman in the world's most erotic car in a dank, dirty New York City alley where anyone who wanted to could stop and watch.

Nora met his eyes again. Zach pulled his fingers out of her and waited. She lowered herself until the tip of his arousal pressed lightly against her wet outer lips. He started to lift his hips, to press into her. Then he heard a click as Nora opened the driver's side door and she stepped out. The cool night air rushed in and Zach struggled to button his jeans back up over his straining erection.

"Better let me take over," Nora said. "You don't need to be driving my baby in your condition."

Zach took a few calming breaths before exiting the car.

He walked around slowly to the passenger side and got in. Nora dropped into the driver's side and turned the engine on.

"You okay?" Nora asked as she backed onto the street and headed toward his apartment building.

"Haven't decided yet."

Nora turned onto his street.

"I'm just following your rules. No fucking until the book's done. I guess I should hurry up and get that book finished."

Zach rubbed his face, breathed through his hands. "Please do."

"Better give me my homework then. If we're going to play again, I guess I've got to get some work done this week. And for some reason I get the feeling you may want to play again."

Zach could still feel her heat on his hand. He could hardly think or speak and she was talking about the book.

"I'll email you tomorrow morning...when I'm lucid."

"Lucidity's vastly overrated. I shall await your email with bated breath." Nora pulled in front of his building.

Zach opened the door and stepped out. Once exposed to the cold night air his senses finally returned to him. He walked around to the driver's side and Nora rolled the window down.

"What was that you said to Søren tonight right before we left? It sounded like Italian," Zach asked, curious about their cryptic exchange ever since he witnessed it.

"*Cloro al clero*. It's pretty common graffiti around the Vatican. It means 'poison the clergy.'"

Zach laughed appreciatively. He could agree with the sentiment.

"Are you ever going to tell me what you were doing when you disappeared for over an hour tonight?" he asked.

"Nope."

"Are you at least going to tell me if it was fun?"

Nora looked at him and didn't smile. But there was dark mirth shining in her eyes as if she knew a great joke that she wanted to tell him.

"I'll tell you this…I didn't have sex with a man. And it was so much fun it oughta be illegal." Zach took a step back as she revved the engine. She rolled up the window.

Then she was gone.

Zach stared after the car and felt Nora take a shard of himself away with her. It was his rule, his proclamation that they wouldn't become lovers until the book was finished. But for a few moments he'd felt no guilt, and the world hadn't ended.

Zach entered his building and took the elevator up to his flat. He was out of his coat by the time he got to his door. He pulled off his shirt, yanked down his jeans and kicked his clothes into the corner of the room before crawling with the reluctance of a weary soldier into the bitter trench of his bed.

Closing his weary eyes, Zach couldn't stop himself from picturing Grace. Some nights she would stop his hands, desperate to undress him herself. Her brief flirtation with aggression over, she would turn timid as her fingers, earnest and nervous, unbuttoned his cuffs, his collar, slipping the shirt off his shoulders so slowly he would shiver. And she would look at him with such wonder, such desire that he, a married man, a graduate of dozens of beds, and so accustomed to the appreciative stares of women that they no longer registered as flattery, would find himself feeling suddenly shy. She looked at him as if she'd never seen his bare chest before, his uncovered arms, his naked stomach and back until he felt he had never been seen like that before and knew, likely, he never had. The next day he would yawn and stretch and stumble through the hours grateful he'd gotten a better offer than a mere good night's sleep.

Zach came hard on his hand and rolled over onto his stomach. God, he missed his wife.

Nora stood at the foot of her bed and stared at the black silk abyss before her. Like many of her characters she slept on black sheets. But unlike them, she did so for reasons more practical than seductive. She wrote in bed and often fell asleep with her pens uncapped and dripping. Wesley's moving in over a year ago put a stop to any overnight guests. These days the only stains on these sheets were from ink.

Nora pulled on her pajamas, grateful to be in comfortable clothes again. What a night...she'd been so stupid to take Zach with her to the Circle. It was a miracle they'd made it out without anyone telling Zach she wasn't just a Domme, but a Dominatrix and that the Circle wasn't where she played but where she worked. He'd stomached the Circle but just barely. Wesley loathed what she did. Zach wouldn't be any more understanding than the kid was.

The kid... The ghost of guilt passed through the room as she remembered Michael. But still...he had been so eager and ready and so desperate to know that he wasn't alone in his strange desires. And if it hadn't been her, it would have been some girl, vapid and foolish and completely unaware of the rare creature she fumbled about with awkwardly. Michael deserved better. He deserved the ceremony and the story.

After they'd finished and she had untied him, he had curled into her arms and cried. She'd rocked him and let him talk. "I always thought there was something wrong with me," he'd confessed. "I thought I was wrong to want this." And she knew he wasn't weeping because of sadness or shock, but because all babies cry when they're born.

Nora glanced around. The ghost was gone. But there was

no way she could sleep in her own bed tonight, not with the memory of Søren's taunts still echoing in her ears.

She padded down the hall in her sock feet pausing outside a half-open door. Wesley lay on his side, his back to her, the sheet draped over his hip.

"I'm awake, Nor," Wesley said without turning over.

Nora tiptoed into his room and sat on the edge of his bed. He rolled onto his back and looked up at her.

"Can't sleep?" he asked.

"There's a monster in my room," Nora whispered unnecessarily.

"Big baby." He threw back the covers. "Get in."

Nora dived in with juvenile glee and wriggled next to him flipping and flopping over like a fish on land until Wesley grabbed her by the arms and pinned her down.

"Why, Wesley. I never knew you cared." She batted her eyelashes at him.

"If you're gonna sleep with me, woman, you have to behave yourself."

Nora tried to ignore how good it felt lying beneath Wesley with his hands on her upper arms and his naked chest in front of her face. She wanted to raise her head, kiss his shoulders, his strong neck.

"Yes, sir," she said meekly.

Wesley raised a hand and brushed her hair off her face.

"Your hair's damp," he said. "You took another shower."

Nora heard the worry in his voice.

"I didn't have sex with Zach. Or Søren. Sometimes a shower's just a shower, Wes," she said, conveniently omitting Michael.

"Was he there?" Wesley asked, letting her go and stretching out next to her. Nora lay on her side to face him. It was funny how much more comfortable she felt in Wesley's far smaller full-size bed than her huge luxurious king-size.

"He was. We talked some. We didn't play. He wanted to but I stopped him."

"You actually told him no?"

Nora sat up and switched on the lamp on the bedside table. She turned her back to Wesley and unbuttoned her pajama top.

"Nora, you don't—"

But Nora didn't stop. She let her shirt fall off her arms. She lifted her hair and showed him her naked back.

"See?" she asked. "Not a mark on me. You can check the rest of me if you want."

She waited for Wesley to speak but instead he grazed her bare back with his fingertips. His touch was so tenuous that it almost tickled.

"Okay," he said. "I believe you."

Nora pulled her shirt back on and buttoned it. She turned off the lamp and lay down again. For a few minutes they lay in silence together.

"You stopped him because Zach was there?"

Nora opened her eyes. Wesley was looking at her. She ran her hands through his tousled blond hair.

"No. I stopped him because I promised you I would."

Wesley took her hand from his hair and held it.

"You did?"

Nora squeezed his hand and met his eyes. "Yeah, I did. Wes, I can't lose you." Reaching out, she laid her hand on Wesley's chest over his heart. She leaned forward and kissed Wesley on the forehead. She wanted so desperately to lower her head and kiss his lips. But she remembered Søren's warnings. She wanted to believe she could be trusted around Wesley.

Wesley rolled over on his side so she could no longer see his face. She tried to settle in and let herself fall asleep. But Wesley's body was so close, so warm and so inviting. Just to tease him, she reached out and ran a finger down the center of his back from his neck to his hip.

"Nora, did you already forget the 'behave yourself' rule?"

"Just returning the favor," she said. "You touched my back. I get to touch yours." Nora ran her finger up his back to his neck again. She delighted in the little shivers she instigated with every pass. "Why are you still a virgin, Wes?"

He's waiting for you to grow up. Nora heard Søren's voice in her head and pushed it away.

"Are you seriously asking me that?" Wesley grabbed a pillow and pulled it tight to his chest.

"I'm very seriously asking you that. I want to know."

"Well, I'm a Christian and—"

"I'm a Christian, too. And I'm not a virgin. Then again, I'm a bad Christian."

"You're not a bad Christian," Wesley said. "You're just doing the best you can."

"That's very gracious of you." Nora grinned at the back of his head. "But you're avoiding the question. Are you really waiting until your wedding night?"

"Not necessarily."

Nora flicked him on his back.

"What do you mean 'not necessarily'? That's not very devout of you."

"I'm not a fundamentalist, you know. I'm a biochemistry major. I do believe that evolution and global warming are real. I just think God's real, too, and He wants us to be, I don't know, honorable with each other."

"Honorable…that's a very good word. So when do you plan on honoring some lucky girl with your virginity?"

"Nora, this isn't a very comfortable topic of conversation."

"Wes, we talk about sex all the time."

"No, you talk about sex all the time. I live with you and am forced to listen to it."

Nora flicked him again. "Come on. Tell me. I want to know."

"All right, fine. If you'll stop flicking me."

Nora started lightly massaging Wesley's neck and shoulders. She thought it would help with his tension but his muscles seemed to get more rigid the more she touched him.

Wesley exhaled slowly.

"I just want to wait until I know it'll mean as much to her as it does to me. As much as it means to me, this might take a while."

Nora stopped rubbing Wesley's neck and instead began slowly caressing his back with her fingertips.

"Remember, I was still a virgin when I was your age. I was twenty before Søren and I made love the first time."

"Were you glad you waited so long?"

"It wasn't my choice to wait. It was his. I was ready and willing much younger than that. But I'm glad that it mattered as much to him as it did to me. I think you'll make some girl very happy one of these days. For your sake I hope she's waited for you, too."

"I don't."

"You don't want to be with another virgin?" she asked, utterly shocked.

"No way. I'd like at least one of us to know what we're doing."

"It's not that hard to figure out, I promise. You just kiss her," she said, dropping a kiss on the center of Wesley's back, "anywhere and everywhere you want to kiss her and touch her anywhere and everywhere you want to touch her. And when she's wet and ready you spread her legs open wide and slowly push inside her and—"

"Stop, Nor." She could hear the strain in his voice.

"I'm sorry. Sometimes I forget I'm not in one of my own books."

"It's okay," he said a little breathlessly. He curled up around the pillow and pulled his legs into his chest. "It's just…you're… I'm…"

"Turned on? I know you are. Your accent gets thicker when you get—"

"Nora, please."

"You can tell me, Wes."

"Yes," he confessed. "Very. I'm sorry. Just give me a few minutes to think about my dead grandmother and I'll be okay."

"Can I help you?"

"I don't think so. You never met my dead grandmother."

Nora laughed. "That's not what I was thinking. Here, just relax. Best thing to do is just get it out of your system." She put her hand on his side.

"I'm not going to have sex with you," Wesley said with vehemence.

"I know. I've met my virgin deflowering quota for the day anyway. Just think of it as a tension-relieving massage." Nora slipped her hand under his pajama pants and caressed his hip. She tapped him where she knew his tattoo was. "Or I could blow your bugle."

Wesley laughed and groaned at the same time.

"This isn't a good idea," he said, although she could hear the need in his voice.

"Then I'll stop. Or I'll continue. Just tell me what you want."

"I want to be able to sleep on my stomach at some point tonight."

"I'll take that as a yes then. Okay?" Nora waited, certain he would say no and send her back to her room.

Wesley took a hard breath.

"Okay."

"Really?" she asked.

"You really told Søren no because of me?" he asked.

Nora didn't have to lie when she answered a quiet, "Yes."

"Then yes. But no bugle blowing."

"Spoilsport." Suddenly Nora found herself feeling something she hadn't felt in months, maybe even years—nervous. She let her hand slip over the hard plane of Wesley's flat stomach, and she could feel the outline of all his muscles. She moved lower and found him. Wrapping her hand around him, she stroked upward.

"God," he whispered as his whole body shivered.

"You've never even let anyone touch you before?" She ran her fingers slowly up and down his hard length.

He shook his head.

"No."

She took him with her whole hand and smiled as he flinched with pleasure. Pressing her body into his back, she kissed only his neck although she ached to kiss all of him.

"You're insanely hard," she said, almost laughing. "You were working on the world's worst case of blueballs."

"Tell me about it." She could hear Wesley trying to be flippant but his voice sounded bated and breathy. She ran her hand from the base to the tip of him; it took a very long time to get there. Not only did she have a gorgeous virgin in her house, but she had an extremely well-endowed one. Yet another thing Wesley and Søren had in common. She closed her eyes and imagined she could hear God laughing at her from on high.

"Wes, forgive the reference to your family's favorite animal, but you're hung like a horse."

"Really?" He sounded pleasantly surprised.

"Definitely." Still stunned by this incredible intimacy Wesley was allowing, Nora tried to keep her voice calm. "Probably a good thing if you never try sex with a virgin. You'd kill the poor girl."

"I think you're about to kill me," he breathed. She loved hearing his voice so hoarse and desperate.

Nora turned her hand again and ran just her fingertips up and down him, grinning as Wesley's breath caught in his throat and his shoulders heaved. She wanted to pretend it was only a massage, but she couldn't stop herself from imagining him inside her, filling her body with his, coming inside her, being his first lover. She forced the image away and focused on Wesley again.

"Wesley, I can do this all night. That doesn't mean you have to. You can come whenever you want."

"I don't know if I can."

"It's just me. We're best friends. You don't have to be ashamed or embarrassed, I promise. Just relax. Come for me," she said, unable to stop giving orders even with Wesley.

Nora tightened her grip slightly and moved her hand faster. Wesley started breathing even harder. His back arched and she heard him inhale sharply. His whole body shuddered for a long time. Nora nearly gasped aloud at the intensity of his orgasm as her own inner muscles contracted with frustrated desire. While he breathed through the climax she held him before reluctantly letting him go. Grabbing a pair of his abandoned boxer shorts off the floor, she handed them to him.

He said nothing as he cleaned himself off and tossed the wet boxers aside.

"Better?" she asked.

"Yeah, better," he said, still panting a little. "Humiliated but better."

Nora laughed and draped her arm over his chest.

"Wes, turn over." Nora could sense Wesley's unwillingness to obey. But he finally gave in and flipped back over. He lay on his side again face-to-face with her. She was relieved to see his eyes were as wide and innocent and unsullied as ever.

She placed her hand on his bare chest right over his heart.

"I'm going to tell you something that is completely true," she said. "And you're going to believe it's true. And then we're both going to go to sleep."

"I'm listening."

"It meant as much to me as it did to you," she said and she did mean it.

Wesley nodded. "Okay, I believe you."

Nora smiled at him, and he smiled back.

"Now go to sleep. On your stomach now if you'd like."

"Good night, Nora," he said and pushed her still damp hair off her face.

"Good night, John-Boy."

Nora kissed him quick on the cheek and rolled over onto her side away from him. She tensed as Wesley reached out and pulled her back against his chest. It took her a moment to even believe he lay so close, that their bodies were shoulder to shoulder, hip to hip. She settled in against him and let him hold her.

After a few minutes his breathing settled, slowing down until his breaths matched hers. He lay quiet for so long she thought he'd fallen asleep.

"I thought you'd be with Zach tonight," Wesley said.

Nora found his hand and wrapped her fingers around his.

"No. I'm with you tonight."

24

Zach spent the entire morning on the phone discussing the details of contracts and upcoming projects at Royal's West Coast office. The meetings would normally have been rather enjoyable and interesting, but with Nora and last night's events on his mind, he couldn't concentrate. He rattled off information by rote, all the while thinking about how a few hours ago, he'd been wandering around New York's most infamous underground S&M club with a Catholic priest and the son of John Fiske, the city's most powerful financier. And then afterward in the car with Nora... He could still remember what she felt like on his fingers and how close he'd been to sliding inside her. Now in the Tuesday afternoon daylight, Zach had trouble believing it was real. He only had Nora as proof—Nora who seemed to pass from his world and into her world and back with frightening ease.

Meetings finally over, Zach got to sit down at his own desk in front of his computer. He discovered that he had twenty-five new pages from Nora and the promise of more to come.

I got up early this morning, Nora wrote. I was sleeping with Wes and he had an eight o'clock class. Microbiology at 8 fucking a.m.? Now that's sadism.

You slept with your virgin intern last night? Zach replied after he read Nora's email two more times to make sure he wasn't missing anything. About fifteen minutes later Nora wrote back.

Don't be jealous, darling. It was completely innocent. Well, mostly innocent. But you'll have to excuse me while I get back to my home-work. I'm not going to give you any excuse to pussy out on our deal.

I think I may live to regret those words, Zach wrote back.

You won't regret a thing once I'm done with you. Now leave me alone. I'm Papa Hemingway today.

Nora was the opposite of Hemingway in every possible way. For one thing, she couldn't write terse prose if she had a gun to her head. For another, Zach actually enjoyed read-ing Nora's books.

Hemingway was the king of understatement, economy of words and brevity. Are you sure you of all people want to use him as a model? Zach replied.

Nora's next email was answer enough.

Yes.

Zach was still laughing when J.P. came into his office.

"Smiling and laughter? This hall hasn't seen nearly as much fog lately," J.P. said. "Do we have a certain writer to thank for this astonishing change of weather?"

"We were discussing Hemingway."

"Yes, a comic genius that Hemingway. How's Sutherlin's book coming?"

"Very well. We've got two and a half weeks left and two hundred pages to rewrite, but if she keeps up the pace, we'll get it done right before I leave."

"Tight schedule there, Easton. That's a lot of quantity to expect a great deal of quality."

"She can do both. She has drive and a strong incentive to get the book finished."

"Yes, her unsigned contract's still hanging over her head, isn't it?"

Zach smiled and leaned back in his chair. It felt shockingly good to smile like that, like he had a wicked secret that was his to keep or tell. This must be what Nora felt every time she smiled.

J.P. must have seen the secret in the smile.

"It's not just the contract that's keeping her working so hard, is it?" J.P. said, stroking his beard with an amused twinkle in his eye.

"We're not sleeping together. Haven't so much as kissed her." He omitted the office floor incident and last night in the car. Technically, they hadn't kissed, not on the lips anyway.

"You can do a lot without bothering with kissing. I was young once."

"Thanks to Nora I have enough disturbing images in my head to last two lifetimes. Please do not add to them."

"At this point," J.P. began, standing up, "I don't really care how you get the book finished. Just get it finished before you go to L.A. and without getting on Page Six, and I'll be the happiest man on the face of the earth. You are still going to L.A., aren't you?"

Zach paused. Of course he was going to L.A. Wasn't he? Then again, leaving New York meant leaving Nora. Leaving London had meant leaving Grace—he wasn't sure he ever wanted to leave like that again. "Yes, I'm going to L.A. It's all about the book, J.P." Zach said.

"Keep telling yourself that, Easton," J.P. said. He turned around and threw a small wrapped box to Zach. "You've got another present, by the way."

Zach caught the box and sighed. His office prankster had continued sending little kinky presents every few days. With some trepidation, Zach opened it. He pulled out the contents and furrowed his brow at them. They looked something like clip-on silver earrings, lightweight and dangling. Hardly kinky at all. Was his prankster teasing him about cross-dressing? Zach put the earrings back in the box and stuffed the box in his messenger bag, not sure what else to do with them. He'd let Nora have them if she liked them.

He pulled her contract out of his top desk drawer and flipped through it again. He picked up a pen and thought about signing it. He could sign it now and not tell her; then when the book was finished, he could show her how much faith he'd had in her all along. A slight exaggeration considering how loath he was to work with her in the beginning, but he knew she would be touched.

Zach thought about J.P.'s question again. Was he still going to L.A.? Why wouldn't he? The chief managing editor position was the reason he took the job at Royal after all. He said he was going and he would go. And he said he wouldn't sign Nora's contract until he read the last page and he wouldn't. And when he told Nora they couldn't sleep together until they were done working together, he meant it.

He refolded the contract with a clear conscience and stuffed it in his messenger bag.

Thoughts of Zach kept intruding on Nora's writing. She desperately wanted to get her chapters done even though she

knew she had too much work to play with him tonight. Then
again, just because she was too busy for Zach didn't mean he
was off the hook entirely. Nora picked up her phone and had
the number she needed after one call.

The phone rang twice before a nervous voice answered.

"Yes, hello?" the girl on the other end said.

"Hello, little bird. Guess who?"

Nora smiled at the gasp she heard on the other end of the
line. Kingsley had fantastic taste in the women of his coterie
these days. He never cared if they could afford the membership dues as long as they had other ways of earning their keep.
Invariably, Kingsley's ladies-in-waiting all had very useful
talents inside and outside the bedroom.

"Told you I'd remember your name, Robin. King told me
about your day job. Do you have an hour or two to do a favor
for me today? I'm an excellent tipper."

"Anything for you, mistress."

Nora gave the girl her instructions and hung up the phone.
She forced thoughts of Zach aside and got back to writing.

Zach checked his watch—almost five-thirty. He'd been on
the phone for the past two hours with his soon-to-be assistant
at the West Coast offices. They'd been discussing upcoming
projects when Mary buzzed him with news of a visitor.

"Come in." A young woman he didn't recognize entered
with a large tote bag and a rolling table.

"Mr. Easton? Nice to see you again," she said.

"Have we met?" Zach asked, standing up.

"Yes, I'm Robin. We met last night."

"Of course, from the—"

"The club." She cut him off before he said the 8th Circle's name.

Zach did recognize her now. Out of her costume and with

her hair up and wearing retro-chic glasses, she looked like a very different person from the provocatively dressed cigarette girl.

"Right. The club. What can I do for you?"

The girl turned and closed his office door, locking it behind her.

"You can take your clothes off, Mr. Easton."

An hour and a half later Zach shut the door behind Robin and sank into his chair. He was glad she'd come late enough in the day that almost everyone had already left. He'd been reluctant at first but a professional massage was a gift impossible to refuse. The girl had marvelous hands and she spent well over an hour working out every single knot of tension in his entire body. His muscles felt as loose as a sea anemone. He owed Nora a huge thank-you for arranging the massage. Since she wasn't quite allowed to put her hands on him yet, she'd obviously gone looking for a loophole and found one.

Zach stretched his arms and enjoyed how calm he felt, how peaceful. It had been over a year and a half at least since he'd felt even remotely this relaxed. His marriage to Grace had begun as a nightmare but had turned quickly into his best dream. But like any dream, it couldn't be trusted. Something dark always lurked around the corner in dreams. And one day that something dark started showing itself even while he was wide-awake. Grace started conversations with him, terrifying conversations he refused to finish. And then something had happened with her, or maybe it had happened with him. All he knew was Grace had started to fade out on him and there'd been nothing he could do. She just slowly shut down on him like a watch someone forgot to wind.

Having Robin's hands on him had been such a strange revelation. He'd shared with Nora an incredible sexual intimacy the night they'd gotten drunk in her office and then

last night in her Aston Martin. But just to be touched by another woman, to have his back touched, his arms and legs…
to be touched in a way that was sensual but not sexual felt
as foreign to him as that night with Nora. Foreign but not
frightening. He wondered if he saw Grace again, would he be
able to be more open to her than before? He'd love to touch
her the way Robin had touched him. He'd love to teach her
a few of the things he'd learned from Nora.

The phone rang and Zach smiled. He had one guess who
would be calling his office this late in the evening.

"Nora, you're the very devil," he said as he put the phone
to his ear. "But I'm not complaining."

Zach heard a slight intake of breath on the other end of the
line followed by a static-filled pause.

"Zachary?" came a voice he would recognize a thousand
miles or a thousand years away.

Zach sat up ramrod straight; his heart raced. Everything
that had been relaxed a moment ago became a live wire of
tension again.

"Grace…" he breathed. "I'm sorry. I thought you were one
of my writers. Nora Sutherlin—she's a loony. I think you'd
like her. But I'm rambling like an idiot. How are you?"

He lived and died through another terrible pause.

"You've never rambled like an idiot in your life," Grace said
in her lilting Welsh accent, and Zach could picture the smile
on her face as she said it. "I've never heard you so friendly
with one of your writers before. You're usually telling them
what berks and idiots they are. This one must be special."

"She's stark raving mad, and I'm terrified of her. How are
you?" he asked again and winced. He really was making an
idiot of himself.

"I'm in the dark, quite literally, I'm afraid. I just walked in the door and all the lights are out. I can't find the torch anywhere. I'm just glad I had my mobile with me."

"Is it a blackout or just our house?" Zach winced again. Was he even allowed to say "our house" anymore?

"Blackout, I think. The whole street is dark. I called the power company. Should be on again by morning, but until I find the bloody torch, I'm afraid to move."

Zach imagined Grace sitting at the kitchen table in the dark debating whether or not it was enough of an emergency to call him. She said she'd just gotten home. But it was nearly midnight in London. He didn't want to imagine where she'd come from.

"Let me think. Did you try the drawer?"

"By the stove? Yes, I looked there first. Found everything but the light."

"No, it isn't there. You're right. It's in the cupboard in the utility room. I remember stashing it there now."

"I'll check."

"Be careful."

Zach heard Grace's tentative footsteps and the sound of a door opening.

"Found it. Second shelf near the back."

"Good," Zach said, desperate to find a way to keep her on the line a little longer. "Be careful if you light any candles."

"I will be," Grace replied, a faint note of amusement in her voice.

"If the lights don't come on soon, stay the night at—" Zach stopped and swallowed. "Stay with a friend. If the lights are off, the alarm might be, as well."

"I'm sure I'll survive the night." He heard the smile in her voice. "If I need more help, I'll ring you again."

"Please do." Zach rubbed his face. "Did you need me? Need anything else?"

Zach heard that pause again. He needed her. He needed her to say she loved him, or that she hated him, or that she wanted a divorce or wanted him back or wanted him dead or wanted him home right now rescuing her from the dark like any good husband would. He needed something from her because he could not and would not go on like this anymore.

"No," Grace finally said. "I have the torch now. Thanks again."

"Sure. Right then," Zach said, his stomach falling and taking his heart with it. "Of course."

Zach didn't hang up the phone. He held his breath and listened, waiting for that awful little click. When it came he flinched as if he'd heard a gunshot. He held the buzzing receiver until the line died and then finally hung it up.

25

Nora woke up on Thursday morning with a smile on her face. She dressed in her favorite suit—her business kink black skirt, her knee-high black boots and a white blouse with a black tie. She heard a whistle as she walked past Wesley's door.

"Did you just whistle at me, young man?" Nora asked, pausing in Wesley's doorway.

"I did," he said as he stuffed his laptop into his backpack. "Where are you going today looking so nice?"

Nora came close to blushing. She knew Wesley was attracted to her. He was nineteen, after all, and she wasn't hideous. But he always tried to treat her as just a friend and roommate. But since their intimate encounter Monday night, he'd been more playful with her, more flirtatious. She was starting to like it.

"I'm going to Kingsley's." Wesley's smile faded. "To tell him I'm quitting."

The smile came back.

"Zach signed the contract?" Wesley looked so happy and hopeful it broke her heart.

"Not yet. But he will."

Wesley came over to her with his backpack slung over his shoulder. He looked so cute and young right now with his baseball cap on his shaggy hair that she wanted to throw him down on his bed and put her tie to better use.

"I've gotta get to class. But maybe we can hang out later today. We should celebrate you quitting your job."

"What did you have in mind?" Nora stepped closer to him. In her heels she was tall enough to kiss him.

Wesley leaned close and put his mouth to her ear. "I was thinking…we could…"

Nora held her breath.

"…rent a movie." Wesley slapped her playfully on her bottom and brushed past her.

"Sadist!" she yelled out and took a breath, her heart racing. The door opened and closed and Wesley's car started. She tried to remember what she was doing. Kingsley—that was it.

Nora drove the Aston Martin to one of Manhattan's oldest and most elegant town houses. It wasn't just a private home but the headquarters of New York's most thriving underground business. She handed the keys to the doorman and climbed the front staircase to the third floor. Striding down the hallway, she went through the double doors at the end without knocking.

Four huge black Rottweilers charged at her.

"Down, kids." She laughed as she petted the massive beasts.

"Brutus, Dominic, Sadie, Max, down," the man behind the desk ordered tiredly and snapped his fingers. All four dogs sat and stared up at Nora as if waiting for her to countermand the order.

Nora left the whimpering dogs by the door and headed to

the ebony desk. Behind it reclined a man she knew no one would believe owned such a posh establishment. He'd pulled his long dark hair into a low ponytail tied with a black silk ribbon. He wore a stylishly rumpled black Victorian-era suit with a long tail and a black vest with silver buttons. His cravat was carelessly tied but that was nothing unusual. On his feet he wore his signature black riding boots. He looked like a handsomely roguish pirate someone forced into a suit and acted liked one, too—the one and only Kingsley Edge in person.

"I was at the window when you pulled up." He paused and sipped his cocktail. "You drove the Martin, *maîtresse*. You really are a tease." He didn't so much speak as he allowed words to saunter out of his mouth.

"I only tease the ones who pay me to tease." Nora came around the desk and sat on the top. Not even Kingsley had an Aston Martin. She liked to remind him of that. "Miss me?"

"I miss you. My bank account misses you."

"Your bank account is bigger than the GDP of Luxembourg, King."

"Oui, maîtresse." He took a bigger swig of his drink. "But Luxembourg is such a small kingdom."

"Cough it up," she said. "I've got news."

Sighing, Kingsley slowly rose out of his chair and strolled across the room. He picked up a small black briefcase and handed it to her. Nora tossed it aside and wrapped her arms around his broad shoulders.

"None of that," Kingsley said as Nora nibbled delicately on his ear. She wanted him in a good mood for the bad news. Her hand wandered down his taut stomach. Damn beautiful Frenchman, she hated to see him pout. "And none of that, either. What's this news of yours?"

"I quit," she whispered.

Kingsley pulled back and raised his eyebrow at her.

"Quit?"

"Oui," Nora said. "I adore you, Kingsley. You are annoying and frustrating, and I don't know what I would have done without you. But my editor's going to sign my contract. It's time I started behaving like a real writer. *Comprende?"*

Kingsley sighed and kissed both of her cheeks.

"Notre prêtre will be thrilled to hear that. And God knows I'll be happy to go a day without him threatening my life and manhood on your behalf. It wouldn't be so troubling except—"

"Søren means it."

"Bien sûr, ma chérie," Kingsley said and kissed her on the lips. Nora tried not to enjoy it but it was Kingsley after all. The man was half-French but his tongue was all-French. "Now that you're a free woman, care to spend a little free time *avec moi?* I'll tip you for old time's sake, *oui?"*

"Je suis désolée. But I'm seducing my editor this week. And besides, we both know you're a terrible tipper."

Nora pulled away and headed to the door.

"Elle?" Nora turned around to face him. Kingsley had changed her name to Nora Sutherlin four years ago. If he ever called her Elle anymore, it was because he wanted her complete attention. He sat on top of his desk with his cocktail again. "I tease you but your books… You make us all proud, *chérie. La communauté. Bonne chance avec le roman, ma belle dame sans merci."*

Good luck with the novel, my beautiful lady without mercy. Nora smiled.

"La belle dame avec merci," she replied with a curtsy, touched by his kind words. Usually Kingsley had nothing but disgust for the other job that often kept her from her clients. *"Merci,* monsieur."

He was still laughing when she left him.

★ ★ ★

Nora drove to Zach's building, parked in the garage and tipped the attendant a hundred dollars to keep an eye on her car. Tipping generously came easily with the ten thousand dollars in cash Kingsley had just given her.

She tipped Zach's doorman with equal generosity and claimed she had something to drop off at his apartment. Good thing Zach had a male doorman or sweet-talking her way inside might not have worked.

Nora found number 1312 and knocked lightly, praying Zach wasn't working from home today. She waited and heard nothing. Opening her bag, she pulled out her small lock pick set.

The lock took less than a minute to jimmy open. With a deft hand she turned the tumblers and felt it give way. She slipped inside the apartment and looked around.

The impressive neatness didn't surprise her. Zach was quite fastidious when he wanted to be. The apartment was austerely furnished, everything dark wood, dark leather and sparse. On the side table next to the black sofa she found a stack of manuscripts and on top of them sat Zach's silver-rimmed glasses that he wore only when line editing. She'd seen them on him only a couple of times and it was good for both of them he didn't wear them more often. He looked so intellectual in them that it was all she could do not to bite him. Only Zachary Easton could make proofreading that sexy.

She glanced at his one bookshelf and saw his private reading was of astonishingly high quality—Stanley Fish and Noam Chomsky. The man read literary theory for fun.

"What a nerd," she said to herself, grinning.

Nora poked her head in the bathroom, inhaling with pleasure the warm scent of his soap and shaving cream. Men simply had no idea how profound an effect their masculine scent could have on a woman. She already felt her pulse beginning to surge with every invasion of his privacy.

Back in the living room Nora glanced at the stack of manuscripts again. Hers wasn't among them. She picked up a small box lying next to his glasses on the stack of manuscripts. It still had some of the brown paper wrapping around it. It must be his latest gift from the office prankster who was anonymously torturing him for working with her. She opened the box and grinned—nipple clamps, she nodded her head appreciatively. She looked at them more closely and made a nervous discovery—they were handmade Eris brand, a kind not for sale anywhere. A local dungeon master gave them to his guests as party favors. They were two-ways—nipple clamps that doubled as clip-on earrings. She even had a pair somewhere. Whoever Zach's office prankster was, he or she was an insider. Nora put the nipple clamps back in the box and set them on the top manuscript where she'd found them. Surely if the prankster knew she was on the underground payroll he would have already told Zach, she comforted herself.

A closed door beckoned and Nora passed from the living room into his bedroom.

There was nothing in his bedroom but the bed itself and a small table with his alarm clock. She appreciated his priorities—a bed was all they'd need. The bed was made, she noted. That wife of his had him so well-trained. She opened the closet and found a white shirt with French cuffs that Zach wore on occasion. She never told him how insanely attractive she found him when he wore it. Knowing him, he'd stop wearing it around her just out of spite.

Nora pulled it off the hanger and laid it on the bed. She tapped something with her foot, and bent and pulled the mysterious object from underneath Zach's bed. It was a copy of her manuscript. Zach had apparently reserved her book for bedtime reading. She took that as a compliment.

Nora pulled off her boots and undressed quickly. It felt delicious standing naked and alone in Zach's bedroom. She put the dress shirt on and buttoned only the two middle buttons. With a flourish she pulled the covers back from his bed and slid between the sheets. She reached for a pillow and placed it underneath her hips. As her legs fell open her mind found its way to Zach.

Zach…Zach knew her books and because of that she sometimes felt he might know her better than anyone. His body was long and lean and his lower back had the most exquisite arch and his fingers and hands were strong and it wouldn't be long before they were on her and in her and he was inside her completely with nothing—not the book, not his wife, not his fears and his secrets—between them. What would it be like to look up into those ice-blue eyes and see them on fire?

Nora came hard on her hand and wiped her fingers on his pillowcase. She looked at the clock and saw it was still early. Zach wouldn't be home for hours. She slipped her hands between her legs again. Time for at least one more.

Or maybe two.

Long after seven had passed, Zach trudged his way home, exhausted from a day at work. He'd felt miserable ever since Grace called. He'd snapped at Mary for no reason and hung up on J.P. in the middle of a call. He'd apologized to both of them and then wished he hadn't. They were so damn sympathetic he felt he was wearing a scarlet *D* for *dumped*. As soon as he turned the key in his lock and opened his door, Zach perked up a bit. He inhaled Nora's perfume, that unmistakable scent of hothouse flowers, and knew she'd been here.

"Nora?" he called out as he dropped his messenger bag by

the door and shrugged off his coat. He saw nothing had been moved or altered. His books were all in place, his furniture, his glasses. Curious, Zach moved toward the bedroom and saw his normally closed door standing ajar. He peered around the door half expecting, half hoping to find Nora lying on his bed. But the room sat empty. Still it was clear she'd been in his bedroom. The bed was unmade, the covers pulled back and the imprint of her body still on the sheets. Zach started to inspect the bed, looking for any note she might have left. The moment his hands touched the sheets the phone rang. This time Zach knew it was Nora.

"Somebody's been sleeping in my bed," he said as he answered.

"And it was just right. How are you today, Zach?"

"Exhausted. But the excitement of thinking my flat had been broken into did wake me up a bit. You know, if someone caught you in the act, you might have been arrested."

"Wouldn't be the first time. Hope you don't mind but I masturbated in your bed."

Zach coughed in response.

"Did you?"

"Three times. I only planned on the one but your sheets smelled so good, just like you. And I couldn't help but notice that you had my dirty little book by your bed. Can't imagine why my book gets such a place of honor...can you?"

"I often read in bed."

"Don't be coy, darling. We both know you've masturbated to my scenes. Haven't you?"

Zach considered lying or not answering at all. But what was the point of either? Nora would know. "Yes," he admitted. "Once."

"I'm flattered. Can't blame you, though. I'm pretty good

on the page. Tell me something," she said, her voice turning to warm honey. "What's your favorite position?"

"I usually play winger."

"Zach, I adore you, but you can't make soccer jokes during phone sex. It just isn't done."

"We're having phone sex, are we?"

"Yes, we are. We've both worked too hard this week. Playtime. This is an easy game."

"No chance I could talk you into a hand or two of whist, could I?"

"Not a chance. I left you a present in your nightstand."

Warily, Zach opened the drawer in his night table. Nora had left him a tube of lubricant. Why were people always giving him lube?

"How kind," he said with a clenched jaw.

"Comfortable? I suggest lying back on your pillows. I wonder if you can guess which pillow I put under my hips when I masturbated."

Zach's heart fluttered at her brash words. He and Grace had been married two years before he could even talk her into performing in front of him. He would have given his right hand to have watched Nora in his bed. Well, maybe his left hand.

Zach ran his subtly trembling hands over his pillows. He flipped one over and saw a small watermark on one that hadn't been there that morning. Grateful Nora wasn't there to see him, he lifted the pillow to his face and inhaled. A thousand sensory memories returned with that one breath. The scent was the unmistakable mark of a woman's arousal, utterly potent and completely erotic.

"My God," he said and heard Nora giggling at the end of the line.

"Thank you. Comfortable yet?"

Zach kicked off his shoes and propped himself on his pillows as Nora had suggested. "Physically I'm comfortable. In other respects, however…no. Not even remotely."

He expected a laugh but none came.

"Zach," Nora began and her voice sounded oddly solemn. "Listen to me. You don't have to be uncomfortable. It's just me. There's nothing that you can say or do that will shock me. You've been inside me, in case you've forgotten. We're both grown-ups who are very attracted to each other. You are an insanely gorgeous, incredibly intelligent man and you have no reason to be embarrassed by this."

"Just a bit out of practice," Zach confessed.

"Practice makes perfect. I'll go easy on you this time. Asking again, what's your favorite position?"

"This is the easy version?"

"This is kindergarten, Zach. Now answer me and be honest."

Zach exhaled and looked up at the ceiling. Better to just get it out.

"I prefer from behind positions."

"Doggie style?"

"Sometimes. My favorite, though, is when she's on her stomach and her leg is sort of pulled up."

"Why do you like it? And don't skimp on the details."

"It's…" Zach searched for the right word. "It's intimate without being sentimental. I suppose that sounds like a load of rubbish to you."

"No, it makes perfect sense. Missionary position is as vanilla as it gets. But from behind positions are fantastic. Some of my favorites, too. When was the first time you tried it?"

"I was seventeen, I think. I was seeing a university student a few years older than me."

"Such a lady-killer. And she was more experienced than you?"

"Vastly. I'd had more than a few wild nights but nothing had prepared me for her. Second time we were together she rolled onto her stomach and made her will known."

"I like this girl."

"She was a beautiful half-crazy bint named Raine of all things, but I don't regret the lessons."

"Raine is making me wet. What do you remember from the first time, Zach?"

"Ah…" Zach closed his eyes and summoned the memory. It had been years since he'd even thought about her. "I re-member having to move her hair off her neck. She had gor-geous dark hair like yours. And I'll never forget taking a fistful of it and pushing it out of the way so I could kiss her back and shoulders."

"Did you bite her?"

"Constantly," Zach confessed. "And I remember bracing myself with my arms over her. My hands were on either side of her and she reached her hand out and wrapped her fingers around mine. I think that's when it became my favorite." He closed his eyes and remembered how often he'd taken Grace like that. She did the same thing, taking his hand while he was thrusting into her. When Raine had done it, it aroused him. When Grace did it, he was undone.

"Understandably. As a woman it's very erotic to be taken like that. You feel, oh, what's the word? Used, I guess. Used in a good way. From behind positions are fairly dominant. I think you have a Dom streak in you, Zach."

"It didn't feel like dominance. Just intimate. I mean…I can't begin to fathom what I mean."

"Yes, you do. Tell me." Nora's voice was even softer now, coaxing him to close his eyes. He wondered if she was in her bedroom and what she was doing to put that purr in her voice. He didn't want to ask, but he did want to imagine.

"The whispering," he said.

"The whispering? What whispering?"

"In that position, his, my mouth is at her ear. It's perfect for whispering…things."

"So he does like dirty talk after all. What do you say when you're on top of a woman and inside her?"

"Nora," he protested. "I can't just—"

"Yes, you can. Tell me. Close your eyes and pretend it's me underneath you. Pretend your chest is pressed to my shoulders. Pretend your hands are locked over my wrists. Pretend your mouth is at my ear. Pretend you're moving inside me. Is that such a horrible thought?"

"No, it's amazing," Zach said, suddenly breathless.

"Tell me, Zach. Tell me what you'd say. Whisper it in my ear…"

Zach took a deep breath, and remembered he was allowed to trust Nora and to trust himself. It was so damned hard to do, but he wanted to trust her, needed to trust her.

He rolled onto his side, unbuttoned his pants and whispered.

26

On Friday morning Zach was stuck in a staff meeting and finding it hard to concentrate for two reasons. Reason number one—the phone call from Grace that had left his heart aching. Reason number two—the phone call from Nora last night that had left his body aching.

"And as most of you know," J.P. said, "in two weeks our Zach Easton will be going west to take over as chief managing editor at the L.A. offices. I'm sure all of you will miss his sunny presence. To quote the old Irish blessing, *may the fog rise up to meet you* or something like that." A gentle murmur of laughter rippled through the room. Only that pompous arse Thomas Finley wasn't laughing, merely smirking as usual.

Thomas he would not miss. But he would miss his assistant, Mary, and J.P. Of course it was Nora's presence in his life he'd miss more than anything from his time in New York. She had become the embodiment of the city to him—reckless and wild, fascinating and beautiful, dark and dangerous, so spoiled and so very generous.

"So two weeks from now," J.P. continued, "in the conference room we'll have a going away party for Easton. I suggested all of us go out to the Four Seasons but someone vetoed that suggestion so blame Easton for his half-assed fare-thee-well." A smattering of playful boos were thrown Zach's way.

The meeting concluded and the staff started filing out. Mary gave him a hug on the way out and said, "Take me to California with you," in a stage whisper in his ear. J.P., standing next to Zach, mouthed, "Not a chance" at her, and Mary departed wearing a faux pout on her face.

There were friendly shoulder pats and a few hearty handshakes from his fellow editors. Zach turned to ask J.P. something when he heard a smug laugh behind him.

"How's Nora's book coming, Zach?" Thomas Finley asked in his unctuous tone. "Coming hard and coming often?"

"The work is progressing very well, Thomas," Zach replied, ignoring Thomas's childish insinuations. "Thank you for asking."

"Cracking the whip, are you?" he asked with a sneer. "Oh, wait, that's her job."

"Finley, that's enough," J.P. said, pointing an angry finger on his way out of the conference room. "Our writers deserve our respect."

"Respect her?" Thomas snorted as soon as J.P. was gone. "If I paid her to put her boot on my back then maybe I'd respect her."

Zach stuffed his papers in his messenger bag.

"I see Mary was right," Zach said calmly.

"Right about what?" Finley demanded, his face reddening.

"About your professional jealousy. I'm sorry if you thought the position in L.A. should have been yours. The fact that you responded to my promotion with juvenile pranks is proof that you barely deserve this job, much less the chief managing editor position. Publishing is for adults, Thomas. It would help if you acted like one."

"Zach, the only reason you got offered that job in L.A. was pure pity. J.P. got wind your wife was dumping you. After all, none of my writers have ever had to sleep their way to a six-figure advance."

"None of your writers have ever earned a six-figure advance. And Nora will earn her advance like every other writer I've ever worked with—by writing her heart out. Nora and I are not sleeping together. The position is mine because I'm better at this job than you are. And this conversation," Zach said emphatically, trying to shove past Thomas who stepped in front of the door to bar his way, "is over."

"Not sleeping together? Really?" Thomas feigned shock. "Let me guess, she's out of your price range."

"You're a child, Thomas."

"And she's a prostitute, Easton."

Zach blanched and opened his mouth to protest but something stopped him.

A wide and vicious grin spread across Thomas's face.

"Zach, Zach, Zach…you really didn't know? Nora Sutherlin's the most famous Dominatrix in this city. I guess she just hasn't sent you the invoice for her services rendered yet."

"I know what she is, what she does in her free time. Her private life is not my concern."

"Private life? Easton—it's not private if you have to pay taxes on it. She does it for money. She is a hooker. Friend of mine shelled out 5K just to watch him tie up and fuck his girlfriend. Do I need to put this in writing for you?"

Zach pushed Thomas out of the way. Finley's cackle followed him all the way down the hall.

Zach stopped in J.P.'s office. J.P. looked up at him with wary eyes.

"Give me your car keys, J.P."

J.P. dug in his pocket.

"What did he say?"

"Nothing I'll repeat until I hear it from her."

Zach took the keys and headed to the door.

"Easton—you're my only new critic, remember? It's not supposed to be about the author, just the book."

"It's never just about the book," Zach said and slammed J.P.'s door behind him.

Nora glanced at her handwritten notes and started typing again. She wanted to quit for the day but knew she had to push through her tiredness. She was getting close to the big crisis in the story and while she looked forward to rewriting the intensely dramatic scene, she also dreaded having to begin the process of ending the book. More than any of her previous books, this one had become her baby, hers and Zach's, and she loved it more than she ever knew she could love something her own hands had made.

Nora started to flip a page in her notes but stopped when she heard someone knocking on her door. The insistent knock came again.

She smiled as she opened the door and saw Zach standing on her porch.

"You're making a habit of this, Zach," she said, quietly thrilled to see him.

But Zach didn't smile back. He stared at her and raised his chin.

"How much do I owe you?" he asked.

Nora's heart dropped through her body and into her feet.

"Shit."

"That's all you have to say?" Zach said, coming through the open door.

"What do you want me to say? I'm sorry I didn't tell you. I was going to. At the club. Then Søren showed up. I chickened out, I'm sorry. It doesn't matter."

"Doesn't matter that you're a prostitute?"

"A prostitute? Is that what you think I am?" she demanded. "Prostitutes would kill to be me. I'm a Dominatrix. People submit to me for money. But they never ever get to fuck me."

"I thought you were this sexy, wild writer, a free spirit. But you aren't a free spirit. You're just a very expensive cheap trick."

"I told you, Zach—my tricks are anything but cheap." She heard the iciness in her voice and Zach gave her a dark look.

"You lied to me," he said with cold, quiet anger.

Nora took a deep breath and forced herself to stay calm.

"Zach, I know you're upset. I know this is a huge shock to you—"

"Are you sick?"

Nora blinked at him.

"Some might say so. I can't say I disagree."

Zach tore from the living room and came back seconds later with a pill bottle in his hand.

"These," he said, shoving her beta-blockers nearly in her face. "My father takes these for his heart trouble that could kill him at any moment. And your M.D. appointments in your date book—are you ill?"

"First of all, you had no right to dig through my medicine cabinet or my date book, but considering I broke into your apartment, we'll let that slide. And no, I'm perfectly healthy. M.D. just means 'My Dungeon' which you've seen. And these are the same pills that a lot of performers take for stage fright and performance anxiety. They reduce hand tremors. My work isn't easy sometimes. They help me get through some of the rougher scenes."

Zach collapsed into a chair and buried his head in his hands. He sat back and threw the bottle of pills across the room. They hit the wall and clattered to the floor.

"I've been quietly terrified for weeks that there was something wrong with you. I thought that was the secret you were keeping from me. I never dreamed you…"

Nora bent down in front of him and reached out to touch his knee. He stood up and brushed past her.

"I can't believe the first woman I allow near me since Grace…" Zach paused and shook his head in disgust. "I thought you were a writer."

"I am a writer," she said, more hurt and angry than she'd been in years. "You know that better than anyone."

"You have sex—"

"I only fuck the women," she admitted. "The men I just beat the shit out of."

"For money," Zach said.

"No, Zach. Not for money," she said and stood toe to toe with him. "For a lot of fucking money," she said, biting down on every word. "You get your paycheck in an envelope. I get mine in a fucking briefcase."

Nora grabbed the black briefcase off her couch and grabbed a fistful of one hundred dollar bills and tossed them in Zach's face. They fluttered to the floor like falling angels.

"I had nothing," she said. "Nothing when I left Søren. I was twenty-eight years old and living with my mother. I could barely eat or sleep or move for months. She finally got so sick of me she kicked me out. I went to Kingsley Edge—"

"Your pimp," Zach said.

"Kingsley Edge, my *friend*," Nora countered. "And he helped me. I'd been a slave and he turned me into a master."

"He turned you into a monster. Søren was right. I should be afraid of you."

"You're afraid of everything, Zach. Afraid to leave your wife. Afraid to go back to her. Afraid to start over. Afraid to have sex with me. Afraid to trust me or yourself or anyone for that matter. And afraid to tell me what happened to you…I was going to tell you my secret. I swear to God I was. I was just waiting until you were brave enough to tell me yours."

"I keep my private life private, Nora. I don't put it up for public auction like you do."

Nora crossed her arms and stared at him.

"Now I'm starting to see why Grace left you. You're a real charmer, Easton."

Zach took a step toward her. "You don't even deserve to say her name, Nora. And all I have left to say is goodbye."

"Fine. I get it. We're done. I said I'm sorry, and you refuse to accept my apology. What about the book?"

"The book?" Zach stepped over several thousand dollars on his way to the front door. "The book's off. It's over."

"What do you mean it's over? It's not finished yet. I still have two weeks."

Zach opened the front door and looked over his shoulder.

"It's over," he repeated. "Royal House can't afford you," he said, kicking a hundred dollar bill out from under his foot. "And neither can I."

The pounding felt amazing. Every hit reverberated through her whole body. It started in her hands and ran though her arms, across her shoulders and down her back and into her feet. She poured herself into every punch, her muscles straining and opening and screaming. She'd almost forgotten how good pain could feel.

"Nora!"

She heard Wesley's voice calling to her from far away and ignored it. She just wanted to keep hitting, keep hurting.

"Nora, stop it!" Wesley yelled, bounding down the basement stairs three at a time. He tried to grab her, but she slipped through his hands and hit her punching bag even harder.

She pulled back, ready for one more punch, but Wesley stood in front of her.

"Get out of my way, Wes," she ordered, wiping sweat off her forehead. It rained off her, down her bare arms, soaking her hand wraps all the way through.

"Nora," Wesley said, taking her by the wrists. She struggled a little but he wouldn't let her go. "You're out of your mind. You're going to hurt your hands."

"I don't care."

"Yes, you do. You don't even have gloves on. You're going to hurt yourself and you're not going to be able to write for a week."

Nora pulled away from him.

"It doesn't matter anymore," she said.

"Why?"

"It's off. The whole thing's off. Some jackass at Royal knew about me and told Zach before I could," she said, panting the words. "He was, to say the least, unhappy."

"He called off the contract?" Wesley asked, looking shaken to the core.

"Yeah. It's dead. He's done with me and the book."

Wesley shook his head. "He can't do that. I'll call him. I'll talk to him."

Nora laughed coldly. "Not even you could sweet-talk him, kid. He said it's over. He meant it."

"There are other editors."

Nora shook her head. "Zach knew my book better than I know it. I can't finish it without him."

"Yes, you can. You've gotten five books published already."

"Gutter stories from the guttersnipe writer," she said, untwining her hand wraps. "And now it's back to the gutter."

"They were good stories. You know I don't like stuff like that and even I enjoyed reading them. You don't need Zach or me or anyone else to tell you how to write. You're a good writer, Nora. You're my favorite writer."

"Your favorite writer," she said and laughed. She took a long, slow breath. "Too bad. I'm now a retired writer."

Wesley's eyes widened in terror.

"Nora...don't."

"I don't know why I even thought about quitting the game. I make more in a month with King than I did on my first and second books combined."

Nora threw her hand wraps on the floor and started up the basement stairs. Wesley followed hard on her heels.

"You don't have to go back. I balance your bank statements. You've got enough money to live on for five years or longer."

"I plan on living longer than thirty-eight. Life's expensive."

Nora stood in the kitchen and pulled a cup from the cabinet and filled it with water. She drank it down in a few hard gulps.

She slammed the cup down on the counter and reached for her red hotline phone.

Wesley reached out and put his hand on hers.

"I'll give you every penny I have." His eyes were black with fear.

"That's sweet, Wes. But you're an unpaid intern, remember?"

With that she hit the number eight on her speed dial and held it down.

"*Enchantée,* madame. To what do I owe this pleasure?" Kingsley asked.

"My waiting list...who's on it?"

"It would take less time to tell you who isn't, *chérie.*"

"Call them. Set it up."

"Call whom?"

"All of them. You're right. Luxembourg is a small kingdom. Let's expand the realm, shall we?"

She expected Kingsley to laugh or thank her. Instead, she heard him exhale and speak in a way she very rarely heard—with sincerity.

"Elle, are you sure about this?"

"Yes."

"As you wish, *chérie*."

"Smile, King," Nora said with a laugh. "Let's make lots of money."

27

Two weeks left…

Zach paced around his flat trying to decide where to begin packing. His flight to L.A. was in exactly thirteen days. He'd arrive on Sunday morning, get settled into the temporary quarters that Royal had rented for him and he'd start work on Monday. There was little to pack so he wasn't sure why he was bothering about it so soon. With his work at Royal New York almost finished, he didn't know what else to do with himself.

He opened a cardboard box and starting packing his books. *The Great Gatsby*…the book that first turned him on to modern American literature when he was a university student. *Atonement* by Ian McEwan…a glorious story, one of McEwan's best. Zach stared a long time at the title of the next book—*Of Human Bondage* by W. Somerset Maugham. Nora had joked about that book once; that she was quite disappointed that no one actually got tied up in it.

When he realized he was smiling at the memory he made himself stop. Everything was over with Nora now—the book, the deal, the promise of a few nights together before he was gone. He was so angry with himself. He thought that once he was settled out in L.A. she would come visit for a few days. He'd offhandedly mentioned the idea a week ago. She asked him if he'd ever heard of something called "Goths in Hot Weather." Apparently leather and tropical weather didn't mix. But she'd said she would consider it…if he begged enough.

He'd been fully prepared to beg.

It was useless. Nothing he did could exorcise thoughts of Nora from his mind. The anger had burned itself out yesterday and turned into a cold, hard fist of anguish in the pit of his stomach. He half hoped she'd call. Even another fight was preferable to the bitter silence that had become the last three days since he'd told her it was over.

Zach went into the bedroom and looked around. Perhaps there was something in here he could pack that wouldn't spur such potent and painful thoughts. He stared at the clothes in his closet and considered packing some of them. But he still had over a week in New York and he didn't have the energy for sorting out what he'd wear from what he wouldn't.

Giving up, Zach sat on his bed with his elbows on his knees. He rubbed the bridge of his nose, sensing a headache coming on. He looked down to the floor and saw the corner of Nora's manuscript peeking out from under the bed.

What hurt more than anything was knowing how good the book could have been. She was almost finished with it. A hundred pages or so was all that was left to rewrite. So close… It would have outsold all her other books combined, outsold all of Finley's dull, dreary pretentious postmodern books combined. It would have been a sensation.

With his heel Zach kicked the manuscript all the way under

the bed. He started pulling clothes from the closet and throwing them into an empty box. He'd just give them all away. Everything. He'd start over completely in L.A.

After a few minutes Zach realized what an idiot he was being. No matter what he did with his things, burn them, bury them or send them by mail, he would take nothing with him to L.A.

He had nothing anymore. And nothing was very easy to pack.

More exhausted than she'd ever been in her life, Nora dropped her toy bag in the entry hall and didn't even pet the dogs. She stumbled up the stairs of Kingsley's town house and stopped at the second floor. She'd been staying with Kingsley since Saturday not wanting to subject Wesley to the torment of knowing how many jobs she was taking in an effort to get Zach and her aborted novel out of her system. Wesley called every day and every day she texted him the same message— I'm fine, kid. I'll be home soon.

Three clients today—two men and one woman. The men were actually the easier gigs. One had a foot fetish and would pay through the nose just to kiss her boots for hours on end. The other was a masochist who was at his happiest when he was tied up, called a "slut" and beaten black and blue. Both were married men, upstanding members of their communities. They came to her to keep their marriages and lives intact. A few hours with her a month and then they could go back to their regular lives until the pressure built up again and they had to let off their secret steam. Women, as usual, were much more work. But at least Nora liked this girl. She was one of Griffin's trust fund friends who hadn't come out to her family yet, afraid they'd cut her off until she straightened up. Nora felt sorry for the girl—she knew all too well how difficult it was to tell the truth about who you really were to the people you cared about.

Kingsley had given Nora the room next to his, after she had reluctantly turned down his invitation to join him in his own bed. Zach had accused Kingsley of being her pimp, but it was just one more thing that Zach didn't have a goddamn clue about. Kingsley had saved her life five years ago. They were friends and business partners, and right now, business was good.

Without even bothering to undress, Nora collapsed onto the bed. She didn't have to wait long before Kingsley made his usual nightly appearance.

"*Comment ça va?*" Kingsley asked as he came into the guest room without knocking.

"*Je suis* too fucking exhausted to speak French, monsieur."

"*J'accepte.*" He sat next to her on the edge of the bed. His hair was unbound and he'd abandoned his suit jacket for the night. He looked ridiculously dashing in the dark vest and knee boots in a gypsy king sort of way. She decided not to tell him that.

"Drink?" He held out a glass of wine to her.

"God bless." She took a very unladylike gulp of one of Kingsley's best merlots.

"The distinguished gentleman from New York called again. He said he'd consider changing his vote if you considered changing your mind."

"Did he consider upping his offer?" Nora hated Senator Palmer. He was a family-values Republican by day and an S&M fiend and pervert by night. When her work got too difficult, she focused on the money. She'd never forget the desperation that had brought her to Kingsley five years ago. She'd learned a long time ago that money didn't buy happiness. But it did buy a roof over your head and that was more than she'd had when she'd started this job.

"He doubled it, *chérie*."

"Doubled it? Our hard-earned taxes at work?"

"What are taxes?" Kingsley asked and they laughed. She prayed the IRS never got a look at Kingsley's books. "What should I tell him?"

"Tell him yes. I don't care. He's at least easy to please. Any idea why he likes getting the shit kicked out of him by a grown woman in a schoolgirl uniform?"

"He was the U.S. envoy to Japan for a few years. Perhaps he's read too much manga?"

"Tell him Wednesday night. And that's it. I need a day off." She stretched out to take the pressure off her aching shoulders. She wished Wesley were here. He had this magic way of rubbing her back that not only made the pain go away, but made her forget how it got there in the first place. Wesley... it had been four days since she'd even seen him. Was he eating like he was supposed to? Checking his numbers? Nora forced Wesley-worries out of her mind. Thinking about him hurt almost as much as her back did.

Kingsley tapped the end of her nose to get her attention.

"You have a day off. Thursday, recall? A certain member of the clergy would have me in the Judas Chair if I dared interfere with your Holy Thursday ritual."

Nora closed her eyes. Thursday...her anniversary with Søren.

"You know, King, you pretend to be all debased and amoral, but I think, deep down, you're a romantic. You have to stop playing matchmaker. Leaving Søren was the hardest thing I've ever done. Going back to him would be the only thing harder."

"*Mais oui,*" King said and stood up. "But as you know, *mon père* was a Frenchman and I have a Frenchman's heart. We French do love our romances."

"Søren and I aren't a romance. We're just a fantasy."

"Bien sûr, ma chérie." Kingsley bowed to her as he backed out of the room. "You are the writer, after all. You would know your genre, I suppose."

Nora reached out and turned off the light next to the bed. She lay alone in the dark.

"I was the writer," she said to the ceiling. "And I don't know anything at all."

Nora stood outside her house and took slow, shallow breaths. They didn't help. She walked to the edge of the porch, leaned over and threw up in the bushes. Life at Chez Kingsley was harder on her than it once was. She'd taken a few too many of her pills, drank more than she needed to, had done and seen things she wished she hadn't. She wiped her mouth and took the house keys from her pocket. She hadn't been home since Saturday. Five days gone and she already felt like a stranger breaking into her own house.

She said nothing as she passed Wesley's room on the way to hers. She was single-minded in her destination. She went to her bedroom and brushed her teeth before sinking into the bathtub fully dressed. That was as much as she could do.

A few minutes later, she heard a gentle knock on the bathroom door.

"I'm in the bathtub," she said.

"I'm coming in anyway."

Wesley pushed tentatively through the door wearing a fretful look on his face. She glanced his way but couldn't meet his eyes. He knelt next to the bathtub and laid his head on his crossed arms.

"You're wearing clothes, Nora."

"I know."

"There's no water in the tub," he said with the slightest smile on his face.

"I said I was in the bathtub. I didn't say I was taking a bath."

"That's true," Wesley conceded. "Nice to see you again, stranger."

"I'm a stranger to myself these days. Don't take it personally."

"Any particular reason you're in a school uniform with your hair in pigtails and sitting in an empty bathtub?"

"Because I need a bath."

"You look clean enough to me."

Nora swallowed and started to rock slowly back and forth.

"I was with a bad person tonight," she whispered.

The smile left Wesley's face.

"Did he hurt you?" He paled at the mention of the idea.

"I hurt him. It's what he paid me for. After he said thank you. He said…" Nora pulled her knees tight to her chest. "He said he's in love with his twelve-year-old niece and it helped to have someone dress like her and beat it out of him."

"Oh, my God," Wesley breathed. "What did you do?"

"Nothing. I wanted to hit him but hitting a masochist is pretty pointless. Wesley?" She finally looked him full in his face. For a moment his brown eyes turned silver and she saw Michael's face floating in front of her. "What if I'm a bad person, too?"

"You're not a bad person. If you were a bad person you wouldn't be sitting fully dressed in a bathtub with no water in it because you're terrified you might be a bad person. The devil doesn't worry about going to hell."

"Only because he's already there."

Wesley sighed. He reached out, pushed down the bathtub stopper and started the water running. He took her shoes off one by and one and pulled her knee socks down and off her feet.

"What are you doing?" she asked as the warm water started to surround her.

"You said you needed a bath. So you're gonna have a bath. Okay?"

Nora nodded. "Okay."

Wesley eased the ponytail holders out of her hair and ran his finger through her long locks to loosen them. The water rose up to the top of her thighs. Wesley took some of her bubble bath off the ledge and poured it in. The scent of orchids filled the bathroom as the bubbles rose in a weightless white wave.

Wesley paused and seemed to steel himself. He started to unbutton her shirt as it was quickly getting soaked. She lifted her arms when he tugged to let him pull it off her. The water and bubbles were up to her chest now. Wesley pulled off his flannel overshirt and in his short-sleeved T-shirt he reached into the water and unzipped the back of her short plaid skirt. She raised her hips so he could pull it out from underneath her. He reached back into the water and found her panties. She tried to meet his eyes, but he looked only at the black-and-white tile as he slid her underwear down her legs and discarded the wet cotton onto the pile with the rest of her clothes. She laughed as he struggled with the clasp of her bra.

"You men," she said. "The bra clasp defeats you every time."

"I think a demonic engineer must have designed these things. I may have to get the bolt cutters." Wesley finally got the clasp undone.

"Watch out. Bras are often booby-trapped," Nora warned.

"You're out of your mind," Wesley said as she slid the straps of her bra slowly down her shoulders. The bubbles were up to her neck now. She tried to let the heat seep in and relax her, but the tension remained.

"You keep saying that. Do you really think I'm crazy?"

Wesley turned the water off.

"I'm the virgin living with an erotica writer. I think it's pretty safe to say we both need our heads examined."

Nora reached out a wet hand and laid it on top of his halo of blond hair.

"You have a good head."

Wesley took her hand and kissed the back of it.

"So do you. And a wet head." He grabbed her by the shoulders and dunked her under the water. She came up spitting and laughing.

"That," she said, dragging wet hair off her face, "was uncalled for."

"It was totally called for." Wesley took a bottle of shampoo off the tub ledge and poured some out in his hands. He began massaging it into her soaking hair.

Nora sighed with pleasure as his fingers ran through her hair and rubbed her scalp. Wesley really did have amazing hands. The combination of strength and gentleness threatened to undo her. If she wasn't careful, she was going to start crying.

"You're pretty good at this, kid. You've given a lot of grown women baths?"

"Nope. But I have groomed many a filly in my day. This isn't that different."

"Thank you for comparing me to a horse."

"You compared me to one," he reminded her with a faint blush.

"That was a compliment. A big one."

Wesley didn't say anything to that. He leaned her back into

the water to rinse the shampoo out of her hair. His fingertips brushed her cheek and forehead.

"Wes, are you okay with what happened the other night with us?"

He gave her a little half smile as he pulled her back up out of the water.

"Of course I am. Is any guy on the planet going to complain about that?"

"I was just worried that maybe, I don't know, you thought I took advantage of you in your weakened condition."

"I had a hard-on, not cancer. I don't think we should make a habit of it, but I don't know." He wiped the soap off her face with a dry towel. "I liked it. Nothing more to it."

"Is there more to this?" She nodded at her naked body hidden under the bubbles.

"Sometimes a bath's just a bath," he said and flicked water at her.

She laughed as Wesley took the bottle of conditioner off the shelf and began running it through her hair. Before she realized it, tears were mingling with the water and running down her face. She knew Wesley saw but he said nothing, just kept scrubbing her down.

"Søren used to give me baths." She grabbed the towel and swiped at the tears. "It's a very dominant thing to be completely clothed while your lover is naked."

"I gotta tell you, I don't feel a bit dominant right now."

"What do you feel?"

He looked at her, looked like he was going to say something to her.

"I'm just glad you're home. Wet and naked isn't bad, either."

Nora leaned back into the water and did her best to rinse the conditioner out of her hair while Wesley stood up and unfurled a clean towel.

"Don't look," she said.

Wesley laughed but didn't object. Closing his eyes he turned his head away. Nora rose out of the water and stepped into the towel. With his eyes still closed, he wrapped it around her. She burst into surprised laughter when he lifted her off her feet and hoisted her over his shoulder. He threw her wet body, towel and all, down on the bed.

"Are you going to ravish me now?" she asked even though she already knew the answer.

"I'm going to dress you. Where are your pj's?"

"The dirty laundry I think. I've been gone a few days. Sort of let the laundry go."

"How about this?" Wesley left her for less than a minute while he ran back to his room. He returned with a clean pair of his boxer shorts and one of his T-shirts. "Good enough?"

"Perfect." She slid the shorts on under the towel. Wesley turned his head again when she dropped the towel and pulled his T-shirt on. Sliding into his clothes felt like being in his arms—they were warm and clean and smelled like a summer morning.

She toweled her hair and squeezed as much water out of it as she could while Wesley pulled the covers back. She crawled into her bed and was relieved by the familiar scent of her sheets, the familiar fabric and Wesley so close by.

"What time is it?" The past few days time had poured through her hands like water. She only knew it was Wednesday because that was the day that came before Thursday.

"Almost midnight." Wesley dragged the covers over her. She sighed with pleasure, feeling human for the first time since last Friday.

"Almost Thursday." Nora saw a veil fall over Wesley's eyes. He knew exactly what tomorrow was.

"You're gonna go see him?" Wesley sat next to her.

She scooted closer and looked up at him with tired eyes.
"I have to."

He nodded. He usually argued with her whenever she said she "had" to do something he knew she didn't have to do. This time he seemed to understand.

"You still love him, don't you?"

Nora smiled sadly up at him.

"Many waters." She ran a hand through her wet hair and let water drop from her fingertips to the floor.

"'Many waters cannot quench love,'" Wesley finished the quote. "'Rivers cannot wash it away.'"

"'Nor will rivers overflow it,'" she corrected. "Catholics use the New American."

"N.I.V.—it's what we use in youth group."

"I won't let him hurt me. I promised you I wouldn't. I just have to see him. That's all."

"Okay," he said. "But you'll come home tomorrow night?"

"Yeah, I'll come home."

Wesley nodded and slid off the side of the bed. He started unbuttoning his jeans.

"What are you doing?" she asked as he took off his pants and threw them on a nearby chair.

"Told you. It's almost midnight. Scoot over."

He stripped out of his T-shirt and Nora moved over to let him slide in next to her. Turning off the bedside lamp, Wesley gathered her to him. She breathed slowly, relaxed onto his chest and melted into his arms. She didn't deserve him, didn't deserve this. He knew she would see Søren tomorrow, and he didn't hate her for it. She might hate herself, but Wesley would never hate her.

Nora traced his collarbone with her fingertips while Wesley slipped his hand under her shirt and slowly kneaded her lower back. She almost laughed at this foreign sensation—for once in her life she lay in bed with a gorgeous young man, and she had absolutely no desire to seduce him.

"We're both wearing your underwear," Nora said after a long silence.

"Could be worse. We both could be wearing your underwear."

She smiled, knowing that even more than the bath, just having Wesley so close to her made her feel clean and sane again. When Søren touched her she became his. When Wesley touched her, she became herself.

Nora's hand slid from his chest to his arm. Wesley had twice the muscle she did. He could hurt someone so much more easily than she could, and yet she knew he would never hurt anyone unless he was trying to protect someone else. She'd seen that with her own eyes.

"Wes," she said as she felt sleep coming for her.

"What, Nor?"

I love you, she thought but didn't say the words out loud.

"Thanks for the bath."

28

Wesley had already gone by the time Nora rolled out of bed the next morning. *Morning?* she thought and then looked at the clock. It was already after noon. She dragged herself from the tangle of her sheets.

She went to her closet and dug through it. Today she would do something she did only once a year—dress conservatively. She found her only skirt that went past her knees, her only black shoes with a low heel, her only blouse that wasn't designed to show every inch of cleavage. She even found a strand of pearls she'd received as a gift from her grandmother years ago and put them on. She pulled her hair back and up, taming the wavy mane as best she could and applied half her usual amount of makeup.

Today she was going to church.

As Nora drove she fought off the twin demons of eagerness and fear that this day always visited upon her. Shortly after three she pulled into the parking lot at Sacred Heart Catholic Church. She'd been christened here as an infant, made her First Communion here, and this was where she first saw Søren over eighteen years ago.

Sacred Heart had thrived under Søren's watch. From barely over a hundred members, the church had trebled in size during his time here. A handsome polyglot only twenty-nine years old when first he arrived, he was everything priests were not usually known for being—erudite, witty and charming. Two other priests in nearby diocese had been removed from their posts for allegations of sexual offenses in the past two decades. Catholic parents brought their children to Sacred Heart in droves. They knew Father S. could be trusted. And although Nora knew who he was with her behind closed bedroom doors, those parents were right to trust him.

It was funny, she thought as she entered through the front doors of Sacred Heart, how little she remembered of her childhood here. Even Father Greg, Søren's predecessor, wavered in her mind as little more than a memory of elderly kindness. Then one Sunday when she was fifteen years old, Søren had come like an Annunciation; it was as if God Himself had hailed her by name.

She paused in the foyer and glanced around. Foyer…Søren always corrected her when she called it that. "It's the narthex, Eleanor," he'd said, hiding his smile. "Not the foyer." Next time she referred to it in his presence she'd called it the "lobby."

Glancing around, Nora tried to sift through the thousands of memories that descended on her. She saw the little shrine to the Virgin Mary in the corner of the entryway and the burning candles beneath her. Nora stood before the shrine, closed her eyes and remembered…

She'd been sixteen years old, almost seventeen, and her best and only friend was a girl named Jordan. Introverted and shy, Jordan had no idea she was also quietly beautiful. They'd gone to the same Catholic high school, had most of the same classes—all the same but for English her junior year. Nora had been in the highest-level class and Jordan, never the writer Nora was, had an easier teacher. Nora would never forget the ashen look on Jordan's face one day after school. It took three days for Nora to drag it out of her—Jordan's English teacher, a married man in his forties, had kept her after class and put his hand up her shirt. He'd offered her an easy A in the class in exchange for the obvious. Nora had been livid and threatened to beat the teacher to death with her bare hands. Jordan had sobbed, terrified that no one would believe her, that no one would help her. After all, this English teacher was also the basketball coach, and the team was having the best season in years. Jordan made Nora promise not to tell the school, and in return Nora made Jordan promise to tell Father S. To this day Nora still didn't know what Søren had done or said to the teacher. She only knew Søren had gone to her school on a Friday and by Monday the teacher was gone.

Nora had raced to church after school that day and found Søren praying here by the shrine to the Virgin Mary. She'd told him how grateful Jordan was, how shocked the whole school was, how nobody knew why the coach had left so abruptly.

Søren hadn't smiled. He'd only lit a candle.

"Was that hard to do?" She remembered standing in this very spot and asking him that question. "Telling that guy off?"

"It was frighteningly easy to put the fear of God into him," Søren had said. "And almost enjoyable. Why do you ask, Eleanor?"

She'd zipped up her hooded sweatshirt and plucked nervously at the ragged cuffs. "I thought it might be hard for you. You know, since you're in love with me."

Søren had met her eyes and she saw she'd actually managed to catch him off guard, one of the few times in their eighteen years she had.

"Eleanor, there are suicide bombers on the Gaza Strip who are less dangerous than you are." He started toward his office. She followed him, nearly running to keep up with his long strides.

"I'm going to take that as a yes," she'd said when they arrived at his office door.

"I've always been an admirer of the Cistercian monks." Søren stepped into his office. "Especially their vow of silence." And he'd closed the door in her face.

She'd smiled nonstop for the next two weeks.

Nora opened her eyes and stepped away from the shrine and out of the memory. Her heels clicked on the hardwood floors grown slick and shiny with age. She thought she'd find Søren in his office working. But she paused outside the sanctuary when she heard the sound of a piano wafting through the heavy wooden doors. Inhaling the muted notes, she slipped inside the nave and stepped quietly toward the chancel where Søren sat at a grand piano.

He didn't look up at her as she came to the piano. She placed her hands flat on its polished black top. Closing her eyes again, she let the subtle waves vibrate through her and into her. The last note shivered up her arms and down to her feet. As the note echoed throughout the nave and back to the altar Nora opened her eyes.

"*The Moonlight Sonata,*" Nora said. "My favorite."

Søren smiled and played a few stray notes.

"I know it is."

Nora returned the smile and leaned forward, running her hand over the smooth black surface.

"Happy anniversary, Søren."

Søren smiled again, one of his rare, genuine smiles that

reached his eyes. Something caught in her chest and she let her own smile fade.

"Happy anniversary, little one," he said, his voice as gentle as the last note of the sonata.

With those four words came a thousand more memories. She and Søren had never, would never marry, had never dated in the traditional sense of the word, but never had they questioned what day would become the signifier of the beginning of their life together. The first time Søren had beaten her and then taken her virginity was thirteen years ago on Holy Thursday, the day before Good Friday, the day when Christ celebrated His Last Supper. Jesus, God Incarnate, had knelt before His disciples and washed their feet on this night. Thirteen years ago tonight Søren had done the same to her. Even as the liturgical calendar changed, they never once considered celebrating their anniversary on any other day but this too-neglected holy day, this last night of Christ's freedom before He was taken, this last night to share a quiet moment alone with those He loved.

Søren began playing the haunting melody again, and she let it draw her inexorably into its insistent rhythms. She watched his hands, his perfect pianist's hands, and recalled all too well how intimately she knew those hands, how intimately they knew her. One courageous strand of Søren's perfect blond hair threatened to fall over his forehead. She longed to reach out and brush it back.

"You played this for me that night," she said as the music faded. Nora closed her eyes and let the past come to her. "You were playing it when I came to the rectory." She remembered that night like yesterday, slipping in through the tree-shrouded back door, following the music to Søren's elegant living room. She stood in silence and watched the priest who would become her lover that night play by the light of a single candle the world's most beautiful piece of music as if it had been written by him and for her. "The next morning I woke up in your bed for the first time."

"The best morning of my life," Søren said.

"And mine." Nora felt the old tug of love and straightened, trying to brush it off her. "When did the church get a grand piano?"

Søren smiled.

"A mysterious stranger had an Imperial Bösendorfer delivered to my home on my most recent birthday. I donated my Steinway to the church."

"That was very generous of that mysterious stranger," Nora said with a sheepish grin.

"Very generous indeed. Although the Steinway still plays beautifully."

"It's had a tricky sustain pedal for ages."

"Yes, and whose fault is that?"

"That is not my fault," Nora protested. "Do you recall what you were doing to me at the time? I had to hold on to something, didn't I?"

Søren looked down at his hands. His fingers hovered over the keyboard playing soundless phantom notes.

"You could have held on to me."

Nora only swallowed, finding herself in a rare moment of speechlessness. Perhaps sensing her discomfort, Søren dropped his hands to the keyboard and began playing again.

"*The Moonlight Sonata* is a strange piece of music," Søren said. "It's been called a Lamentation. You can feel that when you play it, can feel the sorrow and the need in the endless repetitions. It's simple to play but maddeningly difficult to play well. The arpeggios allow great freedom of expression. Too much freedom in untutored, unskilled hands. They say Beethoven wrote it for a seventeen-year-old countess, the

Countess Giulietta Guicciardi. He may have loved her. More likely he was simply trying to seduce her."

"It would have worked for me."

"It did work for you."

This time Nora smiled at the memories Søren's words conjured. Again she slid her hands lovingly over the piano. "My God, the crimes against nature that have been committed on this piano."

"I hope you aren't referring to my playing."

"Never. I know how gifted those hands of yours are."

"Some decorum please. We are in a church, Eleanor," Søren reminded her with only a playful hint of sternness about his lips.

"Forgive me, Father." She composed her features into a pantomime mask of contrition.

"Of course, little one. I can forgive you anything. But don't think you won't be called upon to do your penance someday."

Before she could respond, the unmistakable squeak of sneakers on hardwood sounded outside the door. Another louder squeak followed that one and then the shrieking giggles of children.

"Duty calls." Søren rose from the bench.

Nora walked with him down the aisles and into the hall outside the sanctuary. They followed the sound of the children from the church to the annex that housed the fellowship hall and the church kitchen. Søren led her into the fellowship hall that was part gymnasium, part reception area, and before her was a scene of animal chaos. Her mental description proved even more apt as a boy dressed as a sheep careened by them.

"What on earth?" Nora asked as they found a quiet place near the kitchen.

"The children are practicing for Sunday's Passion play," Søren explained.

Everywhere children ran to parents, from parents, sometimes through parents. As Søren's presence became known, however, the din quieted and order began to reassert itself. She had always admired that about Søren. He let his presence speak far more often than his words.

Nora's eyes stopped on a woman who looked vaguely familiar. As her features came into better focus, Nora placed a name to the face—Nancy James, one of her favorite mothers here. Sometimes it was hard for Nora to imagine that it was only five years ago that she still attended this church, babysat these kids, chatted with these parents. Nora was finally able to catch her eye and smile. It took Nancy a moment but then she returned the smile with full recognition. Five years…it felt like just yesterday, it felt like a million years ago.

"Did they know about us?" Nora inclined her head toward a group of parents. She kept her voice unnecessarily low. With all the children she could have screamed the question at Søren without fear.

"I am still a priest. I believe it is safe to assume they either never suspected or they never cared."

Nora laughed coldly. "Ex-con Elle Schreiber and the sainted Father Stearns? Of course they never suspected."

"Eleanor, they never thought as ill of you as you believed. When you come back, you will be welcomed with open arms."

"I'm not coming back."

A faint smile played at the corner of Søren's exquisite lips.

"And yet you are here."

Nora started to argue, but she caught a glimpse of mirror-pale eyes across the room and froze.

"Michael…" she breathed.

"Yes, he's helping with the Passion play this year. He's quite good with the children. Around them he can relax, which is difficult for him in other situations."

At the moment Michael looked anything but relaxed. His long black hair was pulled back in a ponytail but she could see frustrated strands loose about his face. Children bustled around him frantically. He straightened haloes, retied wings, wrestled the little angels... A shepherd nearly plowed into him and he laughed and slid out of the way.

"Is he okay?" Nora asked, a knife of guilt threatening to cut into her.

"He and his mother started attending here over two years ago. This is truly the most contented I've ever seen him. He's at peace now. Almost happy. There is a new look in his eyes. Relief."

"Relief...that he isn't alone?"

"Yes. I told him about us, who we are, the other world we live in. I realize I was taking a great chance by doing so, but he had listened all too well to his father's words and convinced himself that he was sick and depraved for his desires. But telling only goes so far..."

"Show, don't tell," Nora said with a grim smile and made herself not think of Zach. "It's not fair, you know. It's such a double standard. You let me have Michael and he's only fifteen. But you made me wait until I was twenty."

Søren inhaled slowly. "That was my mistake."

"Miracles do happen. You just admitted to a mistake. What was your mistake? Not fucking me sooner?"

"It was my mistake—" he turned and met her eyes "—thinking we had all the time in the world."

Nora's heart contracted in her chest. She studied Michael from across the room. He was far from jubilant, but she could see his posture had eased and he had a light in his eyes. She would never have guessed from just looking at him that he wore such fearsome scars under his wristbands.

"You owe Michael a small debt of gratitude, Eleanor." Søren interrupted her melancholy meditation. "I had counted the day you left as the worst day of my life. The day I knelt in the back of an ambulance and administered last rites to a fourteen-year-old boy..."

"Knocked me out of first place, did he?"

"Perhaps a tie for first."

"His scars are horrific. I can't believe he survived that."

"It was not a premeditated attempt. He broke glass and slashed fast. He bled profusely but not fast enough that we didn't have time to save him. Still, the attending physician called his survival a miracle."

"I'm glad he made it. He's a sweet kid."

As Nora said the words, Michael looked in their direction for the first time. His silver eyes widened with shock at the sight of her. His skin flushed and a look of pure panic eclipsed his face.

"Søren..." Nora was afraid Michael was about to lose it.

"Just watch, Eleanor."

Michael kept looking at her. But she did as Søren ordered. Michael closed his eyes and took a deep breath. The red faded from his face, his body went calm and slack. He opened his eyes again and met her gaze once more. And then, of all things, he smiled at her.

"He's fine," Søren said. "He is one of us after all."

"You care about him very much. I can tell," she said.

"He's become like a son to me."

"How sweet. Like Abraham and Isaac."

"I know you are still angry that I didn't tell you his age. Had I told you, would anything have been different? Apart from this impressive claim to righteous indignation?"

Nora opened her mouth to protest but a boy of about five or six squealed past them.

"Owen!" Søren called out, freezing the little boy in his tracks. "Come here, young man."

Søren snapped his fingers and pointed at a spot on the floor in front of him. Little Owen slumped over and slunk to the spot. Nora had to bite her lip to keep from laughing. Owen was the cutest little thing with his curly black hair sticking out in all directions.

"Yes, Father S.?" the boy asked and kicked at the hardwood, making his soles squeak on purpose.

"Owen, please examine your shoes."

Obediently Owen looked down. His whole body heaved the most forlorn sigh she'd ever heard come from a child.

"I forgot." Owen looked up at Søren with pleading eyes.

"You forgot to tie them or you forgot how to tie them?" Søren asked.

"I forgot how."

"Eleanor? I believe this is your area of expertise."

"I'll try, but I'm a little out of practice."

Nora knelt in front of him and attempted to demonstrate the bunny rabbit method, the two loops as ears and the loop around the loop… Owen just watched her with his grave eyes.

"Does that make any sense, Owen?" she asked as she stood up again.

"I don't know. It's just so hard. Thank you."

"You're very welcome, Owen."

Nora watched as Søren reached out and placed the tip of his finger between Owen's eyes. Owen's eyes crossed and both he and Søren laughed. "You're dismissed. But do try to stay in the slow lane, please."

Owen took off again, but this time at a more restrained pace.

Nora glanced across the hall, past the tables to where the

parents sat talking among themselves but never taking their eyes off their kids.

"I wanted to have your children once," she said, not looking in his eyes.

"I told you, Michael is like a son to me. And you had him, did you not?"

Nora inhaled sharply. "There's a difference between sadism and cruelty. I hope you learn that someday."

"Remind me which of those you prefer?"

"I'm going, Søren. Thank you for another lovely anniversary."

Nora turned on her heel and strode from the hall. She heard footsteps behind her but kept walking. She only made it as far as the entryway when she heard her name.

She stopped and turned around to face Søren.

"It's hard enough for me to come to this place again and see you," she said. "You don't have to make it harder."

Søren raised a hand to the side of her face. He brushed her cheek with his fingertips. She glanced around to make sure no one was there watching them. It was a habit she'd never break.

"Forgive me. This is difficult for me, as well."

"I didn't think anything was difficult for you."

Søren lowered his hand and stepped out of the sunlight and into the shadows by the shrine of the Virgin Mary.

"Surely you of all people cannot think so highly of me."

Nora smiled and followed him into the shadows.

"The day I first saw you, I thought you were omnipotent."

"You were fifteen, Eleanor."

"I still think that."

Søren's laugh was empty and somber.

"If I were omnipotent you would still be with me, little one. I didn't have the strength to stop you from leaving."

"You did," she said. "But you loved me too much to use it."

"Perhaps I've always loved you too much." Søren turned his eyes up to the Virgin Mary statue. "Our mutual acquaintance tells me you've given up work on your book."

Nora tugged at her shirt cuffs.

"Zach found out about what I do. He killed the deal."

"Surely you can write without him."

"I'm not sure I can. He made me see my book with new eyes. I was just a smutty storyteller before him. For a little while I felt like a real writer."

"Answer a question for me, Eleanor. Why did you begin your work with our monsieur?"

"I had nothing. He offered me a job."

"You could have worked any number of jobs. Why that one?"

"He said I'd make a lot of money working very few hours. I thought it would give me—" She stopped and swallowed. "I thought it would give me time to write."

"Your work with Kingsley was merely a means to an end. It was never meant to be the end."

Nora didn't know how to answer that.

Søren reached into his pocket. He pulled out a small black velvet bag and placed it in her hand.

"What's this?" she asked.

"Your real anniversary gift."

Nora opened the bag and a silver pendant on a chain poured out into her hand. She held it close to her eyes.

"A saint's medal." She laughed. "I haven't worn one of these in years. Who is it? St. Michael? St. Mary Magdalene?"

"St. John the Apostle actually."

"St. John...patron saint of fools and ex-lovers?" she hazarded a guess.

"No," Søren said, his voice and eyes gentle. "The patron saint of writers."

Nora's hand shook slightly and she couldn't quite get the necklace on.

Søren took the medal from her and clasped it around her neck. She closed her eyes and relished the brief moment when his arms encircled her.

"Our Lord Jesus had twelve disciples," Søren said, taking a step back. "After His Ascension all were scattered to the four winds and were persecuted unto death. Oddly enough it was only St. John, Patron Saint of Writers, who didn't die a martyr."

"You always hated it when I played martyr. You know, I'm not sure I deserve to wear this."

"Genesis 1:1, *God said let there be light and there was light…* God created the world with words, Eleanor. Words are the thread in the fabric of the universe. You write because it brings you closer to God. I was foolish enough once to think I could do that for you. I know better now. This is who you are."

"Zach doesn't think so."

"Then he's a bigger fool than I was. I know you, little one. You wrote your way out of hell once. You can do it again."

"The book's not done, not even close, and I've only got a week left before he leaves for L.A. Not that he'll even bother to read it if I do get it done."

"Then in your vernacular, Eleanor—fuck him. Finish the book. Not for me or for Zachary or for Wesley or even for God. Finish it for you."

Nora laughed against her tears.

"Is that an order?"

"Does it need to be?"

Nora thought about it a moment, thought about the energy that now surged through her veins. She had one week before Zach left for L.A. What if she did finish it without him? She could walk up to him and throw the book in his face. The contract be damned. She'd finish it just because she wanted to know how it ended.

"No, I think I've got this one."

"Then go." Søren nodded to the entrance.

Nora almost ran to the door. But she stopped at the last moment and turned around.

"You could have kept me, you do know that, don't you?" she asked.

Søren struck a match and lit a candle under the shrine.

"I would that you had kept me."

Nora didn't, couldn't speak. But it didn't matter if she spoke or not, as long as she could write. She stepped out of the foyer and into the sunlight. She took one last look back at Sacred Heart and knew her most sacred heart remained inside. *Sometimes,* she thought to herself, *I wish you'd kept me, too.*

Wesley was waiting for her in the living room when she got back to the house. He wore a look of profound relief when he saw that she was unharmed. She smiled at how much more thankful he would be in just a few minutes.

"You came home," he said.

"I've got a book to write."

A smile as bright as the sun spread across Wesley's face. But it wavered when he held out her red hotline phone.

"It rang while you were gone."

Nora took the phone from his hands and pressed the number eight. For herself and no one else she would finish the book. But this at least she could do for Wesley.

"Pardonnez-moi, madame," Kingsley began as he answered the phone. *"Mais—"*

"Forget it, King. Don't take this personally, but Mistress Nora is out of business."

"For how long this time, *chérie?*" She heard the laughter in his voice.

Nora looked at Wesley and smiled.

"Forever."

She dropped the phone on the floor. With one quick stomp she smashed the cell phone with the heel of her shoe.

Wesley hugged her so hard he lifted her off the ground.

"Down boy. I don't have a lot of time and I've got a helluva lot to write. Brew coffee and turn off all the phones, unplug the internet, don't answer the door. For the next week, it's nothing but all-nighters."

"I thought you said Zach said—"

"Fuck Zach. I'm writing it for me."

29

One week left...

Zach sipped his coffee and grimaced.

"You know, you should really let me make the coffee, boss." Mary entered his office holding a Starbucks cup. She passed it to him, and he took it with gratitude. "Yours is disgusting."

"You'd think with a doctorate from Oxford I'd have learned how to make a proper cup of coffee somewhere along the way."

"Some of us have the gift. Some don't. Poor you, swilling gross coffee all your life."

Zach grinned at her as she sat in the chair across his desk. "Grace always made our coffee. She had the gift apparently," Zach said. "American coffee is vastly superior to English coffee anyway. She knew some little shop in London that carried the real beans. She got up early to brew it every morning."

"She sounds like a keeper." Mary smiled and then seemed

to realize she'd said something she shouldn't. "I'm sorry, Zach."

"It's all right. It's apparently no secret that Grace and I fell apart. Even that arse Finley knows."

Mary shuddered with revulsion. "I can't believe he went to all that trouble, leaving all those dirty little presents, just to get under your skin. And then all that stuff he said about Nora...I never told you this, but I really like Nora's books."

"Mary, I had no idea you were of that persuasion."

"I wouldn't say I was of that persuasion, but I do love a good story. And she writes some torrid ones."

"Her life is her most torrid story," Zach said.

"You say that like it's a bad thing."

"Mary, her books aren't the only thing she sells."

"Yeah, I heard she was the real thing. I can't believe I've been working for someone who was working with a real live Dominatrix."

"Not simply a Dominatrix. *The* Dominatrix apparently. I can't have it. She's just supposed to write about it. She's not supposed to live it."

"She doesn't write murder stories, boss. She doesn't kill people on paper and in real life. She just..."

"Beats them on paper and in real life," Zach finished for her.

"But they like it. Slightly lower rung on the ladder of horror than murder and rape, don't you think?"

"Mary, you don't mind your husband had other lovers before he met you, do you?"

"Of course not. I had my fair share, too."

"Now, would you mind if you found out these other lovers had paid him for sex?"

Mary laughed at the idea. "I see your point. But still—"

"I can accept it as a private practice between consenting adults. But to do it with strangers for money?"

Mary exhaled and rolled her eyes.

"Boss, do you really think her personal life means she doesn't deserve to be published? That's a little harsh, don't you think? Is this really about her book?"

Zach looked at Mary.

"Please don't share this with anyone—"

"Jesus, Zach, I'm not J.P. You can tell me anything."

"Nora and I… It wasn't strictly business."

She nodded her head. "Well, obviously. Your mood definitely improved when you started working with her. Is that why you're so pissed?"

"She lied to me. That's what I can't get over. I cared about her. For the first time since Grace and I separated I could vaguely imagine myself happy again. Or at least not miserable anymore."

"Maybe she was imagining the same thing with you. Maybe that's why she was afraid to tell you. Or maybe she just wanted you to see her as a writer and not as, I don't know, a character."

Zach sighed. He knew Mary had a point. He just didn't want to admit it yet.

"Tell me something, boss. What do you think is the highest form of art?"

"Literature," he answered without hesitation. "Painters and sculptors require elaborate supplies and tools. Dancers must have music. Musicians must have instruments. Literature needs nothing but a voice to speak it or sand to scrawl it in."

Mary walked to his office bookshelf and pulled down three Royal House titles. She laid them facedown on top of his desk. She pointed one by one at the UPC barcodes on the back.

"Even the highest form of art is for sale, Zach. And you, editor extraordinaire, help up the price."

Zach met her eyes. "You think I'm a prude."

"Prude…ish. Poor J.P. was heartbroken when you told him it wasn't going to work out with Nora."

"I know. He looked like a boy whose puppy just died. But he kept his promise."

"He trusts you. If you say the book shouldn't be published, he won't publish the book. Do you really think the book shouldn't be published?"

Zach stared at Mary. Twenty-eight years old and she was far wiser than he. She was right. At least Nora deserved a chance to tell her side of the story.

"You deserve a raise."

"For what? Bringing you coffee?"

"And telling me off. And coming in on a Sunday to help me clean house a little."

"It's Easter Sunday. You and I are both members of the tribe. Might as well. Besides, you're the best boss I've ever had."

"And you're by far my best assistant ever. Here." He dug in his messenger bag and pulled out Finley's most recent gift to him. "Would you like to have these? Finley's last gift. Earrings, I think."

Mary opened the box and burst out laughing.

"What?" Zach asked.

"Nice nipple clamps, boss."

Heat rushed to Zach's face. "Nipple clamps? I should have known."

"Well, they do look a lot like clip-on earrings," she said.

"But you knew what they were immediately." Zach raised his eyebrow at her.

Mary looked up to the heavens in feigned innocence. "I

don't know. Maybe I am of that persuasion." She stood up and headed for the door.

"You think I should call Nora?" Zach asked. Mary turned around.

"I think you should think about it," Mary said as she left his office.

He picked up the phone and dialed Nora's house number, but there was no answer. He called her cell phone but it went directly to voice mail. He sent her an email that said only, Will you call me please? but got an automatically generated away message back from her. All it said was, To Whom It May Concern: Fuck off. I'm busy.

He sighed and gave up. He could only imagine what she was so busy doing. Even on Easter Sunday, a day that meant nothing to him but he knew was very important to Catholics, she was clearly hard at work at her other job.

He'd tried to call her. It just wasn't meant to be. He considered calling Grace. He picked up the phone again, stared at it, then put it back down.

He sighed, knowing he was caught. It amused him to think that while he was ostensibly in charge of every aspect of her life, Caroline still believed she could control his choice of reading material. Her benign feminine disapproval trumped any act of dominance he could muster.

"In the effort to retain my status as the dominant partner in this relationship, consider the following a preemptive strike—I give you permission to criticize my book," William said to Caroline as she knelt on the ground at his feet.

"Camus again? He's so bleak and melancholy," Caroline chided him. "You can't really think there's something noble about pushing a rock up a hill for all eternity, do you, sir?"

"It's noble because Sisyphus is doing something more than nothing. He knows his task is meaningless and that the world is absurd,

but he continues, refusing to surrender to the futility. It is both profound and noble."

"It's depressing. And Camus was an atheist, right?" she countered, resting her chin on his knee.

"He was, yes."

"Then Sisyphus's something is still nothing. Without God life has no ultimate meaning. Pushing the rock up the hill is no nobler than leaving it at the bottom and just killing yourself."

William smiled down at her as he twisted his fingers into her hair. "My little Kierkegaard...if it were proved to me right now that heaven's throne sat empty and at the center of all that exists nothing but a bleak and empty void...I would still make love to you tonight with the same ferocity as I made love to you last night. Is that not a better response than celibacy?"

She blushed like a new bride. "I think that's a trick question, sir."

"No trick at all." He closed his book and set it aside. "And what are you reading now?"

"I found an old copy of some O. Henry short stories. We read The Gift of the Magi *my freshman year in high school, but I don't think I've read anything by him since.*"

"Ah, yes. The young couple, desperately poor but deeply in love... she sells her only possession, her lustrous long hair to buy a chain for her husband's pocket watch...and her husband sells his only possession, his pocket watch to buy his wife combs for her lustrous long hair. On the altar of love they sacrifice the only things they have of value."

"They have each other," she said, her voice little more than a whisper.

"Oh, yes, of course. They have each other." William pulled his hand from her hair and picked up his book again. "And you say Camus is melancholy."

"Hey, Sinner Still in Her PJ's," Wesley said, peeking into her office. "Can you afford a five-minute break?"

"I need a five-minute break." Nora pushed away from her

desk and looked at Wesley up and down. "A suit and a tie. Very *GQ*."

He bowed at her.

"It's Easter, Nora. Could you not even tear yourself away from your book long enough to go to church on Easter?"

"If I'd gone to church it would have been Sacred Heart." Wesley grimaced.

"Good point. How's the book coming?" He sat in her armchair across from her desk.

"Okay. It's harder not having the daily feedback. I've gotten used to that. But it's progressing. I'm dreading the big scene, though."

"What's the problem?" Wesley loosened his tie.

Nora put her elbows on her desk and rubbed her temples. "It's a mess. It's the most important scene in the book."

"So it's a sex scene."

"Right. But it's really difficult for me to write. My guy in the book is pure kink. My girl is vanilla but trying to be what he wants her to be. But this is the scene where he gives in and tries to be what she wants. It's hard to write vanilla sex when you've never actually had vanilla sex."

"Can I help?"

"You want to help me write a sex scene?"

Wesley shrugged. "I've helped you before."

"Yeah, and you swore you'd never help me with a scene again after the last time. Which I thought was an overreaction on your part."

"You left me hog-tied on the floor while you made yourself a sandwich."

"I offered to share."

"Suit yourself. I'm getting out of these clothes before I suffocate. Holler when you want lunch." He got up and headed for the door.

Nora looked down at the morass of notes about the big scene.

"Wes?"

"Yes, ma'am?" He spun around in her doorway.

"You can help me. I need all the help I can get."

"No comment. Tell me what to do."

"Go change first. Meet me in my room when you're done."

Wesley bowed again and yanked his tie off on the way out of her office.

Nora printed off her most recent draft of the big scene. She'd have to be careful and not let Wesley see the pages or he might be upset by one or two things he read.

She entered her room and found Wesley already lounging against a mound of pillows piled against the headboard of her massive bed with one leg bent at the knee, his arm resting on it. He now was barefoot and wore only jeans and a white T-shirt. With the sunlight in his sandy-blond hair, Wesley looked even more enticing than usual, and for a moment Nora couldn't quite think of what she was doing. He looked at her and didn't smile but only raised his chin slightly as if he knew exactly what she was thinking. Had she seen that expression on the face of any other man she would have assumed it was a come-on.

"So what's going on here?" Wesley asked as Nora hopped up on the bed next to him.

"It's hard to explain completely unless you've read the whole book, which you haven't."

"You won't let me."

"You can read it when it's done. Maybe."

"You've let me read rough drafts before."

"Are we going to argue or have pretend sex?"

Wesley exhaled. "Pretend sex, I guess. What am I doing?"

"Sleeping in bed. She's sleeping on the floor."

"He makes her sleep on the floor?"

"He gives her a blanket."

"Very romantic."

Nora glanced down at her pages, still warm from the printer. "Okay, I'm her. I wake up and have to have you because while I know we don't belong together, that doesn't change the fact that I love you and want to try to make it work."

Wesley nodded.

"You pretend to be asleep," Nora instructed. "Then I'll wake you up. Then you'll let me make love to you."

Nora expected a laugh or a protest but Wesley only tilted his head just slightly and sank deeper into her pillows.

"Okay, Nora," he said, his voice low and serious. "Make love to me then."

Tremors rippled through Nora's fingers as if her hands had fallen asleep and were just now beginning to awaken. To cover her sudden nervousness, she purposefully scanned her scene, looking for a good place to start.

Nora took a deep breath and reached out. Wesley was feigning sleep. His head was turned to the side and his eyes were closed. His blond eyelashes lay on his tan cheeks. She touched his face as gently as she could and his eyes fluttered open.

"What do I do?" he asked.

"He grabs her wrist. Hard but not viciously."

Wesley raised his hand and clasped Nora's wrist. She wondered if he could feel her pulse racing.

"Then what?" Wesley stroked her wrist with his thumb.

"He says to her, 'You know that's against the rules.'"

"And she says?"

Nora paused. The light in the room changed as a cloud swallowed the sun and everything was thrown into pale shadows. The darkening room seemed suddenly and dangerously intimate, but she didn't dare stop. She knew how fragile, how easily shattered such a moment was. Her body tensed. The room held its breath.

"She says, 'This isn't about the game. It's just me now. I want, just once, to be with just you.'"

"And he says?"

"He doesn't say anything. They look at each other in the dark until she says…'please.'"

Nora's and Wesley's eyes met.

"Please," Wesley repeated. "Then what happens?"

"The big moment—he's been in control the whole time, totally in charge. This is when he lets go and gives himself into her hands. He surrenders."

Wesley nodded his head solemnly. "And she?"

"She kisses him." Nora laid her hand on Wesley's chest. "And he lets her."

Nora leaned in even farther, expecting Wesley to stop her at any moment. When he didn't she nearly stopped herself, but after the briefest hesitation she pressed her lips to his. Opening her mouth, she brushed his bottom lip with the tip of her tongue and his mouth opened to hers.

A million times perhaps Nora had imagined what it would be like to finally kiss him. But as they grew to be best friends she'd tried to stop thinking of him like that. Their friendship was too fragile—it rested on the edge of a knife's blade. Her resolve to love him without making love to him wavered at times, but her profound respect for him kept dragging her wayward heart and body back in line. But as his untutored lips trembled under her lips, and his tongue tentatively sought hers, that resolve threw itself onto that blade, sliced itself in two, slid to the ground and died there, quiet and happy and without any further protest.

"What happens next?" Wesley whispered when Nora paused for a breath.

"She pulls the covers off him and kisses him from neck to hip."

"She doesn't take his pajamas off first?"

"He sleeps naked. So does she, of course."

Wesley smiled at her and she saw desire in his eyes.

"Of course."

Nora pulled back a little and watched Wesley. In the space between them hovered a question that only Wesley could answer.

He rose up and with that enviable masculine grace pulled his T-shirt off and threw it on the floor. But he'd been shirtless around her a thousand times. She waited.

Nora studied his hands for any sign of nervousness, but his fingers didn't quiver at all as he gathered the fabric of her silk camisole in his hands and pulled it off her. She watched him study her naked curves. His gaze of innocent wonder was more erotic than any lascivious stare she'd ever received.

"Don't look at me like that, Wes. You gave me a bath a few nights ago."

"The bubbles were in the way." Wesley tore his gaze from her breasts and met her eyes. "You're so beautiful."

"So are you."

Nora fell into his arms again and their mouths met. This time the kiss wasn't remotely tentative. Wesley's lips sought hers again and again, his tongue found hers, his arms encircled her and pushed her onto her back. He gasped as her lips met his skin. He tilted his chin back to give her better access, access that she took eager advantage of caressing his shoulders, his chest and his collarbone with her mouth. She felt unleashed at last, finally free to touch every inch of him as she'd wanted for so long.

"How am I supposed to do this again?" he whispered in her ear.

"You just kiss her anywhere and everywhere you want to kiss her…" she said, remembering the first night she'd slept next to him, the first time she touched him.

"Anywhere and everywhere…" Wesley kissed his way from her neck to her breasts. He paused for a moment and looked at her before lowering his head and taking one of her nipples in his mouth. She arched underneath him and sighed with pleasure. He was eager but gentle. It was the strangest sensation. Her instincts told her to throw him on his back, tie him down and have her way with him. Lying there so passively while he touched and kissed her felt so unusual, as if he was making love to her in a foreign language, a beautiful language to hear, but one she didn't understand.

Wesley brought his mouth to hers again and shifted so that his body was on top of hers, his full weight down on her, his hips pressing into hers. He pushed her arms over her head and she smiled—this she was used to. But instead of holding her down by her wrists, Wesley twined his fingers into hers. Something caught in her chest at the simple gesture of tenderness.

Pausing from the kiss, Wesley pulled back and looked down at her and searched her face as though he couldn't believe she was real.

"Please tell me this means as much to you as it does to me," he begged.

Nora swallowed a lump in her throat. "I'm terrified, Wes. I think it may even mean more to me."

Shaking his head, he smiled. "Not possible."

Wesley released her hands and pulled her into his arms. His body radiated warmth and she couldn't seem to get enough of his skin. She wrapped a leg over his back and Wesley pressed his forehead to the center of her chest. Nora felt a flutter of fear when she remembered this was Wesley and he would never have sex with anyone he wasn't in love with. The only person she'd ever had sex with who loved her was Søren. Søren...

"Wes, stop for a second."

Wesley pulled away from her and she saw the fear in his eyes.

"I wasn't hurting you, was I?"

She rolled up and pulled her legs to her chest.

"No, you weren't hurting me at all. I just..." She panted a little. "I just need a second. I told you, I've never had vanilla sex before."

Wesley laughed a little.

"Are you a virgin, too?"

She met his eyes and smiled.

"Guess so."

Wesley reached out and ran his hand through her hair.

"Nora, I don't think I can do what you do. I've never even had normal sex much less...you know."

Nora took short breaths. "I know. I'll try, too."

She pulled Wesley to her again. She wasn't sure how to do this, how to just let go and let him make love to her. They kissed and he pushed her onto her back. A strange panic set it. This wasn't who she was. Nora Sutherlin didn't have vanilla sex. She didn't do missionary position. The last time she had sex on her back and face-to-face was with Søren, and she'd been in four-point restraints. She didn't know the rules to this game. But she knew if this happened, if they made love right now, he would believe she loved him as much as he loved her. He wasn't just giving her his body. He was giving her his heart.

"Talk to me, Wesley," she begged. He grew more courageous with every kiss. His hands roamed over her arms, her breasts, and even slid between her legs and caressed her through the fabric of her silk pajamas. "Tell me what you want to do."

Wesley placed a hand on the side of her face and caressed her cheekbone with his thumb.

"I want to be inside you." He breathed the words.

She reached between them and unbuttoned his jeans.

"Nora—" She heard a note of panic in his voice.

"We can get under the covers. Would that help?" She hoped he would say yes. Maybe it would help her, too.

"I'm the guy. I'm the one who should be saying that," Wesley said with a rueful smile.

"Don't worry about it. I'm older and a slut. Let me handle it, okay?" Could she handle it? She wanted to stop, wanted to talk to him before they went any further. She hadn't been nervous like this in years. The night she gave her virginity to Søren felt like destiny. This felt like fear.

Wesley laughed. "Okay. Yeah, I would feel much more comfortable under the covers."

Nora scooted off one side of the bed as Wesley slid off the other. As they pulled the sheets back, the pages of her novel fell off the bed and to the floor. Wesley picked them up and glanced at them.

Nora crawled across the bed toward him and wrapped her arms around his shoulders. But Wesley didn't respond. He just kept reading.

"It's just fiction." Nora kissed his shoulder.

"William and Caroline?" Wesley finally tore his eyes from the page. "That's your father's name and my mother's name. Is this about us?"

Nora shook her head. "No, not really."

"Not really?" Wesley took a step away from her and grabbed

his shirt off the floor. Feeling both defeated and relieved, Nora pulled her camisole back on and sat cross-legged on the bed.

"No, it isn't our story. He's not quite me. She's not quite you. It's just inspired by us, by things I've thought about because of our relationship. They're lovers. We're just friends. Or were. Jesus, Wes. Did you plan this?" Nora couldn't quite finish the question; the enormity of what they'd almost done together finally hitting her as she surveyed her disheveled bed.

"You quit your other job. I thought now maybe it might mean as much to you—"

"God, Wesley, it does mean as much to me."

"Or is this just about your book?" he asked, holding the pages in his hand. He glanced down and scanned them. *"The Gift of the Magi.* That's my favorite short story."

"I know. It's what they're talking about the evening before this scene happens, about what people have to give up when they're together."

"So what is his watch? My virginity? I was ready to give that to you."

"Your innocence. So much more valuable and so much more traumatic to lose."

"And her hair, what's that? You've already given up your job with King."

"But I haven't stopped being who I am."

"It isn't who you are, Nora. It's just what you do."

"Even if I'm not doing it for money, it's still who I am. And I can't sell it, not even to buy you a watch chain. It's what writes my books and makes me me. It's the only thing I have of value. And even if you wanted to give me your innocence, wanted to come into my world with combs for my hair, I can't let you do that. So where does that leave us? You tell me."

"With no Christmas presents, I guess."

"I guess not," Nora said, suddenly exhausted.

Wesley weighed the pages in his hands, flipped through them and pressed them to his chest.

"Why did you write this? Write a book about us?"

"Because I guess I've always known you and I can't be together. God, I thought I was going to faint a few minutes ago trying to have vanilla sex with you. I hate that we have this thing between us. It kills me a little bit every day. The book— I don't know. I guess I thought at least we could be together on paper for a little while. It's not much, but it's something," she said, trying and failing to smile.

"Let me read it. All of it."

"You don't want to read it, sweetheart."

"You said it was us."

Nora remained unmoved.

"Please," Wesley said, and Nora heard the slight but desperate catch in his voice. Nodding, she slid off the bed and retreated to her office. She grabbed the binder that held her most recent copy of her novel and returned to her bedroom.

"It's not done yet. I still have about eight or so chapters to write."

"How does it end?"

"I don't know," she lied.

"*The Consolation Prize.*" He opened the binder and read the title out loud.

"Yeah, the consolation prize. You know, it's what you get when you don't win."

"What do you want to win?" In his voice was a quiet promise that if he could give it to her he would.

"You, Wes. But I can't win you without selling who I am to afford you."

"And I can't win you without selling my soul, right?" Wesley asked.

"Now you see why I said *The Gift of the Magi* was a horror story."

Wesley only looked at her before turning his eyes to her novel.

She spun on her heel and left Wesley alone in her room with the book—the book she had written in a reckless attempt to exorcise the demon of love from her heart. Once Wesley finished the book he would know everything—know the good of her love and the evil, know she wanted him and why. They'd been so happy together in the strange little paradise they'd made together, but now she felt expulsion was imminent. And she had no one but herself to blame for her fall.

Nora returned to her office and sat at her desk. Outside, the last gasp of the retreating winter winds paced back and forth across her windows. Wesley was going to read her book. She opened her saved draft and put her hands on the keyboard. What could she do but write? At least now she knew how to end the big scene. William would try to make love to Caroline like she wanted. He would try, but he would fail. And between the two of them a chasm would open up so wide they could not even see to the other side. The moment they tried the hardest to be together is the moment they are forever torn apart.

Poor Caroline, Nora thought and swiped at a rogue tear hiding at the corner of her eye.

Poor William.

30

Thursday night at 11:48 p.m. Nora placed the last period in her book. She saved her document and shut down her computer. She could barely suppress her smile as she floated from the office and looked in on Wesley on her way to her bedroom.

All week after reading her book he'd been quiet, but not angry. Desperately she wanted to talk about what had happened between them on Easter, but she knew she needed to leave Wesley alone to think about it on his own. She could barely sleep at night for the flood of memories of Wesley's hands and mouth on her, how close they'd come to making love. All this time he'd wanted her even more than she'd ever guessed. He'd been ready to give her his virginity, to give her his body. Her Wesley—he'd never have sex with someone he wasn't in love with. Wesley in love with her...what was she going to do with that kid?

The kid in question was supposed to be sound asleep. But he turned over in his bed and smiled at her through the dark.

"You have an eight-thirty class tomorrow," she reminded him. She came in and sat on the edge of his bed.

"It's canceled. Professor Matheny's sick. Or he just wants to start the weekend early. Either way I get to sleep in."

"Congratulations." She ran a hand through his mussed hair. "Can I tell you a secret?"

Wesley propped himself up on his elbows.

"Definitely."

She leaned forward and whispered in his ear.

"I finished the book."

"Are you serious?" Wesley pulled back to look at her.

"Yeah. Just now. It's full of typos but the book itself, it's done. And it's good."

Wesley threw his arms around her. "That's awesome, Nora. I'm so proud of you."

She returned the hug and released him. "We'll celebrate tomorrow night. We'll celebrate the best book I've ever written that no one will ever read."

"Absolutely. But I think someone will read it someday. It's too good to just sit in a drawer."

"Maybe. But I'm not going to worry about it. And neither are you. Bedtime."

Nora started to leave, but Wesley called her name.

"What's up, kid?"

"Tomorrow night when we celebrate, I want to talk to you about something."

"About us?"

"About me. It's not bad, I promise. There's some stuff I want to tell you. A lot of stuff."

"Tomorrow. It's a date. 'Night, sweetheart."

Nora leaned over to kiss his forehead. But at the last second Wesley turned his face up and brought his lips to hers. Too shocked to move, Nora only shivered in that eternal moment as a light, white and winged, brushed over her shoulder and settled somewhere she could not see.

She was still smiling when she fell asleep that night.

Friday morning, Nora awoke and dressed and gathered the handful of things she would need for the day. Last night's smile still remained. Without Zach, without anyone, she'd managed to finish her book. It was done. It was good. And she couldn't wait to start the next one.

And tonight she and Wesley would celebrate her book and maybe finally figure out what they were going to do about each other. But first she had an errand to run. And then she had a book to throw in someone's face.

Zach sipped his tea and strolled around the conference room making pleasant small talk with his coworkers at his going-away party. J.P. had hired a very good caterer, but still Zach was taking a lot of ribbing for his refusal to allow J.P. to spring for lunch at The Four Seasons, especially from Mary.

"Recession," Zach reminded her.

"Tangerine cheesecake," she countered.

"The lady has a point," J.P. said. "It's quite good cheesecake."

Zach set his tea down. He leaned over the buffet spread, took a plate and filled it with some gourmet cheese and a piece of the cake.

"Here," he said, handing the plate to J.P. "You two make your own damn cheesecake."

Zach was secretly touched by how many of his colleagues had bothered to come to the luncheon. He knew free food and a break from the desk and the phone would get almost anyone to an office party, but everyone was talking to him and wishing him well in L.A. He almost regretted how his own grief over Grace had kept him from getting to know some of the other editors better. Americans were a fairly charming group of people. Even New Yorkers, not known for their friendliness, were more immediately affable than most Europeans. He'd decided Americans were quick to like people because they couldn't conceive of anyone not liking them. Even Nora, who made her money being vicious to people, was without a doubt the most engaging person he'd ever met. He recalled how priggish, at moments outright churlish, he'd been to her at their first meeting, and how she'd responded only with humor and a promise to try harder for him. Looking around the party he felt her absence keenly. Had they not fought, she would be here with him right now, toasting her book's completion in public, toasting their attraction to each other in private. Last week in anticipation of their first night together, he'd already bought the wine. He'd even bought a candle. He felt a fool for what had happened between them— even worse than losing her book, he'd lost her friendship.

The congenial atmosphere of the little party dampened considerably as Thomas Finley entered and started talking over his coworkers. Zach ignored him, huddling in the corner and chatting with J.P. and Mary about upcoming projects in L.A.

"I've only handled a few screenplays," Zach said. "And the U.K. film scene is quite small. Hollywood might prove to be rather daunting."

"Faulkner thought so, as well," J.P. said. "He was working with a director, Howard Hawks, out in California. He told Hawks he thought he'd work better from home. Hawks told him that was fine not realizing Faulkner meant his real home, Mississippi. The man just packed up and went back to Mississippi to work from home."

Zach and Mary laughed. J.P. patted Zach on his shoulder and excused himself to the restroom.

"You'd like to go home, wouldn't you, Zach?" Finley said, slapping his hand on Zach's back. Zach repressed a shudder and turned to face him. Of course, Thomas would wait until the second J.P. was gone to start in on him. "England, I mean. I don't know if L.A. is safe for you. Have you ever had a tan in your life? Probably not. No tanning in a fog."

"I plan on working in L.A., Thomas. Not playing."

"Working like Faulkner?" he asked with a smarmy grin. "How many affairs did Faulkner have while out in L.A.? Three? Four? Of course, you're not married anymore, Zach, so I guess they won't count as affairs. Oh, wait…you're still married, aren't you? I'd forgotten. Hard to tell sometimes. So I guess Nora Sutherlin was number one."

Zach locked eyes with Finley. "I am not, was not and have not slept with Nora Sutherlin. She is, was, one of my writers. I try to respect that line."

"Writer? She's a whore, Zach, and we both know it."

"You don't know anything, Thomas," Zach countered. "Call her whatever you want—she's still one of the most promising writers I've ever worked with. I'd far rather work with whores than hacks any day."

"Hacks?" Thomas took an angry step closer. "None of my writers are whores. And they're definitely not hacks."

"I wasn't talking about *your writers*." Zach heard a collective gasp from around the room as the implication of his words sunk in.

"You son of a bitch." Before anyone but Zach could react, Thomas raised his arm to take a swing at him.

But Zach had more fights with drunken football hooligans under his belt than he cared to admit, thanks to his days as a bartender in university. He ducked and swung back, making fierce, hard contact with Thomas's chin. His head snapped to the side and Thomas went down in an instant.

There was a long silence as the room seemed to take in the scene that had just played out before them. And then it was filled with applause and laughter.

"Mary," Zach said. "Did you know that the first rule of S&M is to hurt, but not harm?"

Thomas wiped blood from his mouth.

"Looks unharmed to me, boss."

Without waiting another second, Zach ran from the room and headed for the elevators.

"Where are you going?" Mary called out as she raced down the hall behind him.

"I'm getting my writer back. Or at least her book."

Mary grinned at him.

"Good luck, Zach. Just so you know this is why you're my favorite boss of all time."

Zach fled the building, his right hand throbbing, and hailed a taxi. Suddenly he realized he wasn't sure what he was doing.

He gave the driver his address to his own flat. He'd try calling Nora again from there. If she didn't answer he'd go to her house. And if she wasn't at her house, well, he'd hunt her down any way he could.

Zach stopped in the lobby of his building and dialed Nora's number from the phone at the front desk. If she answered he wouldn't even bother going upstairs.

"Wesley," Zach said, relieved to hear the boy's voice. "It's Zach. I need Nora. Please, is she there?"

"She's gone, Zach. She was gone by the time I got up this morning. What do you want? You dumped Nora, remember? Want to dump her again?"

Zach sighed, guilt stabbing into his stomach.

"I was wrong about her, Wesley. I'm apologizing to her... again."

"This time she really shouldn't let you."

"Believe me, I know. But please, can you give me any idea where she could be?"

"It's Nora. She's probably where you'd least expect."

Zach hung up and tried to think. He decided to go up to his flat to dig out his copy of her book from under his bed and think it out. If she wasn't at home she could be anywhere. With a client, at the 8th Circle, on the moon for all he knew.

Where you'd least expect... Zach thought to himself as the lift climbed the twenty-three stories. Those words reminded him of something he'd heard before.

You merely think you know her. It's one of her best tricks. She flirts, she teases, she confesses everything but reveals nothing. It's the oldest magician's trick—smoke and mirrors, misdirection... You are absolutely certain she's here, Søren had said. Zach slipped his key in the lock of his door and turned the knob. *When all the while she's right over here...*

"Hello, Zach."

It took almost a full ten seconds for Zach to register that Nora stood in his living room. She was wearing a suit and a tie and a smile so defiant he was as nervous as he was relieved.

"You're home from work early," she said. "I was ready to wait it out all day."

"My God, you're here. I just called Wesley looking for you."

"You found me. And I won't darken your doorstep for long. Just wanted to bring you a present."

A sheaf of paper landed with a thud at his feet. Zach bent and picked it up. It was a book—her book—printed out and spiral bound. He flipped through the almost five hundred pages.

"Nora..."

"I finished it, Zach. Without you. Read the dedication."

With trembling hands, Zach opened the front cover and flipped to the dedication page.

"'To Zachary Easton, my editor. Fuck you.'"

"Very nice. I deserved that."

"You deserve this, as well," Nora said and came over to him. She met his eyes and took a deep breath.

"Zach, I'm sorry I didn't tell you about me. I've never had anyone take my writing seriously before. Your good opinion meant so much that the thought of losing it terrified me. I'm done with that part of my life now. I quit the other job and started writing again. Just writing. I know you tore up the contract. I know you're done with me. I know it's too late for me and Royal. But I wanted you to see the book and know I finished it. You can keep that copy. It's the only hard copy that might ever exist."

Zach gripped the book in his hand. He couldn't believe his good fortune. He couldn't believe he had both the book and his writer again.

Nora seemed to be waiting for him to say or do something. When he couldn't find the words, she stepped away, picked up her coat and headed for the door.

"I didn't—"

"Didn't what?" she asked, turning around.

"I didn't tear up your contract. I still have it."

"That's very sweet, but an unsigned contract is worth as much as one in the shredder."

Zach faced her.

"Is it just the hard copy you have? Or do you have an electronic version with you?"

Nora cocked her head at him. She reached inside her shirt and pulled out a thin lanyard from around her neck.

"Flash drive."

Zach held out his hand and she put the flash drive in his palm.

"What are you doing?" she asked as he threw the paper copy on his sofa and plugged the drive into his laptop.

"Today's Friday. My flight leaves Sunday. I've got a book to edit between now and then."

Nora searched his face.

"Are you serious?"

"Completely. I told you I wouldn't sign the contract until I'd read the last page. Good thing I'm a fast reader."

"Then I'll let you get to it."

"Stay." Zach set his laptop aside and stood up. "I'll need your help. If something needs to be rewritten then I'll need you here to do it."

Nora took her cell phone out of her pocket and turned it off. She reached out and locked Zach's door. She walked over to the wall and unplugged his landline phone. She stood in front of the sofa and grinned dangerously at him.

"Okay, Zach. Let's do it."

31

"Okay, here—" Zach shifted his laptop so Nora could look at the screen. "I'm shifting the order of the paragraphs. Caroline would think about his feelings first before she'd allow herself to think about hers. But I need some sort of transition."

Nora reread the page.

"She could look down and notice the bruises on her arms. He gave the bruises to her. It would help her shift perspective."

"Good. Write." Zach passed her the laptop. He went to his kitchen and dug through a box until he found his wineglasses. He opened his almost empty refrigerator, pulled out a bottle of chardonnay and poured two glasses.

"Thank you." She took the wineglass from him with one hand while she kept typing with the other. "Very good," she said after the first sip. "This is fantastic. What's the occasion?"

Zach reddened a little.

"I bought it over a week ago. I thought we should have some wine to celebrate when we finished your book—"

"And when we started sleeping together?" She finished the sentence for him. Zach looked at her and sighed. She'd taken off the suit jacket and loosened her tie. How could a woman look so feminine, so tempting in such masculine attire?

"Something like that."

Nora shook her head, took another sip of wine and finished the paragraph. She started to pass his laptop back to him but she paused and grabbed his wrist instead.

"Your knuckles are scraped." Nora looked up at him.

Zach gave a rueful laugh.

"I clocked my office prankster at my going away party today."

Nora's eyes widened and she burst out laughing.

"That's fabulous. I'm sure he deserved it."

"He called you a whore and I called him a hack. In my defense, he threw the first punch."

Nora nodded her approval. "You punched out a guy defending a woman's honor. You're a real man now, Zach. *L'chaim*," she said and raised her wine.

"*L'chaim*." They clinked wineglasses.

Zach took his laptop back and sat next to Nora on the sofa again.

"I'm proud of you, Nora. You finished the book without me, despite me."

"To spite you," she said. "What can I say? A writer writes."

"And you are a writer now. My writer. You can still be my writer even in L.A. We can still work together." Zach smiled at Nora and she smiled back.

"Work together or sleep together?"

"Is 'both' the wrong answer?"

"Both is negotiable."

He tried to resume his reading but he knew there was more he had to say to her.

"I tried to call you." Zach tore his eyes away from the screen. "Last Sunday. I called every number, emailed you."

"I was working and didn't want to be interrupted. Why did you call me?"

"To try to talk things out with you. Mary gave me what for about you."

"I like that girl. She's one of us. She got me to sign her copies of my books the first day I went to see J.P. She told me my books were her favorite one-handed reads."

Zach laughed and rubbed his face.

"I don't want that image of my assistant in my head, Nora."

"What do you want, Zach?"

Zach studied her face, wanting to memorize every line of it. Who knew how long it would be before he saw her again, if he saw her again? Her green-gold eyes glimmered strangely in the lamplight. What did he want? He knew but wouldn't say it aloud.

Nora tilted her head and gave him a slight smile. She brought the glass to her lips and drank slowly.

She lowered the glass and her lips shimmered wet with the white wine.

Zach reached out, laid a hand on the side of her neck and kissed her. She didn't seem the slightest bit shocked by the kiss. She opened her mouth to him and he tasted the wine on her tongue. The Chardonnay-sweetened kiss was more intoxicating than the alcohol. She kissed back…slowly, deeply and with breathtaking expertise. She bit his bottom lip, teased his tongue, drew him in farther and faster. And then she abruptly stopped and pulled away. She crossed her legs and picked up the hard copy of her novel.

Breathless and aroused, Zach sat next to her and panted a little.

She glanced at him and opened her book to the same page he was on.

"What's next?" she asked.

Zach swallowed and glanced down at his screen.

"Page three hundred and eight," he said still a little breathless. "We need to cut this scene down."

"Swollen, is it?" Nora asked without the slightest hint of irony although he knew now nothing had a single meaning with Nora.

"Quite. We should take care of that."

"Yes, sir," she said and flipped to that page. "I'll chop that scene right off."

Zach yawned and checked his computer clock— 3:37 a.m. He blinked and stretched out his neck. Next to him on the sofa, Nora lay curled up and sleeping. Zach closed his laptop and reached for Nora's hard copy of her book and flipped to the last page—William's goodbye to Caroline— and read it for the first time.

> *My Caroline,*
>
> *If you're reading this endnote then I can assume you've suffered your way through the story, our story once again. I suppose having you relive our time together is the ultimate proof of my sadism, as if you of all people needed further proof.*
>
> *At the end I find myself surprised by how easy it was to write this book about us. I found I missed you so much that a terrible vacuum had formed; all the words came and filled it and for a little while you were home with me again. I didn't want it to end but a story must have an end, I suppose.*
>
> *I have no secrets to reveal on this final page. I loved you. At least I tried to. And I failed you. I failed you with great success. Forgive me if you can. I will not apologize anymore.*

I'm done writing now. I may go into the garden and read until evening. It isn't quite the same without your head on my knee and your ill-informed criticisms of my reading material, but I shall carry on alone, page by page, until the end. And when evening comes and the sun is sitting on the edge of the earth, I will look out, searching for a break in the horizon as that father did once so many thousands of years ago…the father waiting for his prodigal child to return.

I hope you are happy. As for me, I…continue. If you ever miss me, miss… But some things are best left unwritten. Just know I have kept your room for you. I'll say no more. I know I sent you away. I know it was the right thing to do. But I also know that perhaps not every story has to end.

Love,

Your William

Zach turned to look at Nora's sleeping form. She looked so young right now, so defenseless. She looked like a child sleeping on her stomach, her arms tucked under her. What a fool he'd been. First he'd pushed her away out of grief for Grace. Then he'd pushed her away out of anger at himself. Adrift and unmoored, she had tried again and again to throw him a rope to save him from the raging waters. And now he no longer felt like a drowning man at sea. Nora…the siren and the goddess, the ship and the wine-dark sea. She would either save him or end him. Right now, with her words singing in his ears, he didn't really care which.

Standing slowly so as not to wake her, Zach found his messenger bag and dug through it. He pulled out her contract and returned to the sofa. He knelt beside her sleeping form and flipped to the last page. Taking up his pen, he laid the contract on her back and with a sure hand and absolute certainty that the book would outsell anything Royal had ever published, he signed his name, Zechariah Easton.

Nora stirred and opened her eyes.

"Zach?"

"Here." He handed her the pen. "Your turn."

Nora took the pen and only stared at him for a moment. Then she rolled up, took the contract, laid it on his back and signed Eleanor Schreiber on the line.

"It's done," she said.

"It's good. Nora—" Zach placed a hand on the side of her face "—it's spectacular."

Nora smiled. And then the smile was gone. They only looked at each other. Nora leaned forward and kissed him.

He didn't think it was possible but their second kiss was even more intoxicating than their first. He was still on his knees, and she sat in front of him on the edge of the couch. He started to stand, started to push her onto her back.

"No." She stood up abruptly. "I wrote the book your way. If we're going to do this, we do it mine."

Zach didn't have to ask what she meant.

"Safe out and send me home, Zach. Or come with me. Those are your only two choices."

Zach rose off the floor and made the most terrifying decision of his life.

"I'm with you."

Nora headed to the bedroom.

He stood alone in his living room and breathed for a minute. Grace... Her name echoed hollowly in his heart like an unanswered prayer.

But there was no going back. The wind took hold of the sails. Zach followed Nora into his bedroom. She struck a match and lit the single candle he'd left next to the bed.

"A bottle of wine and a candle..." Nora said. "You were looking forward to this night, weren't you, Zach?"

"Yes," he confessed.

She came over to him, unknotted her tie and took it off. She brought it over his eyes and tied it around his head, blindfolding him. He tensed at his loss of his sight.

"Relax." Nora's voice was calm and soothing as if she were talking to a child. "Trust me, please."

"I do," he said and knew he meant it.

He stood still as Nora unbuttoned his shirt and pulled it down his arms. But she didn't take it off completely. She used the shirt to tie his hands behind his back.

Zach sensed her step away. He heard her soft laugh.

"Ecce homo." Zach remembered the painting in the church. "Behold the man."

"Nora..." Zach said, worried he was about to get crucified.

"How do you feel?"

"Disoriented."

"The blindfold will do that. Don't breathe too deeply and don't lock your knees."

He nodded and tried to relax his legs.

"Do you know why I've done this, Zach?"

"No."

"I could say it's because I want you. I do want you. I have rarely been so attracted to someone in my life. But if I just wanted you I could have had you the day we met. Yes?"

Zach knew she expected an answer. He decided to save them both time and simply go with the truth.

"Yes."

"Do you know why I didn't let that happen? Why I stopped you before you could ask me up that night in the cab?"

Zach experienced a mild wave of vertigo. Nora moved as

she spoke and the words seemed to come from everywhere at once.

"Why?" Nora had never made her attraction to him a secret. Why she'd turned him down the one time he'd come on to her was something he'd wondered about since that night.

"Because when you said Grace's name you had so much pain in your eyes. I knew you didn't really want me. You just wanted to not think and not feel for a few hours. Yes?"

"Yes," Zach admitted.

"I do want you, Zach, but I also want to know you."

"You do know me."

"You've kept half your life from me," she said. "I don't want half. I want all. You know my secrets now. Time to tell me yours. It's all or nothing tonight. Say 'all' and we go on. Say 'nothing' and this ends now and forever. You decide."

He felt the floor rock underneath him. On the wood floor and in his bare feet, he imagined for a moment he was on a ship in a storm.

"All."

"Good," Nora said, sounding relieved and yet determined. "Now…tell me about Grace."

"I don't want to talk about this."

"Then say your safe word and end it. But that will end it. It and us. But if you don't want to end it, answer the question."

For a terrible moment Zach considered his options. There were some things he simply did not talk about. But they'd come so far now…it would be a more difficult journey back than forward. Zach took a few short, shallow breaths and used the street sounds below to orient himself.

"Grace was eighteen when we met." He gave up the words like precious possessions to a thief. "I was…older."

"You were teaching at Cambridge then, yes?"

"Yes."

"Grace was your student?"

Zach swallowed hard. "Yes."

"That explains why my relationship with Wes made you so uncomfortable at first. Déjà vu, right? It seems so unlike you, getting involved with a student."

"All teachers nurse attractions to the occasional student. I never intended to act upon it. Grace was lovely beyond words, twice as bright and talented as any student I'd ever taught. She wrote poetry, good poetry. No eighteen-year-old in history has ever written good poetry. But she did."

"What else did she do?"

"She brought me her poetry sometimes and asked for my opinion, my help."

"You were her editor."

Zach laughed bitterly.

"I suppose I was."

"She loved you."

"As much as a girl of eighteen can love her thirty-one-year-old teacher. At the time, I simply assumed she cared only for her writing."

"Eighteen means she couldn't buy booze in the States. It doesn't mean she couldn't love you."

"It does mean I shouldn't have loved her back."

"But you did."

"Foolishly, yes." His stomach churned as he relived that year, that nightmare of a year. "Or what passed for love at the time. But I never acted on it. I loved my work, loved teaching, loved my life."

"What happened?" Nora's questions were as relentless as any assault.

Zach took another breath. He never even allowed himself to think about that time, much less tell another soul about it. It was his burden alone.

"I was in my office late on a Friday night. I had a hundred exams to grade that weekend. I suppose I'd complained about this in class. Somehow she knew I'd be there."

"She came to your office?"

"Yes. I was exhausted." Suddenly Zach was back in that cramped third-floor office again. His sleeves were rolled up; his fingers were tinged with red ink. His head ached from the hours of reading, the endless concentration. He yawned, stretched, heard a noise in the hallway. "I heard footsteps in the hall and looked up. She was standing in my doorway."

"She came to your office late at night. Shall I assume the inevitable happened?"

"It felt inevitable. She came inside without waiting for me to ask her. And then she closed the door behind her."

"What did she say?"

"She said, 'I don't have any poems tonight.'"

"And what did you say?"

Zach exhaled. "I didn't say anything at all."

"This shouldn't be a bad memory for you. Tell me why it is."

"She was..." Zach stopped and let the silence speak for itself. Behind the blindfold he closed his eyes. He remembered how easily Grace came to him, how her body relaxed against his, how his hands fit her thighs as if they'd been made to press them open again and again. And then he recalled her gasp of pain, that brief intake of breath that told him all.

"She was a virgin," Nora said, filling in the blanks.

"Yes."

"It's not your fault that you didn't know."

"It was my fault..." Zach began and felt the guilt on him again like a knife pressed to his throat. "It was my fault I didn't stop. I couldn't stop."

"Did she tell you to?"

"No. But I should have anyway. I had dozens of lovers before then…but never…" Zach said and though the memory was an agony, his body remembered that moment. He could still feel himself inside her tight passage. "I'd never taken such pleasure inside the body of a woman before that night."

"Tell me what happened, Zach," Nora demanded. She wouldn't stop until he told her.

"No, it wasn't my fault I didn't know she was a virgin. But it was my fault she got pregnant."

"Jesus Christ," Nora said, sounding both shocked and sympathetic for the first time. Zach was almost afraid of the next question.

"You don't have any children so I'll assume it was one of three possibilities—adoption, abortion or miscarriage."

"It was ectopic. Worse than a miscarriage."

He heard Nora's slight intake of breath, the wince of pain.

"How bad was it?"

"It almost killed her. She was so young she didn't know what was normal and what wasn't. She ignored the pain for a month. We'd only been married two weeks when she woke up in a pool of blood. One in a million chance, the doctor said, that a girl so young and healthy would suffer that. So young, he said, and he looked at me like a criminal. I felt like one. Eighteen years old and she's hemorrhaging in the emergency ward. Eighteen years old and she has to marry a man over a decade her senior, a man hardly more than a stranger to her."

"What happened after?"

Zach shook his head. "She survived. But I wasn't sure we would or even if we should. I waited every day for her to tell me she was leaving me. We married because she was pregnant. Then she wasn't. But she never left me. Still, that year was hell for us. I had a nineteen-year-old wife I barely knew who had to transfer to King's College in London after I left Cambridge, left before they could fire me."

"But you stayed married."

"We did. How or why, I don't know."

"Because she loved you, Zach. And because you loved her."

"I did. Not that it matters."

"Why doesn't it?"

"Because we're over. She's made that perfectly clear."

"How do you know it's over?"

"Because she left me, Nora," Zach said, letting irritation seep into his voice.

"She left you?" Nora seemed unfazed by his anger. "Aren't you the one who packed up, boarded a plane and moved across an ocean?"

"She left me long before that."

"Tell me." Nora's voice was insistent, hypnotic and musical. Unable to see, Zach felt uncoupled from the ground, unmoored. Nothing seemed real. It was easier to make his confession in this kind of darkness.

"Two years ago Grace told me she wanted us to try again. Try again—as if we were trying the first time."

"What did you say?"

"I said she nearly died because of my mistake, and I would never let that happen again. After that, she started to fade out on me. First she stopped making our coffee in the morning. Another month passed and she stopped reading with me in the evenings. She didn't leave all at once. Just room by room. She left the bedroom last. I told her about the job here. She told me to go if that's what I wanted. But she was already gone. I did leave, but she left me first."

"Can I tell you a secret, Zach?" Nora's voice came from over his shoulder. "I would have left you, too."

"Nora, I—"

"Shut up and listen," she said with such cold, quiet authority that Zach fell silent at once. "You called the first night
you spent with her a mistake. It was that night, that mistake
that brought you two together. What should have been a one-
night stand created a marriage. Can you imagine the guilt
she's been carrying for the past eleven years? Thinking that
because of her you had to leave a job you loved, that you had
to marry someone you didn't, that she ruined your career,
your life, your world. And you call the night that started it all
a mistake? She didn't leave you, Zach. You threw her out."

"She nearly died because of me, Nora," he said, nearly spitting the words. "You can't even imagine what that was like."

"She was eighteen, an adult. It was her decision as much
as yours. She came to your office. You think she came for
a cup of tea and a chat? She wanted you. She got you. And
I can promise you even waking up in a puddle of her own
blood it never once occurred to her that it was all a mistake.
Making love to her a mistake? That's a worse slap in the face
than Søren ever laid on me."

"Why...why are you saying all this, Nora?"

"Because you need to hear the truth. The truth that your
guilt didn't punish you. It punished her. You were so afraid
to hurt Grace that everything you did ended up harming
her. No more, Zach. No more fear. You will not be afraid
anymore, afraid to hurt a woman with your own passion and
desire. Remember that night at the 8th Circle?" Nora asked.
"Do you remember what I told you I was?"

"A Switch." As long as he lived he'd never forget that night.

"Yes. And that means I can give pain but I can also take
it. Aren't you tired of the pain?"

"Yes," Zach breathed.

"Good," Nora said and tore off the blindfold. She yanked
his shirt down and freed his arms. "Give it to me then."

Zach grabbed Nora, nearly tearing her clothes in his frenzy to get them off. He pushed her back against the wall and unzipped his jeans. She wrapped her legs around him, her arms wound around his shoulders. With a fierce, unforgiving thrust, he pushed inside her. He had never let himself be so brutal with a woman in his life.

"Hurt me, Zach. Better me than you." He did as she instructed; he couldn't do otherwise. He drove into her again and again, thrusting harder each time. He bit her neck and breasts, dug his fingers into the soft flesh of her hips and thighs. She submitted to his every merciless thrust without complaint. The more vicious he was with her, the more she responded with gasps and moans of her own. Nora's body clenched around him and he came inside her with the ruthless force that only thirteen months of miserable celibacy could deliver.

Zach wasn't finished with her, though. There seemed to be no end to his need. He pulled out of her and forced her to the floor. He pushed his hand into her body, needing to feel her wetness on his fingers. He knew that she was wet not only from her desire but from his own passion that he'd poured into her. She writhed underneath him. He pulled his hand out and moved to take her again. But Nora lifted her arms to shove him off. He grabbed her by the wrists and pinned her down, her arms by her head. She held her legs together tight and Zach pried them apart with his knees. Shocked by his violence he could only stare down at her.

"Good boy," she said.

Zach let her hands go. He pushed her over onto her stomach and penetrated her from behind. She arched beneath him, taking him in deeper, goading him on with her hips, her cries. She came so hard that he felt the spasms in her stomach rip through him. He seized her by the wrists again and held her down. Over her, inside her, he pushed in so hard and so far she cried out. Still, he did not relent, could not relent. He was all force and no restraint. Nora had tied him up and set something else free.

With brutal, bruising strength, he impaled himself completely within her and came so hard even Nora flinched from the ferocity of it. He collapsed onto her prone body, resting inside her, not ready to leave her wet warmth. They lay coupled together, swallowing air and saying nothing. Zach brushed her hair over her shoulder and kissed the back of her neck. He closed his eyes and rested his head on her back. Her skin smelled so warm. He could stay here forever if he kept his eyes closed.

Zach pulled out of her slowly and rolled onto his back. He lay on the floor next to her and studied the play of candlelight on the ceiling and willed his thumping heart to settle. Nora moved to his side, leaned up on her elbow and looked at him.

"Did I hurt you?" he asked after a long but strangely comfortable pause. He could see the faint red welts on her arm.

"Yes. A lot. I'm very impressed."

Zach laughed but the laugh rang hollow even to his own ears.

"She left me, Nora," he said, his throat tight as a fist. "God, she left me and it's all my fault."

He rubbed his forehead but Nora took his hand and pulled it away.

"I know she left you. But I'm here."

Zach inhaled slowly, exhaled even slower. He turned and cupped Nora's face in his palm.

"I don't deserve either of you."

Nora gave him a wicked smile.

"Don't be so hard on yourself, Zach. That's my job." She

came up on her hands and knees. "You're still in charge. Tell me what to do."

"Tell you what to do? Where to even begin?"

Nora grinned at him still on her hands and knees over him. "Use your imagination."

His imagination gave him a very good idea.

"Stay," he ordered.

"Yes, sir."

Zach reached for the drawer of his nightstand and pulled out the lubricant that Nora had given him.

"Why, Zachary, you surprise me."

Zach nearly groaned aloud as he pressed into her. She was so tight around him he could barely breathe.

He pushed hard and Nora flinched.

"Sorry," he said, smiling at his own eagerness.

"No, you aren't." He heard the laughter in Nora's voice.

"No," he admitted. "Not this time."

32

Shortly before dawn, Nora dragged herself out of Zach's bed and dressed quietly in the dark. She found her tie that she'd used as a blindfold and hid it away where Zach would find it later. Last night certainly deserved a memento.

Nora gazed down at Zach's still sleeping form. She could scarcely believe what had passed between them just two hours earlier. Someone, something, the real Zach who had been hiding for the past ten years and six weeks came out the moment she'd ripped off the blindfold. Last night she didn't spend with Zach, her prim and proper editor. Last night she spent with the Zach who'd been a lady-killer as young as thirteen, had drunken threesomes during his university days and had taken the virginity of his eighteen-year-old student on his Cambridge office desk. Nora's whole body ached from last night's brutal sex. Without her toy bag they'd had to make do with just his hands to pin her down, his knees to hold her legs open, his hand over her mouth to gag her cries. It was some of the roughest, dirtiest sex she'd ever had in her life. She couldn't stop smiling.

On her way out of his apartment she stopped and picked up her contract still lying on the sofa. She glanced through it, making sure all the i's were dotted, all the t's were crossed. The advance wasn't going to make her rich, but it would keep her very comfortable for the next few years while she focused solely on her writing.

Nora drove home and dragged her exhausted body into the house. Although she longed for sleep, something nagged at her, something that told her that in her excitement over finishing her book with Zach, she'd forgotten something very important.

Nora entered the hallway that led to her room but stopped in midstep. Wesley stood outside her bedroom leaning back against the door. In his hands was a small box of Tiffany blue. From his stance it appeared he'd been waiting for hours, maybe all night. At first his eyes shone with relief; but then as he took in her tousled hair, her disheveled clothes, a terrible realization dawned on his face. His arm fell to his side, the box dangling by its ribbon from his slack fingers.

"Zach?" Wesley asked.

"Yes," Nora said, cold with fear and shame.

Wesley only nodded. The box tumbled from his fingers and fell to the floor. He didn't seem to notice.

"Wes—" Nora began, desperate to explain. Their date, their celebration, was supposed to have been last night. But she'd stayed with Zach instead, stayed and finished her book. She wanted to explain all this to him, but Wesley only brushed past her and disappeared into his bedroom. Nora tried to follow but found his door locked. She stared unbelieving at the knob for a tortured eternity. In all their time together Wesley had never once locked his door.

In quiet shock, she walked to her room but stopped to pick up the box from the floor. With trembling fingers she opened it. Inside the box she found two silver hair combs, delicate and ornate. Nora's heart cracked like glass in her chest. Wesley's innocence, his father's watch, the only thing he had of value…this was his way of telling her he would sell it all to be with her. He'd been waiting all night to give himself to her, and she'd crawled home bruised and stained from a night with Zach.

Nora entered her bedroom and collapsed on her bed without undressing. She was too tired to sleep, too broken to cry. She curled up into a ball, clutching the combs in her hands so hard the metal prongs bit into her skin. She held them tighter, let them hurt her more. Finally it hurt enough she could sleep.

Morning's relentless assault finally defeated Zach's resolve to sleep Saturday away. He opened his eyes reluctantly, knowing from the silence that Nora had already gone. Everything hurt, but he couldn't care less. Had there ever been such a woman in all the world like her?

Zach got into the shower with as much reluctance as he'd left his bed. The hot water burned his skin. He couldn't remember when his body had been this raw from so much sex. He lingered in the shower, needing the heat on his sore and aching muscles. After getting out he toweled off and dressed carefully, cursing himself for behaving like an eighteen-year-old lad in his forty-two-year-old body.

By midmorning he remembered Nora had unplugged his phone last night. He plugged it in and checked his voice mail. One message—most likely from work, he guessed.

"Zachary, it's me." At the sound of Grace's voice Zach's hands went numb and his legs turned to stone. "I'm in New York. Not sure why." Pause. "That's a lie. I do know why.

You don't seem to be home. I stopped by and knocked but no one answered. I called Mr. Bonner. I may try what he suggested. Anyway, I'm only in town until tomorrow morning. I wish you'd get a bloody mobile. Never mind. I'm staying—"

Zach grabbed a pen and scrawled the name of Grace's hotel on his palm. He considered calling to see if she was there but didn't want to waste a second. He threw on his coat and raced from his apartment. If the lift had broken the sound barrier on its way down, it still wouldn't have been fast enough for Zach. She'd come by his flat? When? Probably when he was in the shower. Of all mornings to take an hour-long shower, he cursed himself again. Traffic was blessedly light, but it still felt like a lifetime passed before the taxi pulled in front of her hotel.

Zach shoved money in the driver's hand and raced into the hotel lobby.

"Could you ring Grace Rowan's room please?" Zach asked the hotel desk clerk.

"I'm sorry, sir, but we have no one registered under that name."

Zach swore under his breath. Had he heard Grace wrong? Unless…

"Try Grace Easton."

"Ah, yes. I'll call her room for you."

Zach sagged with relief. The clerk dialed her room number. After what seemed an interminable amount of time passed, he hung up the phone. "I'm sorry, sir. She doesn't seem to be in. Would you care to leave a message?"

Zach decided his course of action that instant. "I'll wait for her."

He found a seat in the lobby that afforded him a clear view of the entrance. He stared at the elegant revolving doors, trying not to let their endless spinning hypnotize him.

Now that he was finally at her hotel his heart was still racing as if he'd run the whole way there. Why was Grace here? What on earth had she come for? He knew her. She'd always been brave enough to deliver bad news face-to-face. But he'd already heard the bad news. So why?

It didn't matter, he told himself. Whatever the reason he would get to see her. That was reason enough to wait in the lobby. Forever, if necessary.

Two hours after falling asleep with the combs in her hand, Nora crawled from her bed and showered and dressed in a daze. Numb from exhaustion, exhausted from shock, she entered the kitchen on feet made of lead. Wesley was there loudly opening and closing cabinet doors.

"What are you looking for?" she asked between slams.

"My coffee thermos. The blue one with the lid." His voice sounded tight and strained.

"Did you check the dishwasher?"

Wesley stopped, wrenched opened the door of the dishwasher and yanked out the top rack.

"Dishwasher," he said, as much to himself as her. "Right. Of course. How could I have been so completely stupid?"

Nora winced and sat down gingerly at the table. It hurt to be in the same room with him. Wesley leaned against the counter for a moment and just breathed.

"Are you mad at me?" she asked in a small voice.

"I want to be. I oughta be." He shook his head. "No, I'm not mad at you. Just myself."

She nodded and met his eyes.

"Are you sad at me?"

He released a cold, empty laugh.

"Yeah, I'm sad at you." She could tell he was trying not to cry. She tried, too.

"I'm sorry, Wes. I am. God, you said you wanted your first time to be with someone who knew what she was doing. Obviously when it comes to you I have no idea what I'm doing."

"I don't care. There's no one else I want to be with. But if you want to be with Zach...I just want you to be happy. That's all that matters."

"Listen, last night with Zach—it was about the book. I went over to his apartment yesterday to throw the book in his face, to show him it was done. I was going to leave. He asked me to stay, to help him finish editing it. We got it all done in one night."

"I saw you when you came in. You didn't just work on the book. I'm not completely stupid about everything."

"You aren't stupid about anything. I am. I'm the one who forgot to call, who forgot we had plans. I was just so shocked that Zach had changed his mind...that he wanted to read the book. Wes," she said and Wesley met her eyes. "He signed the contract. We celebrated."

"I thought we were going to celebrate."

"We still can. We—"

"I wasn't talking about dinner and a fucking movie, Nora." Nora flinched at the sheer agony in his voice. "I wanted us to be together."

"Wesley..." she began but couldn't find another word to say.

"I'm sorry," he said and ran his hands through his hair. "I didn't mean to yell. This is...I don't know. Last Sunday on your bed, Nora, I can't even tell you how that made me feel."

"I never felt anything like what I felt with you, either," she said and remembered that abject panic she felt when she and Wesley had come so close to making love.

"Felt what?" he asked, crossing his arms over his chest. He

looked cold and tired. She wanted to wrap her arms around him until they both felt warm again.

She laughed a little. "Performance anxiety."

"Performance anxiety? Nora, you don't have to perform with me."

"I think that's why I was so scared. I don't know how to be with someone like you. I don't know the rules to this game."

"It's not a game."

"Then how will we win?".

Wesley didn't answer, just stared past her.

"I guess that answers my question," she said.

Wesley took a deep breath. "I'll try. I'll try to be what you need me to be. I know I'm not like you, but I can try. It's worth it if I can be with you."

"But it wouldn't be you with me. It would be some version of you that was trying to be what I wanted. I won't let you sacrifice who you are to be with me." Wesley shook his head and headed for the door. "Wesley, please—"

She started to stand up, wanting to go to him.

"Don't." He raised his hand. She froze where she was. "Don't apologize and don't explain. I'll live with this. I just need you not to talk about it."

"I'm so sorry," she said, her voice hardly more than a whisper.

"Hey," he said with false levity. "At least it's not Søren."

Nora shrugged and clenched her teeth.

"Wes…will you let me give you the combs back? I can't imagine how much they cost and I know—"

"Keep them." He grabbed his coffee mug and headed to the door again. He paused next to where she sat huddled in her chair. "They'll look beautiful in your hair."

Nora rested her head on her knees. Her stomach rumbled

from stress and hunger. She hadn't eaten since yesterday afternoon, but the thought of food only made it worse.

"I gotta go," Wesley said. "Study group."

"Be careful."

Wesley left without another word. The door shut. She
heard Wesley's car start and pull away. And she knew she was
alone. Coughing on purpose, Nora tried to relieve the pressure in her throat. She rose and poured a cup of coffee and
half-considered spiking it with whiskey.

Sipping at her coffee, she swallowed the bitter heat gratefully. She needed more sleep, she decided, or another shower.
No, she realized. What she really, who she needed was—

The doorbell rang jarring her from the dangerous trajec-
tory of her thoughts. She set her mug on the table and went
to the door.

Nora opened the front door to find a woman standing on
the porch. Her hair was an elegant shade of red and her fair
skin was dusted with becoming constellations of pale freckles. Lovely beyond description, she looked a year or two shy
of thirty, but her shining turquoise eyes glowed with a wisdom and intelligence well beyond her years.

"Hello," Nora said.

"Ms. Sutherlin," the woman said and with the first lilting
words out of her mouth Nora knew exactly who she was.
"I'm so sorry to trouble you. I'm—"

"My God," Nora breathed, "you're Grace Easton."

"I am," she said. "How did—"

"Welsh, beautiful, freckles. I don't see that combination
much in this neighborhood." Nora smiled at her, sensing that
this meeting was somehow preordained. "Please come in."

33

Nora poured her coffee down the drain and replaced it with tea. She filled another cup and placed it on the kitchen table in front of Grace.

"Milk?" Nora offered.

"Thank you, no. Zachary always called me a heretic for drinking my tea without milk."

"It's not very English of you," Nora teased. "But then again, you're Welsh."

"My father is, and my mother is Irish."

"I can tell." Nora envied Grace her red hair and exquisite freckles. "Can you do an Irish accent, too?"

"A bit. But I grew up in Wales. Zachary can actually do the better Irish accent."

"Really?" Nora asked. "That jerk. He never told me he could do other accents."

Grace smiled and sipped her tea.

"He's a man of many talents," Grace said. "You're being very kind to me. I know I must seem like a lunatic showing up at your home like this. I'm leaving tomorrow morning, and I can't seem to find him anywhere. I called Mr. Bonner. He gave me your address. He said you and Zachary work together on the weekends sometimes."

"We did. But the book is finished now, thank God."

Grace nodded and took another tentative sip of her tea. Nora took a drink of her own and noticed a bruise beginning to purple on her wrist.

"So it's work then that brings him here so often?" Grace asked, fixing Nora with a surprisingly firm stare.

"We're friends. Good friends."

Grace looked down and her eyes appeared to study the tiny ripples in her tea. She seemed nervous as a bird, her delicate fingers fluttering over the rim of her teacup.

"I meant to come sooner. I tried to leave yesterday morning but my flight was delayed."

"Why are you here?" Nora asked and Grace met her eyes.

"Zachary leaves for California tomorrow. I could hardly stand it when he was in New York. California seems like the other side of the world. His mornings would be my nights." Grace breathed in and exhaled slowly. Nora stayed silent and let her talk. "I should have come weeks ago. I called him…I told him there was a blackout, and I couldn't find the torch. There I was with every light on in the house lying to him just to hear his voice."

"Sounds like something I would do." It was easy to see why Zach had loved this woman so fiercely. She had a poetic beauty to her, a gentleness that belied her undeniable fortitude.

"There was something in his voice when we spoke, something that frightened me. He sounded farther away than just an ocean. I talked myself in and out of coming. Now I have to wonder—am I too late? No, don't answer that. I'm sorry."

"I'll answer any question you ask, Grace."

"I shouldn't ask. I forfeited my right to ask the first night I spent with Ian. I say the first night as if there were dozens of them instead of just three rather humiliating awkward affairs. It only took a week to realize what a foolish mistake I'd made. But I was so young when Zachary and I married, and it was under such horrid circumstances."

"I know. Zach told me. I'm very sorry."

Grace gave Nora a quivering but determined smile.

"He must care about you very much to have told you about us. Even his best mates, he never told them."

Nora shrugged. "I beat it out of him."

"I think he's always been embarrassed by it, by me."

"No, I promise you he wasn't. I think he was only ashamed of himself. You were young and he was your teacher—"

"My teacher, yes." Grace laughed. "Every girl I knew was half in love with Zachary. He talked to us like we were equals." She smiled at a memory. "He wore the most dignified, scholarly ties every day."

Nora conjured the image last night of Zach blindfolded with her black tie.

"Zach in a tie is quite a sight to behold," Nora agreed.

"A suit and tie every day." Grace grinned. "He was so bloody proper and so handsome strolling the grounds with the ancient old profs hoary with beards quoting Shakespeare and Marlowe from memory…we'd all nearly faint when he strolled past, suit jacket over his shoulder and carrying that staid leather briefcase. We girls had our own ideas about what to do with those ties of his."

"You're a woman after my own heart."

"The first night with him—" Grace stopped. Her voice drifted far away. "I thought I was on a suicide mission. I went to tell him I was in love with him. I thought for certain he'd throw me out. Instead, he made love to me. I know I should have stopped it, should have warned him I wasn't on birth control, but I didn't want him to stop. The moment he kissed me I felt like I'd won the world. And even after all that happened, I still felt the same. But it isn't easy to be married to someone when you have this terrible banshee voice in your head screeching that he only married you out of guilt."

"There was guilt, I'm sure. But there was love, too, and more of that than anything."

Grace sat quietly for a moment and seemed to collect her thoughts.

"I know you may not believe me, but I've loved Zachary all this time. Even during the worst days. Even those awful nights with Ian…that's when I missed him the most."

"I believe you." Nora tried to give her a reassuring smile. "Five years ago I left the man who had been the center of my universe for thirteen years. Trust me, I believe you."

"Thirteen years." Grace sounded stunned. "How did you survive?"

"I wasn't sure I would. Sometimes I'm not sure I did."

Grace nodded her understanding. "Ever since Zachary left I've felt like a shade. I walk through the empty house and catch glimpses of myself in the mirror or the windows, and I'm surprised to find I'm still there." Her voice dropped to a whisper. Her eyes held unshed tears. "I scare myself sometimes."

Nora took a sip of her tea and found she could barely get it down.

"I scare myself, too."

"I suppose I should be glad Zachary and I stayed married as long as we did. I never believed he loved me. I wanted to. And he certainly did everything he could to show that he loved me. But even after seven years, eight years, I still doubted it. So I pulled away hoping—"

"Hoping he would come after you."

"And I let him go…"

"Hoping he would come back."

"But he didn't come back…" Grace finished the thought.

"I'm sorry," Nora said, not knowing what else to say.

"I think…I don't know what I was thinking at the time.… I believe I had the idea that we had to end before we could start again. Nonsense, of course. A romance novel fantasy, I see that now. No offense."

"None taken. I write erotica, not romance novels." Nora grinned but her smile faded from her face. "Ask me, Grace. I know you need to."

"I rang his flat. No one answered. I stopped by this morning and knocked. No one came to the door. Was he with you?"

Nora sensed her claws instinctively wanting to show themselves. But for some reason she harbored none of the hostility she usually felt for a rival.

"I won't lie to you, Grace. He was with me." She leaned forward to gaze earnestly at Grace. "But I won't lie to myself. I think he was with you, too."

Grace stood up slowly and walked to Nora's kitchen window.

"When I called him…" Grace began and exhaled. Her warm breath steamed up the cold glass of the window. "He didn't call me Gracie like he always had."

"Gracie," Nora repeated. "That's cute. You should start calling him George."

"For King George?"

Nora laughed. " For George Burns and Gracie Allen. They had a legendary marriage. Might work."

"I fall in love with him a little bit more every time he calls me that. We'd been married a year and one day it just came out—'Gracie, come read this.' It was the first time I felt truly married to him. And it was such a relief after a lifetime of being called 'princess.'"

"Horrible nickname."

"It gets worse. It's a terrible joke. My parents honeymooned in Calais so I'm Grace Calais. Princess Grace and Grace Kelly... Madness."

"Your middle name is Calais?" A memory came to Nora like a face remembered from a dark dream. She stood up and walked to where Grace still stood at the window.

How do you choose your safe word? Zach had asked.

Pick anything. The street you grew up on, your favorite food, the middle name of the long-lost love of your life...

"I did lie to you, Grace," Nora finally said and waited for Grace to meet her eyes. Nora reached out and put her hand on Grace's arm. Grace covered Nora's hand with her own. "He wasn't with me last night at all."

Long after Grace had left, Nora sat at the kitchen table and stared at nothing until her eyes watered.

Wesley and Zach...somehow without trying she had lost them both. Zach would turn from her and Wesley she had turned away. A realization came upon her with the unavoidable force of the night after the day. She rose from her chair and returned to her bedroom. She threw open the closet door and pushed back the racks of clothes. On the back wall impaled on a nail hung a set of deep red rosary beads with a small key hidden behind the crucifix.

She took the key and dropped to her knees. From the farthest corner of her closet she pulled out a wooden box the size of a small Bible. With shaking hands she opened it and took from a bed of blood-red velvet the white leather collar that had once bound her to Søren, the collar she had not worn in five years.

Rising from the floor she left the key in the lock and left the box on the floor. She left no note for Wesley and she left on all the lights. She threw on her coat, found her car keys, and taking nothing with her but her collar, she left. She pulled out of the driveway at breakneck speed and not once did it occur to her to look back.

34

Zach had heard of sleeping with one's eyes open but not of dreaming that way. But after a two-hour wait, two hours with his eyes on the hotel entrance, he knew his mind must be asleep. And when Grace walked in, saw him and smiled as if the two years of the cold and quiet hell they'd been living in had vanished into thin air, he knew he could only be dreaming.

He stood up and shoved his hands in his pockets, afraid if he didn't he'd drag her to him.

"Hiya," he said, not knowing what else to say.

"Hiya." It was her, her voice, his Grace.

"I was waiting for you."

"I see that. I tried to call you. Several times. When I didn't hear from you, I called Mr. Bonner. I told him it was an emergency. He gave me—"

"He sent you to Nora's, didn't he?"

"Don't be angry at him, please."

"I'm not. So you met Nora?"

Grace nodded and hazarded a smile.

"Had tea with her. We talked."

Zach was afraid to ask, more afraid not to. "What did she say?"

"She said I should call you George."

"She would say that. Gracie, I—"

"About Nora," Grace said, cutting him off. "I think she might be the only woman in the world I could ever forgive you for."

"Say the word," Zach said, "and she'll be the only woman you'll ever have to."

Grace smiled, but the smile broke in two as she collapsed into his arms. He held her to him and pressed his lips to her hair. She said nothing and that was fine. The weight of her slight body against his, her head on his chest...it made him feel safer than any words she could have spoken.

"Forgive me, too," she said. "Please."

"No, Gracie." He swallowed hard. "Nothing to forgive. Tell me something, please."

"Anything."

Zach pulled back and held her by the shoulders. He searched her face, still unable to believe she was here.

"Did I lose you, or did I never have you to start with?" he asked.

Grace shook her head. "You never lost me, Zachary. And you always, always had me."

Zach's heart rose so high he thought it would burst from his chest.

"I lied to you," Grace said, and looked up at him.

Zach's hands went cold. "About what?"

"The day when I called about the blackout...the lights weren't really out."

"They weren't?" Zach almost laughed.

"No," she said and pressed her head against his chest again. "The lights were never out."

The sanctuary at Sacred Heart sat empty but for the heady air still radiating warmth from the hundred or more souls who had left barely an hour ago. Nora faced the altar and inhaled the familiar smoky scent. She thought of the book of Revelation and how in it the prayers of the church rise before God in the form of incense. She said her own silent prayer and released it like smoke into the sky.

"I'm afraid you've missed Saturday morning Mass," a voice as familiar as her own said.

Nora turned around and found Søren with a pewter pitcher refilling the fount of holy water at the entrance to the sanctuary.

"But we celebrate Vigil mass at five o'clock this evening if you'd like to come back."

"Søren, you are ubiquitous." Nora came to him. He set the empty pitcher aside.

"I prefer the term *omnipresent*," he said.

"You would."

Nora didn't bother attempting to fake a smile for him. She knew him, knew he would see right through it. She waited and let Søren study her. His knowing eyes on her face felt as intimate as a touch.

"You look tired, little one," he said.

"I am tired."

"Tell me."

"I have such a great gift for ruining things. It even impresses me sometimes."

"Self-pity does not become you," he chastised her in the same tone he used to silence unruly children in the hallways. "And while you have a gift for creating chaos, I have never known you to be willfully destructive. Now, what is this about?"

Nora gave him the faintest of smiles.

"I finished the book."

"I had no doubt you would."

"Zach even signed the contract. Then we celebrated."

"Of that I have no doubt, either," Søren said with a wry smile. "So why is there so much sadness in your eyes?"

"I met Zach's wife today."

"Ah, the once and future Mrs. Easton. What did you think of her?"

"I think he'll go back to her."

Søren nodded. "That was inevitable."

Nora swallowed. "And last night meant nothing."

"I'm sure your night together meant a great deal to him. More than you may ever know. The same wind that blows us off course can turn and carry us home."

"She is his home. I could see that in her eyes. She's perfect, Søren."

"Perfect for him perhaps. To me, Eleanor, it is you who is flawless."

Nora's heart beat heavy in her chest. Søren's love never ceased to humble her.

"I'm as flawed as it gets."

"You are human. And that is the better part of your beauty. But you always knew your editor longed for his wife more than anything. This can't be a surprise to you. What else?"

Nora was afraid he'd ask her that. But Søren had been her father confessor for eighteen years. Now she needed his absolution more than ever.

"Last Sunday...Wesley and I almost made love."

"You have been busy, haven't you? Why only 'almost'?"

"He stopped first, and then I stopped it all. Søren..." she

said in a hoarse half whisper, "I broke the rule—I think I harmed him."

"Little one." Søren cupped the side of her face. "I'm so sorry."

"I have to make him go, don't I?"

"For his own good, yes. That, I'm afraid, was inevitable, as well."

Nora nodded, feeling none of the anger she usually experienced when Søren proved himself insufferably right as he always did.

Søren laid two fingers on her temple. He traced the line of her face from her forehead to her lips.

"You always knew Zachary loved his wife. Yes?"

"Yes." She remembered the ghost of Grace that haunted his eyes from the day they met. "I knew…at the back of my mind, the back of my heart."

"Where you love Wesley, yes?"

"Yes."

"And me?" he asked, his voice soft and earnest in that way it so rarely was with her these days. "Where do you love me?"

Nora did not hesitate before answering. She closed her eyes and whispered, "Everywhere else."

Søren looked at her as if he'd already known that would be her answer, as if for all eternity it would be her answer. Perhaps it would, she thought.

"Come to my office," Søren said. "We can talk about it."

Nora smiled. "Your office. I remember when you'd make me cocoa and help me with my math homework on that bench right outside your office."

"I always knew when you were working on your math homework. The litany of profanities echoing through the halls was always an excellent indicator. Shall we? I'll see what's in the cupboard."

He held out his hand and Nora reached into her pocket. She laid her collar on his waiting palm.

"I didn't come here for the cocoa." Nora met his eyes. For perhaps only the second time in eighteen years, she saw she'd surprised him.

Søren said nothing, merely closed his fingers around her collar. She'd seen those same fingers wrapped around his rosary a thousand times. He held her collar with the same love, the same devotion, the same grim determination to make heaven bend to his ear.

Without a word, Søren turned on his heel.

Nora followed him through the sanctuary and through door after door. A final door opened to a shadowy tree-shrouded pathway that led from the church to the rectory. How many times had she furtively stolen from the church to his home? A million times, she thought. A million was still not enough.

Secluded by a copse of old-world elms and oaks, Søren's rectory stood graceful and quiet in the sheltered sanctuary created by the trees. A small two-story Gothic cottage, it afforded him both beauty and privacy—two very precious commodities.

Nora waited in submissive silence as Søren built a fire in the living-room fireplace. Glancing around, Nora saw the secret signs of their long association: the Bösendorfer piano she'd given him as a gift last December 21 for his forty-sixth birthday, the tassel of an embroidered bookmark she'd made for him at church camp the summer she turned sixteen peeking out from a volume of John Donne poetry, a lock on the bottom door of a cabinet under one of the bookcases. Only she and he knew what he kept behind that lock. And on the fireplace mantel were ten slight scratches in the wood left by her desperate fingernails on a night he had shown her no mercy. She knew she might add another ten there tonight.

Søren came to her and gazed down at her face. She kept her eyes respectfully lowered. It had been the first submissive act he'd taught her.

"Why are you here?" he asked.

"To give myself to you, sir."

"You wish to be mine again?"

"Yes."

"Completely?"

"And utterly, sir," she said. "Without conditions or constraints." The words came so easily to her she knew they must be true. Coming back felt as easy as falling, as simple as death.

"You weren't mine last night, were you?" Søren demanded and Nora blushed.

"No, sir," she whispered.

"You were with your editor last night. Yes?"

"Yes."

"And did you do as I told you? Did you make him hurt you?"

"Yes, sir."

From the corner of her eye she saw him raise his eyebrow at her in clear skepticism.

"Show me."

Nora held out her hands and displayed her wrists, the purple bruises on her skin.

"He held you down," Søren said. "Your arms were over your head."

"Yes," Nora said, amazed how Søren could read that simply from the angle of the marks.

"What else?"

Nora unbuttoned her blouse and let it fall to the floor. She unzipped her skirt and stepped out of it. Without shame or fear she shed all her underclothes, as well. She stood naked before Søren and waited. He studied her body with appraising eyes. Stepping behind her, he raised her hair off her back.

"He bit your shoulder, I see. Several times. He took you from behind."

"Yes, sir."

"Anal?"

"Once."

Søren moved to her front again. He reached down and slipped his hand behind her knee. He raised her leg, inspecting the inside of her thigh with the perfunctory expertise of a judge at a dog show.

"Finger marks," he said, releasing her leg. "And knees. You fought him."

"I made him work for it."

"Did you?"

"Yes, sir."

"Will you fight me tonight?"

"No, sir. Not now or ever again."

Søren said nothing as he continued to study her naked body.

"A few bite marks, a few bruises...I'm afraid your Zachary is something of an amateur in the art of pain. Isn't he? Not like us."

The vicious slap landed across her cheek with such speed that Nora gasped as much from the shock of it as she did the pain. She inhaled and tasted blood in the back of her throat. She swallowed it and met Søren's eyes.

"No, not like us...sir."

Søren smiled and snapped his fingers. Without a moment's hesitation she dropped hard to her knees. He wrapped her collar around her throat and buckled it at the base of her neck. She breathed into its grip; let it hold her throat like a hand.

Nora heard the air divide in half and she braced herself for the blow.

How easily you forgive, Eleanor. How freely you absolve the sins of others. Tell me, little one, when the time comes, how will you absolve yours?

With the first lash of the whip Nora felt a strip of fire burn across her back. She cried out from a pain so ferocious she nearly choked on it.

Like this, Søren, she dared answer only in her mind. *This is how.*

Yawning, Zach stumbled into his flat. He'd spent all night with Grace at her hotel talking it out. In all his life he'd never been so grateful for a sleepless night. He glanced at the clock on the wall—10:38 a.m. He smiled at the clock. He'd missed his flight to L.A.

He'd already called J.P. and told him he needed some time to decide what to do next. Thankfully, J.P. didn't seem the least surprised. Zach had gone with Grace to JFK and seen her off. She'd kissed him goodbye, something she hadn't done when he'd left almost eight months ago. He floated home on that kiss and curled up with it on the couch. He would sleep first, catch an hour or two then call Nora. He didn't know what to say. But he knew she would understand.

Before he could close his eyes the phone rang. Zach grabbed at it, nearly dropping it in the process of trying to answer it.

"Yes? Hello?"

"Zach, it's me. Wes."

"Wesley, what is it?" Zach asked, coming fully alert again at the sheer panic in the boy's voice.

"I'm at the hospital. I had to bring Nora in."

"My God, what happened?"

Zach heard Wesley cough like he was gagging on something. But it only took one word to explain all.

"Søren."

The ride to the hospital was nearly as torturous as the ride to Grace's hotel had been the day before. Zach found the emergency ward where Wesley said they took Nora. He stood in the middle of the vast antiseptic room prepared to do battle with any doctor or nurse who dared ask him to leave. He wasn't sure exactly where Nora was, what curtain to look behind. He listened, hoping to hear her voice or even her tears, anything to lead him to her. Instead, he heard her laugh.

Zach followed her fading laughter and heard the low rumble of a man's voice. After a moment a man in a dark blue suit emerged. Zach saw a flash of gleaming metal on his belt. After a quick, steadying breath, Zach slipped through the curtain.

"Good Lord, Nora," he said as he took in the bruised and bandaged sight before him.

"Hey, Zach. What the hell are you doing here?"

"Wesley called me in hysterics. I can see why."

"He overreacted. Nearly dragged me here kicking and screaming. He thought it was a broken rib, but it's just bruised. Seriously, it's not that bad." She adjusted the pillow behind her.

Not that bad? Her cheek was purpled and her bottom lip was cracked and swollen. He saw red welts on both wrists and even around her neck.

"A bruised rib? You must be joking."

"That was my fault, though. I flinched wrong. I'm a bit out of practice. This stuff just goes with the territory. No big deal."

"No big deal? That was a police officer, wasn't it?"

Nora flashed him her old arrogant smile, a smile undiminished by the fissure of blood on her lip. "That's Detective Cooper, my friend on the force. He works with the community, keeps us out of trouble."

"You're a madwoman, Nora. Why did you do this?"

Nora gave a cold, hollow laugh, grimacing as the movement seemed to hurt her.

"Remember that day in my kitchen," she said, pausing to catch her breath. "That first day we were working on my book. You asked me what Wes's story was."

"Yes, I recall. Why?"

"I told you I'd put the first randy bitch who laid a hand on him in the hospital. Turns out it was me. Hey, never let it be said I can't keep a promise."

"Nora...you will be the death of me," Zach said, wanting to laugh, too, but finding it utterly impossible.

"You keep saying that. And yet you're still alive. What the hell are you doing here anyway? Where's Grace?"

"I dropped her off at the airport."

"You let her leave without you? Are you insane?"

"I can't just bloody go—"

"Yes, you bloody well can," Nora countered. "Just go. Don't pack your toothbrush. Don't call work. Just get on a goddamn plane and go get your wife back. For good this time."

Zach stared at the tiles on the floor. His eyes followed the spots of black and white, letting them swirl together and become gray.

"Go, Zach. You have no idea how much I want to keep you here. Selflessness is not in my nature. Go before I change my mind."

"What about Wesley?"

"He'll be fine, too. We'll be fine. And we finished the book. Your job is done."

Zach looked up and met her eyes. "You must hate me."

"I understand. Trust me."

Zach felt a terrible tightening in his chest. "I couldn't have gone back to her, wouldn't have known how if it wasn't for you. I'm sure that makes no bloody sense whatsoever."

"Oh, it makes perfect sense." Nora laughed. "I taught you how to leave me."

"I'm so sorry."

"I'm not. Søren told me you were still in love with Grace. I should have listened."

"Søren…why?" Zach shook his head.

"Why?" Nora scooted back on her pillow and briefly closed her eyes. "Why? Søren has loved me since the day we met. He's loved me since I was fifteen years old. He's loved me without fear, without guilt, without failing and without flinching every day of my life." She opened her eyes again and looked at him. "He's the only man who never hurt me."

Zach searched for words, any words, but couldn't find them.

"Nora, I—"

"It's okay. Really. You have to go. You're wasting time. You've had your bags packed since the day I met you. But it was never to L.A. you were going. We both know that. Go home."

Zach stood up and walked on shell-shocked feet toward the door.

"Zach?"

Zach turned around. Nora was looking at him.

"It meant something to you, didn't it? Me? My book? Last night wasn't just—"

It took less than a second to get from the door to Nora's bedside. Zach took her face in his hands and, careful of her bruises, kissed her with the passion of a man who knew the next woman he kissed would be the only woman he'd kiss for the rest of his life.

"Yes," he said, breathlessly. "It meant something."

Nora nodded. "You're still my editor, right?"

"Always."

"I have an idea for a new book. But I'll need your help."

Zach touched the unbruised side of her face.

"Just remember, show, don't tell." He winked at her.

Nora laughed again, her wicked, dirty, perfect laugh.

"How much are they paying you for this?"

The drive home from the hospital felt interminable. Wesley didn't speak and Nora was afraid to shatter the silence. He pulled into their driveway. She got out of the car and felt a sudden wave of dizziness as the painkiller the nurse gave her kicked in when she stood up too fast. She thought she was about to go down, but then Wesley had her in his arms and carried her into the house.

"You shouldn't have left the hospital." Wesley set her on the couch.

"I've left AMA before. You have to or they'll start calling in for psych evaluations and other shit you don't need."

"You sure you don't need one?"

"I had a feeling that deep down you thought I was actually crazy," Nora said.

Wesley sat in the chair next to the couch. He leaned back and covered his face with his hands.

"I'd like to think you weren't in your right mind when you did this to me."

Nora leaned back into the couch cushions. Every breath she took hurt, but not from the pain in her ribs.

"I didn't do it to you," she said. "I did it for you."

"That makes no sense, Nora."

"You promised me you'd leave me if I went back to Søren. Leaving me is the best thing for you to do."

"You want me go?" he asked, his voice soft with shock.

"No. Never." She hated the look of relief on his face. "But I need you to. I can't keep you anymore."

Wesley ran his hands through his hair. His face was red, his eyes rimmed with unshed tears. "Let me keep you then."

"No, sweetheart, I can't. I—"

"Do you love me?"

"Wesley, it's not morning until you're awake. And it's not night until you're asleep in your bed under my roof. And I could go on and on but hope is a horrible thing, and I love you too much to give you any. I need you to do something for me."

"Anything," Wesley said. "Everything."

"Please," she begged. "Keep your promise."

Wesley opened his mouth to speak, to protest, but he turned his head at the sound of a car honking discreetly outside.

Nora met his eyes.

"That's for me," she said, standing up.

"You're really going back to him?"

Nora faced Wesley. All she wanted to do was take him in her arms and hold him until all their pain was gone. But there was no time for that anymore. And his pain and hers weren't going anywhere anytime soon.

"Wes, I don't think I ever actually left him."

Nora grabbed her purse by the door and dug inside it. She pulled out her wallet and wrote a check to Wesley.

"Here." She handed him the check. "Back pay. Should cover your tuition and anything else you need for the rest of the semester."

Wesley took the check and methodically ripped it into pieces.

"I never needed or wanted your money. All I ever wanted was you. Nora, please—"

Nora looked back at Wesley and wished she hadn't. She knew this would be the last time she saw him, maybe forever. She wanted her last memory of him to be happy... The day they'd danced around her living room when her fifth book hit the bestseller list... The night they'd stayed up until 3:00 a.m. to catch the meteor shower... That Saturday last summer he took her horseback riding for the first time... Last Sunday when he wanted to give her his virginity and there was nothing more in the world she wanted than to take it. But she knew she'd never forget the look he wore on his face, the desperation, the broken eyes.

"Don't go," he begged. "I love you. I've always—"

Nora stopped his words with a hand on his chest over his heart. He covered her small hand with his much larger one. She took a shallow breath.

"I was wrong, Wes. About the watch chain and the combs... You're the only thing I have of value."

"Nora—"

"Don't forget to check your numbers. And stay away from carbs, okay? And do your homework and—"

Nora closed her eyes and tears poured down her face. She inhaled hard and met his eyes.

"I will," he promised with a hollow voice. His eyes were wide with shock.

She pulled away from him and left the house carrying nothing but her bag. A gray Rolls-Royce was waiting on the street.

"Bonjour, maîtresse," Kingsley said from the backseat.

"No, it isn't a *bon jour,* monsieur." She collapsed against him, her head on his knee.

"I know, Elle." Kingsley put his hand on her flushed forehead. She winced at the pity in his voice, the pity in his touch.

"Where to? You said you needed to hide out for a few days. My town house? The Circle?"

"Take me anywhere," she said.

"Anywhere?" he asked.

Nora closed her eyes as the painkillers finally bested her desire to stay awake. Sleep came for her and she let it take her, not falling into it, but flying.

"King…just take me home."

35

There was no such thing as London fog—never had been. Zach laughed to himself as he recalled his Royal House nickname. He thought he was the only London Fog anyone would ever see. But tonight it was a real London fog—clean, pure, swept in from the southern seas that wrapped its gray arms around the never quite sleeping city and around Zach as he stood outside the house he and Grace had shared during their marriage.

Almost eight months had passed since he'd crossed the threshold of his own home. He stood in the shadow of a streetlamp and imagined Grace inside. She was most likely reading, her knees tucked up under her chin in that battered but comfortable armchair they used to play-fight over. Zach slipped his hand into his pocket and felt a rush of silk against his fingers. He pulled out the black tie Nora had used to blindfold him. He stared at it. How had it gotten into his pocket? Who knew with Nora? Magic most likely. Zach considered throwing it into the nearest rubbish bin, but thought better of it.

Perhaps…maybe…one never knew…

Zach shoved the tie back into his pocket and strode forward up the three steps to his front door. He raised his hand to knock, but the door flew open before his knuckles touched the wood.

And there stood Grace wearing one of his shirts and not much else, and no woman in the history of the world had ever looked so beautiful standing in a doorway.

"Hi, Gracie."

Grace grinned at him.

"Hi, George."

Nora awoke and knew neither the time nor the place. She knew only that she had slept for a long time and that wherever she was, she wasn't afraid.

"Where am I?" she asked, trying to orient herself. She only knew this was not her bed, not her usual darkness.

But it was a familiar darkness. She remembered this darkness and knew it remembered her. She inhaled the scent of hardwood so clean and comforting, savored the soft sheets wrapped around her naked body. The bed that held her now had held her before.

She saw a square of white break through the blackness, felt the bed shift with a familiar weight.

"I'm here, little one," came a voice made for coaxing secrets from the heart. "Sleep now. We'll talk when it's time."

"Yes, sir," she said, now knowing where she was. She surrendered to sleep again.

The most familiar darkness...her darkness...she was home.

★ ★ ★ ★ ★

The End or is it…?
Watch for THE ANGEL,
Coming soon from Mills & Boon® Spice.

Her only weakness, his deepest desire

Two worlds of wealth and passion call to Nora Sutherlin
and, whichever one she chooses, it will be the
hardest decision she will ever have to make.

Wes Railey is the object of Nora's tamest yet most
maddening fantasies. He's young. He's wonderful.
He's also thoroughbred royalty and, reuniting with him
in Kentucky, she's in his world now. But Nora's dream
of fitting into Wesley's world is perpetually at odds
with the relentlessly seductive pull of Søren—her owner,
her lover, the forever she cannot have. At least,
not completely.

The Original Sinners

The Siren • The Angel • The Prince • The Mistress

www.millsandboon.co.uk

0513/MB417

Discover more romance at

www.millsandboon.co.uk

- ❤ WIN great prizes in our exclusive competitions

- ❤ BUY new titles before they hit the shops

- ❤ BROWSE new books and REVIEW your favourites

- ❤ SAVE on new books with the Mills & Boon® Bookclub™

- ❤ DISCOVER new authors

PLUS, to chat about your favourite reads, get the latest news and find special offers:

- ❤ Find us on facebook.com/millsandboon
- ❤ Follow us on twitter.com/millsandboonuk
- ❤ Sign up to our newsletter at millsandboon.co.uk